I0621620

Strange Beginnings

Vamp Squad Series: Book 1

by Miriam Matthews

Strange Beginnings
Vamp Squad Series:Book 1

By Miriam Matthews

Published by Miriam Matthews
Edition 2.2015.v1HC

Published in digital format by Miriam Matthews, 2.2015.v1DIG
and available at most digital providers.

*This book is a work of fiction. Any reference to persons, living,
dead or undead, or places, events or locales is purely for the
purpose of enhancing the story. The main characters are
productions of the author's imagination and used fictitiously.*

ISBN-13: 9780991455546
ISBN-10: 0991455541

Dedication

To the people who have chugged along with this series, supporting me, badgering me and challenging me to get the first book in this series done and out!

To my mother, Miriam who spent endless hours reading and editing… and whose name I stole and plastered across the covers of my books!

To my husband, Timothy. Your love and support and hours of arguing over words and semantics has made me a better writer.

To the ladies of the Alaska Romance Writers of America, *thank you* is such a small word for the years of support, critiquing, encouragement, brainstorming, etc. I love you all!

Note to Readers

Foreign words have been phoneticized from the actual language text, if the text is not written with the English alphabet.

TOP SECRET

Center for Disease Control (CDC)
Medical Alert (Report Date: 22 JULY 1954)

Vampticious Meticulosus Deliriotum *n*
(Also called VMD or Vampire Virus)

1) A contagious virus causing an individual-specific genetic mutation following a death-like comatose state. The VMD virus is transmitted through blood-to-blood transfer, the VMD T-cells retain the base genetic strain of the parent virus thus providing a genetic link to the parent and progeny virus and host.

2) A virus that causes death and then rebirth as a vampire – in European folklore; a dead person who rises from the grave to live off the blood of humans by biting the neck and sucking blood through extended fangs.

MISCELLANEOUS INFO: Infected individuals initially enter a coma which imitates a death-like state while VMD begins to mutate the genetic code and physical body. As the virus grows and multiplies, more mutations occur and initial mutations become enhanced. Continued introduction of the parent virus speeds the process while increasing specific side effects including; (1) bone and joint pain, (2) muscle growth and extreme cramping, (3) development of extended canine teeth as a feeding mechanism, (4) the need for additional amounts of plasma and blood products to sustain mutations and tissue repair, (5) enhanced metabolic recovery rates, (6) increased cerebral tissue functionality (up to 98% tissue usage), (7) heightened cell replacement, (8) low body temperature accommodating hyper-metabolic rates, (9) temporary psychosis including Obsessive Compulsive Disorder, Narcissistic Personality Disorder and/or Sexual Addiction, (10) VMD specific-allergic reactions (sun, silver, some kinds of water, garlic, etc.)

PROGNOSIS: Genetic mutations of VMD are irreversible and continually adapt to accommodate the apparent survival instinct of the virus (unsubstantiated theory; Dr. Helga Anderson, US Services Institute of Genetic Study, Walter Reed National Military Medical Center, Bethesda, Special Projects Department). Mutated individuals seem to develop extraordinary abilities, however, individuals lack adequate melanin in the skin causing a severe allergy to ultraviolet radiation (sunlight). In reaction to this allergy, VMD initiates a sleep cycle in its host causing extreme exhaustion and weakness during daylight hours. A mutated individual's cell structure no longer contains the human genetic code instead possessing deoxyribonucleic acid, or DNA with 3 chromosomes in a triple helix design.

*******************CLASSIFIED: TOP SECRET **********************

TOP SECRET

*******************CLASSIFIED: TOP SECRET **********************

Chapter 1

Strange Beginnings

In the beginning,
God created the heavens and the earth.
Now the earth was formless and empty.
Darkness was over the surface of the deep,
And that's just the way we liked it.

Gnaeus Julius Agricola, Grand Master, Vampire Council of Elders
Orsova, Romania 1003

On the border of Russia and Kazakistan...

"Incoming!" A shout ran through the company like wild fire.
Yuri lie prone in a ditch watching for the line of Taliban so-called
'freedom fighters' that were most assuredly on their way across the
dusty expanse in front of him. Soon they would appear like a
shadow out of the filthy mist and what was left of his company
would die, quickly. They were outnumbered and short of
ammunition, a deadly combination in a deadly position.

"Captain Milassoviech, your orders?" Sergeant Kraznikoff
asked hopefully. Yuri had grown up with Kraz in Siberia, playing
together as children then competing good-naturedly as young
comrades, racing across the wild steppes on their ponies.

They had also enlisted in the army and trained together until
Yuri's parents scraped up the rubles to purchase their son a
commission. Kraz's parents were not quite as fortunate or as
forthcoming. "Survive," came the stalwart answer. "It's a bit late
for formalities, Kraz. Your duty is now to survive, as is mine."

The first grenade exploded a few yards away accompanied by
anguished screams and a hail of rapid gunfire. Twelve men left to
face thirty or more crazed terrorists.

"Yuri, comrade brother, I shall do my best to follow those

3

orders." Kraz rose slightly to peek above the ground. "They come. Luck and life to you, moi-ya tovarish."

With that, the fight was on. Terrorists dressed in a ragtag assortment of everything from smock-like dishdashas to military pants and shirts charged in a rush, overrunning the diminished company pinned down in their hastily dug ditches. Kraz was one of the first to take a bullet and fell to lie motionless behind Yuri in the cold sand.

"Kraz! No, damn it. No!" Yuri returned fire aiming his last remaining bullets carefully, taking out as many of the oncoming soldiers as he had ammunition. Kraz's death would not go unrewarded and each bullet found a target with Yuri's blessing. Oblivious to the carnage around him, each target he aimed at went down and did not get up. Each bullet took him closer to an empty magazine and the deadly, yet unavoidable end that awaited.

A hot searing piece of metal slashed across his forehead and still he fought. Too soon the trigger of his AK-47 clicked. No more rounds. Empty. Yuri crouched, holding the rifle as a bat ready to take at least one more Islamic pig with him to his impending end. A bullet slammed into his shoulder and still he held on. Two enemy fighters slid over the bank and into his ditch. He swung and heard the resounding crack of a skull, sweet music to his ears. He swung again and missed, scrambling down the ditch after the retreating fighter. Mid-swing on the third try he heard another crack. Pain exploded in his brain and the sky lit up a strange sharp white color. Then his entire body vibrated. A wild humming sound filled his ears and everything went black.

A deep voice floated through the blackness to tickle the throbbing pain within Yuri's head. "Check the names. We must find the Milassoviech man. He is the one I am paid to take." The fighters scrambled to do the bidding of the tall brutal man who was their leader. Teffas Hamza stuck his rifle muzzle beneath Kraz and lifted, flipping the dead soldier over.

"Hmmm. Not this one." He fired into the corpse and walked away.

"Over here. I have found the Milassoviech!" An excited shout sent Hamza sprinting across the field.

"You are sure? This is the Milassoviech? Quickly, his tags, show me." The young fighter pulled Yuri's body into a sitting

4

position and fished beneath his uniform for the identification tags that would display his name.

Handing Hamza the tags, the young fighter was curious, "Why is this man's death worth so much? Who is he?"

Hamza slammed the butt of his rifle into the subordinate's head. "Do not question me. This is Milassoviech."

Yuri groaned, semi-conscious and bleeding from his shoulder wound.

"And he is alive. This is better than dead, much better. Tie him. Bring him with us." The smile that seemed to light Hamza's face frightened the soldiers around him more than the battle they had just fought.

*****

Castle Vyrubova, Vilyuchinsk, Kamchatka Krai, Siberia, Russia...

Natalia gasped in agony. Her head felt like it had been hit with a fireplace iron and her shoulder burned as if she'd been struck with a hot poker. What was happening? She stumbled across the old tile floor to her bed and fell onto the mattress. She was dizzy and having trouble forming thoughts. Wild splashes of color played across her visual path and bright flashes momentarily blinded her.

Holding her head, she rolled over and buried her face in the down pillows that lie in disarray at the top of her sumptuous bed. *Breathe Natalia*, she told herself, and took a deep freeing breath. The pain disappeared as fast as it had appeared. Her vision cleared as she sat up testing her limbs and neck.

What in the world was going on?

Vampires don't get sick.

Natalia sat for several minutes monitoring the minds of those around her. It was early evening, dark outside, and she could walk where she wanted without risking exposure to the damaging rays of the sun. She rose slowly testing her limbs and balance. Nothing was left of the strange pain that had, moments ago, invaded her mind and body. No nausea or vertigo remained. How odd!

She descended the long stone staircase that led to the common rooms below her private quarters. Some of her staff worked late into the evening hours and they would still be at their tasks. Petra, the night keeper and her human familiar, assistant and confidant, would be at her desk. Maybe she would know if Natalia were ill or experiencing some kind of strange manifestation. Petra had an intuitive nature that was amazing and Natalia valued her friendship, as well as her homegrown advice. Petra had been a servant at the castle since childhood and knew more secrets than Natalia could remember telling. Petra was also highly educated, a member of the local Polit Bureau and an accomplished research assistant.

"I thought I would see you soon, Natalia. There is something strange in the air that puzzles me. I felt a... I do not know. Did you feel it too?" Petra smiled as she rose to greet her friend and employer.

"Possibly for you it was strange, for me it was horrendous pain. But very short." She kissed each cheek before warmly hugging Petra. "Any ideas? I am baffled. Nothing like this has ever happened to me before. I can't seem to think straight, like a cloud swirling in my mind." Natalia took her usual seat in the worn, comfy rocking chair next to the ornate coal stove. Her fingers traced the Italian patterns on the tiles that decorated the warm stove.

"Tell me what you felt and when." Petra sat and spun in her modern office chair, crossed her legs and focused her attention on Natalia with a worried expression clouding her crystal blue eyes. Russian to a tee, Petra's creamy cheeks glowed red from the heat of the room.

"I was just standing in my bedroom. I woke several hours ago, took a shower as usual and dressed. All of a sudden a pain hit my head. Then a burning sensation appeared in my shoulder. I got dizzy and lights flashed in my eyes. It was horrible and got worse before it just ended. Thank God it disappeared quickly." Natalia spoke carefully.

"Who flashed lights in your eyes?" Petra pointed the security remote towards a series of camera pictures on a large television screen.

"No, not from outside, from within, like pin pricks of light behind my lids. I was alone." Natalia pulled a thick afghan over her legs and tucked her feet beneath her. Spring in Siberia was always a good reason to cuddle beneath a wool knit blanket made by loving hands. For a vampire the warmth was unnecessary but the cuddle was divine.

"From inside your eyes? Strange. Let me check the area for an interloper. A rogue could be responsible for attacking you if he or she were strong and skillful enough." Her fingers hit the keyboard with vicious accuracy. Petra was extremely protective of Natalia. "No other vampire has come into our territory since that wandering rogue, what, fifteen years ago? The Council of Elders usually alerts me to any company that may be headed our way. It is in their best interest to keep our politics and potential conflicts quiet. And, it's just good manners." Petra had considered herself a member of the vampire's collective society since she first learned of their existence as a teen. Despite a touchy and volatile relationship, she was ultimately trusted by the Council, as a human asset.

"You amaze me, Petra. I am lucky to have you with me. You're a good friend with whom I don't have to pretend or cover my true nature." Natalia smiled, her eyes glowing a soft deep red with emotion. As an employee, Petra was hard working and loyal. As a friend, she was simply family.

"Just keep those beautiful teeth to yourself and I will be happy. Of course, a little extra in the paycheck is always a great incentive, Nat." Natalia could see Petra's grin in the reflection of the woman's huge panel of computer screens. When had she purchased a thirty-six inch monitor for Petra?

"Pah! You make more than the Prime Minister now. How much can one woman spend when she never takes a vacation, and dresses in hand-me-downs from her sister-in-law? Really, Pet, you need a life." Natalia rocked slowly, completely comfortable in teasing her assistant who could be a great beauty with little effort.

"Focus, for heaven's sake. No one on my loops has knowledge of uninvited visitors. The sensors around the castle show no alerts. Security has been uninterrupted. The stock market is up forty points; Velechee's still carries your favorite shoes and perfume. There is no sunspot activity. The northern light envelope is minimal this night, and I do not need a vacation or fancy clothes. I have a life that I love here with you. I am safe and appreciated. Oh, and minimally paid for what I do."

The last three keystrokes pulled up the castle's extensive

security system. "Nothing unusual on the horizon. Tell me again what you felt."

"Ah, I do not believe it will help. It was like nothing I have ever encountered in all my years alive, or dead. Do you think it could be..."

"Yuri?" Both women spoke at the same time.

Chapter 2

The Course of a Life

A horror to be sure,
With no cure.
War changes the course of more than one life.
Bringing destruction, hatred and strife,
Such a boon for the wicked liar,
A pleasure for those who watch in silent desire.

Emilliano Frabriaci, Librarian
The Human Chronicles
1943, Orsova, Romania

Yuri fell the last four steps, landing painfully on his shoulder. For the misstep he earned a slamming kick to his already black and blue ribs.

"Get up, Infidel!" Two soldiers, one on each side, grasped his arms roughly hauling him to his feet.

Yuri's wound opened with a fresh flow of warm blood. He groaned, leaning heavily on a guard. In the five days since his capture he'd drifted in and out of consciousness more times than he could remember. The trip across the Caspian Sea from the southern border of Russia had been a grueling and storm-tossed trek in a very small, leaky fishing boat. Someone patched his shoulder with a dirty compress at some point, but time for Yuri had become a shadowy memory of night and day. It no longer applied in his world, a world of agony punctuated with moments, hours or days of blank unconsciousness.

The last two days, or so he thought, were a nightmare that just seemed to get worse and worse. The back of the lorry in which he rode, bound and gagged, hit every conceivable bump and hole in whatever road it traveled. Stinking of sweat and blood, Yuri lie on the wooden floorboards praying for rescue first, then praying just

9

for survival.

He stumbled on without thought or purpose. He was in some kind of cave system, that much he knew. They descended through an old dry well that had steps carved into the man-made walls, circling to the bottom. Yuri tried to lift his head occasionally as he was dragged from one room to another, down steps, up steps, along a passageway, then down more steps. It went on forever. He lost track after a while, the dark passageways leading to heavenly release in the black world of unconsciousness, on the floor of a cold cell.

*****

Kraz had crawled what seemed like miles. His head was clear but his body ached and cramped like a son of a bitch. Every time he tried to stand nausea ripped through his gut and he fell to the ground once again. How many hours had it been? Five? Eight? Twenty-four?

The bullet lodged in his side stung and burned but was crusted over and bled no more. The huge deep purple and blue bruise in the center of his chest was clearly evidence he had broken bones and some kind of internal damage. He paused to rest and touched the Russian Orthodox cross beneath his tattered and blood stained uniform. It literally saved his life, deflecting a point blank shot from one of the attacking terrorists.

Kraz groaned and began to crawl once again. He had to find help soon. He needed food and water and medical attention. He could feel life seeping from his body slowly but surely. If he didn't get help he wouldn't last much longer.

Hand, knee. Hand, knee. His fingers touched something soft and smooth. A shoe.

"Materish, ahhhh!" The small scream brought another pair of shoes running toward him. Kraz couldn't find the strength to raise his head, to reassure the tiny owner of the shoe that he was harmless.

"A you-tha may," he whispered through cracked and swollen lips.

*****

10

Natalia dozed in her rocking chair next to the coal stove as Petra searched for answers. Thoughts of the last time she had listened in on Yuri's conversation with his parents played across her mind.

Conversation?

Well, it was actually more like a screaming match, with a few broken dishes and some torn clothing thrown in for fun. Yuri's mother pleaded with tears and histrionics. Yuri's father wielded guilt like a horsewhip, attempting to brow beat his son into remaining home and safe. When it had finally come to fists and hateful words, the older man stormed from the house in anger. But in the end, neither could convince the young man to give up his desire to enlist just to "show the world the true worth of a Romanov." Years living in the shadows wearing an assumed name to protect his real identity did little for Yuri's self esteem or prospects for any kind of future. Stuck in a tiny Siberian town, the energetic and intelligent young man rebelled, enlisted with his friend and went off to be a soldier, unwittingly leaving the safe haven of Natalia's protective influence. Though she could hardly blame him for wanting a life of his own, she agonized over the distance and her inability to watch over him.

As The Watcher, Natalia's hands were tied. She could not follow the headstrong Yuri *and* protect his parents at the same time. Through her contacts she could ensure he serve only in remote non-combat assignments, somewhat insulated from danger and possible identification. At the time, she had done the best she could and hoped it was enough. Now she wondered. If this unexplainable pain was connected to Yuri, why hadn't she ever felt it before? What trouble could the young Captain be in?

As she sat patiently, desperate for news, Petra contacted the Council of Elders and was put in touch with the Librarian, a very old and very smart vampire who kept the historical archives for vampires as a species. It was an especially proud moment for Petra, knowing the Council did not offer contact with the Librarian as a rule, especially to a human.

Natalia knew a little of Emilliano Frabriaci. He was an unusual man, even for a vampire. He loved a good mystery but he loved negotiating for his services even more. Everything had its

11

price and he was a consummate, masterful dealer. Neither Natalia, nor Petra had ever met the man, but over the years, Natalia shared many secrets of vampire society with Petra and she knew a little of his existence. In his mind and beneath his hands lie the entire known history of vampires. Natalia knew it would cost her a great deal to request a consult on her painful problem.

Petra hit the enter key and sent the request with a heavy sigh.

Natalia stirred, glancing up. "What, Pet? What's wrong."

"Nothing's wrong. I just sacrificed my first born for you, my dear. Go back to sleep. I won't have an answer for awhi-" The speaker chimed and the light flashed on her menu bar indicating she had an incoming e-mail. "Okay, well maybe not."

Natalia peered over her shoulder as Petra opened the file. "Petra? What have you done?"

To: *Natalia A. Vyrubova*
Cc: *Petra Phillamonov*
Interesting symptoms. 3 Possibilities. Proposal?
E.

"What does that mean, Pet? And why did he write to me?" Natalia was curious but wary as well. She worried about the lengths to which her loyal assistant would go to serve or protect Natalia.

"I used your name and account because I wasn't sure he would respond to a human. He's a weird little fellow, the Librarian, you know. I sent him a query on your symptoms. The cryptic reply means he has three possible answers." Petra looked over her shoulder and winked. "Don't worry, Natalia. We will find the answer to this puzzle. I promise."

"If anyone can, you can, Pet. And what does *Proposal* mean?" Natalia raised an eyebrow.

"My first born, that's what it means." Petra frowned in thought. "Fortunately I don't have a first born to offer up. What do you think the boy would like? What little carrot can I tempt him with to help us?"

Natalia thought. "Think out loud. Tell me about him, Pet."

"Well, he's Italian, originally from Venice, I believe. He treasures information above all else. I've heard he likes old manuscripts and loves double Dutch chocolate malt balls, a good pizza pie and AB positive. He has no affiliation beyond serving the Council, that I know of."

"Wait, you said he was from Venice? He likes old manuscripts? I wonder…" Natalia leapt from her chair and ran from the room. "I have an idea, I'll be right back." Her voice drifted down the stairs as she flew up the steps.

Petra stared after Natalia. "You have my first born stashed upstairs?"

In a vampiric flash Natalia was back, reverently holding an ornate wooden box about the size that might contain an expensive pair of running shoes. The sides of the box were covered in carved Roman script.

"This, my wonderful Petra, is much better than your first born and much more expensive. It's been in my family forever. My aunt used to tell me that it was the glass pen that Emperor Constantine the Great used to create the plans for Constantinople. See the initials here on the barrel: FVC for Flavius Valerius Constantinus. As a Librarian, Frabriaci may just be interested in ancient writing utensils. What do you think?"

A brilliant smile flashed across Petra's face as her hands flashed across the keyboard. "I think we may have found the bait, Nat. Start counting. I will know how interested he is by how long it takes to get a response. Start-" she hit the send button, "now."

Natalia glanced at the old Black Forest clock that hung above the coal stove just as she heard the computer chime. "Me thinks the man is interested!" Natalia grinned just as wide.

"I guess so. God bless v-speed. Let's see what good old Emilliano has to say about a two-thousand year old Murano nib." Petra returned to the keyboard and opened the file.

From: *Natalia A. Vyrubova*
To: *Emilliano Frabriaci, Librarian*
Cc: *Petra Phillamonov*
FVC glass pen (320 AD). Constantine the Great.
N.

From: *Emilliano Frabriaci, Librarian*
To: *Natalia A. Vyrubova*
Cc: *Petra Phillamonov*
Acceptable. Exchange 24 hours. Council conference room.
E.

"Looks like we're going to Romania, Pet. Pack light it's going to be a whirlwind trip and Yuri's safety may depend on our speed." Natalia placed the box on Petra's desk with a pat and danced up the stairs.

"Well, I'll water the plants, feed the dog and be right with you! Hey Nat, keep in mind I'm only human right? RIGHT?" Petra yelled into the hallway then muttered to herself, "Here we go again."

*****

Pavel Kraznikoff lie beneath a hand woven quilt watching a spider in the corner spin silk around a stunned fly. Every few seconds the fly would struggle half-heartedly, then give in to the venom coursing through its pathetic body and lie still as the spider continued to work, packaging its next meal. Pavel felt quite like that fly. Just this morning he had struggled to sit but failed, confined by the weight of the quilt and the softness of the feather bed in which he lie. He could remember lying in this bed for at least seven days. How long had he wandered or crawled before being found by the family that now cared for him? He had no idea and could not even speak to his savior, who seemed only to converse in some tribal form of Kazahk. He could show his appreciation, and at every turn kissed the palm of the child who found him. She would giggle, hide her face then babble endlessly on.

Tomorrow he would try once again to rise. Tomorrow, possibly, he would be the spider and not the helpless fly. He closed his eyes and let his mind drift toward home. It was a bitter sweet thought without his life-long friend, Yuri. There was no point in rehashing the recent past. Yuri had been taken and there was absolutely nothing Pavel could do. Did he even still live? Pavel

14

had no idea who had taken his friend. He did know Yuri had been set up and sold by someone in the army or possibly some politician. What little he overheard convinced him of that.

Rubles had been exchanged and now Pavel was alone. Tears welled, seeping from the corner of each eye to roll towards his ears, then drop to the pillow beneath his head.

He was alone and afraid.

Chapter 3

Of Knowledge

With age comes experience and knowledge,
Not always good things.
But in the world of knowing and doing,
The truth shall give such wings,
To deeds and thoughts of dark or light.
Oft the choice is die… or fight.

General Mario Velario, European Allied Forces
1947, Roma, Italy

Through a well-guarded cave at the edge of the river below a sheer cliff, stood the doorway to the Council of Elders. No human could have accessed the entrance without vampire help. The river ran wildly mere inches from the mouth of the cave. The catacombs below were black and foreboding, discouraging any human from pursuing exploration. Guards at each juncture made sure humans brave enough to test their courage did not find their way into the Council of Elders.

Together, Natalia and Petra entered the long passageway that led beneath the Danube River and across to the submerged island of Ada Kaleh. It had become the home of the Council of Elders shortly before being completely covered by river water when a dam was constructed farther down the Iron Gates. A huge gorge, called the Iron Gates, was aptly named for the formation that contained the powerful flow of the Danube. Tamed by the new dam in the 70's, the original island was home to an old fortress with a mosque. The town's inhabitants were resettled, mostly in Turkey, during the building of the dam. When the island was vacated, the Council took over sealing entrances and covering structures to make the perfect home away from home.

Over the years, the Council built connecting tunnels from the

Romanian side of the river through ancient and secret exits, then proceeded to excavate and build whatever they wanted. Closeted away from the curious eyes of the local humans and safe beneath tons of flowing water, the entire Council moved into their new home, finally collecting the world's store of vampiric information in one secure location.

Natalia and Petra trudged along between their respective escorts deep within the catacombs that led to the submerged island. "Are we under the river, Natalia? I hear running water above." Natalia nodded but did not speak. *Petra, do not speak to me unless I speak first. These guards of the Council are very traditional and will not think twice about killing one more human. There is serious protocol here.* Natalia used her mind, focusing in a tight contained thought, to communicate with her assistant.

Petra glanced at Natalia and briefly nodded. It was amazing Petra had even been allowed to enter the catacombs. She was prepared to spend the night comfortably on the rocks above the entrance, instead of entering the protected domain of the oldest and most powerful vampires on the face of the earth. When their escort of five huge hungry looking vampires emerged from nowhere indicating she and Natalia should follow, Petra had just about fainted. Only Natalia's strong mind and firm hand kept her upright and moving, at first. At the rate her heart was hammering in her chest, she seriously doubted she'd make it to motherhood, to have the first-born she'd joked about bartering away.

Petra skipped over a damp drainage ditch and looked ominously at Natalia. *Calm yourself, Pet. These tunnels have transported many more humans and vampires than you could ever imagine over the years. They are sturdy and more solid than would seem from the inside. Wait until you have seen the complex, you will not know you are beneath sixty feet of flowing Danube and much more solid rock. It is magnificent and most comfortable. I have only been here once. I am anxious to see what has been added.*

Petra nodded and continued along, no more secure than before Natalia's mental message. Soon dim light illuminated parts of the tunnel. As she walked she tried to observe everything around her; the carved stone walls; the man-made bricks; the strange symbols and writing on the walls, heavy metal doors that looked like they belonged on the space station instead of plastered into ancient arched entries, alcoves that held who knew what, the bones left to rot.

Bones?

Left to rot?

Petra was used to being around Natalia and those gleaming fangs, but what had she gotten herself into here in this place where a human had the same status as a juicy piece of rare prime rib?

Natalia shuddered and grabbed her right hand to stem the momentary burning sensation. "Petra, it's happening again. My hand, the fingers burn as if placed in a fire." Natalia pulled her hand to her chest and held it for several seconds, agony written all over her elegant features.

Petra could do nothing but stand and hold her friend. "Is it passing like before?"

"Yes, but the pain! Oh Petra, what is happening?" A tiny blood red tear appeared at the corner of one eye. Petra had rarely seen Natalia cry. The vampire kept her emotions tightly locked away from everyone. Petra was stunned.

"It passes but I feel the fog again. I…I…I am…I cannot focus and my thoughts are tangled. Pet?" Pet felt Natalia shiver as she stood holding her friend.

*****

Yuri sat tied to a broken chair. He had no feeling in his extremities. The plastic tie-wraps that held him tight to the wooden frame long ago cut off all circulation. He took a shallow breath and felt pain warm his sides. It burned like hot coals in his gut but told him he still lived.

"Russian Infidel, you do not die easily. I have had the pleasure of your company now for what, seven days and still I see defiance in your eyes." Colonel Fashiam shook his head. "You should let yourself die soon. It will end the pain. The longer you hold out, the longer you will feel such agony. You will die in the end anyway. Honestly, it has been ordered and I shall obey." The Colonel bent and clipped the tie-wrap that held one of Yuri's arms to the frame.

The rush of blood and feeling was overwhelming. Yuri tensed against the taunting pins and needles that raced up and down his

18

arm like fire in his veins.

The Colonel motioned to his subordinate who stood ready with a heavy metal pipe. "The right hand this time, Khaleel. One finger at a time, please."

Yuri could not resist the scream leaving his throat. He was a soldier and a man, but the pain was intolerable and beyond his voluntary control. This was so unfair. It had just begun to feel again when the pipe contacted his little finger with the force of a sledgehammer and he heard his bones crunch. He screamed wildly.

The next contact did not make a crunch. It sounded more like a slug when its body ends up under the sole of some careless gardener's boot; a squishy, mushy splat. He screamed again and knew his ring finger would be next. Yuri closed his eyes as tight as he could and prayed. He had eight fingers and ten toes left. How long could he last before the Colonel's word crept into his prayers?

*****

Pavel leaned heavily on the homemade wooden crutch, as he attempted use of his legs one more time. So far, so good. He had taken five steps this morning and now he was on his seventh of the afternoon.

Finally! He was the spider. He took another step and fell as his knees gave out. Pavel hit the soft dirt and lie for a moment just breathing in the freshness of the earth upon which he lie. He had been in bed for days and his muscles did not want to work. He lie in the warm sunshine feeling its heat on his back. He smiled and tasted small particles of dirt that stuck to his face and lips. Pavel heard high pitched giggles behind him and twisted to see the little girl who had saved his life by finding him in a ditch.

How long ago?

More than a week?

Less?

The little dark haired girl dressed in a colorful smock tied with braided wool, tugged at his shoulder. "Ca'-chee va. Ca'chee va nah ha Pavel." She at least knew his name. "Manshx va tinlan ach, Pavel."

"Okay, okay. I'll get up in a moment." Pavel rolled over and watched the little girl's hair move in the breeze. It hung almost to her waist and gleamed in the bright sunlight. Even though he lie in the dirt, almost helpless, with a small child laughing at his predicament. Today, he was the spider!

*****

Petra sat quietly, hands folded in her lap as she watched Natalia presenting their part of the bargain to the Librarian before the Council. The Librarian, Emilliano Frabriaci, stood on a dais in the middle of the cavernous chamber, dwarfed by high stone arches and magnificent stained glass windows lit from behind. Each of the huge eight windows depicted some scene from vampiric history, lauding a hero, defining a battle, or demonstrating caution in surviving the vamp life-style. Natalia stood before the Council Grand Master speaking the required words.

"The agreement to provide Librarian Emilliano Frabriaci with one writing utensil of ancient origin has been met. In accordance with our payment, I would ask the Council for assistance with a matter that may, or may not be of concern to all vampires. It is surely of concern to us." Petra was not surprised that Natalia used the royal 'we' in speaking to the Council. All mistresses and masters spoke in the plural as a matter of power and respect for their coven members and human familiars.

Gnaeus Julius Agricola eyed the woman before him, looking down his long Roman nose from his position high on the Council bench. Natalia waited, her eyes demurely downcast and without challenge. Grand Master Agricola was an ancient and powerful vampire but more than that, a solid and fair leader. He was known for keeping his word and standing solidly behind pro-vampire policies. The Council had the responsibility for trouble shooting problems and keeping peace between covens. But more than that, the Council, and more pointedly, the Librarian, was charged with gathering the global information database on vampires as a species and society. He kept records on everything from genealogies, medical anomalies, food banks, and power lines to worldwide financial interests. Modern vampire life and society was not that much different from humans when it came to politics and finances.

"Mistress Vyrubova, your half of the bargain is met. Present

20

your request to Librarian Frabriaci." The Grand Master stood dismissingly, the rest of the Council following suit. "Emilliano will tell me of his findings." Agricola shambled along behind the long bench with his Council in attendance. Petra thought he looked old and fragile, but she knew better, way better.

The Librarian snatched his box and strode out of the rotunda with a tight giggle. Natalia almost ran to keep up with him. *Pet, let's go. Come on. This place is huge and I have a feeling the Librarian won't bother looking for us if we get lost in this maze. I am completely amazed at what has been added since I last came here, almost thirty-five years ago.*

"Yes, ma'am." Petra's whisper echoed off the cathedral styled ceiling as if she had shouted the words. "Holy shit!" She ran after Natalia and the Librarian.

Pet! Watch your mouth, child. Natalia was trotting now to keep up, trying to figure out what the Librarian was mumbling about as he caressed the wooden box he held.

Through long corridors. Up and down ancient stairs. Up and down new stainless steel stairs. Along catwalks above bottomless pits or simply across rough walkways, the place seemed endless, and still the Librarian continued at a breakneck pace. How did his skinny little legs carry him so quickly?

Without warning, Frabriaci halted in front of a cast iron door engraved with the kind of symbols Petra saw in the entry passageways. The glyphs curled and meandered through a tangle of intricate border patterns that outlined the tall door. All three hinges were ornately carved and solidly welded holding the oiled door securely in place, and probably had for centuries. Frabriaci waved his hand in a pattern over several glyphs and Petra heard the distinct clicking sound of a lock disengaging. Then the door simply disappeared. Petra gasped.

Ignoring the human's noise, the Librarian strode through the doorway as Natalia grabbed Petra and hauled her after the quick willowy man before the door reappeared in place with another loud click. Once through the doorway, Natalia released her hold on Petra as she froze in place. The room was completely round, like a giant cylinder and at least five stories high. The total surface of the one circular wall was covered with shelving literally cram packed with books, scrolls and bound manuscripts. Some of the lower shelves actually contained heavy stone tablets separated between modern sheets of cushioning neoprene. A mammoth computer station resembling a techno-octopus with a fifty-two inch monitor sat in the middle of the room surrounded by tables and chairs stacked with all kinds of documents, magazines and boxes of old fashioned slides, reel-to-reel tapes, film reels and photographs. In a tiny alcove beneath a massive arch, sat a slight woman with strawberry blonde hair that fell to the floor and puddled at her feet, tangling around the legs of her stool. She was engrossed in a scroll, not actually touching the skin, but following the fluid calligraphy with a metal pointer. Petra stood in place just taking in the overload of sensory input.

"Natalia, look at this place. The answers to the world's mysteries may lie right here, right before our eyes." Petra spun in a circle with her arms out wide.

"Down, girl. Unless, of course, you really want to sacrifice your firstborn child, I wouldn't dicker with the Librarian. He's ruthless." Natalia smiled as she approached the man to whom she would pose her question.

"Oh, yes. I do believe I enjoy being called ruthless. However, I enjoy being *it* even more. Now, Mistress and accompanying human, what do you seek from the Librarian?" He slid a pile of books from the seat of an ornate fifteenth century chair with a flourish. "Sit, sit, sit." He stood at his computer terminal, glancing every few seconds at the screen which hung from a frame on a thick cable. "I *am* listening."

"Ah, sir, a few days ago I, ah had this... thing happen." Natalia was nervous and in awe of the tall, very slender vampire who stood in flowing robes similar to those of a priest or Turkik magistrate. They did nothing to disguise his seemingly frail and almost wispy form. His pure white hair hung to his shoulders, shimmery and so thin Natalia could see his scalp and chin through its fine curtain.

"May I?" Petra jumped in when Natalia stalled. "Perhaps, I could-" Petra found her throat clamped shut by a childish hand that commanded incredible strength. She choked and croaked at the tiny woman who was just inches away, hovering above the floor in midair.

"Humans do not speak to the Librarian without permission.

22

You do not have permission." Like a faerie floating on the wind, the girl's strawberry hair drifted and coiled in a nonexistent breeze. Her diaphanous robe billowed about her tiny emaciated frame and her sweet smile revealed a gruesome display of spiked teeth and long fangs. Petra tried to gasp in fear but the woman-child's grip kept all air from entering her lungs.

"Cliona, dearest, do let the human go. She has my permission to be here, and so may lend some help with this *thing* that seems to be bothering Mistress Vyrubova. Sheathe your claws my lovely." Frabriaci placed a gentle bony hand on Cliona's shoulder, and the woman released her hold on Petra's throat.

In less than a heartbeat, Natalia was at Petra's side catching her as the gasping human collapsed. *Breathe, Pet. Just calm yourself and breathe.* "Ms. Phillamonov belongs to me and I will not have her damaged in any way. Do I make myself clear?" Natalia growled, barring her fangs in anger.

"Of course, of course. Do calm down. Cliona shall keep her distance, won't you, my sweet child? Now go to your desk and continue your studies. We shall discuss your behavior later." He directed the girl to her alcove with a stern dismissal. "Now Mistress, perhaps your human and you, yourself can explain what this *thing* is you would like me to comment on. I have only had a simple e-mail from you on which to think."

Natalia pulled Petra to her feet and helped her sit on a nearby stool, easily tossing its contents to the floor. "She requires water."

"I have sent for bloodwine. It will be delivered directly." The Librarian returned to his computer screen and waved away Natalia's concerns.

"She is human, she will need water or human wine. She cannot drink bloodwine, Frabriaci, and you of all vampires should know that. Your disrespect and lack of concern for my assistant is surprising and unsettling. I must be assured she is safe here or our bargain is off." With her anger had come strength and Natalia was not going to let the issue go until she was satisfied Petra would be treated with respect and care.

"Yes, yes, yes. I have ordered both and here it is. Please, human, help yourself." Frabriaci would only be pushed so far as a host.

"Her name is Petra Phillamonov. Please address her as such."

Natalia left no room for argument, as she poured a glass of golden wine and handed it to her assistant.

From deep in the alcove Natalia heard a childish taunting voice. "She serves her human. How disgusting. The little pet has her heart, I think. Does she allow her pet in bed with her as well, I do wonder."

"The point, Mistress?" Frabriaci poured himself a tall glass of bloodwine and considered the two women who had come to ask his counsel.

"I was in my chamber standing in front of a window when all of a sudden, I felt such pain. It came and went so fast but still it was horrible. It has happened several times since. We have ruled out tainted blood, illness, of course, intruders and rogues. It happened again, not over an hour ago, here in the entrance. You mentioned three possibilities in your e-mail response." Natalia also poured herself a glass and paced as she spoke and drank.

"You are sure you have ruled out the things mentioned, without a doubt?"

Natalia glanced at Petra to see if she was recovered enough to speak. Petra nodded and Natalia sent her a quick mental message. *You may speak for yourself. I believe he will listen without interference from that weirdling in the alcove.*

Petra quickly explained what she had researched shortly after Natalia's odd experience.

"Now that I have heard more, I no longer believe there are three possible answers. However, two still remain with merit. The first I have doubts about. That would be the theory of an incredibly strong vampire's mental attack. But again, that could not happen here, under our protection." Frabriaci scanned his computer monitor before continuing. "The second theory revolves around your own family, Mistress Vyrubova. I have known of vampires who 'feel' or sense events in the lives of their family members. These are usually very old and very strong vampires with close ties to their families. This does not seem to fit your profile either. Hummm… Interesting."

Natalia took a chair and sat near Petra after clearing the seat of miscellaneous papers and a box of half-used number two pencils. "I can assure you I have no family left. The only ones to whom I am in the least attached are in my village, or serving in the military, a desk job. I do not understand. Vampires do not contract illnesses, or at least we didn't in the past. In any event, the pain passed too rapidly to be any kind of illness, and there does not seem to be any lasting side affects."

"Natalia, I can always try to scan your mind to see what is affecting you. It is one of my many gifts, to enter a mind and body to 'see' what lies beneath the skin and within the mind's matter. An unusual gift, to be sure, but then we are the same in that respect, I have been given to understand." His comment on Natalia's extraordinary power to compel minds was not common knowledge. In fact, Natalia was under the assumption that the only one who really knew of her unique powers, was the human who sat next to her sipping wine.

"The procedure is very stressful and can cause extreme fatigue. That presents a problem with your human, Petra, here with us. You will be extremely hungry. Do you understand?" Frabriaci glanced knowingly at Petra.

Petra rose to the occasion. "My Mistress will not hurt me, I am confident of that. I should be here to help Natalia if she needs me." Petra smiled at her Mistress with that set jaw that told Natalia nothing short of moving heaven and hell, would get Petra out of the room. "How long will it take? Will she be in pain?"

"The choice belongs to your Mistress, human. You do not know the power of blood lust. Natalia, what is your decision? How much do you trust yourself with your human, Mistress?" He watched Natalia carefully as she considered her choice.

"Petra will stay."

A tiny voice drifted around the room. "Petra will stay. Petra will stay. Petra will pay."

Chapter 4

The Brave and the Dead

If the better part of valor is discretion,
Then what of the coward's choice?

Unknown Author, Konstatin Station,
Omoag Bandon, Russia

Pavel stood on the ridge above his village, tears of both happiness and regret streaming freely down the man's face. He was home.

Home.

It was such a small word that meant so much. He would wait until dark to approach Yelizovo, until all of the streets were empty by decree. He did not want the authorities or even the neighbors near the farm to ask questions until he could see his parents and explain his arrival. He was sure news of his death had been delivered to his family. It had been almost three weeks since the battle, he figured. Some days still ran together in his memory.

Had Yuri survived? Where had he been taken? Guilt ate at Kraz as he hobbled toward a rock outcropping that would provide cover for the day. He was so hungry his stomach ground against his backbone. When was the last time he had eaten?

When was the last time Yuri had eaten?

With that thought Kraz no longer wanted food. Guilt was an effective tool to drive away his hunger pangs.

He crawled into a cave-like space beneath the rock and curled around his crutch, propping his bad leg a little higher than his body to keep the constant swelling down. One quick look told him he would be safe and out of sight, if someone should come along while he slept. He had no possessions left, not even a pocketknife with which to defend himself. He had left all but his clothing with the family that found and cared for him as a gift of thanks. They

26

had done the best they could but his body healed of its own accord, not quite correctly, but healed enough to make his way home.

His lips smiled and he shivered, sinking into the cold. Cold was good. Cold kept the pain away, at least the physical pain. He shivered again and tried to relax against the hard dirt. Unfortunately the pain in his mind would not depart with his body heat.

Yuri was gone.

Who knew where.

Pavel's parents thought their son dead. His country had betrayed Pavel, and would hunt him to the ends of the earth if it were known he survived. Even his identity would have to go. He would be without his life-long friend, his family and his name. Nothing would be left to him, and that was as it should be. He was the one who lie, feigning death. He was the one who had let his friend be captured.

He lived.

He suspected Yuri had not.

Hot tears fell against his frozen cheeks. He must find out, know for certain. He owed that much to his friend. He must be sure before he abandoned all hope.

*****

"Colonel Fashiam, have you tired of your little toy?" Teffas Hamza sat outside the small café in Torkham with a man he only called friend. "It has been some three weeks and still the Russian survives. He is a strong man, that one." Teffas' smile was a scary, animalistic thing.

"Ah, Teffas, only you would respect a pathetic prisoner who lives, despite impending death. I have considered the method long and hard, well, for me anyway. I do believe I shall simply slit his throat. He is no longer much fun to torture. Most times he is not even aware of what is being done to his body. I honestly think his mind is gone, but there are times I see a flicker. I am driven to see what is left."

"And you have called me an animal, Fashiam?" Teffas Hamza chuckled, then sobered, looking around the market place. "Albani has requested my assistance to set a summit. What do you know of this?"

"Nothing Teffas, but I will find out quickly. My General does not often leave me out of his confidence. It does not bode well for me, my friend. I question my position within the ranks with this new information." Fashiam watched Teffas adjust his bulk, then leaned closer to his friend. "Possibly I should not spend so much time with the Russian. He will die on his own soon enough. I shall endeavor to be more efficient from today on. Son of camel dung, the Russian Captain can rot in his hole." Fashiam studied the fly buzzing near his cup. "Tell me Teffas, what do you do with all the money you get for your dirty deeds? You must be a very wealthy man. Does Albani take a cut of your profits?"

"Fashiam, I am sure General Albani would tell you if you asked." That nasty smile was back giving Teffas' face a grizzly and maniacal gleam.

Colonel Fashiam knew better than to question Albani on anything. His position was tenuous at best. He was one of only three people who knew the true extent of Albani's holdings in the caverns beneath Hafsa Tokar. If Albani had any reason to question Fashiam's unwavering loyalty, the Colonel would simply disappear. The next unwaveringly loyal man would take his place, just as loyal and just as expendable as Fashiam. The Colonel was beginning to realize he had grown fat and complacent in his impregnable stronghold.

"I do not believe I am that curious, Teffas." Colonel Fashiam threw down a hand full of puls, enough to pay for both of their drinks, then rose to leave. His men appeared from their positions around the café. "Allah keep you, my friend. I must now go to find out why I have been left out of these new plans and what it may mean."

Teffas Hamza watched the depressed Colonel saunter off. He was sure Fashiam would not be long in his position. Albani was clear that the Colonel, while still trusted, had shown poor judgment in bringing the live Russian into the stronghold. The General was not pleased, and that was the first reading of the Qur'an at Fashiam's funeral. Teffas found some amusement in his thoughts. Albani had accumulated untold wealth stored in a mammoth cavern structure attached to the stronghold by a secret passageway. The hills were full of such caverns and were handy as secret warehouses. Albani, Teffas and Fashiam were the only three living men who knew what filled one such cavern. Teffas was not opposed to making it only two.

*****

The Librarian caught Natalia as she fell to her knees. "My foot, my God, it feels like someone has smashed my toes. Aughhhhhh!" Frabriaci lowered the vampiress to the floor where she curled, tearing at her boot and stocking. "Do something. It is getting worse, Librarian. Petra, help me."

Petra was by her Mistress' side in a flash, or as fast as a human could move. "Natalia, hold still. Let me remove your boot." Petra quickly pulled Natalia's ruined boot from her foot, tugging the stocking off as well.

"Natalia, there is nothing wrong." Petra's fingers prodded feeling for fevered tissue or injuries. "Your skin is not even warm. In fact it is cold, just right for a vampire. Can you move your toes?"

Natalia sat up, stunned. "It is gone. What is happening? There is not even residual ache. Not an itch, nothing." She looked at her assistant, then at the Librarian, then towards the roof where Cliona hovered, mildly interested, only from the standpoint of enjoying the scene of someone in pain. "It was there, horribly there. Then it was gone."

"Sorta like your boot, Nat. Hope you packed another pair." Petra held the shredded boot and limp sock with a pattern of small yellow boxes circling the cuff. "Sponge Bob? You have got to be kidding, Nat." Petra mumbled under her breath, gaining a dirty look from her mistress.

Stow it Pet. And they were a gift from Brianna on my human birthday. The Admiral's daughter has developed an unhealthy attachment to this Bob fellow and to me as well. My socks, my secret, okay?

The Librarian looked puzzled, considering Natalia's last little experience in pain. "I must enter your body to find the source of this disturbing event. If our species is developing a form of sickness, then I must know what it is." He spoke more to himself than to his visitors. "Cliona, you are charged with protecting the

29

human."

"Her Mistress says the human does not need protection. Why would I disbelieve this woman?" Cliona snickered from on high.

"Do not pout, child. Obey me." The Librarian's stern voice filled the room like a thunderstorm.

Cliona floated to stand next to Petra with a sniff. "Yes, Librarian." Effectively chastised, the faerie-like vampire kept her position as Frabriaci knelt next to Natalia on the floor.

"This is not painful but will be facilitated if you relax and assist me. You shall feel a pressure and may become nauseous but the effects will fade when my power departs. I will be quick. It will tax me as much as you." Frabriaci placed a hand on top of Natalia's head and closed his eyes.

Automatically, Natalia's eyes closed as well. Petra thought it was like watching a puppet show. Whatever Frabriaci did, Natalia did as well. As his hands moved across her body, her hands followed. When he gasped, Natalia gasped with the same depth and strength of the action.

One minute.

Two minutes.

Petra watched Natalia and Frabriaci along with her watch. How long could this go on? Natalia's face grimaced and she moaned in a weak, tiny voice. Petra took a step forward, only to find herself jerked back and restrained in an iron grip.

"Stay, human." Cliona commanded as if Petra were some kind of misbehaving dog on a leash.

"He's hurting her. He said it wouldn't hurt."

"Shut up, human. Pets know nothing of our ways." Cliona moved her free hand and Petra's lips would no longer work, her vocal cords instantaneously incapable of making sound. She stood, restrained and mute as her Mistress moaned and mimed the movements of the Librarian.

It seemed that the process went on forever, but Petra knew it was less than five minutes by her watch.

All at once, Frabriaci withdrew his hands and sat heavily next to Natalia, breathing deeply, obviously fatigued and breathless. Cliona left Petra's side to fetch bloodwine for her master, concern clearly written all over her pale, child-like face. Concern for Frabriaci only.

"Emilliano, drink my darling. Why do you push yourself so far, husband." Cliona knelt, caressing the Librarian's feathery hair as she fed him small sips of the wine.

"Husband? Holy shit!" Petra's lips were working again. She was astounded. Tiny, faerie-vampire Cliona? Emilliano Frabriaci's wife! "Isn't that just rich."

Natalia opened her eyes. They shone blood red and her nose twitched compulsively. She needed blood and it stood just a few feet away. Warm and alive, the blood coursed through a live heart that beat frantically.

"Natalia, it's me, Petra, your assistant." Petra watched her Mistress rise and stalk toward her with a glazed look in the vampire's eyes. "Nat?"

"Oops." Cliona smiled and stroked her husband's hair as he recovered what little color the bloodwine could provide in a pinch.

Natalia shook her head but stood her ground, observing the human as if she were a starving child contemplating an oatmeal or chocolate chip cookie, both a good choice. She took another step and shuddered. The bloodlust washed over her mind and she took another step trying to straighten.

Petra's high voice fought its way through the waves of lust. "Natalia? You can resist this. I love you, my friend. Fight." Natalia felt a cool glass pressed to her hand.

"Drink, Mistress. It will stem the tide and possibly your pet will survive." Cliona stood next to Natalia with a full glass of bloodwine. "Drink, Natalia."

Natalia raised the glass to her lips and drank deeply of the wine. She could feel the blood enter her system, dampening the hunger and stilling the need to feed. Her fangs retracted and her eyes cleared. Petra stood close, refilling her glass, urging her Mistress to drink again.

"You took a terrible chance, Petra. I could have killed you, my friend, but thank you. Thank you for being here and trusting me. And refilling my glass! I do believe the alcohol is having more of an effect than the blood. I feel very... giddy." Petra grabbed her swaying Mistress, guiding her to a chair where Natalia plopped down with a giggle, holding her glass out for more. The specially distilled alcohol mixed with blood had the same effect on a vampire's empty stomach, as several stiff shots had on a human

31

who had not recently eaten.

Petra looked to Cliona who shrugged and nodded. Once more, Petra filled Natalia's glass, crossed the room and then filled Frabriaci's empty glass.

"It is not your job to serve the Librarian, but I thank you, human. I mean Petra. He is weak but will be fine." Cliona helped Frabriaci to a chair where he sat, slumped but aware. She perched on the arm of his chair, not willing to leave her husband's side quite yet. A tiny pale hand stroked the white hair of the Librarian with what appeared to be love.

"Mistress Vyrubova, I do believe I have solved the mystery of your phantom pain." The Librarian took a deep breath and another gulp from his glass.

Natalia chugged the contents of her glass and giggled as it fell from her hand. She kicked her legs out in front of the chair in which she sat and giggled even more. "Silly me, I seem to have destroyed my favorite pair of Prada leather boots. Oh well, Pet, time to go shopping." Natalia stood and sat back down very quickly holding her stomach.

"Do vampires, per chance, vomit?" Petra was watching Natalia wildly searching for something; her Mistress' head bobbing as the slightly soused vampire swallowed hard.

"It is probably the wine and my husband's ministrations. Do not let your Mistress foul the archives, Petra. There is a wastebasket near the computer. Quickly!"

Petra heard Natalia gulp and saw her lurch for the basket. She failed to make the distance but hit the computer terminal with incredible accuracy.

"Guess that answers my question." Petra plugged her nose.

Chapter 5

The Care and Feeding of a Vampire

When faced with a hungry vampire, quickly find a source of food that does not include your own body fluids or biting.

Be careful when administering bloodwine to a vampire, unless you just like cleaning up a bloody mess.

Petra Phillamonov, Administrative Assistant to Natalia Vyrubova
Vilyuchinsk, Kamchatka Oblast, Russia

Petra tried not to smile at the filth that came from such an innocent looking mouth, as Cliona dashed for a cloth and cleaning solution. Pet assisted Natalia back to her chair and placed the plastic basket solidly between her legs. "Not a big drinker, boss?"

"Agh! I feel like someone danced on my gut. I think I'm..." Natalia bent and buried her face in the basket. All kinds of icky noise and coughing came from the inside of the clean white plastic container.

Petra found a carafe of drinking water with fresh lemons on the tray where she had gotten the wine, and poured a small glass for Natalia. "Here, rinse, you lush." Petra deserved the glare she got from Natalia, as the vampire rinsed her mouth and spit into the bucket.

"Thanks, Pet. What would I do without you?" Natalia smiled sheepishly.

"Bite the brat." Petra grinned as Cliona floated through the door, rags in one hand and a bottle of cleaning solution in the other.

Cliona floated right to Petra and dumped the items into her hands. "Serve, servant." Cliona returned to her perch next to the Librarian and grinned right back.

"Oh yeah, vamp-hearing, how could I forget?" Petra set to

33

cleaning Natalia's mess from the keyboard and screen. It wasn't as bad as cleaning up after her little brother, when he had been ill. There were no chunks.

"Pet, I can clean..." Natalia tried to rise and fell backwards with a gasp, grabbing once again for the plastic basket.

"I can take care of this, Nat. Stay where you are so this is all I have to clean up." Petra was almost finished when the Librarian finally spoke.

"I apologize, Natalia, I should not have stayed so long within the confines of your body. You are a truly fascinating vampire. What I saw..." His voice trailed off and his head hung once again.

"Dearest, let me find you a snack. I will return. Do not rise until I come back. I will be but a moment." Cliona actually disappeared in a bright, whispering flash.

"Wow! Vampires can teleport?" Petra was amazed at the length and breath of vampire skill.

"Some, not all. She worries overmuch about me. I shall be fine, in time. Natalia, while she is gone I must tell you. The pain is centered within another, not only you. It is a connection I found to a man, a human man. He is in great distress, physical pain. The connection is so strong, you feel remnant pain of his existence. Until now, I did not believe such a connection could exist, especially with a human. I am at a loss to understand this. Who is this man called Yuri?"

Petra tried to hide her reaction as she scrubbed the desktop with foul smelling detergent, probably selected purposefully by Cliona just for her. The Librarian could not help but pick up on the almost inaudible gasp.

"This man is known by you, then." Frabriaci watched Natalia from behind the shiny hair that hung shielding his face.

Natalia squirmed but answered. "Yes, he is the man I have pledged to protect. He is the last male heir to the Russian royal family. I have protected his family for a hundred years and now..." The pain on Natalia's face more than communicated her inner turmoil.

"Ah, yes. The Romanov legacy. So where is this Romanov? Why is he in such pain?"

"I do not know. Yuri enlisted, against his parents' wishes, in the army." Natalia paused and hiccuped. "I gave the Milassoviech family enough money to purchase a commission as an officer in an attempt to keep him as safe as possi..." Another hiccup interrupted her explanation. "Assigned to a desk somewhere. Last I knew he was an aide to some politician in Moscow." Her words slurred as she continued. "Safe as could be, at least so I thought." Natalia spoke quietly, thinking.

Cliona reappeared with another carafe of bloodwine and a bag of pure blood.

"You should find this person in question to gain resolution to your problem. And, thank you, Natalia, for a most intimate tour of your fascinating personage." Frabriaci smiled and licked his lips a little more enthusiastically than was required. Cliona glared at Natalia and hissed. "I shall be interested to know how this unique problem has arisen and if it bears scrutiny by the Council... for our own protection, of course."

"Good advice, sir." Petra had completed her impromptu maid service and set the supplies next to the half full wastebasket. "I think Natalia should rest and eat before we leave, considering her somewhat inebriated state."

"I am not ine, ienee, inbeeniated...drunk! I can take care of myself." Natalia stood up and this time remained upright but, swaying back and forth. She glared at the wastebasket and placed a hand over her mouth. "I will not. I will not...yes I will." She grabbed the basket and vomited for a third time. Wiping her mouth with a clean rag, she vowed, "No more bloodwine for a while. Pet, let's find our quarters and put me to bed."

"Of course. Right away. Sir, is there a place we might rest for a while? Then we will be glad to get out of your hair." Cliona hissed but pointed to an alcove across from her own.

"My dear, you are correct. They will be safe in our guest room. Well, Natalia will be safe anywhere in the Council chambers, however, Petra should stay close. Would you please find some human food for the girl and something for Natalia? As Petra has pointed out, I do not believe she should have any more bloodwine. It doesn't seem to sit well with her."

Recovered, the Librarian rose and moved toward his computer station, sniffing and scrutinizing the desk. He ran a finger across the surface and smiled at Petra. "Thank you Petra. A most disgusting chore, most efficiently accomplished. Everything I have heard of you has been validated." His crinkly face broke into a grin and he winked.

He winked!

A disgusted Cliona pulled Natalia from her chair and dragged the giggling, wavering vampire across the floor and through the alcove, kicking its door open with a surprisingly strong foot. Petra skipped after her, smiling her thanks back at Frabriaci.

He had winked at her! The most intelligent and one of the most powerful vampires in existence had winked at her.

Wow.

Was that good or bad?

Cliona released Natalia onto one of the beds that sat against a wall. Natalia promptly crumpled with a wild half giggle then curled up in a ball and dropped into a noisy sleep. Her snores reverberated throughout the room. Cliona sneered and left as quickly as a vampire could, in the veritable blink of an eye.

Petra hugged her arms to herself and wandered around the room, literally. It was shaped like a cylinder, a smaller version of the rotunda outside their door, and at least two stories high. The wall above the wainscoting was all bookshelves, full to the brim. Like the main library, this room held any number of rare or lost manuscripts. The books, pictures and miscellaneous papers were stacked in disarray. Petra's head spun. What a wealth of knowledge existed in this room alone, not to mention the main library. What other alcoves existed, crammed with books and scrolls, lost tablets, etc? She was in heaven in the middle of what could easily turn out to be hell, for a human, at least. That wink had begun to bother her.

She started at the doorway and began reading titles. The spines boasted all languages and styles of writing. Some of the printing was barely distinguishable, some looked new and bright. As Natalia slept, Petra read as much as she could, as fast as she could.

*****

Kraz woke freezing and stiff. The sun had gone down and the hills were dark under a clouded sky. He could smell rain and the familiar tang of pollution from the power plant at the base of the hill. He slithered out from under his rock, just like the cockroach he felt he was. It was time to face the music and see his parents. They would be home, tucked in for the night like all farmers in the area who rose before the sun and spent all day in the fields. He was from a poor hard-working family, unlike Yuri whose father wore a suit and lived in the lap of luxury. The kind of luxury that included a commission for his only son.

Kraz struggled to stand and tried to stretch a little. Pain shot from his hip to his toes and back again. His chest struggled to expand and contract; his arms grasped the cliff for balance. His head swam at the quick movement.

Slowly, his crutch stoutly lodged in his armpit, he began the long walk to the main road far below. He would not actually walk the road but travel parallel to it, until he found the gravel track that led up the valley. There stood a cozy, thatch-roofed farm house with blue shutters perched above the bank of the fast flowing Avacha River. It wasn't much, but it was home. His heart twisted in his weak chest. It was a pain more of the mind than the body.

It seemed like an eternity before he heard gravel crunch beneath his crutch and tired feet. Close, almost there. Again his heart lurched crazily. Would they even know their own son?

He was a ghost of his former self, now scarred and misshaped. One hand was useless and the other missing two fingers. An angry red gash marred the previously handsome features, that now seemed frozen in a perpetual frown. He had gone away a tall, striking, cavalier boy, ready with his equally handsome friend, to take on the world. Now he returned, a broken and bitter man without even a name he could answer to.

Would they know him?

Would they want him?

Pavel forced back the tears. He had to conquer this weakness of mind and spirit. He straightened and took the road up the valley. It was late. He didn't expect anyone to be up and awake. He would sleep in the barn until sun-up, maybe see his father first, saving his mother the initial shock of seeing him again. He was twenty-five, and looked to be an old man of sixty, older than his own father.

One foot, a crutch, then another foot. One foot, a crutch, then another foot. He could smell smoke from the peat fire, the peat fire that burned on his own mother's hearth.

One foot, a crutch, then another foot. He heard the river water flowing over the stones that he and his siblings played on as children.

One foot, a crutch, then another foot. Off to his left a horse whinnied at the approaching stranger. His horse. His Vadiem. Cossack grazed not to far from the gate, his beautiful white coat gleaming despite the dark night. Another reminder of Yuri. How many times had they ridden across the hills together, laughing, racing? Vadiem snorted and chortled, now trotting along to the fence, calling to him in that peculiar horsey way. At least his horse knew him and seemed pleased at his homecoming.

One foot, a crutch then another foot. A door creaked open and a short burly man moved to stand on the step. "Who goes there?"

The voice teased his mind and flowed around his body like the caress of a mother's arms in the dark. Pavel stood still letting the feeling seduce him with its precious touch.

"Who goes there, I say? Do you not have a tongue in your head?" The man held a staff topped with a vicious looking gaff hook.

"Father?" Pavel's voice cracked as he collapsed.

*****

Natalia rose with the moon feeling mildly hungry. Petra sat in a rocking chair asleep, a book open on her lap. In the center of the room on a Louis the XV table sat two bags of blood and a bottle of bloodwine. Just the sight of the wine made Natalia's stomach lurch and grumble. She did take a bag of blood and sip it slowly gauging the effect it had on her system. Other than the taste of human blood, something she detested, she felt fine and so did her stomach. She finished the snack and started on the second.

"Petra, wake up, dear. We should go." She gently squeezed the shoulder of her sleeping assistant.

Petra jumped, then calmed, finding only she and Natalia in the room. She yawned. "I think I just drifted off. Natalia, you can't believe this book. Look." She shut the book, placing her finger between the pages to keep her place. "This is a genealogy of vampire society. It's amazing. There are names here that I read in the history books. They were vamps. Incredible. How long have vampires been around, anyway?" Petra stretched.

"Since time began, I think. Or I guess since man has been around. The virus that mutated humans and created vampires has been in this world for a very long time. Who is the first name in the book? Or did you skip to the end as usual?" Natalia knew Petra's habit of reading the end of stories before beginning the book.

"Lemurius, an Atlantean. Atlantis really existed, Nat! But more importantly, I found the root of your line. Wanna know who it was?" Petra's eyes glowed with excitement.

"No, I want to go. The longer we stay, the more chance someone may challenge me. Understand, it will be a challenge for you. Let's get out of here, now." Natalia finished her blood and wondered why it was placed there for her. She had a sneaking suspicion. If she was completely recovered, a challenge would have no reason to not be answered. Natalia did not want to engage in a challenge fight in this place where the odds were stacked against her, and there was no safety for Petra if she lost. It was better to leave quickly and quietly. "Shit! I am missing a boot."

"Nah, your boot is still here. It just doesn't look like a boot any more." Petra held up a few shreds of leather. "Shame. I love Prada."

Natalia kicked at the lone boot at the base of the bed on which she'd slept. Pulling the sock from her foot she moved silently across the floor barefoot and listened for movement in the main library. "I'll just have to go without. Any damage will heal almost as quickly as it occurs and I will move more quietly. Too bad you can't do that. It would be helpful. We may face resistance in leaving."

Petra's nose was buried in the book but at Natalia's words, Pet looked up with concern.

"You think someone wants to... to bite me?" Petra was instantly terrified. It had not occurred to her that another vampire would covet Natalia's property. She was just a nondescript human, a glorified secretary, in an isolated castle, in the wilds of Siberia. She wasn't even good looking. What attraction did she have for these vampires who could have anyone they wanted?

"It's not specifically *you* they want, it's my property they may want to take away from me. It's a kind of power thing between vampires. Like humans and their possessions. Why do humans steal from each other?"

"Okay, I get it, just one more second. I think I have found something really cool." Petra squinted, speed reading two pages, then placed the book in an obscure location low on a shelf nearly behind a box of ragged scrolls. "Let's move. Anyone out there? How will we find our way out? Don't we need permission to leave?" Petra was wary but ready to go.

"Shhh! Think to me and do not speak. I can send messages to you mentally. But no noise, please." Natalia opened the door to their room and tiptoed to the edge of the alcove. The coast was clear. *Let's go. Quietly.*

We'll get lost, Nat!

"Did you think you could leave without the Librarian's permission?" Cliona hovered two stories above the alcove, a tablet in her hand. She gracefully descended to eye level and smiled engagingly at Natalia. "Did you, Mistress?"

"I was hoping to avoid long goodbyes, Cliona. I need to search out the person who has attacked me. If it can happen to me, it can happen to any one of us." Natalia bent the story a little to add a dramatic punch. The less Cliona really knew about the true story, the better. "I have agreed to forward what I find to Frabriaci. He is as concerned as I about these attacks."

Cliona squinted at Natalia, as if she was trying to discern truth from fiction and could not grasp the fleeting concept. "Emilliano sleeps. He was more exhausted than he let on. I will not wake him."

"And that is a good thing, Cliona. Did you know he actually winked at my human? I think he is interested in Petra. What think you?" Natalia taunted the faerie-vamp. She knew Cliona had a huge jealous streak, more like a jealous river – the Nile River.

Cliona snarled and growled hovering closer to Natalia's face, her eyes glowing blood red. "Then I suggest you remove your pet before I do." She pressed a small, elongated stone into Natalia's palm. "Hold this like so." She held Natalia's hand out and flattened the palm. "It will direct you through the catacombs by its glowing end. Follow it faithfully and you will return the way you came."

"Thank you, Cliona. We will go as quickly as possible. How will I get this back to you?"

The tiny woman shrugged indifferently. "Leave it at the entrance. It is only a stone. Outside of the complex it has no power." Cliona cocked an ear. "It is clear outside this chamber. Go. Do not bring that human here again. I will see that Emilliano has nothing to lust after." Cliona hissed ominously as Petra slid by behind Natalia.

"Thank you, Cliona. I owe you a debt that will not be forgotten." Natalia's appreciation was waved off by the woman who floated toward the ceiling, replacing the tablet she had been studying on a shelf several stories above.

"Luck be with you. I certainly won't be." Cliona's parting words worried Natalia more than the distrust she had for Cliona's graciousness.

Nat, do you think she was truthful?

That doesn't matter. We don't have a choice. Natalia was straining her senses, checking the way the glowing rock indicated.

Always the practical one, aren't you. How are the feet holding up? Petra was moving quietly and as fast as she could and still felt like the world could hear the thunderous echo of her steps.

Can you not sweat so much? Every vampire in this place will smell you. It's a sweet nectar and very appealing, Petra. Whoa... Stop! We have guards ahead. Natalia froze as Petra slammed into her back.

Two guards lounged near the exit from the catacombs that led to Romania beneath the Danube. As Natalia stopped, she could hear the two sit up and sniff the air. They were so close. Almost free. Now it looked like there would be trouble.

I can't control my sweat glands. You know that. Can't you compel them, Nat? Like you do with humans? Adding the taste of fear to Petra's scent made her almost irresistible. Even Natalia's mouth watered and she did not, as a rule, feed on humans.

I have never tried to compel vampires. Who knows? I can at least attempt it. Natalia focused her thoughts and heard the two guards slump, falling immediately asleep.

Petra peered around Natalia at the two huge sleeping vampires. One snored like a chain saw, the other gurgled as he slept fitfully. *Obviously it worked, my Mistress extraordinaire.* She slapped Natalia on the back and took off at a quiet trot down the tunnel to freedom.

In a flash, Natalia was in front again leading the way, zapping guards to sleep as they fled through the connecting passageways.

As fast as her feet moved, her mind moved even faster.
Yuri, I am coming!

Chapter 6

Death's Choice

Like the birth of a babe, Death comes of its own time.
We write of its stealth, in story and rhyme.
But those who walk the path can only wait,
To bow and beg entrance at the gate,
Of the one who decides the beggar's fate.

Heaven or Hell, if truth be told,
For the beggar, both in riches hold.
One of goodness or one of the dark,
A place to remain, to make a mark,
Passing time until a new start.

Cliona MacDougal, Librarian's Assistant
A Visit With Death, unpublished romance manuscript
Orsova, Romania

Yuri lie shivering in the dark on the dirt floor of his cell, finally praying for death. Days before, he had lost track of time. Now his world was filled with freezing cold, hunger, thirst and pain. When he was capable, he would crawl to the stonewall and lick at the tiny trickle of moisture that seeped between the rocks. It was not much but sustained his pathetic body. Once or twice, he had even tried to chew some of the moss that grew there. Now even that was impossible. Most of his teeth were gone, knocked from his head by continual pummeling. His jaw was probably broken in several places as well, but that was of no consequence now. He didn't want to eat. He wanted to die. He closed the one eye that still functioned and drifted to a better place, a place far away from his cold cell and brutal captors.

*****

Natalia sat at the end of the long dining room table conversing as if she were a lady holding court. Petra Phillamonov sat at her right and the Admiral sat to her left. His daughter sat next to him swinging her legs, and trying to act as adult as she could at the ripe old age of ten. Petra's brother and head of Natalia's estate security sat to his sister's right with his stunning wife, Rivka. It was a cozy group and the laughter flowed freely despite the tension that colored Natalia's presence.

"So, Admiral Zakharenko, you have located our person in question?" Waiting until after dinner and a suitable time to catch up on family news, Natalia posed the question. Mikhail Zakharenko was an old friend and Admiral of the Pacific Fleet stationed at the base just kilometers from Natalia's home. As soon as the Admiral was assigned to the base, Natalia made it her business to renew their ties. He was one of the few humans aware of what she was. At times he had even asked for her assistance. In return he kept her secrets. Watched after her welfare and allowed her to live near the base undisturbed. It was a symbiotic relationship.

"Natalia, my friend, please call me Mikhail when we are together like this in your home. And yes, I have found an answer, but you will not like it." The Admiral shifted in his seat, glancing at his daughter's wide-eyed look of curiosity.

Rivka, astute as always, interrupted with a pretentious bored sigh. There was serious business to be conducted. A child's ears needed to be elsewhere. "Oh la, la, la. Business is so boring. Brianna, would you not prefer to go with me to the high dome and NOT talk of business." She waved an immaculately manicured set of nails toward a candle, playing with the flame, intriguing the young girl.

"Oh, Papa, could I? That way you and Natalia could talk as long as you want and I won't have to listen. I mean, you won't have to worry about me being bored and kicking you under the table. Accidentally, of course, I mean." The child smiled up at her father with a mischievous grin.

"Of course, my moishka. You and Rivka run along. But please, do not throw rocks off the tower at my guards. They are nice men and do not need head wounds today."

44

Both Rivka and Brianna giggled as they dashed from the room, a fleeting "yes, Papa," dangled in the air for a second then disappeared with the girls.

"Your Manager is most talented, Natalia. In fact, I have to admit I envy you your staff. I do believe that at this table sit the most gifted and tenacious researchist I have never met, and a security specialist whose system my men have never been able to circumvent. Especially an efficient and ravishing estate manager. One who is more than willing to leave the discussion just to distract my daughter with silly games and covert attacks on my guards. How did you gather this group together? How do you command such loyalty?" The Admiral chuckled at Vladimir's dark look.

It was well known that Vladimir loved Rivka with every fiber of his being. He did not take well to any comments, good or bad, about his wife. Natalia immediately thought of Cliona. The faerie-like vampire definitely had a human rival in the jealousy arena.

"They are my family. At least, my family by choice, Mikhail. I do not have to command them. Besides the obvious family ties, I pay much too well for such silliness. We work together as a team. Now, about Yuri?"

"He was, until several weeks ago, attached to the office of Leonid Reiman, the Minister of Communications and Information Technologies of the Russian Federation. Along with his friend, Sergeant Pavel Kraznikoff, a local boy, Yuri served as a military consultant. According to my information, both the Captain and the Sergeant were somehow transferred to an active unit on the border between Russia and Kazakhstan." The Admiral drew a handful of papers from the breast pocket inside his jacket. "I could find no explanation and no official orders. And, Natalia, he is no longer with the Office of the Minister of Communications and Information Technologies. No one there would discuss him, or even admit to having worked with the good Captain. This is highly unusual. I am not a man to be put off easily. So I did a little more checking…" He slid the papers towards Natalia.

"What I found was a classified document that charged Yuri with insubordination effectively removing him from his post and placing him on personal leave. According to the Army Personnel Department, Yuri was to be on restricted leave until further

45

disciplinary action could be taken. He should never have been with that division on the border. The interesting fact among all of the smoke and mirrors is this; the charges were dated after Yuri and Pavel had been transferred. Someone is making paperwork to cover their moves and they were not as careful as they should have been. That also tells me they suspected no one would look for the Captain and his friend for some time."

"So he is now in Kazakhstan? Is that what you are telling me?" Natalia was confused, but the Admiral noticed Petra's face fell like a rock.

"No, my dear, what I am telling you is that your Captain was supposed to be in Moscow on leave, when he was much farther south. Unfortunately, he got caught up in a battle on the border. The division he ended up with, was mostly wiped out during an engagement with Muslim terrorists. It was about three weeks ago. According to my sources, Captain Milassoviech is missing and presumed dead. Of the one hundred and thirty-eight men in the division, only three are known to have survived. The radioman, his flagger and a cook. Not a good showing for Russia's best. Which tells me, it was staged and the outcome assured."

"He was sent there to die! The government sent Yuri to be killed, assassinated by enemy action. How convenient." Petra stared at her plate and shook her head slowly. "We have a Moscowgate on our hands."

"Pet, what do you mean? What gate?" Her brother was not as versed in Americana slang as Petra who'd spent inordinate hours surfing the Internet, and reading news from across the world.

"It's an American saying used to describe a government cover-up, Vlad. The division was destroyed to cover up the ordered assassination of Yuri Milassoviech. Admiral, do you have the specific dates of the battle and the coordinates?" Petra was on to something. Natalia could tell by the intense look on her assistant's face.

"I believe they are in the report, maybe on that third page with the fact sheet. The Army is very good about documenting numbers and locations of their dead. Someone has to inform the families."

"Maybe, just maybe, if I can get a valid DOTA and lat/long, I can find a satellite that retains enough scratch to actually get a digi of the AI." Petra grabbed the papers, rifled through them and tore from the room.

Natalia smiled weakly. "Will someone please tell me what she just said?"

Vladimir was on his feet shoving chairs out of his way. "DOTA is date of terrorist action and lat/long is latitude and longitude, coordinates of the firefight. Scratch is Petra's nickname for data, a digi is a digital download and the AI stands for area of interest. When she talks in acronyms even I need a translation sometimes. I'll let you know when to break out the vodka." He was gone, running up the steps after his brilliant sister.

Natalia rose and walked the Admiral to her salon. He glanced up the stairs toward the office into which the two siblings had disappeared. "Even I can't get digital downloads more than three days old, unless someone has recorded them for a specific purpose. Maybe I should steal her away from you, my dear."

"Mikhail, you know you could never afford her. She has resources all over the world and networks with some of the best minds on the planet, besides being my best friend! How would that look to the Ministry of Defense? Besides the military would squelch her enthusiasm. Look what it has done to you." Natalia chuckled and poured the Admiral a glass of Matryoshkina. The local vodka was known for its pure distilled flavor, and Natalia knew Mikhail enjoyed his vodka.

"True, true. When I left for the Navy, a young idealistic boy, I thought I could serve my country and be a hero. Now I am old and tired, and simply want to live long enough to retire. Maybe I'll fish away my twilight years. Surely I would make more fishing and finally enjoy myself. Ah, for the true freedom of the sea." He downed the glass and held it out for more. "Perhaps if I drink enough, I will forget that I am simply one small screw in a huge machine. It rolls along with or without me... and sometimes over me."

They talked and he drank far into the evening. At some point, Brianna returned with Rivka, wind-blown and out of breath, her hands scraped and sore from throwing rocks from the tower. When she promptly curled up next to her father and fell fast asleep, Rivka covered the little girl with a blanket. Then she stole away to clean the dirt smudges from her own face and hands. Natalia could tell by the twinkle in Rivka's eyes that the girls had had fun, and there would be at least a couple soldiers with sore heads in the morning.

*****

Pavel woke to the delicious smell of roasting bacon and boiling potatoes. From his makeshift bed near the fireplace, the aroma of fresh baked bread settled on him like a favorite childhood blanket, warm and comforting. His youngest sister, Ylena sat cross-legged at the bottom of his bed playing with a set of matryoshka dolls. Pavel carved and painted them for her before he left to join the army. She sang softly to each doll as she joined the halves and placed the smaller into the larger.

"You are awake, my son. It is good." His father rose from the large table in the middle of the cozy kitchen. At one point his entire family filled the table for their meals, Ylena, Irina, Sascha and Pavel with his parents, a close and loving family. "Malinka, come quickly. Pavel is awake."

Malinka dried her hands on the dishtowel and scurried across the kitchen, a mother's smile lighting her soft round features. "Pavel! My boy. I thought I had lost you." She bent and kissed her son on the cheek. "Welcome home, son." She kissed him again and sat on the edge of the bed just looking at the scarred and wounded man who lie in her son's place.

"Mother, I can not stay. Father, no one must know I am here." Tears welled in Pavel's eyes. "I am…" He could not go on. He could not tell his parents he survived a battle with horrendous injuries to return as a deserter. "I left. No one knows I am alive. Yuri…" The tears began in earnest. "Yuri is gone."

Pavel sobbed quietly as his mother fretted, adjusting the blankets and comforting the son she was unable to help. "Yuri is gone.

I could do nothing." He mumbled.

"War is such a hateful business. Do not blame yourself, my son. I'm sure you fought bravely. Look at your wounds. Pavel, how could you have done more than you did?"

Pavel's father stood, his arms wrapped around his wife's shoulders. "Rest now, my son. We will say nothing of this to anyone. Understand, children?" He turned back to his son. "Just rest, Pavel. Leave this family's safety to me."

"Papa, please, I do not want to endanger my family. I must go."

"Pavel, dear brother. Look in the mirror. No one will recognize you, even if we call you by name." Irina sadly handed Pavel a rusty edged mirror.

It was true. No one would recognize this emaciated, scarred version of him. He closed his eyes and blocked out the view.

"Irina, take it away. How could you?" Ylena chastised her sister, and carefully crawled to sit beside her brother. "Do not worry Pavel." She petted his head like she would her favorite puppy. "I will take care of you and never tell anyone you are my brother. It will be our secret." Ylena was only ten and full of love for her family, her dolls, her animals, the flowers in the garden, just about everything. Pavel smiled and patted his sister's hand before drifting off to sleep once again.

At least in sleep he did not hate himself.

*****

Twenty-two long and exhaustive hours later, Petra hit pay dirt.

"Nat, I've got it. Come quick." Natalia lounged in the courtyard garden enjoying the early spring evening, trying without success to calm her nerves. She awakened from her day sleep drenched in cold sweat and shaking like a leaf.

The nightmare still twisted in her mind. She stood before the Council of Elders begging for the life of a human, her Yuri. Slowly, each of the Council members turned and walked away. Cliona giggled in the background. The feeling of helplessness was as palatable as the bloodwine she sipped.

Natalia shuddered, more from the emotion than the cool, brisk evening. The sky was clear, and the moon shone almost as bright as daylight. The nightmare was gone, but the feeling remained.

With vamp-enhanced hearing, it sounded to Natalia as if Petra was screaming in her ear. *Be right there, Pet.* Natalia ran up the stone stairs that led to Petra's office. She had experienced several more 'events' in the past twelve hours and remained close to home, someone with her at all times. The pain was inconsistent and fleeting, but horribly crippling nonetheless. She'd actually fallen on the stairs last week when a terrific pain consumed her right leg for the space of five minutes. One of the maids found her sitting on the landing weeping, rocking back and forth holding her leg. It passed, as had they all, only a memory of the agony left behind. Something terrible was happening to Yuri and Natalia could only guess and wait.

"What did you find?"

"Look! I isolated the satellite, and found the back scratch storage. In about seven point two minutes, we should be able to see a three-hour window during which the battle was supposed to have taken place. I can zoom in to point three-three-six resolution. We won't be able to see features, but we should be able to count men and watch what happens. Pull up a chair."

Natalia grabbed the rocking chair and slid it behind Petra. "Alright, let's go to the movies. I am dying of curiosity."

"That's impossible. You're not alive, Nat." Petra watched the bar fill indicating the download's progress.

"That's a matter of perspective, my dear."

"Okay, here we go." Petra punched the view button and sat back with Natalia hovering on the edge of her seat behind.

The screen filled with a fuzzy, pixilated image then cleared to indicate bodies outlined in light gray. Pet zoomed in as far as she was able. Natalia could almost make out battle gear on the soldiers. She could see their rifles and backpacks but could not make out personal features or rank.

There were twelve men moving. Many more bodies lie immobile, some so close as to seem almost carefully placed. That had to be Yuri's company – the Admiral said there was only a handful left at the end. Which one was Yuri? Natalia strained to see something more in the figures on the screen. Pet moved the view south and east. According to the scale at the bottom of the screen, a mass of moving figures marched less than a kilometer away heading toward Yuri's location.

It was about to begin.

"Watch the synchrometer on the left. About what time did your first pain appear?" Petra pointed the mouse to the two imbedded circular dials that ticked away the minutes indicating past and present time.

"It was close to eight o'clock our time." Natalia absently rubbed the shoulder that had burned.

Both women sat intently watching the approaching enemy and the Russian troops The troops were severely out numbered and pinned down along a ditch of some kind. It seemed Yuri and Pavel had only minutes to live now. "Oh my God, Petra. I can't watch. In just minutes…"

"Natalia, it's not like you don't know the outcome. Come on! Be strong like a vampire should be. Watch, here it goes." The figures met and fought. It was over in a matter of minutes. The Russian troops had been slaughtered. They lie sprawled about the landscape, unmoving.

"Look. The enemy soldiers are searching for something. They are checking the bodies. Oh-ho, what do we have here? Someone has found something." Petra's running commentary didn't help Natalia at all. They both watched the same screen.

"That one must be the commander." She pointed to a figure on the screen and left a small smudge mark where the form had been. "The others run back and forth to him, see? Now he is looking at one of our men, the guy who chased around swinging his rifle during the fight."

They both watched as the Russian soldier's body was lifted and dragged to the man who appeared to be the Commander. Some conversation must have taken place, then an enemy soldier removed something from the Russian and gave it to the Commander.

Identification tags.

They were trying to find a specific person. The commander nodded and pointed to a truck that had driven close to the group.

"They're taking the body, Nat. Why? He's not one of their own. He's a Russian, I would bet my life on it." Natalia looked puzzled and shrugged at her assistant.

Petra gasped and Natalia looked back at the screen. "He moved, Nat. He is alive – the Russian soldier moved."

"Yuri!" They both whispered in unison.

"My Yuri is alive." Natalia could hardly believe her eyes, but finally had an answer. The remnant pain was her connection to Yuri. He was still alive. As long as the pain continued to periodically afflict her, Yuri was alive!

Chapter 7

<u>All That Is Left</u>

When all that is left to hang onto is hope,
Life is an endless, sliding slope.
Toward death in release,
It's a strange kind of peace.

How far must one slide before strength will wane,
And the mind, in its vastness, gives into its pain?
Now that my friend,
Is a question for the dead.

Dr. Serious McBain, Professor of Philosophy
Oxford University, 1879, Oxford England

Petra sat back in her chair and rubbed her eyes. "Well, I guess that explains your remnant pain. You are connected to Yuri and he is in pain off and on. Somewhere." She continued to keep one eye on the screen. The Russian soldier was loaded into the back of a large truck, along with a few of the enemy soldiers, and the one they suspected of being Commander. The truck headed southeast.

Petra moved her stylus on the draw tablet marking the truck on the screen. "The computer will track the truck during this scratch then search for the next adjoining file and switch satellites automatically now. We'll see where it goes. Then, maybe we'll have a clue as to where Yuri has been taken. This is one heck of a program. By the way, it cost you an arm and a leg."

"I don't care. What is money compared to finding the truth. How did you get this program?"

"Ah hah! Your money, my secrets! Actually, Natalia, Emilliano helped. He has a huge-"

"You made a deal with the Librarian?" Natalia interrupted Petra. "How much did that cost me?"

"Actually I made a deal that cost you nothing. Some day it will cost me, but that is beside the point. He simply pointed me in the correct direction." Petra was more closed mouth than Natalia had ever seen. Something was going on between Petra and the Librarian. But Petra was not about to reveal whatever it happened to be, just yet.

Natalia let it go and looked back at the monitor. "Oh Yuri, what have you done? Why did you leave?" Natalia curled her feet beneath her and hung her head. She had secretly watched this man since his birth, saw him grow to manhood and was subsequently forced to watch him fight for the right to be what he wanted - a soldier. Headstrong and bold, Yuri was now in desperate trouble through no fault of his own.

"What is it with you and that man, Natalia? I know you're his protector and all that, but really! He's human. And... well, you are not. You watched him grow up. Isn't that a little like pedophilia with a really big ick factor?" Petra studied her Mistress. The vampire was in obvious distress, and not necessarily because of the remnant pain from the Captain's injuries. Her heart was breaking bit by bit the longer Yuri remained missing.

"I can no more explain it, than I can understand why I am the first to have this connection and its remnant pain. I have always felt...close to Yuri. Then, as he grew into such a handsome and virile man, I..."

"Ah Petra, I do not know my own thoughts anymore." Natalia let the tears fall. "I think I have a handle on it, then...my mind goes all haywire. All I want is... him. I dream about him. I think constantly about this man of my heart. I fantasize, Petra. Wonderful, beautiful fantasies of us together, somewhere safe and peaceful. Some place with sunshine, and flowers, and children." Natalia took the tissue from Petra's extended hand. "Then I wake up to reality and I am cold and sterile. I am a vampire. He is a human. Never the twain shall meet. Right?"

"Right. Just keep that in mind. NEVER the twain shall meet." Petra hated hurting her Mistress, but reality was reality. "I'm sorry Nat. I'm a realist. Take me for instance. You could clean me up, put me in heels, and hang jewels off every limb of my body, but as soon as I opened my mouth, every man in the room would run away screaming 'geek' at the top of their lungs. That's life. That's my reality and just like you, I have to face the facts of it." Petra stood and stretched. She was somewhat uncomfortable having 'girl talk' with her boss who just happened to be a heart broken vampire over the age of one hundred. It was time to give Natalia a little space.

"Can you keep an eye on the monitor for me? I need something to eat. I'll run down to the kitchen and be right back." Petra kissed Natalia's head gently. She really did love the vampire like a sister. A quick departure would allow her Mistress to gain control over her emotions in private. The two had shared much, but the topic of Yuri was still a touchy subject. Petra had no doubts Natalia was in love with the handsome Captain, and therein lie an insurmountable problem. Like philosophers said; a fish could love a bird, but where would they build a home? In Natalia's case, it was more like; a tiger could love a steak, but who would end up as dinner?

"Sure. Go. I'll watch." Natalia moved to Petra's chair and began scrutinizing the monitor.

Petra tried to lighten the mood. "Ah, Nat, don't touch anything, okay? Remember the last time?" Natalia chuckled and waved Petra toward the kitchen below.

"Don't worry. I finally figured out that pesky delete key."

"Just don't touch the keyboard. Please!" Petra headed for the kitchen at a run. "I'll be right back."

Finally, Natalia sat alone with her feelings, just watching. She watched a four-week old video of a truck carrying a Russian soldier, probably Yuri, to a destination unknown. Four weeks was a long time for a human to live with the kind of pain she'd felt. Panic rose in her throat and she almost gagged. She had to do something, quickly.

The monitor blinked, its picture turning to lines, then static flickered across the screen. The computer beeped several times, then a yummy male voice spat from the speakers.

"Switching to MODIS.SIR-C 67902.16 gs in five, four, three, two, one." The screen flickered, blurred then cleared to show a red dot on a truck moving southeasterly. Natalia sat patiently, watching her Yuri being taken deeper into Kazakhstan.

Petra had pinned a huge map of the area on the wall opposite her desk. Natalia began to draw Xs that corresponded to the movements of the truck. The initial conflict occurred on the banks of the Ural River, just south of Orenburg in the Volga Federal District. The truck was now half way to the town of Oral in Kazakhstan. Within a couple hours they could possibly reach the seaport of Atyra on the Caspian Sea, and then he would be lost. A boat, a plane, another truck or car, Yuri was being taken south, into lawless and feudal regions controlled by tribal warlords.

How did this happen and why? It was a puzzle Natalia was intent on solving, then she would find Yuri and bring him home.

Petra came through the door, an enormous sandwich and a bag of chips in one hand and three bottles of Coca Cola in the other. She had become addicted to the American soft drink when she gave up smoking Marlboro Reds, the European version of the American killer. Natalia was glad Petra decided to live a more healthy lifestyle, but chips and coke? Really.

"I've been tracking the truck on your map. I don't know what we will do if they change transport." Natalia crossed her legs, a nervous foot continually wiggling against her chair.

"Calm down, Nat. Now that we have a fix, we can follow just about anything. It's an art. An art at which I happen to excel." Petra motioned for Natalia to get up from the chair. She plopped down and settled her stash of food on the shelf next to the desk. "You might as well find something to do. I'll monitor the progress, and let you know when I have anything new. Maybe have a talk with the good Admiral. Let him know what we found." Petra's attention was on the fading screen once again.

"That may be a good idea. I'll see if he has time for a late dinner." Natalia waited for a response but Petra was glued to the monitor as the computer switched satellites again. "How is it you came up with that program again?"

"Mmmm. Dinner, a good idea." Petra waved Natalia toward the door. "He likes Matryoshkina." Petra commented absently.

As Natalia trotted down the stairs she could hear the digital voice listing the next satellite followed by a very enthusiastic, "YES!"

Admiral Zakharenko answered his cell phone on the first ring. "Ms. Vyrubova. How nice of you to call." Natalia could hear Brianna in the background chattering noisily. "My daughter is also glad you called. We were just going to see if you wanted to join us for dinner. Brianna is cooking something special for me and I am not sure I can handle it on my own." She heard the loud groan from Brianna. At ten the little girl loved to cook and tended to mix everything she could find together in her preparations.

"Mikhail, please extend my thanks to Brianna but I have already eaten. I should like to join you for a light drink however. Would that be convenient?"

"Of course, my dear. You are always welcome in our home. Will you be bringing Brianna's playmate, the charming Rivka?" Natalia was sure the Admiral was the one who wanted to see Rivka, more than his daughter.

"I am afraid it will only be me. Say one hour?"

"Lovely, if I am still alive, we shall have drinks on the veranda. Shall I send a car for you?"

"Thank you, but I will have Vladimir drive me. Will you arrange passage at the gate for us? I do so detest having to wait with a gun aimed at my new car." The last time Natalia had driven to the base, a young private was so afraid the huge SUV would storm the gates, he stood in front of the car with his rifle aimed at the chrome grill until the Admiral's Aide came to escort Natalia's vehicle through.

"Oh yes. We can't have our young soldiers frightened by your magnificent car with its truly intimidating smoked windows." He was remembering the last episode and chuckling.

"Thank you, Mikhail. I will see you both in about an hour." Natalia closed her cell phone and ran to change clothes and find Vladimir.

Dressed in elegant casual, Natalia found Vlad tinkering with his classic motorcycle in the expansive garage below the castle gardens. "You know Rivka hates that machine. Vlad, why do you work so hard to keep it spotless, then never go for a ride?" It was a question she knew the answer to. Vlad did not ride his motorcycle because it frightened Rivka no end. But still he loved to polish the metal until it gleamed, taunting his wife just a little. "Can I drag you away from your toy long enough to take me over to Vilyuchinsk for a visit? I shouldn't be more than an hour or two, I would think."

"Of course, just let me get cleaned up a little." Vladimir was always interested in going to the military base. It served some perverse need of his to oppose the government's authority and strut around as a free agent instead of a conscripted soldier like all young men of the country.

Natalia had to laugh. Vladimir was such an elitist, and she indulged him no end!

The evening had just begun when Mikhail ran for bicarbonate of soda, much to his daughter's dismay, and much to Natalia's amusement.

"I was so careful. Maybe I shouldn't have used so much chili powder. But papa said he liked his goulash spicy." Brianna sat next to Natalia on the brocade divan wringing her hands and swinging her feet. "I should ask Ylena again how her mother makes it."

The little girl was so serious about her recipe, Natalia bit her tongue to keep from laughing out loud. "Does Ylena cook for her family too?" It was hard to keep the giggles away as Natalia tried to enter into a serious conversation with the ten-year old about something she herself had never done.

"Oh yes, especially now that they have a real war hero living with them. He has a big scar on his face, and has to use a crutch to walk. Ylena says he won the war and walked all the way home from Kak-za-stand, where ever that is. She cooks for him and he loves her food."

Natalia's heart lurched and she froze. "A war hero?" she croaked.

"Yep, a real war hero. Her brother Pavel is in the army too, but he isn't a hero yet. He's a sergeant. He went away last year. She got to ride his horse every day until the war hero came. Now he rides it a little." Brianna prattled on as if her words had not made a bit of difference to Natalia.

"Does this war hero have a name, Brianna?" Natalia whispered the question.

"Of course, Natalia, everyone has a name. But his name is secret! Ylena said her father told her she could never say it out loud to anyone. That's why it's a secret, right? I better go see if papa is feeling better." She hopped off the couch and ran up the stairs. "I'll be right back, Natalia. I made cookies for desert."

Natalia groaned, contemplating the gastrointestinal delight that awaited Mikhail's reappearance. Halfway up the stairs Natalia heard Mikhail's voice warning Brianna to slow down on the steps.

The girl was enthusiasm incarnate.

When the two came down the stairs, Mikhail's color had returned to normal and he was rubbing his stomach with relief. He held Brianna in a tight bear hug and the girl was giggling.

"Brianna was just telling me about her friend, Mikhail. Brianna, what was her name again?"

"Ylena Kraznikoff. She lives in Yelizovo by the big airport. She can see planes landing from their farm." Mikhail set his daughter down. "I'll get the cookies." She skipped into the kitchen. The admiral groaned quietly and rubbed his belly again.

"Brianna's friend has a war hero staying at their home, a recently wounded war hero. The girl's father is keeping his name a secret. What do you think about that?" Natalia watched the information soak into the Admiral's brain. Natalia smiled when Mikhail put the clues together and an obvious light came on in his mind. Ylena Kraznikoff plus a recently wounded war hero who could not be named, staying at their home recovering, equaled Pavel Kraznikoff. He had somehow survived the massacre and made his way home. He would know what really happened, and possibly, where Yuri had been taken.

"Brianna, maybe we should visit Ylena with you. I am sure her mother will help you with your goulash recipe." Natalia saw the girl's face light up at her suggestion.

"If you are there, can I ride her brother's horse, papa? If the war hero isn't riding him?" Brianna was already planning the visit to her benefit. "Maybe we can go tomorrow when I do not have school." She held out the plate of cookies she had lovingly made with her own hands. Mikhail and Natalia each took one just as lovingly and tried to smile through the first bite. Tomorrow would most likely be a revealing day; Pavel Kraznikoff and intestinal distress.

On the way home, Natalia thought seriously about a little fly-by over Yelizovo. She was horribly impatient for news and could very easily have compelled the 'war hero' to tell her everything. Unfortunately, there were many farms with families outside Yelizovo and she had no idea where Brianna's friend lived. She had no choice but to be patient. And flying in the modern age was just a tad more risky than it had been in her early years. One did not have to watch so closely for incoming aircraft!

58

"Vladimir, I'll be visiting a friend tomorrow afternoon, with Brianna and the Admiral. If you are free, I'd love to have you drive. Brianna loves to ride in my car and play with the gadgets back here."

"Of course, Natalia. I'll make sure the cabinet is stocked with prianik medoviy. She loves Rivka's honey cookies. And some Matryoshkina, for the Admiral? What's in Yelizovo, anyway?" Vladimir was extremely observant and a master at planning, no, designing lives. If there was a special snack or preferred drink of an individual, Vladimir knew what it was and that item magically appeared. Everything ran smoothly with the delicate touch of his hands and the undying gratitude of his Mistress.

"Well, I am beginning to believe that Yuri's friend, Pavel, the boy he always called Kraz, has returned home from the front. He may be this mysterious war hero who is staying with Brianna's friend's family. I don't know for sure, but there seems to be some secrecy about this man's name. He rides Kraz's horse. If I remember correctly, Yuri and Kraz used to race on the steppes. They would always try to out do each other."

Natalia's mind wandered, remembering the young Yuri, so handsome, so strong. The Milassoviech family knew her as 'The Watcher'. The one who kept a vigil and protected the last descendants of the Romanovs. But, even they did not have personal contact with the strange woman who moved and watched from the shadows. Ever since Tsar Nicholas had become aware of Natalia's peculiar condition, he accepted her for what she was, and what she could do for his family. His gratitude and acceptance was all Natalia needed. However, with the Tsar's recognition, also came wealth and land. In the end, she could not stop the violence of the Bolsheviks, but she did what she could for Nicholas and his family while they lived. After their execution at Ykaterinburg, Natalia retreated to her home in Siberia. That was where she remained, watching over the last living relatives of Nicholas and Alexandra.

When Larisa and Pyotr produced a son and a daughter, Natalia's job increased ten fold. Yuri was a precocious and strong-willed boy who grew into a handsome strong-willed man who roamed the steppes looking for excitement. Olga followed her mother's way, remaining close to the church and her father.

At some point, Natalia's job became her pleasure. Watching Yuri challenge the world on his own terms struck a cord in her dead heart.

When had Yuri's image become the object of her fantasies?

When had the boy become a man, and in her mind, the critical connection to what was left of her humanity, her heart?

Maybe that was why she experienced the pains. Who knew? But it was a theory that seemed to make sense. Though the pain was horrible, it was a good horrible if it meant Yuri lived.

"Possibly this man will know what has become of your Yuri and my sister can begin sleeping again." Vladimir snorted. "She has not left her office in days. She runs to the kitchen to fix food, then runs back to eat in front of the monitors. Cook is insulted. Petra needs a bath. I am sure you have noticed, enhanced smelling, and all."

His smirking statement drew her from her thoughts. "You've got to be kidding! I didn't know. I'll talk to her, Vladimir."

"And you think that will help? When my sister is on the hunt, the world better watch out. Maybe you could stun her, or compel her to go take a shower and go to bed. You know she even agreed to let that old vampire have some of her blood in return for a satellite connection? It's all on the up and up. She won't let him bite her or anything. Just…well, sort of like a transfusion, you know, by a tube or something." Vladimir glanced in the rear view mirror at Natalia's gasp. "Ah, you didn't know, did you? Oops. I'm in trouble now. Don't tell her I was the one who ratted her out. Okay?"

"An old vampire? The Librarian! Damn. I can't believe she did that. Just to help me? That girl is loyal to the nth degree but bartering her blood? Now I really am going to have a talk with her. And, no. I won't mention your name, but thank you for telling me." Natalia was close to tears. "It's risky business, wheeling and dealing with the Librarian. No one has ever done anything like that for me…ever." The whispered response was so soft Vladimir almost missed it.

"Now, don't get all weepy on me. Last time it took a whole day of scrubbing to get the blood stains out of the upholstery and carpet." Vladimir handed back a box of tissue. The Mitsubishi touring SUV was his pride and joy. Spacious and luxurious, he cleaned and polished it almost every day, spending hours waxing the surface until it gleamed.

"Vladimir Phillamonov, you sure know how to keep a girl straight. No turning my head with sweet nothings. You cut right to the upholstery!" Natalia just had to chuckle as she wiped her nose and eyes.

"So what time is the big trip tomorrow? Dinner with the Admiral and little Miss Brianna again?"

"She said something about the day and riding Pavel's horse. If tomorrow is overcast I can handle it with v-screen. I will need to eat first. Maybe the afternoon, then return to the castle for dinner. Will you arrange it for me?"

"It would be my pleasure, Madame. We are home at last. Please, Natalia, Petra will kill me if she finds out I told you about the blood thing. She's merciless, and didn't want anyone to know. I caught the e-mail as she sent it. I asked and she stalled. Then she told me because, well, mostly because she loves me and I am her brother. We have no secrets from each other." Vladimir helped Natalia from the car as if she were a stately lady. His smile was one of convincible beauty, handsome and sophisticated.

"More like she told you because you threatened something. I know you and Petra as well as your own mother did." Natalia poked a finger at the man's chest accusingly.

Vladimir chuckled, "well, there is that." Companionably they walked up the main staircase to the front entrance of the house. The massive doors dated back to the sixteenth century and could have protected the place from a legion of marauding Cossacks. Huge iron bands encased the weathered planks that extended from an iron panel at the bottom, twenty feet up to domed marble arches covered in Cyrillic script. The castle included a main house, a chapel, and the stable with a garage beneath the courtyard. Typical Russian onion domes on all four corners, it was surrounded by a thirty-foot wall. In recent years, an entry large enough for an RV had been cut in the old wall and an automatic gate had been installed. The castle was virtually impregnable by ancient standards. Security was virtually impregnable by modern standards. That was Vladimir's specialty for which he drew a very lucrative salary.

"No matter how many times I walk through these doors, I still love the feel of old world wood and iron. A throwback to my childhood, I guess. But it is a good thing the hydraulic system you developed works so well, or I would be the only one in Russia able to open them with one hand."

The entryway was a cavernous rotunda with painted ceilings and stained glass insets. The floor was a picture of parquet madness that wound its way into a wooden mass of floral tangles in the center of the room. A winding marble staircase extended around and up the side of the room connecting the five floors of the main structure and the wings that extended north and south from the rotunda. The staff offices were located in the southern wing and the living quarters were in the northern wing. Natalia's personal suite was on the top floor with easy access to the roof gardens and a small, personal Orthodox chapel that composed the top domes of the castle. All together, it was a huge complex that served her well but appeared warm and cozy in its individual components. Natalia and Rivka had redecorated the entire place a few years back and the young wife made several changes that lent a family feel to the castle, despite its size and grandeur.

The one thing that Natalia refused to compromise on were the beautiful wooden doors. So Vladimir invented a system to open and close the mammoth wooden pieces with the touch of a button. It was a handy for those who lacked the strength of Natalia's kind.

"I shall find Petra straight away and speak with her, and, I will keep your name out of it." Natalia ascended the stairs with the grace of a royal princess.

"Thanks, Boss!" Vladimir was off toward the kitchen and cook's newest delectable treat.

Chapter 8

Reflections

In the mirror I see,
A small piece of what I used to be
Once a creature totally whole,
Now a man without a soul.

How does one recoup such a loss?
A healer, a magician, a man of the cross?
Without it, there is no hope,
Of regaining sanity, placing life in scope.

I believe I am destined to die a raving maniac.

Gellar Manson, Author, Reflections On My Life
Minnesota Asylum for the Criminally Insane

Ylena skipped behind her brother as he hobbled toward the stable where Vadiem awaited. Again today he would ride for a few minutes until the pain consumed his body and he could stand it no more. Each day he rode a fraction of a moment longer. Despite the cost, Pavel was willing to endure any amount of pain, to grow stronger, to grow closer to his goal. When he was whole, he would find Yuri and bring closure to the guilt that consumed him. He would never forget the name of the man who had taken his friend; Teffas Hamza. The name was etched in his brain. He repeated it over and over again, every day as he lie helpless and recovering. It was a name that haunted his night terrors and drove him during the daylight hours.

"Pavel, why do you ride when it hurts so?" Ylena missed nothing when it came to her beloved brother, the war hero.

"I must, Ylena, and do not call me Pavel. Someone may hear you." Pavel worked to saddle his horse as the horse stood still and

63

relaxed. Somehow, Vadiem sensed what Pavel needed and was willing to be patient for his old friend.

"What shall I call you then?" The young girl's warm smile melted her brother's heart.

"Call me Timonov. It is our mother's family name and mine as well. It is a good name and can be our outside name for me. You may call me that any time, anywhere, but not Pavel, never again. Agreed?" Pavel spit on his hand and held it out to secure the deal.

Ylena grinned, spit and clasped her brother's hand shaking it vigorously. "Deal, Timonov. Vadiem wants to go. Let me help you." She scurried around the stable, pulling tack from the walls and tossing it to her brother.

"Slow down, Ylena. I cannot yet move that fast." Her energy was amazing. Pavel groaned as he tried to catch the bridle she so eagerly threw to him. "Vadiem can wait a moment longer." He laughed. It was the first time he had laughed in a great while. To his ears it sounded more like a croak than a true laugh. Life was moving back into his mind and body, slowly but surely, however his heart – it remained frozen in a muddy ditch somewhere near the border of southern Russian and Kazakhstan.

"I hear a car. It must be Brianna. She is coming to visit today so we can share recipes. Can you finish saddling Vadiem on your own?" Ylena was already deserting her brother for the expected visitor. Ten-year-old devotion only lasted until another ten year old came to play.

"Surely, Ylena. I will ride up the road and back today. I will not be long. Remember our agreement?"

"What agreement, Timonov?" The imp giggled and ran from the stable with a quick wave.

The instant the car stopped moving, Brianna was out and flying toward her friend. The two girls hugged and kissed cheeks like all little girlfriends did, exuberantly jumping up and down.

"Natalia, you were a girl once, how do they do that? Jump, hug and kiss all at the same time!" The Admiral laughed from the back seat of Natalia's car as he watched his daughter and her friend.

"I was a little girl over one hundred years ago, Mikhail. I'm not sure I remember. They do resemble little puppy dogs, all wiggly and licking each other." Natalia giggled trying to remember her childhood. It had been so long ago, before...

"Ylena's mother is coming to the car. I will stay inside. It is better that a government official does not appear out of nowhere to ask questions." The Admiral slumped down in the seat as Natalia got out and prepared to meet Gospazhaw Kraznikoff.

Immediately, she could feel the ultraviolet attack on her sensitive skin, despite the v-screen she applied earlier. It was a good thing the day was overcast and thick clouds threatened rain. The afternoon was cool, and great dark clouds helped blot out the direct sun.

"Madam Vyrubova, a great honor to have you visit. Ylena has been looking forward to Brianna's visit. Please do come in for tea and potavietsa." Brianna's mother bowed briefly, and motioned toward the house with an eye on the stable across the road and the grand car parked near.

"My pleasure. Please call me Natalia. I am sure Brianna and Ylena are not so formal." Natalia followed Gospazhaw Kraznikoff into her home. It was small but clean and warm, smelling of oranges and cinnamon, brewing Russian tea steeped on the stove.

"I am Malinka Timonov Kraznikoff. Please call me Malinka. I feel very honored to call such a grand lady by her Christian name. Please, please, sit down." Gospazhaw Kraznikoff tittered as she prepared a plate of nut rolls and tea for the two of them.

"Brianna is learning to cook and wanted Ylena's recipe for goulash. Such a small thing but I cannot deny the child. She is such an inspiration and so energetic." Natalia waved her hand across her face like a harried mother.

"Ah, children these days, so much energy, so much talking. Ylena is the youngest of my four and a joy, but also a trial. She never seems to stop."

Natalia chuckled, playing the part of one overworked mother sharing with another over tea. "You have four? How do you do it?"

"Pavel, the oldest, is serving as a soldier in the army." The words caught in her throat but she continued. "Irina is in her last year of school. She plans to study at the university in Vladivostok next year. Sascha is at the trade school in Petropavlovsk and Ylena; well she is our little one and, of course attends school with Brianna. One day she wants to be a singing star the next she wants to be a doctor. God only knows what she will become."

"Your son is away in the army? I thought I saw a young man by the stable." Natalia was fishing for answers but in a calm and friendly manner. She nudged the woman's mind with warm and companionable feelings. Natalia watched as Malinka tried to configure her thoughts and pull the false information from her mind.

"He is, a… injured soldier. A relative…recovering from wounds." Malinka struggled to pronounce each word, as if something had a strangle hold on her tongue. "More tea?" The question was quick and so was Ylena's mother. She hopped up and grabbed the teapot from the stove.

"Yes, thank you, Malinka. I should love to congratulate your soldier on his survival, and thank him myself for serving our great country." Again Natalia pressed the woman's mind, finding it hard to break through the wall that was a mother's need to protect her child.

Malinka fought for control of her thoughts and words. Her brow wrinkled and the stress of the mental battle was clear on her weathered features. A beautiful woman in her prime, Malinka now resembled a wrinkled old woman who could not remember her own name.

"Is he at home, now?"

"Ahhh…, I…think he has gone for a ride…on his," she paused, searching for the correct wording, "my son's horse." Malinka sat down, exhausted as if she had labored for hours.

"Not to worry, Malinka. I can see him another time." Natalia calmed the woman with a compelling thought of security and secrecy. Malinka had been good, but not good enough. Natalia caught the tiny slip of *his horse,* seeming to ignore it. It allowed Malinka to think their conversation had just been small talk between two women. "Thank you for the tea, Malinka. I shall send a driver for Brianna in a few hours, if that is acceptable." She placed a friendly hand on the woman's arm. "Malinka, it is a hard time for us all. I am sure you worry about your son endlessly. Were I in your position, I would as well. Things will be fine. I know this."

Tears dropped from a bent head. "Thank you, Natalia." Malinka snuffed, then dried her eyes on her apron and rose to show Natalia out. "Brianna is welcome to stay as long as she likes.

Possibly she can help Ylena prepare dinner and sleep here tonight. It will save your man a long drive. We have room and the girls will have a wonderful time."

"That is a fabulous idea, Malinka. Thank you for suggesting it, and thank you again for the tea. I will check with Brianna before I leave. She will be so excited." Natalia strolled toward the car waving to Brianna. The girls came running, a frown plastered on Brianna's face.

"Are we leaving so soon? I have not had a chance to ride the horse. Can't we stay a little longer, please, Natalia?" Brianna pleaded, tugging on Natalia's coat.

"Ylena's mother has asked you to stay until tomorrow. Would you like that?" Seeing the expression light Brianna's face, she wondered why she even asked the question.

"YES! Ylena, I can stay." Already Brianna was running toward the stables, dragging her friend with glee. "I can stay the night."

Vladimir let Natalia into the car as she laughed out loud. "You have lost your daughter for the evening, Mikhail. She will be torturing the Kraznikoff family with her cooking tonight, then sleeping over with Ylena." Between laughs, Natalia tried to communicate the plans to the Admiral. "I hope that is okay. You are her father. I should have asked."

"No, no, no. It is fine. Better the Kraznikoff family than us, and she has stayed with Ylena before. Did you see the alleged war hero?"

"Unfortunately, no. He was not at home. But Gospazhaw Kraznikoff is protecting him. Of that I am sure. She said he was out riding *his* horse, then corrected herself. She could hardly talk to me about him, and I compelled her as much as I thought safe. She is a very strong woman, seriously worried about her son, with incredible maternal instincts." Natalia rubbed her temples with elegant fingertips. "I think I shall return later this evening and have a talk with the brother. Alone.

"What do you think he knows? He must have been near the fight. I wonder how he escaped the massacre? I certainly hope we are not looking at a cowardly deserter. That, I could not ignore." The Admiral was a loyal Navy man and hated cowards, but he was also a father. He could look the other way for a man who had

67

survived such horror.

"Pavel was Yuri's best friend. Yuri would not have tolerated a coward or a dishonorable man as his friend. I think there is more here than meets the eye." Natalia was confident of Yuri's choice of friends. "I intend to find out what that might be. Tonight. Vladimir, let's go."

They rode in silence all the way back to Natalia's home, each thinking about Yuri's possible whereabouts, and what connection Pavel had. Natalia was antsy to get the Admiral on his way and return to the Kraznikoff farm.

It seemed like hours later, Admiral Zakharenko's car finally whisked him toward the base leaving Natalia to morph and fly to the farm. In moments, she touched down behind the stable and crept quietly around to the front. Although Yuri had never physically seen her, Cossack knew her well, but Vadiem trotted away with a snort.

Lights burned brightly in the windows of the farmhouse and with her enhanced hearing, Natalia could detect the loud laughter of little girls, the bubbling of some culinary concoction on the stove, and a quiet mother's directions warning the girls to be careful. Two other youthful voices chatted in one of the bedrooms and a snore was audible from a chair in the main salon. Natalia searched for the mental pattern of Pavel and could not find even a thin thread to follow. He was either not at home or drugged into a deep enough sleep his thoughts were submerged and inactive.

Cossack whinnied and nudged the hand that had stopped scratching his head. Natalia whispered, "Shush, Cossack. I am here to find Yuri." At the mention of his master's name, Cossack shook his head and snorted softly, continuing to search out Natalia's scratching fingers.

She placed her cheek against the proud animal and rested against his neck. It would be a long night, but she would wait for Pavel to show his face.

Within the hour, Pavel did show his face. Natalia sat in the corner of the stable petting a stray cat. Before he even gained the farm gate, Natalia picked up his thoughts. He was walking without crutches and in terrible pain. He was also deriding himself because he was weak, and not fit for human company. He was definitely Pavel Kraznikoff. He was carrying the heavy burden of guilt stoutly on his shoulders.

Natalia sped to the gate in a flash. She positioned herself just beyond a huge birch tree, in the shadows on the edge of the drive. As the soldier approached, Natalia spoke. "Pavel, I am a friend. I need to talk with you. It is urgent." She kept her voice soft and compelling.

Still Pavel nearly jumped out of his skin, falling to the fence. He grasped the rough wood to keep his balance. "Who is there? Who are you? Why do you call me Pavel? I am Timonov." He clung to the fence breathing hard.

Natalia could hear his heart pounding in his chest. She could feel fear racing through his blood. "I am The Watcher, Pavel. I am sure Yuri told you of me. I watch over him, and protect his family. Do you know of me?" Natalia used the name that Yuri had learned as a child. It was the name of the entity that always seemed to be there, on fringes of reality, watching and protecting.

"Yes... He spoke of you, but I thought he was mad, dreaming. I had no idea The Watcher existed. Oh God, forgive me, Watcher." Pavel crumpled to the ground sobbing.

Natalia crept from the shadows and gently lifted Pavel to his feet. "And what is it I must forgive, Pavel? What can you tell me about Yuri's disappearance? What happened? Why have you returned... like this." She indicated his wounds.

"Watcher, I am a miserable excuse for a friend. I let them take Yuri. I did nothing but lie there in the mud, like the insect I am."

Natalia lifted the man, and carried him like a child to the bench by the farm's gate. Sitting him gently on the bench, she prodded, "Start at the beginning and tell me everything. It will cleanse your soul, and give your heart forgiveness." She caressed his cheek, wiping the tears from his face. "Tell me, Pavel."

She compelled the man to recall everything in detail. They sat alone for almost an hour, talking quietly beneath the cloudy night sky. When Pavel had recounted everything up until his night beneath the rocks above his village, the clouds parted and starlight illuminated the valley with a crystal clarity that cast magical bluish shadows across the road.

"He said my duty was to survive. That is what I did, in a way. This..." he pointed to his legs and arm, "does not feel like survival to me. But what else can I do? I will never think to kill myself. I

69

would be damned forever. Father Petrovick would not allow me to be buried in the churchyard. I can not do that to my family." He pulled the cross from beneath his shirt and kissed the center divot, the remnants of his saving grace.

"Pavel. Look at me." Natalia's eyes burned a deep red as she concentrated on the man's mental processes. "You are absolved of guilt in this. You were a good friend to Yuri. You are now responsible for helping to find him. You have done your part in this. Now go on with your life. Heal. Let your mind and your body recover so when Yuri comes home, you two can ride again across the steppes, together. Now, go home and sleep well. No more nightmares. Heal, Pavel." She reached up and closed Pavel's eyes. Before leaving the man, she impressed a deep calm into his mind, a peacefulness that he would need to begin to truly heal.

Morphing, Natalia leapt skyward, carefully watching for air traffic. She would be home in seconds with the name of Yuri's captor, Teffas Hamza – a vile name for a vile individual. Vile or not, the name was a key and a beginning.

From Pavel's recollections, Natalia now knew that Yuri's capture had been arranged and paid for. The contract was to kill the Captain. Found alive, Yuri had been taken south as a captive. What tortures had he endured? Where was he being held? Natalia was determined to find him, alive or…there was no *or* for her. She would find him alive.

She touched down between two flowering bushes on the roof garden just outside her bedroom. Stepping lightly through the French doors, Natalia dashed for Petra's office and her talented assistant.

Petra sat with her feet curled beneath her, munching on crackers and cheese as she watched information stream by. Natalia froze at the doorway to her office, amazed that a human could follow the information that flew across three separate screens. Petra chewed in time to the flicker of pages, taking in what she needed and disregarding the rest.

"Petra, how do you do that?" Natalia flounced across the room and plopped in her rocking chair.

Without even pausing a single screen, she replied, "Do what?"

"That! That reading thing you do. Reading at mach speed on more than one monitor. How do you do it?"

Petra sat up suddenly and hit F7. One screen stopped with an article about smuggling goods across the Caspian Sea. After a second, she hit the key again. The information flowed once more. "Nope. Nothing new there."

"Pet, stop. I have news. Make it stop." Natalia was bursting with excitement. Petra hit some key sequence and the monitors immediately froze.

"Okay, I'm listening." Natalia had her complete attention, at least for a second or two.

"I talked to Pavel Kraznikoff tonight. He told me everything he could remember," she snickered, "and some things he couldn't. In any event I know what happened. I know the name of the man who took Yuri." She grinned in excitement and her fangs glistened in the reflection from the bright monitors.

"Nat, the fangs, please! I'm still listening." Petra was completely comfortable with Natalia, but watching her talk with fangs was unsettling.

"Teffas Hamza. That's the man's name. Teffas Hamza! Can you check him out?"

Petra spun her chair. "On it, Boss." She opened a program and typed in the name with three variations of the spelling. The computer sounded chime after chime as its hi-tech fingers did the walking through the techno-yellow pages. The American euphemism came to mind as Petra sat, walking her fingers back and forth. She was not the most patient person to wait out an info search.

Pretty soon, Petra's feet were moving with her fingers as wrinkle after wrinkle appeared on the woman's forehead. "Go, go, go Teechno."

Petra named each computer she used. Beesch, Mancha, and Teechno; pest, eater and fatty. Petra was a very unique individual who had an unusual and unique relationship with her machines. Even for a human, Natalia thought her strange in the way she could manipulate data,... and follow a cyber-clue.

"Got it! Holy shit, Natalia. He's hooked up with the Taliban forces in Afghanistan, an aide to General Albani, but a civilian. Look at this. It's a map of the area with the general location of Albani's headquarters. We're sunk, Nat. No one gets in or out of that territory, and it's riddled with caves. You might fly in, but you won't find anything on your own. We need help. Let me see what I can come up with." Petra's fingers were working the keyboard.

"Hang on a minute there, super comptrooper. Search but no more bartering blood. You can't afford to dicker with the Librarian. I don't trust him. I value your services above trading on your life."

"He told you, didn't he?" Petra did not take her eyes off the articles she was scanning. Multi-tasking was Petra's middle name.

"The Librarian? No, he didn't tell me. Nothing happens in my home that I do not know about." Natalia sniffed.

"Vlad, not Emilliano. Come on, keep up, Nat. Lately you seem to have trouble just following a conversation. In fact there is sooo much that goes on here about which you have no clue. Did you know Rivka is pregnant? Cook is taking online classes from a chef in California. Old Nikos quit drinking two months ago and is dating Cook…"

"He did? She is?"

Mikhail has a crush on you and…" Petra's fingers continued to fly across the keyboard as she detailed the castle's private soap opera.

"What?"

"-and has asked Brianna if she wants a new mom? Which would be awkward to say the least. And…"

"No more. I give in. I guess that's what I get for sleeping away the daylight hours. Lately, it has been more like nightmaring away the daylight hours." Natalia hung her head then looked up with a smile. "My staff sleeps around with each other, and my assistant plots the demise of my status as a single woman of means!"

Natalia was aghast.

Her cook, Svetlana, was dating Nikos? The world must soon be at an end. Online classes?

Rivka expecting? Such a joy and Natalia had no clue.

She sighed heavily, suddenly exhausted. She'd done nothing but concentrate on finding Yuri for weeks now, and things had slid right by beneath her nose.

"So, I'll get my brother later. Right now we need help, serious help. Natalia, I have to make a request of the Council. Emilliano and I have become… ah, Internet-close, so to speak. I think I may have impressed the old sucker. Anyway, he might have a way to contact Albani, or some way to get close. I don't know, but I have to try." Petra scrutinized another article then moved on quickly.

"No blood contract, Petra. The Librarian is a crafty and very old vampire. He will not play straight. No more bartering your blood, understand?"

Natalia grabbed Petra's chair arms and spun the woman to face her. "Understand?"

"Yes, I do. I wasn't going to barter blood. I have something more desirable, anyway. Emilliano will be in my debt after this." Petra dropped her feet to the floor and walked her chair back to face the monitors.

"And what would that be?" Natalia was wary, but curious. "What could you have found that would trump your own blood?"

"Cliona's genetic pedigree. I finally found it when we were there. You slept. I read. Very fast. It was extremely interesting. Emilliano has wanted to formalize his 'marriage' to Cliona for about a thousand years, but has never had her pedigree. The Council of Elders won't accept their marriage without proof of her lineage." Petra snickered. "I happen to have that lineage and proof of her sire. It was right under his nose all the time. He'll cave. He adores that little brat. She adores him and calls him her husband. Go figure. I assume that is an acceptable trading card, Boss?"

Natalia grinned. "Completely. See what dear Emilliano has to say. I think I'll find Rivka and congratulate her."

"Would you let her know, I'm going to kill her husband when I see him." Petra was back tending her screens and the flashing information that ran without end.

"I have no idea why you would do such a thing, my dear." Natalia commented under her breath as she departed, before Petra could respond.

Chapter 9

How To Get What You Want

Find something that someone wants, a LOT!
Dangle it before the nose of that someone.
Wait for it....
Make your demand.
Grab the prize.
Run like hell!

Unknown Author
Men's Room, Unknown Location

Petra sat impatiently tapping a broken pencil on the desk as she awaited the response from Emilliano. The finish on the desk had disappeared beneath her obsessive tapping months ago and now she worked a small hole in the wood.

Her computer chimed. "You have mail," the digital voice spoke sounding suspiciously like Maxim Galkin, Russia's newest sensation and host of Dve Zvezdy, the celebrity contest for singers that had taken the nation by storm. Maxim's handsome and often radiant face covered Petra's walls and research notebooks.

"Thank you, Maxim. I love you and want your body." Petra opened the file and just had to squeal in delight. It had taken the Librarian three minutes to read her request, accept the barter, and respond. Three minutes was a long time for a vampire, so she scrutinized the answer and conditions. "Okay, transmitting the file now." Petra poked the send button and off went her part of the bargain.

She saved the e-mail for her records and began to formulate questions. She was restricted to five. Only five questions. In exchange for a very long lifetime sealed to his ladylove? It didn't seem fair. Time was of the essence. Petra did not want to haggle. She wanted action.

"Question number one; if Yuri has been taken to General Albani's stronghold, how can we find the location?" Petra chewed the eraser off her broken pencil.

"Question number two; if the stronghold is located, what is the best way to rescue Yuri?" She threw the pencil away and grabbed a handful of crackers.

"Question number three; will the Council assist in Yuri's rescue?" Two questions remained. Petra thought hard and long before formulating the next one.

"Question number four; if the Council will not/cannot help, who can/will?" Petra swallowed hard.

"Question number five; what are the chances Yuri is alive?" It was a question she was afraid to ask, and even more afraid to have answered.

Petra re-read the questions, trying to determine if she worded them succinctly enough to get straight information. Would the Librarian find a way to couch his answers in some unintelligible form? Finally, taking a deep breath, she hit the send button. Now, it was waiting time again. Something she did less than well.

Out of her seat and down the stairs in a flash. She hit the kitchen door just in time to see her brother heading for the courtyard. "Hey, Vladimir, you dirty Cossack. Come back here!"

Vladimir heard his sister's voice and ran for cover. He knew if he ran, she would lose interest in favor of food in the kitchen. She hadn't had a full meal in three days. His feet barely touched the old stone steps as he sped towards the castle wall's mandoor, and his personal safety exit.

True to form, Petra could not pass up the fresh baked bread and sweet cream butter Cook prepared for the humans in the castle. Thick, rich borscht bubbled on the huge stove. The smell of cooking cabbage and onions filled her nostrils chasing away murderous thoughts about her brother. A crock of honey sat handy in the middle of the long baking board on the island in the kitchen. Petra slid onto a stool near the block table.

"I am famished, Svetlana. Do you think I can catch dinner now? I have a very important e-mail on its way and I need to get back to the office as soon as I can." Petra rubbed her eyes and slumped on the stool.

"Chit, chit. You need to have more breaks and eat better, Pet.

You will waste away to nothing before our eyes. The Mistress would not approve." With a disapproving look, Svetlana filled a large bowl with borscht, placed it on a long platter with several slices of bread and enough butter for the entire loaf. "Here, eat now and I will bring you black cake later when it is done."

"You made black cake? With Turkish coffee liqueur? What is the special occasion?" Petra loved the chocolate cake that tasted of coffee and cinnamon. Cook only made it for special events.

"Nothing special. You should not ask so many questions, young lady." Cook's cheeks turned a cherry color and she hurried to the pantry.

"Ah, Nikos likes black cake, huh?" Petra heard a fit of giggles drift out of the pantry.

"You know, Vladimir does not really care for black cake so may I have his share, Svetlana?" Petra snickered. Vlad loved black cake as much as she did, but it was pay back time for his lack of sensitivity about private things.

Cook tromped from the pantry, her hands full of bags and jars of ingredients. "Petra Annichka, your mother, God rest her soul, would be ashamed to know her daughter could lie so unconvincingly! Do you think I have spent my entire life buried here in this kitchen, deaf and blind? Mistress took you in and raised you better than that, God rest her soul as well, if she still has one." The cook crossed herself and began measuring flour into a huge bowl.

"Of course she still has a soul. You know as well as I do that it was not her fault Father Grigori made her a-"

"Chit, chit! Do not mention that vile priest to me, Petra Annichka Phillamonov. That ungodly creature, should he burn in hell!" Svetlana spit on the floor and ground the saliva into the old stones with the toe of her boot. "Now, off with you, young lady. And no more tales about your brother." From the looks of the batter Cook was stirring up, there would be plenty of black cake for everyone, and extra for Nikos.

As Petra rounded the end of the hallway she could hear her computer chime inside the office and Maxim's yummy voice announce her arriving mail. An hour had not yet passed and the Librarian was sending his answers. That was either really good or really bad. Petra was afraid to look. She bolted down the hall and flung herself into the office. Maxim's face danced across her screen, his brilliant smile shining from each monitor.

"Alright Maxim, wish me luck. I have a sneaking suspicion I may need it." Petra went to open a file and smiled smugly. Instead, the old nipper's name appeared in her chat box. She clicked in the box and said a prayer.

Question number one; if Yuri has been taken to General Albani's stronghold, how can we find the location?

Answer: You cannot.

Question number two; if the stronghold is located, what is the best way to rescue Yuri?

Answer: All out assault or stealth.

Question number three; will the Council assist in Yuri's rescue?

Answer: NO.

Question number four; if the Council will not/cannot help, who can/will?

Answer: Contact Elizabetta Zoeltel, 011.207.598.6500

Question number five; what are the chances Yuri is alive?

Answer: Slim to none.

"So, Maxim, my love-for-all-time. We have a phone number and a woman's name. What does this woman have to do with Yuri and why should I contact her? Ummm, I wonder?" Petra planted a dry kiss on the paper lips of her Maxim poster and stalked off to find Natalia. Maybe, the name Elizabetta Zoeltel meant something to her boss.

Natalia heard Petra's footsteps long before her face graced the entryway of Natalia's personal quarters.

"Knock, knock. We need to talk." Petra took her usual place on the window seat near the garden entrance.

"Somehow, those words have never made me feel very comfortable. If I were a man, I would be running right now." Natalia stood in the middle of her bedroom, sword held high, initiating a sequence of deadly moves. Although her VMD maintained the health of her body, she still practiced the old ways of fighting with a sword. It kept her mind and body sharp as a tack, a tack that wielded an even sharper point.

"I'll cut to the chase. Know anyone named Elizabetta Zoeltel? Why would Emilliano give me her name and phone number if we need help? By the way, the Council of Elders has officially refused to provide assistance."

"Do say." She shot Petra a dry look. "I would not have expected them to dirty their hands with human problems. The only time they actually take an active interest in anything, is when it concerns the security of vampire society. Or, when someone breaches the rules such that they cannot ignore the offense. The Council has not been known, through the centuries, to be anything but self-serving." Natalia set her sword aside. "So, this Elizabeth who?"

"Elizabetta Zoeltel, sounds Romanian or Gypsy."

"This Elizabetta Zoeltel will help us? Obviously I don't know who she is, or why the Librarian gave you her name. However..." Natalia slid a hand beneath several pillows near the top of her bed, searching for her cell phone, "We'll find out in short order."

Petra read the number out load as Natalia punched the glowing buttons. "It's an American international access prefix and area code." The number rang twice before a soft voice answered on the other end.

"Hello, this is Elizabetta."

"Elizabetta Zoeltel? My name is Natalia Vyrubova. The Librarian gave me your number. I need your help."

Chapter 10

Consumed in Darkness

So different, the way it seems,
But soon, deep within your dreams,
I will come, bearing my heat
For me, you are but one small treat.
I compel your heart to love only me,
Within your mind, only I do you see.

Come my child, be mine forever.
From humankind I will sever.
Your mind, your soul, your heart, your life.
Consumed in darkness, free from strife.
You will be mine. You cannot resist.
Come to me child, die in bliss.

Father Grigori Yefimovich Rasputin
1894, St. Petersburg, Russia

One week later…

Natalia jerked awake, somewhat disoriented, but relieved to find herself safely wrapped in a down sleeping bag on the cold floor of a cave.

Right.

She chased the clinging tendrils of confusion from her mind, organizing random thoughts into coherent sense. That damn nightmare always had the same effect on her. Huddling in the warmth of her bag on the mountainous northern border of Pakistan, Natalia struggled against the debilitating memories. As the strangling fog of fear receded from her mind, she delicately wiped a blood red tear from her cheek and licked the finger clean, hiding all evidence of the recurring nightmare which had begun that brutal

Russian winter of 1906.

Stretching chilled limbs, Natalia chided herself. She had no time for this foolishness over a hundred years in her past. A secret smile crossed her lips at the thoughts that always followed, the memories of her human life.

She was no longer a naive, virginal girl of the royal court. The sweet child, Lady Natalia Andresiecha Vyrubova, companion to the Tsarina's children, had ceased to exist long ago. Her carefree days of lace frocks, exciting troika rides over the frozen Neva River and lawn games in the brilliant sun ended decades past. Those days were long gone. Covered in the dust of a century or more. Isolation and patience, watching, and honing her skills had made her independent and strong. She was proud of surviving the lonely years, and what she had made of herself in that time. All the while she never lost sight of her pledge to the Tsar and his family. It was her reason to exist.

Enough wandering down memory lane, Natalia mentally admonished herself. Like the mighty Volga River that flowed endlessly to the sea, so her life now flowed, endlessly as well. She could do nothing but accept who and what she had become. She did all in her power to fulfill her promise to protect the Romanovs and their descendants. The thought brought her full circle, back to the cold cave floor, her warm sleeping bag, and a wild-ass scheme to rescue the last male of her beloved royal family. She thought about Petra and Vladimir, enjoying the warmth and comfort of her Siberian Castle, fighting over the last bit of black cake. It brought a smile to her cold lips.

Amazingly enough, she was now part of an American military team that had a mission to accomplish; a mission that paralleled her own goal. She could tolerate that. In fact, it was a win-win situation for her and the undercover operatives. She needed them to help rescue Yuri. They needed her to get into the Taliban stronghold. It was a symbiotic relationship for the moment.

"Fuck you, Rasputin," she whispered. Her secret smile was back, but this time, for a different reason. Natalia stretched and rolled to her stomach, pillowing part of the sleeping bag beneath her head. It was close to sundown. Soon the entire team would be up and on the move. Comfy for the moment, her thoughts turned, begrudgingly, to the mission at hand.

She and Elizabetta had adroitly manipulated a human, an American Army Colonel, into thinking he had convinced Natalia to join the group, recruited for her unique skills. In reality, after weeks of searching, she had been unable to accomplish the rescue of Yuri on her own. Then there was Elizabetta Zoeltel with her Vamp Squad. A new option reared its risky head. They needed her and she needed them; as long as the Colonel agreed, she was good to go.

The group's mission was to destroy a subterranean stronghold and exterminate the group of Taliban generals meeting there. Natalia clenched her jaws in frustration, feeling her fangs grow with the fire of her anger. History would not be allowed to repeat itself here, in this desolate corner of sand and donkey dung. The Romanov line would not end in a dank cave if she had anything to say about it.

Restlessly, Natalia rolled onto one elbow watching the last rays of daylight turn to brilliant red with the approaching sunset. Through the mouth of the small cave where she and the Squad slept, the bright red turned to a deep wine then disappeared across the dirt and stone by inches, in slow retreat. From recluse to military operative, in one short week, her mind still reeled in the turmoil of it all but her resolve was absolute. She would save Yuri.

She'd bet her fangs on it.

Chapter 11

<u>The Dawn of Night</u>

It moves on silent feet,
Its approach meant to greet
Those who roam the night,
In search of human delight.

Velvety fingers caress the dark
Hiding the sign, a vampire's mark.
Beneath the dream, you give a thought
To all that man has ever sought.

Monsters walk within their domain,
Ever bolder without restrain,
Innocence gone, a life replaced
Within the dark, always encased.

Madison Creed, Mistress of the Coven
1698, Salem, Massachusetts

The five women in the team slept away the day, secure in the dark of a cave on the border of Pakistan and Afghanistan. Not far from the famous Khyber Pass, they holed-up safe, in the depths of the earth, protected from the damaging rays of the sun and searching eyes of the local tribesmen.

Elizabetta stirred, waking to the angry remnants of Natalia's nightmare. As Mistress of the newly formed coven, she was privy to all stray or unblocked thoughts of her vampire family members. Now Natalia as well. Delicate auburn eyebrows wrinkled as she stretched and yawned, feeling the chill of the stone floor seep into her five hundred year old bones. It matched the temperature of her heart, stone cold as well. It was an old Romanian joke.

She cast a quick glance at the newest member of the Vamp

Squad, trepidation winding its way into her conscious thoughts. They needed Natalia, a de-facto member of the squad, but she had only been convinced to join the squad in order to rescue a prisoner in the stronghold they planned to destroy. Whether she chose to remain after the mission, was anyone's guess. That question sat at cross-purposes with the Mistress who remained bent on keeping her own coven safe and together.

Recruited for her particularly strong ability to compel human minds, Natalia was little more than a hundred years old, but her strength was incredible and unexpected, for one so young. Elizabetta had read Natalia's case file. What was revealed was explicit and detailed. Having grown to know the woman much better over the week of grueling training they all endured, Elizabetta had come to know Natalia as a friend and dedicated individual. Elizabetta learned that somehow, Natalia gleaned her sire's power when she took his life. History would never record Natalia's part in her infamous sire's death. However, Elizabetta found long ago that history was just a fairy tale. A fairytale written by men for whatever purpose required a particular substitute for the truth, at the time. Many years, living in isolation in an old Siberian castle had provided Natalia with time to practice and experiment. The woman had developed mind control into an incredible art, while using her powers to protect the last of the Russian royal family. Her staff was talented, and operated an international conglomerate from their castle.

How nice.

Natalia seemed to have set herself up amazingly well. She was highly recommended by the Librarian for their mission. How did that come about? As far as Elizabetta knew, the Librarian had no hand in human affairs, and only a mild interest in those of non-affiliated vampires.

Elizabetta shook the invading cobwebs of Natalia's nightmare from her own mind. At least, history was somewhat correct about my sire, the notorious Count Vlad, she thought. He was portrayed as the maniacal sadist he truly was. Her mind fuzzed slightly, the feeling she came to understand as Natalia's way of mentally knocking before entering.

Abruptly, and without the need for eye contact, Natalia sent Elizabetta a mental warning. *Frenchy's at it again. You may want to put a lid on the broadcast, Chief.*

Monique Merchant, wrapped in a fluffy down sleeping bag, moaned some seductive French phrase, obviously entangled in another erotic dream. Natalia could feel Elizabetta mentally contain and isolate the sleeping vampire's thoughts. It would have cost her no effort to completely extinguish the nasty little mental transmission, but as the newest member of the team, Natalia deferred to the established leader, preferring to keep her cards close to her chest. These people had no need to know the length and breadth of her powers. Not yet anyway. Natalia snickered to herself, catching a mental whiff of Monique's fantasy before Elizabetta slammed the proverbial vampire steel door securely shut.

Most times, Monique's sexual tastes were way too grisly for the members of the group to handle. Elizabetta was fairly efficient at playing Earth Mother and Ultimate Nurturer. The Vamp Squad's support team rescued Monique after a century and a half of torture and sexual abuse. Once secure at Olney Farm, the military safe house in Maine, Monique healed quickly with little physical evidence of her persecution. Her mental wounds were still open and often weeping. During the week at the Vamp Squad's secret complex, beneath the cozy farmhouse in Maine, all the vamps would pick up snippets of Monique's warped desires and sadistic sexual fantasies.

Natalia heard Monique moan again and watched a moist tongue lick full pink lips. A true loner, she had plenty of reservations about the collection of vampires that she joined. But so far things seemed to be going fairly well. Whatever the complexities and odd assortment of individuals, she needed them to save Yuri. Isolated and without regular contact with her own kind for so long, she had become a student of human, as well as vampire behavior. Natalia gained a certain internal entertainment from any opportunity to watch the interaction between the team's members, and often sat quietly just observing. Her brow wrinkled in mental questioning; fun to watch but would she bet her and Yuri's life on them?

That was the question.

"Yo, Monique, wake up girl. You're killing me." Susannah kicked the swaddled lump next to her. "Geeze Louise, I have a hard enough time controlling my appetite, without sharing your bizarre shit. Snap out of it, Frenchy."

Natalia, now fully recovered from her hellish nightmare, chuckled inwardly at the fledgling's comments. Susannah had been a vampire for only a couple years. She was only nineteen human years before her turning, a spoiled nineteen years at that. Her lack of common sense and impulsive teen desire for the wild world of adult choices led her to a premature death. It also lead her to life eternal as a vampire. She struggled every day to appear like she was in control of her cravings.

Sometimes she was successful.

Other times…well…those were other times. Of the five operatives, Susannah was the biggest risk, and the biggest baby.

Monique's slim arm snaked from beneath the down sleeping bag and caressed Susannah's bare shoulder. It was a seductive but nurturing move that truly defined the French vampire's relationship with her coven sister. Natalia was stunned the first time she'd realized Monique's bisexual nature. The French vampire was unable to separate normal everyday behaviors from a warped sexual world within which everything existed for sensual pleasure. Actually, Natalia reconsidered, Monique was trisexual. She would try anything sexual, at least once. And probably had.

"Ma petit chéri, I think you like my little dreams, est-ce que c'est vrai?" Monique mewed, drawing her manicured nails down Susannah's arm, entwining her fingers with the other young woman's. She slithered from beneath the fluffy bag and planted a tender kiss on Susannah's lips. Natalia thought the word "slither" was really the best way to describe Monique's moves as a rule, all slinky and sexual. Even waking from a full day of sleep, Monique's lips were wet and soft, her breath a sweet combination of floral and spice. Voluptuous as a human, Monique possessed a figure built to tease and fire a man's lust. As a vampire, she could drive a man mad with desire, especially when she locked her knees and did a perfect impression of Marilyn Monroe's sexy strut. There were times Natalia envied that knee thing. Unfortunately, she wielded a sword much better than a wiggle.

Rising from her sleeping bag with grace, Natalia smoothed her outfit and readjusted the neckline and bangles of her low cut dance costume. Though she hated the brutal side of her earlier existence, she had long ago come to the conclusion that being a vampire definitely had its perks. No aches and pains, no illness, no scars, no wrinkles and no cellulite.

Natalia stretched, flexing her sword arm and testing her reflexes. Toned muscles responded easily as she engaged in a programmed sequence of exercises, similar to a martial arts kata. She reveled in the strength and flexibility of her enhanced body, undeterred by the fact that any male, living or undead, would consider her an incredible beauty. Her full, firm breasts accentuated a slim waist and narrow hips. Her legs, though muscular from years of physical training, were long and shapely. Without thought or contrivance, she projected an aura of danger mixed with sensuality, whether in casual step or in the midst of battle. Her rich dark hair hung in soft swirls well below her shoulders, framing an aquiline face with prominent Russian cheeks and deep red lips that begged for a man's kiss.

The only flaw in an otherwise completely sensual presence was Natalia's eyes. So dark as to appear almost black, years of isolation and loneliness were reflected in the cold chocolate depths. Tsar Nicholas called her his 'Dark Angel'. It was a fitting title for The Watcher.

Natalia concentrated on her steps and tightened the circle of movement as she thought about the results of research on Vampticious Meticulosus Deliriotum, or VMD. How different her life would have been, had she only known about the virus that infected and changed her so dramatically.

Had her sire known the truth?

What would happen if the world knew the truth?

What will happen now, that the American government knows of VMD?

Surely the times, they were a changin'. The Russian government remained ignorant of VMD and the race of vampires that lived beneath the radar, under the noses of the KGB and Polit Bureau. A select few, like Admiral Mikhail Zakharenko, knew of their existence but remained silent, preferring to protect and use vampires for their own purposes. Natalia, better than anyone alive, knew Russian politics and fangs didn't mix.

Natalia rested against the cave wall to catch her breath and frowned to herself recalling the old days, the legends and myths that surrounded her as she grew, matured, and embraced what she thought was the vampire lifestyle. The days of panic and horror ended with the life of her sire, but the uncontrollable desire for blood and sex took many years to master. The onset of modern medical research liberated her mind and her heart, but not her life. People still walked in fear and shunned the monsters of their childhood nightmares. Modern society held the lore of vampires tight to its Judeo-Christian bosom, and reveled in the stories by Anne Rice, Stephen King and Sherrilyn Kenyon.

For a society of mutated humans, it was a nasty cross to bear, causing vampires to live in secret, and guard their own existence at all times. For Natalia, it was a blessing that made her the Romanov family protector and virtually immortal. It also gave her the Council of Elders and the Librarian. For that, she would always be grateful.

"So young. So sweet, ma petit d'amour. You will learn, little sister." Monique deposited a quick peck on Susannah's nose and rose to test the movement of her recently healed limbs against the chilly air of the cave.

Natalia watched from hooded eyes, as Elizabetta intervened before the friendly morning wake-up became an all out frontal assault... or orgy. One never knew with Monique, and there was no excuse to tease Susannah, the fledgling, a vampire barely able to control herself. Memories came flooding back as Natalia remembered those days again… the intensity of every emotion, but mostly, the overriding desire for sex and blood. It would be many years before Susannah would understand her powers. Many years before she could control the lust that drove vampires to first seduce, then kill their victims. Fledglings, without control, took more blood than a body could afford to give up. But vampires had something human's didn't; unlimited time. Susannah would learn, if Elizabetta didn't kill her first.

"All right ladies, let's get this show on the road. Our contact will meet us in an hour at a club in Torkham. The plan says we'll hook up with General Albani's man. He will take us to Michni Kandao, then up the Khyber Pass and off into the hills somewhere. It's a steep trek going toward the summit at Landi Kotal. Once we're off road, we'll be hiking all the way. Not a real problem for any of us, but we have to at least, act like human women to preserve our cover story. The stronghold is a system of caves beneath a village called Hafsa Tokar. No one has ever been able to accurately chart the entire system. We don't know for sure where the entrance to the cave system is located. With a guide, we should be fine and we can avoid trouble with the Shinwari clan. Albani's man will pay a bribe; it's part of the bargain for our *entertainment* services. Let's get this place sanitized."

Though Natalia was new to the squad, she'd picked up much of the lingo used by military operatives in her short tenure at Olney Farm. Both played out in the strange balance of colloquial speech and modern idiomatic sayings that seemed to be just one quirky part of the team, some of whom had several centuries under their bejeweled belts. The rest of the women rolled out of their sleeping bags and began picking up various possessions, stowing gear and hiding wires, explosives and detonators in their specially designed bags. Provided by the best military intelligence department, the bags looked just like Tajikistani traveling bags, but contained expertly concealed compartments to hold the necessary tools of the trade, not the entertainment trade either.

Elizabetta was definitely in command of the Vamp Squad and acting the part. She directed the preparations like a pro, even though Natalia knew Elizabetta had never been involved in an undercover operation before. Natalia watched Susannah twirl and undulate, practicing the sensual moves of a belly dancer. Her mind turned to the heavy burden Elizabetta had assumed and the immature teenager in her charge.

To the amazement of the entire Vamp Squad, Colonel Maddox, their commanding officer and originator of the idea of the squad, had not fought to keep his daughter off the team. Instead, he encouraged Elizabetta to mentor Susannah through this first critical stab at success as an operative of the group. Maybe he was hoping she would learn some responsibility and maturity on the mission.

Natalia had her doubts that would ever happen, finding the teenager's whiny demeanor somewhat frustrating. More to the point, it was probably some requirement to include Susannah. After all, she was the one vampire whose existence was the root of the initial idea for the Vamp Squad in the first place.

During Natalia's intense preparation for the mission, she'd been briefed and questioned extensively on their cover. They would be posing as a Tajikistani dancing troupe. The Vamp Squad's cover established them as a traveling group for hire. The entire squad studied and memorized the identities of the five Taliban generals who would be attending the secret summit hosted by General Abdul Haseem Albani. He was the second-in-command of the Afghan Freedom Fighter's Jamiat Ulema-e-Islam, one of the oldest and most established guerilla groups in the country. The squad reviewed the late Osama Bin Laden's Al Qaeda organization because it would be sending a representative to the summit with a proposal for cooperation. The Vamp Squad would be there as entertainment with a blast, a very real blast. Natalia's part was to share what information she had on Captain Yuri Milassoviech. A Sergeant Miller did recon in the area and filled in the blanks. The cover was solid and worked well only because Albani's religious fervor seemed to end with his zipper and bank account. When it came to Albani's top men, fanatical Islamic beliefs existed only to justify their violent acts, and Jihad war on money and oil.

Silliness drew Natalia's attention once again to Susannah and Monique, giggling wildly as they danced with each other. Their costumes swirling and billowing as they undulated together, Natalia moved to the side clapping a rhythm in the darkening grotto, her sword abandoned for the moment. It wouldn't hurt to blow off a little steam before the real show started. The relationship between Susannah and Monique had developed quickly once Monique was healed, and became a working member of the squad. Their peculiar preference for each other's company seemed to center around sexual play and mischievous games of all sorts. The beautiful blondes could have been sisters if some two hundred years had not separated their births. Natalia envied their closeness and carefree antics at times. At other times, well...again, those were other times. Natalia had a kind of family that awaited her return. However, there had never been anyone with whom she could be silly, or giggly close since her turning.

"These outfits demean the female spirit." MorningStar whispered in Natalia's ear. The fifth and last member of the squad was a Native American before her encounter with a 'skin-walker'. Natalia had studied the profiles of all the team members, as had each operative in turn. Before MorningStar's turning, she was a proud and self-reliant member of the Kanza people in the old west of America. Still, over two hundred years later, Natalia imagined how wearing revealing outfits to ensnare a man's mind was still an insult to MorningStar's Native spirit and female sensibilities. The American Indian vampire stood straight as a rod with a frown marring her desert-exotic features.

"Nyet, cestra. If the Generals believe this rouse, we are 'begrisch', winners. And we will wear the burqa to cover our delicate skins. Such a country is made for our kind, da?" Blood red lips split into a wide smile displaying pearly white canine fangs.

To her dismay, Natalia still had problems displaying her fangs when she was happy, excited or having fun. They just seemed to pop out and shine of their own volition. It was somewhat disconcerting, and a little embarrassing. No one else in the squad seemed to have that problem.

"Cheloveky! Bah. Men are ruled by their eyes and their cocks. You will see, sister." Natalia laughed and briefly hugged MorningStar. Apparently Native Americans seemed to lack a certain sense of humor as MorningStar stood stiff and uncompromising. Natalia could only shrug sheepishly, her smiling fangs glistening in the darkness.

She moved toward the mouth of the cave, leaving the revelry behind. It was a long walk to the marketplace in Torkham, but walking wasn't what the team had in mind. Before they departed the safety of their subterranean haven, Natalia needed a little alone time with her thoughts. The sky was velvety black and called to her with its welcoming arms. Night had always been her friend and lover, her escape.

Perched on the sheer edge of the rocky precipice that defined their cave entrance, she reverently fingered a miniature photo of Yuri hidden in a concealed pocket in her dance costume. She could almost feel his presence as she stood just beyond the mouth of the cave and cast her thoughts into the warm night.

He so resembled her beloved Alexei, that her cold heart was moved to almost human pain. Though she had hidden the royal children, Anastasia and Alexei, for the span of their human lives, she could not save the rest of the Russian royal family from their fate. She had been able to destroy the rotten disease called Rasputin, but it was too late to stem the tide of political plague the mad priest began. Through the decades Natalia served the

Romanovs faithfully as she watched over their children, and their children's children with honor and love, keeping the secret of their true identities as well as the secret of her own existence. Only Alexei left behind a secret family to carry on his line. Two generations later, Yuri and his father were the last direct descendants of the royal family.

Delicate fingertips caressed the picture hidden within her skimpy garment. She had a connection almost as tangible as an anchor line to this man, this great-great grandson of Tsar Nicholas. Always there, just beyond his human ability to perceive, Natalia clung to Yuri as her last tie to the Romanovs and the human world, as the embodiment of acceptance and love.

First as a child, she adored the robust blonde baby. Then, as the child became a strong and virile man, she protected and cherished her Yuri from afar. Somewhere, over the years, she came to love the man who shared the beautiful eyes of the Tsar she worshiped as a young girl. He was the lifeline to what was left of her humanity and her heart's light, despite her love for those who composed her family-by-choice at home.

Right or wrong, just seeing his picture stirred her blood and brought back haunting memories of what she lost; the loss of her human genetics, of love, of life. Natalia felt a warmth settle within her core. It was a feeling she had not had for some time. She fought the seemingly inappropriate feelings for this man who had been the purpose of her life since his birth. But, she could not deny their sexual nature any longer. Petra called it the 'ick' factor, but Natalia only felt a kind of detached love. At least until now...

Though her fantasies often wore the face of Yuri, they were entirely of her making and she knew them for what they were, a poor substitute, a safe whimsy. She would have given her immortality to be a real part of Yuri's heart. An impregnable wall called VMD always separated them, VMD and her sire's brutal and perverted practices.

Natalia knew she could never truly love any man in the complete sense of the word, having been wounded so deeply by her sire's torturous ways. He took more than her virginity and her life. He severed the connection between her soul and her heart.

When Yuri ran off to join the Russian army, she remained in the shadows, watching, guarding, and fantasizing about the handsome Captain who stole her heart as a child and held it as a man. Again she wondered how she had lost track of him? He was safe and secure in Moscow, then he was gone. She would always dream about… and protect him. That was her life; her job and she joined this Vamp Squad to ensure she did just that. Elizabetta's voice drew her from her own mental meanderings.

"Let's get going. Make sure you've left nothing behind. Not even a dirty tissue. Burqas all around, ladies. We can't strut about in these cute little outfits." Elizabetta tossed the voluminous sack over her head and let the folds cover her costume. Black against black, she was almost invisible to the human eye. "Not a bad method for sneaking around." Elizabetta depressed a small, jeweled button on her belt activating the team's communication system, with its series of cyber-implants. The tiny implants, which had been surgically placed in the neck of each squad member, were state-of-the-art communication devices that would allow the women to talk with their support team, even through hundreds of feet of rock. Designed for fighting in the Afghan mountains, the support team would be able to stay in touch once they arrived in Torkham and set up camp. "All right. Report in, by the numbers."

The Vamp Squad tested their equipment with success. Thanks to Natalia's unique abilities, the vamps did not need to keep in touch through electronic means, but their military support team was human and did. The Operational Support Team, better known as *The Babysitters*, was still making its way across Peshawar Province in Pakistan, at the speedy rate of a meandering mule.

"The Babysitters are on their way, masquerading as merchants. Colonel Maddox, Captain Devlin and Sergeant Miller are approaching the target area from Peshawar City. They should come through the Khyber Pass in the morning and be in Torkham early on, ready to lend whatever support we need." Elizabetta was reviewing the strategy that everyone knew by heart and could literally recite in their sleep. It wasn't necessary, but apparently comforting for Elizabetta, and probably adequate remediation for Susannah. The teen had demonstrated a certain lack of retention for anything that didn't show up as a text message or involve shopping.

Twenty-eight miles was not far, as the vamp flew, but the famous Khyber Pass was twenty-eight miles of twisting, windy roads, through thirty-four tunnels, across ninety-two bridges eventually connecting Pakistan and Afghanistan. The Orient Express had long since given up rolling over the tracks of the pass due to tribal squabbles and civil war. The precarious road through the pass rose to some three thousand five hundred feet before dropping into Torkham and the Dakka Plain beyond, in Afghanistan. Dry as a bone and tight as twenty-five feet in some places, full of holes and washouts, it was not a road for the faint of heart or those overly concerned with being ambushed. And it was definitely a challenge for three mortal men dragging donkeys. Natalia was sure The Babysitters were up to it. She couldn't wait to see how the fastidious Captain Devlin handled the dirty beasts and red dust of the Safed Kohl Mountains. She just had to chuckle thinking about the Captain who trimmed his hair daily and washed his hands, at least a hundred times each shift. Devlin and donkeys? It was almost worth coming to Afghanistan, just to see.

Elizabetta took Susannah's hand. "Stay with me and keep physical contact, Susannah. You have much to learn about your new form. It will come slowly. Let me control our form and flight." Although they appeared to be close in age, Elizabetta was born a vampire in the late fourteen hundreds, and Susannah had been turned at nineteen. No matter the chronological age, Natalia, like Elizabetta, Susannah and the rest of the team's members, looked to the casual observer to be around their mid twenties. With the "infection" that caused vampirism came virtual immortality, as the aging process was slowed to almost nothing. While different for each, a vampire year was equal to about one hundred human years and as the vampire aged, the process slowed even more. With age also came strength, but a fledgling of two years would not yet be able to levitate, materialize, feed or compel effectively without her Dama's assistance. "Your father would be very angry if I let you act before you are ready," Elizabetta smiled at the young woman.

"Yeah, right, Daddy, I almost forgot. Always Daddy. What's the worst that can happen? I am immortal aren't I?" A petulant vampire was not a thing of beauty. Natalia shook her head. This woman-child should never have been turned. What was her sire thinking? A quick glance at Susannah's well-endowed figure provided the answer; thirty-two D!

"Listen to your Dama, child. Had your father not come for you, you would be now beneath the ground in perpetual darkness, approaching insanity from the pain of hunger, and desire unsatisfied. Be thankful he is *always* Daddy, and *always* there for you. You had no sire to show you the way or feed you. Do you understand? You would not have survived on your own, little sister?" Natalia was hard on Susannah, but with good reason.

Two years ago, when Susannah was left sireless, her father, Colonel Maddox formed the Vamp Squad, as much to serve his country as to provide for his daughter's unique needs. That was, of course, once the stalwart Colonel came to grips with the fact vampires actually existed. His lovely little girl had joined their ranks. He was a gruff, hard man to feel close to, but always a father. He was always there for his daughter. A daughter who flaunted her independence one spring break, and lost her human life because of it.

Susannah was more fortunate than Natalia had been. Natalia's parents died of a fever when she was seven years old, leaving her in the care of her loving Aunt Anna. The loving aunt who took her to court to play with the royal children, and worship in Father Grigori's church.

"Stay high and keep our cover up. We'll set down outside the market and walk the rest of the way. The whole town is about six dirt streets with blockhouses ringing the market. No one speaks but me, unless one of you has mastered Pashto. Keep your faces covered - all the way. Make sure you have no stray blonde hairs sticking out anywhere." Elizabetta's gaze fell on Monique, their leader's arched eyebrow raised in punctuation. "Muslim men are crazy for light colors. We don't want to blow our cover on some careless incident before we even get a bite at the mission." Natalia chuckled as Elizabetta smirked at her own joke. Natalia was beginning to develop a grudging respect for the coven leader and her sharp sense of humor.

"Yeah, yeah, yeah. You sound more and more like my dad all the time." Susannah pulled a face and scuffed her toe in the dirt.

"And you sound younger each time you open your mouth, little one. You must learn to be more serious if you are to remain with the team. Your father has placed a great deal of responsibility at your feet. See that you do not trample on his decision."

Elizabetta's stern reply stopped the fledgling in her tracks. Natalia watched the interchange with some delight. Susannah needed discipline, and their coven leader was the one to accomplish the task, though Natalia did not envy in the least Elizabetta's burden. Elizabetta had been the first vampire to come to Olney Farm and mostly as a surrogate mother to Susannah. It was only later, when Colonel Maddox became aware of the super-human abilities of vampires, that he hit on the idea. An undercover squad of military operatives comprised of female vampires was a streak of genius. The idea was a healthy portion of fatherly love, and, of course, patriotic ingenuity sprinkled with political prowess. The Squad would work for the government, and the government would protect and provide for the squad, i.e. his daughter. A win-win situation, as long as the government didn't welch on their deal and the vamps didn't bite.

Right.

Where was that turnip truck when you needed it?

Monique made a flamboyant display of tying her hair back while Susannah made sure her own golden blonde tresses were well contained beneath the drab burqa. Natalia and MorningStar joined the group as they launched skyward, morphing wings as they leapt from the precipice outside their secret little hole in the desolate Safed Kohl range.

Below them, the craggy mountaintops reached toward the skimming vamps. Dusty red peaks tested the strength and skill of those who dared the heights.

Exalting in the freedom of flight, Natalia dipped and swooped, soaring circles around the broken and bare mountaintops. She mentally nudged Susannah. *Learn little sister, and soon you will be like this, free and filled with the power of what you have become. You will be able to take any shape just by willing it. You will also be able to levitate by yourself as we do. It will happen for you if you are serious and listen to Elizabetta.* Natalia loved the feeling of flight and tightened her mental string of thought, sending Susannah an emotional burst of pure joy.

Too soon, they touched down in the shadows outside the disheveled marketplace. Each member of the squad morphing in different ways as their limbs contacted terra firma. Susannah stumbled, but held her ground with a hand from Elizabetta.

Susannah threw Natalia a sheepish glance and psyched her sister shakily. *So when does the motion sickness go away? Every time I fly I just want to barf.*

Soft giggles emanated from behind more than one burqa as Susannah straightened and sent a burst of peevish anger to all the vamps. The town was quiet and no one seemed to notice anything unusual in their arrival. Not many people ventured out into the night since the fighting had begun in earnest. People disappeared in the darkness in Torkham.

Completely covered by their coarse robes, the women huddled close together, silent, as they traversed the marketplace heading for their rendezvous and the appointed contact.

The Shinwari Baba Club was frosted in soft shimmering light that spilled up the stairs of its entrance. Oil lamps hung from the rafters, hundreds throughout the underground rooms. Dug halfway into the ground for temperature control and security, the place looked like some scene out of a sci-fi fantasy flick. Natalia thought immediately of the bar scene in Star Wars, an old American movie she had seen on satellite in her village. Vlad added a satellite dish when he could no longer get some of the more modern, but politically incorrect programs he loved. Their little family missed nothing from the world of western media. With such a strong resemblance to the bar in the movie, she would not have been surprised to see an alien in the establishment. Wild western music played over an ancient crackling loudspeaker. Most of the patrons sat in small groups around hashish hookahs, puffing their minds and bodies into oblivion. For a hundred years, the sweet smoke had filled the club, infusing the very stone and wood of the place with its sickening scent. MorningStar wrinkled her nose and swallowed hard as the group moved through the sparsely populated main room. The owner's makeshift office hid behind several hand painted screens depicting erotic scenes of belly dancers.

Amazing, I think I'm wearing that costume. MorningStar mentally communicated to the rest of the women.

God, don't psyche me with jokes, unless you want me to giggle behind this getup. Susannah admonished her sister-in-arms, or sister-in-burqa, as the current costume demanded.

MorningStar smiled behind her veil, feeling the mind tickle that told her Susannah was mentally laughing. *By the Spirits,*

96

Monique, look at that one. It is the image of what you wear, only without the jewels. I do not believe in coincidences. This is odd indeed.

Pipe down all of you. Sgt. Miller did recon here when he established himself as a trader from Pakistan. You know that. He has been here several times. It's not surprising our costumes resemble these works of art. Natalia shot Elizabetta a surprised glance but was still disgusted, with the screens and with Sgt. Miller. What a sick joke.

But then, that was Milo Miller, one big sick joke on humanity. Miller had to have been the role model for the character Klinger on MASH. It was the first program she had ever seen on a Russian television broadcast from America's state of Alaska when the Freedom Exchanges of people and technology began in the eighties. She loved the little hairy man who wore dresses and continually got out of everything – just like Miller. Only not the dresses – Miller was a soldier's soldier, and would never have considered wearing anything but manly clothing displaying his compact physique to its best advantage.

Elizabetta stepped discreetly behind the screen, Natalia close on her heels, followed by the other members of the Squad. Elizabetta let the hood of her burqa slide to her shoulders, her auburn hair glowing amber in the lamp light. As the rest of the women did the same, Hamza stumbled to stand.

Natalia knew Ameer Hamza was expecting operatives he would guide to the Taliban's stronghold, but she was sure he never suspected he'd be taking *five* women operatives up the Khyber and into the mountains without any other men. His mouth hung open for several seconds before he recovered and spoke. "Welcome, Allah shines his wisdom upon us this night. Be at peace in my humble abode."

"And peace be with you. We come to seek your guidance Master Hamza, in all things." Elizabetta responded with the prearranged code phrase that would let Hamza know they truly were the operatives he was expecting.

Placing a finger to his lips and peering around the screen for anyone listening, he whispered, "Quickly, come with me. You should not be seen in this place. Only certain women come here and for one purpose." Hamza leered as he led them through a secret panel behind his desk and down a flight of ancient stone stairs worn by a hundred years of foot traffic. "I was not expecting five women. If, in fact, that is what all of you are, we will have to change our plans. Five women cannot make it up the pass on foot. The way is too rough. My brother will be with us and he will not tolerate lagging. I had expected, maybe two dancers and their men." He looked speculatively from the burqa clad figures to the soft, glowing faces of each woman, now with hoods pulled back. The basement was crowded with supplies stacked in disarray. The chamber stunk of stale alcohol, sweet hashish and lamp oil. The mixture was as offensive to Natalia as Hamza's attitude about women.

Hamza stood, shifting his weight from one foot to the other. He dressed in an ornate salwar kameez with a gold embroidered tarboush covering what little hair he had left on his balding head. His dirty, gray beard swished back and forth leaving a trail of little hairs and dandruff across the dark fabric of his garment. The portly little man continually rubbed his hands together as if he were washing away any knowledge of the night's activities.

"We are trained operatives, Hamza. We go where we need to. We will not cause any delay."

Hamza, upon hearing Elizabetta's accented pronouncement, surveyed the women with distain.

Natalia reached out to the mind of the skeptical man, as Elizabetta spoke. Compelling the mind, after all, was Natalia's true strength, the reason she had been recruited, the way she would liberate Yuri. A slight touch and Hamza would be compliant. A stronger touch, and he would do exactly what they wanted with no memory of this night. A somewhat tight grip and the sniveling little pig would curl up in a ball and die. She felt Elizabetta stay her powerful hand.

No, Natalia, your touch is too invasive for this one. Let me. He is a weak, fearful dolt and we cannot afford to lose the information within his little mind. Though Elizabetta was not as strong a compeller as Natalia, it took little skill or power to control this little rodent of a man. Elizabetta sought and found a thin strand within Hamza's thoughts and wound it around her finger, tugging delicately.

"I was told you were to guide us, Hamza." Elizabetta looked

quizzically at the little man. "The American government is paying you to guide us. What is this about your brother?"

Natalia's talents allowed her to see other vampire's efforts as if they were tangible and clear to the naked eye. She watched quietly as Elizabetta worked her magic. Hamza leaned toward Elizabetta and smiled, his silly expression reminding Natalia of a puppy that found its precious chew toy. It took little encouragement to get him moving, and loosen his tongue as well. Natalia smiled at the finesse with which Elizabetta directed the man. It was a good lesson. She promised herself to be more subtle with her power in the future. Sometimes a switch, in the right hands, was as effective as a club.

"My brother, Teffas Hamza, works for General Albani, not I. Together, we will guide you to the stronghold. Let us go, then." Hamza smiled solicitously, grasping Elizabetta's elbow to lead her through the barrels and boxes of the basement storage room.

With vamp speed, Natalia held Hamza's throat in her grip. "Teffas Hamza is your brother?" Her eyes gleamed bright red, obviously overcome with anger. The sound of the name made her blood boil with hatred. Teffas Hamza was Yuri's captor, a man who had taken money for a life.

Hamza squealed like a frightened pig, flapping his pudgy hands up and down, incapable of gaining his freedom from the livid woman.

Nat, let go and wipe his mind of this incident. We need him and his brother to find Yuri. Elizabetta squeezed Natalia's shoulder in concern.

With regret and necessity, Natalia released her hold on Hamza and blanked his mind as she took her place behind Elizabetta.

Monique coughed and held a pink tipped nail to her nose, nodding toward the stairs with urgency.

As they climbed steep stairs to the rear exit, he whispered conspiratorially, "we will go to my brother's home. He is a very important person in General Albani's organization, but truly misguided. We fight on different sides in this war for our country. He fights for opium and his bank account. I fight for my country and freedom. When we reach his home, I will not leave you in his hands, if it can be avoided. You are to dance for many men. This you can do, no?" Hamza continued to leer at the women as if he could see through their covering robes. Natalia sensed Elizabetta tug at his mental connection a little more aggressively and watched as the greasy little man turned to trudge along more quickly, mumbling to himself.

Stay close ladies. We need a male escort in this country to safely walk about without trouble. The group closed ranks and followed Hamza as he wove his way through the alleys and dark streets of Torkham.

To the casual observer, it appeared as if a man was escorting his wives home for the evening. *Watch how we go and memorize waypoints, so we can transmit them to The Babysitters. They'll want to know where Hamza's brother lives and where we end up. We must be sure to communicate any change in the original plan.*

This is so double-oh-sevenish. I love it. Susannah mentally giggled. *Make my martini shaken not stirred.* The young girl affected a psychic attitude of a female James Bond sharing her little fantasy with the rest.

Quiet, Susannah. You are not only too young to have a martini, but way too inexperienced to drink. Look what happened the last time. Elizabetta touched the young girl's burqa close to her neck and the tiny indentations left by her sire's fangs. *You may be close to immortal, but you are a fledgling. Learn and live, child. Or know destruction. This is not a game.*

It was hard to see Susannah's refreshing enthusiasm squelched. It had been a hundred years since Natalia felt that twinge of excitement about life without the continual color of fear. But Elizabetta was the Mistress of a coven, and the weight lie heavy on her shoulders when it came to Susannah. Natalia could see their Mistress act like a mother with all of the protective maternal instincts in bloom, as well as all of the headaches. This undercover military stuff was new to Natalia and stimulating… and dangerous. She definitely shared Susannah's excitement, if not her quirky sense of humor.

"Come, come, come ladies. My brother is a very impatient man, armed as well. Fear his temper. He is not easy with women. They are for him, two things, a place to stick his chuta'ha, and as an extra pack animal. Have care with your tongue and give him much space." Hamza spoke in hushed tones as he led them through the shadows. "Do not speak with his woman. She will feel his wrath if you do."

As they approached a square, three-story blockhouse at the end of a dusty street, Hamza added, "act like good Muslim women. Keep your eyes down, speak respectfully and quietly. Do not shake hands or touch Teffas in front of his family." He indicated Elizabetta with a tentative wave. "Your Pashto is very good. You sound like a northerner. Almost like real Tajikistani. It is good."

Huffing and puffing along, Hamza led the women up a short hill to the end of a row of clay block structures and around to the back of the last and largest building where a jumble of rocks served as stairs to the back veranda of the block style house. Up on the stone-arched terrace, a man in a traditional black salwar kameez sat at a small table smoking a hashish pipe. Three little boys played nearby with small wooden soldiers, sticks and rocks. They acted out battle scenes and giggled as their soldiers died horrible deaths at the hands of their conquerors. By the door to the structure, a small girl completely covered by a thick shawl, sat silently in the dirt, invisible to the male eyes of the household. A tall woman, buried beneath the weight of her burdens carried heavy trays of food and drink to serve the man who sat leisurely enjoying his hashish. The smell of curry, tallo spice and human sweat was almost overpowering, even at their distance.

The blissful domestic scene would have been perfect but for a sense of fear that permeated the air, along with the smell of sweat and spices. Natalia could taste it. Like an overpowering scent, dread burned her eyes and gouged at her throat. Her breath caught in her chest, and she stumbled. *There is something wrong here, Betta. Have care. This one's mind is hard like steel. There is much hate in this place.*

The women ascended the makeshift steps behind their guide, carefully picking their way up toward the veranda. Natalia hung back pretending to stumble in the rocks. The closer she came to the man in black, the more difficult it became for her to focus and move. Pain surged within her body. Her joints ached as if they had been stretched beyond their ability to function. Her fingertips burned as if held over a fire. Heat sizzled behind her eyes. It was all she could do to remain upright, and not scream in agony. The smell of blood assaulted her senses.

Old blood.

The blood of the Romanovs.

A growl began deep in her throat, and Natalia felt her fangs extend of their own volition. This man had taken Yuri's blood. In fact he reeked of it, as if in the taking, it had somehow marked him. She could smell it, taste it, feel it on him like a physical presence dripping from this monster's putrid soul. Her gag reflex kicked in and she swallowed hard to stem the response.

Natalia, what's wrong? The entire squad felt her white-hot surge of hatred mixed with nausea. Elizabetta was instantly worried.

Susannah stumbled under the psychic outburst of such violent emotion but quickly regained her footing. *Nat?*

Beneath her burqa, blood red tears trickled down a deathly pale face. *He bears the blood of Yuri Milassoviech. He will die!* Natalia scrambled up the rocks in a flash, like an animal in the grip of a bloody hunt.

No. Elizabetta restrained the thoughts and movement of her compatriot. *Control yourself. We have a mission. We need this man. We need him to do what we have come here to do. Natalia, think! We cannot find Yuri without him.*

Natalia slowed, her movements resembling a stalking leopard, as she approached the man on the porch. *I can force his mind to give me what I need, then slaughter him like the pathetic animal he is.*

You might find the location, but that will not get us through the door, my daughter. Focus on the mission. Focus on your personal desire. We are a team. You will have this piece of garbage. I promise you will have him when we have accomplished our task and are safe once again. Patience, Natalia. Elizabetta concentrated a line of mental will toward Natalia. The Mistress calmed Natalia with her thoughts, assuring the infuriated vampire.

He will die by my hand, or fang. I will have his blood. Natalia felt focus return to her mind and air to her lungs as she attempted sarcasm. *He will pay in kind.* A sort of mental purr touched the other members of the Squad as Natalia retracted her fangs and reined in her violent thoughts. *And he will know exactly what bit him.*

Alright, but first we have to get into the stronghold and complete our mission. Elizabetta cautioned her operative. *You're smarter than this, Natalia. Put a lid on those wonderful powers of yours and settle down. We'll get our job done and if Yuri is still alive, we'll find him. We'll get him out.*

He lives still. I can sense his heartbeat. Natalia touched the hidden picture beneath her burqa. Her connection to the descendent of the Romanovs was strong but she could not compel his mind or touch his thoughts. Not yet. Soon.

"Babidev, Teffas Hamza, peace my brother. I bring the dancers you asked for. They are from Tajikistan. There are five, brother." Hamza motioned excitedly to the string of women who followed him. He was visibly nervous as the squad effectively huddled in the manner of Muslim women of the trade. "They are said to be the best, my brother. You will see." Stammering, Hamza backed up rapidly, as his brother stood, knocking over the chair he had been sitting in just seconds before.

Teffas was much taller than his well-padded brother and wore a red tarboush with fancy beaded embroidery on his head. The fez style cap was decorated with symbols of Islam and camouflaged a receding hairline. Teffas Hamza could have passed for the ethnic lead in Lawrence of Arabia had the sneer on his face not totally destroyed any semblance of appeal. The children scrambled, ducking into doorways and crannies. It was clear, this false domestic scene did little to disguise the true nature of the head of the household. Teffas was a bully who got what he wanted with brutal force.

With the reflexes of a cobra, Teffas snatched his brother by the front of his kameez. Grinding out his words between clenched teeth, Teffas warned his brother, "they had better be. Your life, and mine, depend on it. General Albani is a harsh man. He does not accept inferiority. They will go with me. You will remain behind, brother." The man in black glared at the women with their bags. "At the pass they will walk. If one drops behind, she will be shot." His crisp kameez fit like it had been especially made with typical Pakistani care for the tall man. Obviously, Albani's man had access to a wealth of goods that came over the border, probably with Albani's blessing and assistance.

Teffas motioned to the woman near the doorway. She appeared silently with two baskets and helped Susannah and Monique attach leather straps to their shoulders to carry the small

103

containers. Whispering, she indicated the baskets carried water, bread and goat cheese for the trip. Natalia inclined her head in thanks, knowing better than to speak to the poor woman who obviously endured her husband's brutal attentions with no hope of escape. The squad's bags were heavy, but carried easily with the enhanced strength of VMD. The bags contained dancing costumes, musical instruments and much more. Each costume concealed several pounds of C-4 explosives and det cord. High-tech ignition devices were hidden in the bag's construction. As long as no man tried to heft their bags, the team would be safe. In a Muslim world, Natalia knew there was little chance a man would ever carry a woman's bag. The Babysitters bet on that cultural custom with complete faith. Sgt. Miller spent enough time in the region to bet the Team's safety on it.

Dead man walking. When all is said and done, this one is mine. Natalia was steaming and the other members of the squad could feel every stab of anger as they filed out of the building, toting their bags as if each weighed little more than nothing.

In front of Teffas Hamza's block home, a banged-up, dusty troop carrier awaited them. Its engine sputtered and coughed in the cool evening air. They un-shouldered their baskets, slipping out of the decorative straps with ease. Handing up their bags to each other as they climbed aboard, they settled in.

Natalia could see Ameer Hamza scurrying down the road toward his club, as far from his brother as he could get, and as quickly as it could be accomplished. His rapid footsteps caused little poofs of dust at his retreat. She was sure, if she could have seen his face, she would have seen relief written across his pudgy features in huge capital letters. So much for staying with the women!

Such a hero! He cannot get away fast enough, the little rat. Look at him scurry as if a cat stalked his fat little body. One small chomp for a cat, one large relief for mankind. Mental laughs resonated within the minds of the team members as Natalia shared her joke with them. Ameer Hamza was as bold as brass in his own element but could not hold a candle to his vile brother.

Chapter 12

<u>Blood</u>

It is the connection that binds,
A source, a need, the desire reminds,
All night dwellers of its precious gift,
In life and death a focus, a shift.

The drops do pour
From a victim sore.
To feed, to strengthen
A death to lengthen.

Selina Okanoviech, Coven Huntress
1994, United States

A totally disgruntled and aching group of vampires bounced around on the bare benches in the canvas-covered back of the troop carrier that picked them up at the home of Teffas Hamza. Each, a proud and immortal individual with collective powers to amaze and confound the mind… and each, with bruised and battered backsides.

Not only does he bear the blood of a human Natalia has promised to protect, but he has the audacity to… ouch… to provide this wonderful method of transport. Merde!

The truck hit a rut and bounced everyone several inches into the air.

Can we not fly and just wipe this indolent's mind when we arrive? This time, Monique was the one who acted petulant and whiny. Obviously sore, her self-centered nature was most apparent when she was uncomfortable and dirty.

Natalia smiled behind her hot, dusty veil. Go figure, a vampire with cleanliness issues. What a lot they were; gorgeous and graceful Elizabetta, always calm and in control; fierce Natalia

105

ready for battle at the drop of a sword; quiet, but proudly stoic MorningStar; Monique, the clean freak sexpot, and spoiled Susannah, child terror with fangs. What was she doing in the back of an Afghani wreck that passed for a truck, with gun toting terrorists and four vampires bent on blowing up a giant cave?

The truck hit a deep rut and they all bounced again. Susannah squeaked and Monique moaned in what could only be described as a kind of sensual pain.

It wasn't long before they were all sore. The road was full of ruts and potholes. The way twisted and turned every few feet, and the driver often had the truck perched precariously on the crumbling edge of the broken pavement to avoid bombed out sections of the road. All in all, that wasn't so bad, but when the truck pulled off the patchy pavement and headed into the hills on a goat path, things got truly dicey... and bruising.

Soon we will be walking, then, you can complain about your feet instead of your behind. This goat trail can't go on forever. And remember, if you fall behind you will be shot. The last comment was almost a sneer, as Elizabetta inclined her head toward the rest of the guards with special meaning. Like any of the squad would fall behind! Even Susannah had more strength and stamina than their entire escort put together, as long as the sun was down, and the land was enveloped in darkness. A couple bullets, while they would hurt for a while, could not kill a vampire.

Rounding a tight curve Natalia gasped. She clutched her chest, then doubled over in obvious pain. Susannah and MorningStar lurched to catch her, as she slid to the floor of the truck, curled in a tight ball.

Natalia, what's wrong? Elizabetta was instantly on alert still only communicating through their mental link.

"She is ill? Sick from the movement? Weak females." Teffas Hamza reached to cuff the woman on the floorboards, and found his hand stayed by Elizabetta's strong grip.

"She will be fine. It will do no good to hit her. If we are to dance for your men, we should do so without marks." Elizabetta replied in a calming manner. She took a chance, staying the man's hand, but a chance she was willing to bet on, combined with a little metal softening.

"You can dance without her. If she falls behind, she will be shot."

"So you have said. We will take care of our own. Do not worry." Teffas could not see the rage cross Elizabetta's face behind the veil of her burqa as she spoke humbly to the man in a soft voice.

Natalia? Elizabetta's mind communicated much more than just words.

I'm... I'm ok. I felt such pain. For a second I thought... His heart had stopped. Shaking, Natalia groped for Susannah's arm, huddling against the younger woman's body. MorningStar crouched, her strength steadying the two on the bottom of the truck, as they bounced and lurched along. *His heart stopped and I felt the agony of death touch his soul; but it has passed. He lives. Maybe not for such a long time. We must hurry or it will be too late.*

Gasping for air, Natalia was helped to the bench by Susannah on one side and MorningStar on the other. They sat close, helping her remain upright. *He is in terrible pain, but I cannot call to him.* Natalia crumpled in pain, wincing as her dance belt pinched and gouged her middle.

We move as fast as we can without revealing our special talents. Can you send him strength? Elizabetta was reaching for any solution to assist the Russian soldier. They had to maintain their cover, but she also knew Yuri was on the verge of death.

Natalia took the hands of Susannah and MorningStar. *I can try. I will need help. How long before we reach the caves? Lend me your power. Relax. Let me enter.*

Nat, you can do that? Susannah's naiveté was so endearing, unlike her temper tantrums.

I can try. I have not done this for some time. It was a trick of my sire. He increased his power by taking from his minions. He forced their mind to open as he would force their bodies to open. He was brutal, and truly repulsive. I have polished my technique over the century living alone but with support and protection from my neighbors. I only take as much strength as a person is willing to give. I found long ago, drawing strength limits my need for blood. Sharing the knowledge of her unique skill and the way she had acquired it, demonstrated just how much she had come to trust the other members of the Vamp Squad in the short time they had been together. It was also a testament to what she could and would do to save Yuri.

Will it hurt? Susannah asked in a thin mental query, like a child asking the nurse about her first vaccination.

Natalia patted Susannah's arm that circled her shoulders reassuringly. *No, little sister. I would never do something that would cause you pain. It's like lending me some of your endless energy. You can help by clearing your mind and thinking 'toward' me, if that makes sense.*

The two vampires settled on the bench on either side of Natalia, relaxing their guard and clearing their minds enough to let her intrude, usurping their strength and consuming bits of their power. As far as Natalia knew, she and her sire were the only two vampires that could channel energy. She had learned the term v-channel from him early on in their vile relationship. Though he had not taught her all of his demonic tricks, he gave her what knowledge would benefit his needs. Unfortunately for him, he gave her just enough to end his pathetic life. The rest, she knew to take from his lifeless body when she took his head.

Like sharing a sandwich or drinking from one glass, Natalia concentrated and drew what she needed, filling her being with as much energy as she could, without draining her comrades. The power burned but she held it within, rolling a ball of current like a carnival hawker rolls cotton candy on a paper cone. Spinning and winding, it grew into a massive ball of pure energy, tearing at Natalia's nerves and igniting her mind in white hot flames. Yet, she had learned to hold energy many years ago, and the pain was nothing compared to her desire to help Yuri.

Her head fell to her lap as she focused the energy, forming a thin line of power. Like spinning fine wool from raw fluff, Natalia spooled the line into a useful tool. Directing it through the corporeal world, she sought out the man who had so completely captured her heart.

Reaching out to the faltering human life that lay, cold and still in a cavern deep within the mountains they traversed, she found what she sought.

Yuri!

Her soul cried for the pain-wracked mind she so tentatively touched. Natalia plucked at a thin satiny chord of emotion, insinuating herself into his psyche, mentally feeling for any connection, any glimmer of life to infuse with strength. She reached for, and found neurological pathways that remained receptive. Then she moved farther into his body. Once within, she soothed the battered senses and infused the man's tortured tissue with what life force he could accept. Like lightning in a spring storm, flashes of energy connected them for an instant, here and there, as Natalia forced Yuri's body to accept her ministrations, all the while reinforcing his need to survive. Panting from the effort, she continued the contact, repairing if she could, but mostly patching the results of his captor's unrelenting torture. When there was no more she could do, she remained within reaching for the rage that had sustained this man for so long. Rage was powerful. It provided a will to live, if only to assuage one's anger in revenge. If she could reach it…

Then she was there, deep in his subconscious mind, touching the raw emotions churning like a molten core. Natalia caressed his anger and watched it flare to life. Releasing the rest of her strength into this maelstrom of feelings, she could sense Yuri jerk awake, stronger, but still in grave condition.

I am coming for you. Hold on for me, my love.

*****

Captain Yuri Milassoviech lie on the cold stone floor of his cell wishing for death, and hating his weakness in that wish. In the desire to end his pain, and thus end his life, Yuri had given up. He was a Russian soldier. He was a Romanov. He was a dead man. Soon…

How long had it been? Days? Weeks? Months? The endless pain continued on and on. It was impossible to escape. Even unconscious, he felt the twisted agony of a body pushed beyond its limits. He could no longer move from the wall with its trickle of life sustaining water. His limbs lie broken and crushed. The joints were battered to a pulpy mass of bruised and bleeding tissue. What was left of his hands hung at the end of useless arms connected to something resembling shoulders. Eyes, swollen beyond recognition, no longer saw. Lips, unrecognizable, sealed with leaking and crusted body fluid, held his crushed jaw and teeth.

Lungs seeped blood into a torso that filled with the clotting liquid, slowly killing the organs contained within.

Soon…so soon…

Yuri drifted on waves of throbbing agony. Soon he would dip beneath the waves, and it would be done. He raged at the unfairness of it all. Escaping his parent's smothering hand. Running off to join the army to find his future. Fighting to prove the value of a true Romanov? Yuri succeeded only in wasting his life.

How had it ended this way?

Who had betrayed him? His own men? A government official in Moscow? The new, kinder, gentler KGB? He would have wept for himself had he a tear left to fall, an eye left to generate tears. Cold enveloped his soul as he felt the icy fingers of death grip his heart. A final beat and it would be over.

So easy…

Light exploded within his brain.

Go to the light.

That's what everyone said. Right? He would go to the light, to his end. It should have been so easy…

But something was wrong. The light was not an end, it was more pain. The intensity increased, sizzling through his mind and body. It was a shame his throat had become a dry paper-thin image of itself days ago. He would have laughed at the irony. Feeling the pain in each elemental cell of his body, Yuri cried out soundlessly, praying for release from the relentless fire.

Slowly, a soft voice rose from the essence of his pain. Like a Phoenix rising from the ashes, it grew into awareness, so near the edges of his sanity that he only knew it for what he wanted it to be… an angel… his angel. She called to him and his body yearned to give up, his mind fought for release.

"I am coming for you. Hold on for me, my love." She whispered to his heart.

Searing heat drove through his groin. Oh, the cruelest pain was its strength of need. The iron grip of consuming desire to live crept its way into his soul. It held him. He grasped at the weak tendrils of life.

An angel, or The Watcher?

She was coming for him.

He held on.

*****

Natalia sat up, panting from the sheer effort of what she had done. Yuri would survive a while yet. How long was anyone's guess, but she had given him time, precious time. Her heart bled for what she found. But just possibly, she had given him enough to sustain his poor life until they arrived. She had no idea what she would do then.

Her plan to rescue Yuri now floated like a wispy dream, just beyond her reach, beyond any touch of reality.

Ka-chort-tu, she swore in her native tongue. The man she promised to protect lie inches from death and miles beyond her reach. Pent up frustration raged within her mind. Every option for a rescue seemed to slip through her fingers in the wake of discovering Yuri's true condition.

Nat? Elizabetta surveyed her team.

Da. Ohn zheeve. He will live... for a time. Betta, we must hurry. How long before we are there? Natalia was exhausted but still frantic to reach Yuri, before it was too late.

In a quiet, subservient voice Elizabetta queried Teffas, carefully forming the Pashto sounds. "How long before we arrive? My dancer is sick from the movement, and this camel track is making her worse. She will not be able to dance if this continues."

"If she can not dance, she is of no use to me. We go one hour more. Then we must walk until sunrise." Teffas pointed to the ailing woman with his rifle. "She will walk or die."

Elizabetta swallowed a growl and settled back on the bench. *We'll ride for about another hour then walk for several hours- most likely til sun up. Thank goodness for these ugly burqas. We will be fine in the sun, if it comes to that. Fine, but very hot. Maybe, we can push Teffas Hamza to make better time if we keep on his heels. There's no way we can send anyone on ahead with this man dogging our every move. His men watch us as if we are their prisoners, not the hired entertainment. I am beginning to wonder if Ameer Hamza dealt us a bad hand?* Elizabetta's worry was evident to the team and not, by any stretch of the imagination, beyond reason.

He'll be okay, Nat. Susannah encouraged her sister, patting her hand, *you'll see. I saw him through your eyes. It was weird, but he'll make it. I touched him with you. He heard you. I know it. It was so amazing and so exhausting.* Susannah hugged Natalia warmly.

Natalia closed her eyes and, for the first time in almost a hundred years, said a prayer, for Yuri, and for herself.

Chapter 13

Angel of Death's Promise

Angel, come to me and bring me death.
A promise of endings, cessation of breath.

In this world there's no end of pain,
Life concludes in death's refrain.

Come to me, take me there.
Willingly I go, to death's repair.

Angelica Mossen, Daughter of Darkness
1965, Ireland

They walked, and walked, and walked some more. For hours they trudged across rocky hills and down steep cliffs carrying their carpetbags as if they weighed nothing. For a vampire, hours of walking was an insult and an aggravation, but it maintained their cover, so on they went, following in the manner of good Muslim women.

Near dawn, the small group entered a tight canyon with sheer walls extending high into a night that was visibly losing its fight to remain dark. In a country where water is a scarce commodity, it was clear the canyon was cut by floods, but not a drop of moisture had touched the floor in at least a hundred years. Small clouds of dust accompanied each step and a thin blanket of reddish-brown dirt covered anything exposed to the air. The well camouflaged entrance to the stronghold lie somewhere ahead, as Susannah and MorningStar shepherded an unfocused Natalia up steep stone steps carved in the side of the gorge wall. An ancient path, this trek had echoed footfalls for hundreds of years. Worn and polished by constant traffic, the stairs, cut from the solid granite of the vast walls of the valley were smooth and rounded, and seemingly

113

endless. It appeared to Natalia, the other members of the squad climbed with little effort. She was still tired from v-channeling and trudged along, head hanging in exhaustion. It was becoming more and more difficult to focus and contain her fear for Yuri. Her mind seemed to have no control of its own as stray tendrils of power projected her thoughts indiscriminately. Twice she felt Yuri, and staggered. The closer they climbed toward the stronghold, the more frequently Natalia felt his pain and tried to reach out to communicate. Frustration competed with exhaustion to steal Natalia's optimism, and dampen her spirit, yet still she mentally pursued a connection, no matter how faint.

Teffas Hamza visibly labored to keep ahead of the women. His men straggled behind, their guns hanging limp but ready. For big bad terrorists, they looked more like scared rabbits, constantly scanning the terrain, jumping at each odd sound. Teffas panted as he walked, but Natalia knew he would no sooner slow down or call for a rest, than admit he was on the verge of complete fatigue. After walking a good portion of the night, his gasps for breath had become audible half-way up the canyon. Still he pressed on, snorting in disgust each time he turned to find the women following close on his tail.

As they approached a cleft in the canyon wall, a tired Natalia used her skill to monitor and channel mental communications as each member of the squad shared their observations. Elizabetta counted guards from beneath the concealing garment she wore. There were few along their path because the hidden entry required little security. Anyone could be seen approaching from several well-disguised hidey-holes along the way. The group walked some five miles up the deep canyon in single file. No one would be able to sneak up on this stronghold, that was for sure.

That presented a problem, both for exiting the stronghold and for a rapid retreat if they ran into trouble. No help would be available unless it was by air. Air extraction would be risky in the deep canyon with little room for landing. They could always morph and fly out if the sun was down, but the less exposure humans had to vampires, the better. There was no chance of flying in the daylight. Their human cohorts could not morph and fly should their involvement become necessary. Susannah was tired and running seriously low on energy. MorningStar was silent as was her usual way but often reached out to caress stones as they walked. And not for the first time, Monique grumbled about her sore feet.

I will never forgive this General Albani. Pour être fou, crazy! My poor soles will never recover. I shall be the first crippled vampire in all of history. I will hide my feet forever. No man will ever again suck my toes and kiss my feet. I am ruined. The others, who knew she would heal almost as fast as her "poor feet" became injured, ignored Monique's complaints.

With you it is always sex isn't it, Frenchy? Gawd! Susannah had a way of drawing out the last word that made her sound like the proverbial valley gal. Natalia was not surprised at the young vampire's comment. She knew Susannah was continually amazed that everything came down to sex for Monique. Monique bathed to be ready for sex. She fed to have energy for sex. She dressed to attract both men, and women, for sex. She learned to use a computer to surf the net for sex. Ack. Hers was a base life of sex… or more so, a life based on sex. *We're here so now you can quit complaining. This place and these guys creep me out. Let's do the job and get out as soon as we can.* For Susannah to criticize Monique for complaining, was a bit like the pot calling the kettle black.

Several men in the same black Kameez style dress stood on guard at the entrance to the stronghold. Had the men not marked the entrance, anyone could have easily missed the shadowed opening. The guards wore the typical plaid smagh tied with a Bedouin egal. Susannah mentally giggled. *How can you expect to be taken seriously about terrorism, with a plaid tablecloth tied on your head? I mean, really.*

Because the guns are very real and very serious, Elizabetta's comment was a bit dry. Armed with an odd assortment of automatic weapons, the men observed the women passing, with lecherous stares and crude comments flowing freely.

Natalia was exhausted and paid little attention to the pitiful humans. Elizabetta mentally translated the guard's directions for the women as they were escorted through the line of men toward their quarters. Once inside the main cave system, crudely paved walkways and concrete stairs replaced carved steps. They walked through lit corridors noting communication devices and cameras at regular intervals. This was no accidental hidey-hole for ragtag terrorists, as it had appeared from the outside. Rather, it resembled a well-planned, stoutly constructed and easily defensible military base. Winding through a series of tunnels and cavernous rooms, Natalia began to question whether The Babysitters had any idea what really lie behind the seemingly crumbling and rough entrance. She mentally cataloged the corridors and turns, as she and the rest of the squad watched the backs of their guards ahead in the glaring light.

Obviously, this stronghold had housed many generations of fighters, travelers and possibly ancient settlements as well. It was apparent that new tunnels had been added in recent years using some form of power tools, and had been reinforced by modern materials. The grooves and slices that crisscrossed the walls and floor often contained wiring or pipes. In some places fluorescent lighting cast a shadowy brilliance that was easily swallowed by the darkness just inches beyond the limit of the light. Cold inky black depths of irregular openings and natural breaks in the walls, concealed what lie just out of the light. For a human woman, the trek would have been intimidating and anxiety producing. For the Vamp Squad, it was like homecoming, with the added security of safety from the damaging rays of the sunlight outside. The cool damp air was refreshing and Natalia's energy and spirits rose a bit, as they moved deeper into the stronghold however, her worries for Yuri continued.

Hold on for me my love. I am coming for you. I am close. Natalia broadcast her message throughout the tunnels, seeking and finding the frequency of the surrounding rock to use as an amplifier. *If you can hear me, hold on Yuri.*

A weak mental sigh came to her from far away. It resembled the sound of a small animal that lie, pitifully dying, alone and abandoned. Natalia would have cried, but for the bloody tears that would give her away. Facing the end of their trek, she was only slightly aware of the great wood and iron door that opened to their quarters. Ushered in at gunpoint, the Vamp Squad complied, acting as if they were frightened dancers instead of highly trained undercover military operatives.

As he prepared to leave the women to their own devices, Teffas Hamza paused and glared at each in turn. He instructed them not to leave until they were sent for, or, of course, they would be shot. With a sneer, Teffas swaggered through the cemented doorframe, issuing orders to secure the females.

The huge door creaked shut and Elizabetta motioned them to silence with a finger to her lips until an audible click told them all that a lock had been set. *A guard has been posted outside. Only speak within our minds.* As they settled in, communicating only through psyche speak to ensure no one could hear them, Elizabetta reinforced the warning for complete silence.

Natalia had regained some of her strength and was feeling better out of the reach of the coming dawn. With renewed strength came renewed anger, and a serious desire to kill their escort, just for the hell of it. Projecting her desire to the others like a perfectly tuned radio broadcast, she vented vehemently. Everyone was under stress and strung to the max. *How dare these fools threaten us? They do not know that within hours their pitiful lives will end in darkness and great pain?*

Once beyond the touch of the sun's dangerous rays and inside the stronghold, Susannah quickly recovered her immature sense of adventure, if not all of her strength. The spoiled nineteen-year-old often acted more like thirteen going on five. *Doesn't that bastard know any other way to threaten a woman? I will shoot you!* Susannah slumped across the room pretending to aim a gun at the rest of the women and mow them down in a spray of bullets. "Ratta-tat-tat-tat". *You all dead. Now, get up or I shoot you again*! Her little skit was not the least bit funny and earned her a serious scowl from Elizabetta, and a quick signal to remain silent.

Susannah, focus. This is serious stuff. Can you feel Captain Milassoviech, Nat? Elizabetta was in commander mode and seeking any intel their extended senses could provide. Effectively chastised, Susannah stood with her head hung, tired and silent.

I have never lost complete contact. He lives. He is here, but I will not be able to find him in this maze without a guide. The way is too convoluted. Even Yuri does not know the way to his cell. Natalia's growing panic was clear to the entire squad. The iron taste of fear settled on each tongue with the weight of a human soul. Natalia could not only mentally communicate but share emotions as well. *The sun will rise soon and my powers are strong, but they will wane during the daylight hours, even in here. Betta, we must find him soon. The strength I sent may not be able to sustain him through another day.* Pacing the floor, Natalia's restless anxiety would have been catching, had the night not been so close to conclusion. Everyone felt the effects of the on-coming day-sleep.

They had walked through the entire night, well into the early morning. Already the imminent dawn was beginning to draw from their powers. All vampires could feel the pull of the daylight hours, whispering of sleep and renewal in the depths of complete rest. Being the youngest vampire of the group, the effects of the day/night cycle showed mostly in Susannah. Vampires of greater age could resist the call for limited periods of time, but newly turned vamps, like small children, needed their rest and could not remain awake for long periods during the day. Still completely covered in her dusty burqa, Susannah quietly curled in a ball on a straw mat in the corner, and immediately settled to sleep.

A knock rattled the loosely hinged door before it unceremoniously opened to reveal three armed soldiers. "Come, you will speak to Colonel Selaff Fashiam." Teffas Hamza was back, carrying a seriously beat up AK-47. He motioned with the barrel of his gun toward the entrance. "Now."

Monique, stay with the little one. We will return soon. "My daughter is tired from the long trip. We will go. She must sleep. Her sister will remain to watch over her."

Teffas Hamza did not object, only motioning the remaining women with the tip of his gun. Elizabetta, Natalia and MorningStar filed out, following the armed men while Monique poked at the filthy mats, dislodging a huge cockroach.

Ah oui, leave me here with the vermin. Merci beaucoup! Monique squealed as a particularly large roach jumped from the mat and scuttled across the wall. Without breaking step, a guard spun and fired. The deafening noise of the gunshot signaled the end of the roach. Monique screamed, huddling against the rough wall, her hands clasped to her ears. The man snickered in personal enjoyment at the girl's obvious distress, then continued after the departing group. Susannah slept on, seemingly undisturbed as their guard closed the door on a hysterical Monique.

The noise of gunfire had awoken Susannah, but she lie, feigning sleep. Silently she watched the blonde vampire crouched against the cold wall following the departure of her squad mates. Jerked from day-sleep, her limbs were much too heavy to immediately move. Susannah understood through shared mental pictures, Monique's years of incarceration had taught her to fear and hate all manner of bugs. Being chained to a cell wall in a crypt, below the ground for a hundred years tended to do that. Susannah almost laughed, more in irony than in humor, as her sexy sister vampire pulled the dusty burqa tight to her legs and wrapped her arms about herself.

A vampire afraid of little bugs? Holy shit. Her veil had fallen loose and filthy red tear stains dried on her perfect, creamy skin. Monique reminded Susannah of one of her porcelain dolls on whose face her older brother, Kyle had drawn tears with a magic marker. Perfect skin and translucent beauty now were somehow broken. Even though he had been a pain at times, she still missed her brother, dead these last fifteen years.

As Susannah watched from beneath hooded eyes, Monique's lids seemed to grow too heavy to remain open, and finally closed. Sleep called to Susannah as well, and she closed her eyes, relaxing, sliding effortlessly into day-sleep once more.

Susannah, asleep yet aware, cringed and tried unsuccessfully to shield herself as Monique fell deeper into fitful sleep. The beautiful golden haired vampire twitched as she unconsciously shared technicolor pictures of bug filled dreams crawling through her sleep soaked mind. Not yet strong enough to protect herself in day-sleep, Susannah saw and felt everything Monique did.

"Ewww! Frenchy, quit. You have some insect phobia, honey. Keep your head in your head, for my sake." Startled awake once again, Susannah whispered across the cell where they both lie. The nightmares that bled across the room began to infect Susannah's peace of mind with an irreversible adrenaline rush. Finally, unable to sleep, she stood and paced the floor, squishing invisible bugs that crawled from Monique's nightmares.

For several minutes Susannah paced, stomping non-existent insects, controlling the growing fire in her body.

She could not sleep.

She was bored.

She was desperately hungry.

At Olney Farm, she had never been allowed to become truly

hungry. It was a built-in protection for the humans with whom they worked on a daily basis. Now wide awake and restless, the need for blood was becoming overpowering, and she stood in the middle of the room listening to a human heart beating just beyond the door. She reached for her carpetbag that held a hidden container of synth-blood, but the heart so near sang to her with a rhythm that could not be ignored. Her mouth watered and she felt fangs grow, just a little. She knew she was not supposed to be able to feed without the help of another vampire.

Yet the smell… so enticing.

The beat… so inviting.

The need… so overwhelming.

She wanted it.

She needed it.

Crouching like a cat, Susannah crawled toward the door on all fours. Like a stalking feline, she moved through the silence without disturbing as much as a single air current. A petite hand caressed the door, as her cheek pressed delicately against the ancient cast-iron hinge, fighting the urge that drove her mind and body, inching toward insatiable insanity. The tangy essence of male existed on the other side of the barrier just waiting to assuage her every need. Like a virgin, desire and curiosity drove her on. Her moist tongue ran across growing fangs as the vampire's thoughts wormed their way through the door and into the mind of the man who slouched on guard just inches beyond the thick wood barrier.

The fledgling was slowly loosing her grip in the wake of blood lust.

Susannah had never fed from a human source. Since her turning, she'd been protected and shielded by her father. Along with the trusted staff at the farm, her entire world was contrived and controlled. At Olney Farm she always had a full supply of refrigerated blood and synthetic nutrients at her disposal. She never had to experience the horrific hold her need for blood could produce. Though she was not sure she knew what to do, the irresistible craving for warm, living blood drove sense from her mind. It was replaced with an animalistic need for the delicious liquid, and the excitement that seemed so enticing.

It was the same kind of desire that drove her to engage a handsome lone man on a secluded beach in Florida. That fateful night ended her short human life. It changed the face of reality for a nineteen-year-old college bound girl on the verge of womanhood. It changed the face of reality for a father and a select handful of the country's military leadership as well.

Her mind tumbled and burned. The glossy red, manicured nails she was so proud of, drew deep furrows in the wood beneath her hand. She slid her tongue across now fully extended fangs and smiled sweetly. Pouting lips formed around a purr and Susannah giggled. Rubbing her cheek on the wood like a kitty loving its owner, she finally gave in. The nature of the vampire she was took complete control and quietly reached to acquire what it desired.

*****

Natalia walked behind the other two members of her squad, barely aware of each footstep she took. Her senses concentrated on a familiar thread of thought floating amid the maze of stone through which they moved. Yuri was somewhere within the stronghold, alive, but not for long. Frustration at her inability to pinpoint his location, niggled at her brain. His pain-wracked thoughts stabbed at her consciousness like a needle thin stiletto, dissecting each microscopic nerve ending with perfect precision. Every step she took shook her concentration, causing her the vampire version of a mental wince. She stretched her senses to search for the location of the man she was sworn to save. His essence surrounded her and permeated every breath she drew. She could taste his agony like burning acid on her tongue. She could hear his heart falter, beating ever closer to the end, to the extinction of a romantic fantasy that had, for so long, been her only connection to human love, despite the little family she had gathered in Siberia.

She could not let him die.

She could not find him to save his life.

Her footsteps faltered as the group started up shallow steps, the crumbling rock and cement edges sliding beneath her sandal clad feet. MorningStar turned in time to catch Natalia as her knees gave way. *Nat?*

I'm ok... just a little trouble concentrating. Yuri is slowly losing the battle, Betta. He will soon be dead if we do not find him.

I have no more strength to offer from this distance and I cannot locate him. Natalia's frenzied response exposed Elizabetta to Yuri's thoughts for a second.

It was a second longer than the leader needed.

I got it Nat. Believe me I got it! Elizabetta stumbled but continued to climb. She heard the guard at the rear of their procession swear, grumbling about the weakness of women. "I'm sorry but we are all tired from our trek. We walked all night and must rest as soon as possible. Then we can dance for your men." Betta took a shot at explaining their apparent clumsiness as she sent a mentally empathetic ghost to dance within the minds of the guards who escorted them.

"You will sleep when Colonel Selaff Fashiam says you may. You will dance, when he commands. You will not speak unless spoken to." Teffas Hamza spun, cuffing Elizabetta as he spit the evil words at her.

Behind the coarse dark burqa, the guards could not see Elizabetta's eyes flash blood red. Her fangs appear with the growl that issued forth from her painted lips. At the same time, Natalia struck out with a psychic blow. So powerful, the three men who made up their escort crumpled to the ground, instantly stunned into an unconscious state.

Hamza lie in a heap on the ground for a second, only to be lifted by one very irate vampire. Natalia reached for Betta, as the Squad leader raised the cataleptic man to his feet with one hand. His head lolled to one side, exposing a tan neck covered in three-day-old stubble. Betta's fangs sparkled in the cold yellowish light generated by a series of tungsten panels strung along the tunnels. Tossing aside her veil in one swift movement, she sank her fangs into the man's neck.

"Betta. No!" Natalia's hoarse whisper resounded off the walls sounding like a roar in the enclosed space. *We need him, Elizabetta.*

Withdrawing her fangs slowly, Betta smiled and licked her lips. She clearly enjoyed the act of retribution, more than the taste. No one had ever been allowed to hit her. "I know. I am no untried fledgling. Unlike you, my daughter, who can compel at will, taking a little of his life source connects me with this piece of offal. I will now be able to control his sick little mind with ease, for a time. As

122

much as I feel soiled by taking his blood, it does have a somewhat satisfying, ah... flavor." Two small puncture wounds on the side of Hamza's neck were already closing, stemming the tiny trickle of red that had appeared. Elizabetta smiled and dabbed delicately at the corners of her mouth, dropping the dead weight from her slender hand. Teffas Hamza fell to the floor with a heavy thud as MorningStar knelt to sample her guard's blood. Her shining black hair hung straight and long, like a shimmery curtain hiding the truth from view.

"Just a little, Kanza girl. Natalia, help yourself. It will give you more strength, even though you don't need the same kind of connection we do to compel a man's mind. You will, however, need all the strength you can muster when we find Yuri." Elizabetta instructed the squad in hushed whispers that seemed to echo forever. "Quickly. We will need to awaken them, and then wipe their memories of this encounter."

Within seconds the squad took care of their guards and were back, acting the part of chastised females, on their way to meet Colonel Selaff Fashiam in the main chamber of the cave system, their escorts none the wiser for the interlude.

The Colonel, when they found him, sat in an alcove decorated in decadent bad taste. His makeshift office was located in the stronghold's club, a large man-made cavern off the main passageway to the soldier's quarters. Filled with pillows and hand-woven tribal rugs, men relaxed around low Pakistani style tables, laden with food and drink. There was clearly no shortage of anything in the stronghold.

The Colonel's private area was off to one side with a direct view of the entryway. The Colonel and five of his cohorts sat on low couches covered in some indistinct and aged pattern of velvet. The couches circled a large round table made of thick planks banded together atop a huge wooden spool that once held industrial wire. Through the yellowed lacquer finish, a teal logo with the recognizable cursive G and E could easily be seen.

General Electric? Here in an Afghan terrorist hide-out? And, I left my camera back at the hotel. FOX News would love this. Where is Shepard Smith when we need him? Natalia sighed and sent a mental chuckle to Elizabetta. Everyone at Olney Farm knew Natalia had been infatuated with the cute broadcaster since she saw him on television, and heard his characteristic giggle her first day at the farm.

In the center of the makeshift table sat a huge, ornately carved brass hookah. Several of his men sucked on pipes attached to the main urn that gurgled and perked with each intake of breath. Embroidered tapestries insulated the dank walls and soft lamplight glowed from clefts carved high in the stone near the ceiling. Secure in their rat hole, the soldiers laughed, relaxed, high on opium and falsely confident at the end of a long night of partying.

Colonel Fashiam himself, sat in the center of the group, a buxom, scantily clad woman curled in each arm. His shirt gaped open where one woman's hand caressed and played with a patch of thick graying hair on his chest. He smiled greedily showing rotting teeth between bulbous lips. Burying his hand in her hair, he shoved the woman's face into his crotch as his men laughed uproariously. She proceeded to giggle, unzipping his fatigues. Sucking loudly on his engorged cock, the second woman licked and sucked a hairy, sweat covered nipple. The Colonel drew a deep lung full of acrid smoke and moaned loudly in an overt display of entertainment, mostly for the benefit of his men.

"Ah-hem." Teffas Hamza cleared his throat loud enough to interrupt the party in progress. In front of this officer, he affected a completely different demeanor. Elizabetta could smell his disgust as he spoke, but his words were professional and courteous. "Colonel, I am sorry to interrupt but I have the dancers. You wanted to see them for yourself before I return to the village." He grasped Elizabetta's arm, dragging her before the man, as he ripped the burqa from her body. "This one is their 'manager', so she says." Teffas dropped the burqa at her feet.

"Go my friend, Teffas. I have faith in your choice and can see with my own eyes. The women will do. Return to the bed that warms you." Colonel Fashiam waved Teffas away. Teffas Hamza was one less man who would share in the entertainment. The Colonel chuckled as the scowling man quickly left.

Temper well in check, and now prepared for just about anything, Elizabetta stood her ground, swaying seductively before the Colonel and his men. Natalia knew the show must go on and Betta was in good form.

In perfectly accented Pashto, she propositioned the man. "So you like what you see? We will dance so well for you and your men. You will like our dances," she purred, adding a touch of sexual stimulation to her actions.

"We…entertain very…ah…well… Your men will be pleased." Her hips moved rhythmically back and forth as she spoke accentuating her words. At the same time her torso moved in the opposite direction, causing her well-endowed figure to undulate like a snake, charming the eyes that watched. Rich auburn hair hung in soft waves well below her shoulders. Green eyes glimmered as she caught the attention of first the Colonel, then each of his men. They leaned closer as she spoke and moved. Her soft deep voice lulled the men as much as her body's movement.

"You will find us more than acceptable, Colonel." In the way of a very perturbed and powerful vampire, Elizabetta's eyes flashed blood red as she swallowed against the bile that rose with the thought of "entertaining" this sicko-pervert, and his troops.

These twisted terrorists deserved everything they will get, and more. *Betta, the eyes! Calm down.* Natalia mentally cautioned, as she worked the room, touching each mind with excitement and desire. It was a game to end all games, Natalia thought and almost laughed at the hypocrisy of it all. Finally she concentrated on compelling the Colonel's mind into acceptance, working her mental magic that would keep him on the edge of interest but firmly planted in his seat. She stood undulating with her sisters, tempting the men with their bodies and their minds - men who were already dead.

They just didn't know it yet.

Chapter 14

Food for Thought

Voracious appetite for life-blood so red,
But resigned to packaged meals instead.
Safe and protected within a rank defended,
Two lives, two cultures, beliefs upended.

The Book of Mending, Human vs Vampire
Professor Demetri Valasnikoff, PhD
Moscow University, 1976

Monique's eyelids felt like lead and all she wanted to do was sleep. It was daytime outside their subterranean accommodations and all good vampires should have been tucked into their coffins for a long day's sleep, if in fact, vampires really slept in coffins.

Which they didn't.

She, personally, always preferred a feather mattress surrounded by handsome, cuddly young men. However, at this moment, Monique found herself huddled against cold rock, wrapped in a coarse, stinky burqa fearing for her sanity in the midst of a vivid, bug-filled nightmare. If that wasn't enough, there was something more, something beyond her own discomfort floating toward consciousness. There was a new kind of fear invading her dreams. A youthful panic drew her from slumber. Slowly she lifted her lids hoping to find only a sleeping sister vampire, knowing intuitively, that wasn't what she would find.

Unfortunately, her intuition was right; Susannah was not sleeping peacefully on her dirty pallet. She sobbed softly, rocking over the body of what used to be a guard. It was pasty white and emaciated beneath the black uniform it wore. Where the neck had been was a gaping hole. At the end of a slim sinew of tissue dangled a head, flopping back and forth in time with her sobs. The dead white eyes stared blankly into space with a curious smile frozen on its blue lips.

Susannah sat holding the figure, like a little girl holding a broken doll. Close to hysteria, her face and hands were covered with dark reddish brown stains. Crimson tears streaked her face leaving little red paths to her chin where long platinum hair lie plastered and matted in drying globs of clotted blood. Had it not been for the fledgling's tear-stained face, Monique would have considered the scene literally scrumptious, something fit for a vampiric Hallmark card that said 'Bon Appetit'. But then, Monique knew her idea of 'totally yummy' was a bit different than the everyday Joe's. She yawned and unwrapped her legs, carefully watching for representatives of her recent 'bugmare'.

"Oh chéri. What have you done, little one?" Monique spoke the words, knowing the guard would not overhear them now. "I think we have a petit problème." Monique took the mastery of understatement to new heights.

Susannah paused between sobbing hiccups and looked up at her sister. "I didn't mean to… I was so hungry. I just wanted…" The sobs began again. Susannah was close to becoming unhinged.

The feelings had been the same for Monique when she first fed on live blood. But then, the outcome had been a whole lot different because she had a sire guiding, encouraging her, hiding the evidence.

"I couldn't help it Monique. I was… I can't explain it. I just couldn't stop. I think I killed him. He's dead, isn't he?" Her sobs began anew.

Monique could not keep from giggling at Susannah's innocent and naive statement. The man's head was dangling from a virtual thread. Of course he was dead. Very dead indeed. Even VMD could not repair the body beyond a certain point.

"Oui chéri, he is dead. But do not worry your little mind. We will take care of this together. What are sisters for? Come, come, come. We shall find a place to hide the body, and no one will ever know. What is one less stupid man in this place full of such? Come now. Cease the tears and help me tidy up a bit."

Now that the door to their cell was unguarded and open, they had no trouble leaving their quarters undetected. The two women took the guard's body down through the tunnels, deep into the bowels of the stronghold. Susannah tiptoed ahead to make sure the

127

way was clear, spotting and disabling each camera as they moved. Monique hefted the man as if he weighed nothing, all the while thanking whatever demon or deity had given vampires superhuman strength. At each junction they took the downward path hoping to find an empty room or sink hole in which to dispose of the body. As they progressed, the characteristic dank smell of deep caves increased. The dirt and stone oozed moisture upon which mold had begun it's sunless life, adding to the musty smell that permeated the tunnels through which they snuck. They moved silently, hoping their luck would hold, and they would have only one body to dispose of, by the time they finally found a secure place.

Deeper the cave system wound and Susannah shivered as the air grew cold and even more damp. Only a few years past humanity, Susannah still maintained many human characteristics. She was immune to the cold, but shivered out of habit. *Monique, have you any idea where we are? Where we are going?* Susannah was beginning to worry if they could find their way back. Her skills had not progressed to the point where she was secure in their extended use and her natural reserves were low. The lighting and surveillance ended several hundred yards back and now the vamps moved through the blackness, using only the enhanced sight VMD provided. The tunnels this deep were ancient and mostly of natural creation. The walkways were uneven and rounded, causing the women to move more slowly than they had above.

I feel water near. Watch for an underground stream or well. Reach out with your senses little one. Listen and feel. Like casting a fishing line, throw your senses ahead, then, mentally reel them in. See what you can catch, ma petit. Monique placed a light hand on Susannah's shoulder establishing a connection. *Like this.*

Susannah felt, saw and understood through Monique's touch. It was easy, once you could see how to do it, she thought. This vampire stuff was pretty neat... except for the blood thing. That was just gross. She had even disgusted herself and that was fairly hard to do for a modern nineteen year old who loved movies like Die Hard, Pumpkin Head and Texas Chainsaw Massacre!

As they moved deeper, she experimented with her ability to cast her senses. After a minute or two of practice, Susannah found she could almost 'see' around corners and through walls. Down another tunnel she paused, startled, feeling a mind she knew, she squeaked, "Monique, he's here. Yuri. I touched him once before, when Natalia took my power. I feel the same man here, close. Just up here. Hurry." Susannah was running now, her vampire vision serving her as naturally as if she were in a brightly lit hallway. She skipped over rocks, and hopped down two more short flights of steps. "Here. Behind this door. He's alive."

"Ach, oui, easy for you to run. You are not carrying a body on your shoulder. Stop, Susannah, do not open that door. And keep your voice down. First, we get rid of your little mistake here, no? Then, we see to Yuri." Monique passed the excited girl and turned a corner, disappearing from view. Left alone in the dark, Susannah quickly caught up to a smirking Monique.

At the end of the short passage was a crumbling brick casement with an old wooden bucket on a rope. The wood was damp and soft from years of mold growth. It crumbled at first touch. "We have found what we need, little one. A well. No one has used this in many years. Look, it is filled with mud. Perfect for hiding things, oui?" Monique unceremoniously pitched the guard's body into the well, wiped her hands on the hem of her burqa and turned Susannah around by the shoulders. "Go." Swatting the fledgling on her rump like an errant child, they returned the way they had come.

Susannah paused at the door behind which she believed she had sensed Yuri. "I think he is in here Monique. The door is locked," she whispered.

"Hah! A door is never locked to a vampire. You have much to learn, little one." Monique grasped the hook that served as a handle and wrenched. With a groan, the ancient iron gave way and the door swung open on squeaky hinges. "Voilà! Easy, no?"

Both, Susannah and Monique peered into the cell with trepidation. A huddled mass, just barely resembling a human lie in the middle of the tiny, frigid room. Crusted wounds covered the naked form, limbs twisted and laying at odd angles. The face was unrecognizable. Had this once been a man?

Even the genitalia was mutilated beyond comprehension. It was truly a miracle that the heart of this poor creature continued to beat.

Monique covered her mouth and nose with a sleeve, closing her eyes to the scene before her. The years of sadistic torture she endured at the hands of the monks of San Salvador of Leyre was nothing compared to what this man had obviously suffered. "Oh, mon Dieu." She murmured. "Les bâtards. C'est terrible'." Monique's French pronunciation of the word 'terrible' made it sound even worse to Susannah.

"Oh man, Natalia's gonna be really pissed. Terrorist or not, these guys are dead meat. Should we move him?" Susannah was trembling, trying hard to swallow the saliva that gathered in her mouth, teasing the contents of her rolling stomach.

"No, chéri. He is so close to death, we would but hurry it along. We must find Nat and bring her here. Possibly, she can do something other than end his misery. But I do not think it so. Come, little one." Monique pulled the door closed and pushed Susannah up the passage leading out.

"Natalia's gonna really be pissed." Susannah ran along with Monique right behind, retracing their footsteps back to their dirty pallets and a mess they would need to clean up before anyone returned. There would be no rest for a weary vampire this day.

"I think, even the most soulless of vampires would never do such a thing to any human. If Natalia is angry, then let it be on the heads of these depraved dogs. I, for myself, will turn a blind eye to anything she might do to them. There was never a more deserving group upon which to vent one's détestez, the hate, n'est pas? Hurry, we have much to do before the others return."

Susannah did not need encouragement. She ran, naturally casting her senses ahead now to detect soldiers or guards, shutting down the cameras with a wave of her hand, a trick she'd just perfected in the need of the moment.

Within minutes Susannah and Monique stood, scuffing bloodstains into the dirt, crunching the clumps to dark dust, and praising Muslim women for their stylish choice of black burlap as casual wear. Not only did it absorb bloodstains extremely well, it scratched the skin raw, and lie in bulky folds that complimented the feminine figure!

"You gotta love this stuff. Exfoliate while you move. What a concept. In the states we fill burlap with potatoes, not people. And I complained when my dad bought my undies at Sears instead of Victoria's Secret. Frenchy, next time I see my father, remind me to thank the Colonel for not shopping in Afghanistan." Susannah's whispered commentary ended abruptly as she sensed the approach of others. Quickly both women huddled on a pallet together as if they had been resting all along. In the nick of time, Monique gave a mental shove to the lock on their cell door and heard it fall into place with a click.

Almost immediately, the click sounded once again as the heavy wooden door was unlocked and the three missing members of the Vamp Squad stumbled into the room, pushed at gunpoint, by a particularly burly soldier. "Do not leave. Obey or you will be shot." Backing into the tunnel, the soldier slammed the door; an audible click meant the lock was back in place once more. The guard retreated a distance, then leaned against the tunnel wall for a smoke.

Just shoot me and get it out of your system, Natalia mentally growled as she sensed the retreating soldier pause. Of course, he could not hear her mind-speak, but he did feel a quick pain in his groin as if someone had slapped his testicles. Nat smiled at the muffled groan from the other side of the thick door.

Nat, we found Yuri! Both supposedly sleeping vampires broadcast at the same time.

Ouch. Not so loud, please. You found Yuri? How? Where is he? Natalia rushed over to the two women pulling them to their feet. *Show me!*

Slow down Natalia. We need to be careful. Elizabetta cautioned an excited Natalia. She cast her senses beyond the door, checking for the guard who had been previously posted outside their quarters. *Where is our guard?*

No one spoke and immediately, Elizabetta turned to stare at Monique. *Okay, spill it.*

Ah, we had a petit problème. But it is taken care of. We must be concerned with Yuri, Betta. He is very bad. He will not survive long. We must help him. Monique was doing her level best to shift the focus from their 'little problem' to Yuri, hoping they would not have to explain what had happened to the guard.

She was completely unsuccessful.

Did the little problem have anything to do with the missing guard? And maybe some blood? His? Undeterred, Betta sniffed the air and scuffed through the dirt. A dried bloody clump crunched beneath her sandals.

Caught, Susannah immediately teared like a much younger child than she really was. *I didn't mean to do it. It just happened. It was an accident Betta, I promise. We took care of it. We dumped him in an old muddy well. That's how we found Yuri, way down in the cave tunnels. He's a mess. I told Monique that Nat was gonna be really pissed.* Susannah wiped a dirty streak from her face and released a little hiccup to reinforce the fact that Natalia was not gonna like what she found at the end of the tunnel. *There were no lights. It was really creepy. We were lucky to find him at all. If it hadn't been for, well you know. I promise it won't happen again. Really. But we did find Yuri.* Susannah looked so hopeful, it was almost comical. Her sweet teenage face was pitifully tear-stained, cute dimples punctuating her almost genuine frown.

In the first place, sinking your fangs into a neck, and draining a human body is not an ACCIDENT, little one. Elizabetta assumed the worst and turned to Monique. *I left you to watch over this one, not have a party as soon as I turn my back. This is not a game Monique, and Susannah is a fledgling. I hold you responsible.*

Ah. Elizabetta, you know she cannot feed on her own yet. And obviously, she didn't drain the human. Monique scuffed the floor with a dainty toe overturning several un-crunched clumps of what used to be the guard's blood. *The little one made a mistake. I was simply so exhausted, I fell asleep when I thought Susannah slept as well. She could not resist.* Monique kept her eyes on her dainty sandaled feet as she spoke, continuing to scuff the dust in a covert, but casual attempt to hide the copious amount of evidence.

What exactly did you do, Susannah? Elizabetta was angry at the irresponsible behavior of her squad members when so much depended on them and the critical success of this first mission.

Betta, can we hold the motherly disappointment talk for later? Yuri's life is at stake here. Natalia was building up for a blow out. She could not stop feeling the man's life trickling away, like the ticking of a timer set to a count down.

Yes of course. But this WILL be addressed! All right, MorningStar, you're point. Monique, next. Susannah, you're with me, like a second skin, young lady. Nat put the big, hairy guy down the corridor to sleep. Bring our equipment, and let's use this little outing to do some remodeling. It was more than apparent to Natalia that Elizabetta was angry when she yanked on the door and it came away, as if there had been no lock or hinges on the frame. So much for covert operations. Elizabetta handed the door to Natalia, stomped down the passageway and dragged the sleeping soldier into the room. Placing him on one of the dirty straw mats near the wall, she arranged his arms in a sleeping position as if he had gotten tired and curled up for a nap. *Nat, follow up. Be careful. Let's go.*

I can blank out the cameras, Elizabetta. I figured it out all on my own. Just today! Susannah's blatant attempt to gain the good graces of their leader was pathetic, but cute. Her effervescent charm was so refreshing and completely infuriating at the same time. Natalia just had to smile.

The squad moved down the tunnel like a well-oiled military machine, quickly, and quietly. Their bags still contained several hundred pounds of C-4, along with everything they needed to blow the stronghold into the next century. The contents were carefully wrapped in silky dancing costumes, jangling belts and decorative zils. The weight was not an issue, but slinking around with the cumbersome equipment was not easy.

The squad had little trouble finding their way to Yuri's cell, with Monique and Susannah as guides. Natalia wouldn't have had a problem in any event, the girl's vampire signature was everywhere, and as clear as a neon sign. As they neared the level that held Yuri's cell, Natalia was consumed with dread. She felt his heartbeat but could not feel his mind. A great black void existed where thoughts should have flowed like currents in a vast river. Dumping her bag on the floor inside the cell, Natalia did not need a flashlight to see Yuri's condition. What she did need, was Elizabetta's restraining hand on her shoulder.

Rage filled her mind and ignited such revenge, that she shook from the need to slaughter those who did this terrible thing. It would have been easy to simply stroll through the stronghold frying the minds of those who came within touch of her extraordinary powers.

How would the world see such a thing? Natalia had covered her abilities so well for so long. Now was not the time to reveal the length and breadth of her skills. C-4 would do just as well, and keep the warfare easily explainable, on a definitely human level. Her temper cooled with the breaking of her heart.

What lie before her was no longer a man. Its heart labored to beat. Gurgling lungs struggled to separate what little air they contained from the blood, suffocating the drowning tissue.

"Moi-ya Yuri," Natalia whispered close to what used to be ears as she reached out to touch the man's mind. Mired in such agony, it resisted the slightest wisp of acknowledgement.

"Nat, will he live?" Elizabetta queried softly. "Can you help him?" The squad leader knew Natalia would not leave Yuri behind, dead or alive. They had made plans to liberate the Russian, but had not banked on finding a mostly dead soldier who was barely clinging to life. He was in such bad shape, he would not be able to help himself at all. If he survived being moved, he would be totally dependent on them, slow them down or even compromise the mission. Not to mention, he was currently buck-naked.

Handing Monique a checklist for setting charges tightly folded in plastic, she directed, "Susannah, MorningStar, set the charges on the next level above while we take care of Yuri. Be careful and NO BITING. Do I make myself clear? You know where the charges need to go. We can't afford mistakes. We might be immortal, but I don't relish the idea of spending eternity under a million tons of rock."

The three vamps nodded and returned to the tunnels above to take care of business, each relieved to be away from the sight and feel of the tortured Captain. They had practiced their mission enough times at Olney Farm, it was now second nature to set and string explosives. Their fingers developed muscle memory and could accomplish the intricate task, with or without sight. The actual destruction of the stronghold would have to wait until the Generals arrived, but there was no harm in setting the stage early.

The Vamp Squad's intel indicated five Taliban officers were expected on the morrow, along with their security contingents. All in all, an Al Qaeda representative and the generals, with their traveling aides, would be attending a summit to organize a strategic and collaborative assault on the Afghan Parliament. General Albani's hope of providing a good show for the newly formed ISIL organization sweeping Syria, would lead to an invitation of some kind. With the changing political climate of the American government, Albani was convinced it was time to retake the country and begin expanding his Jihad once again. In order to accomplish such a feat, the Taliban, Al Qaeda and ISIL would need to work together. This summit was supposed to be the new beginning.

The Vamp Squad was there to make sure it was a new ending.

Chapter 15

The Turning

Tis a wondrous thing to feel the pull
From human life to a new kind of whole.
The next step in man's evolutionary ride,
Forced to believe tales from just one side.

The need, the burn,
The sensual turn,
From less to more,
Men oft abhor.

But little do they know what is on trial
The wily grin, a vampire's beguile.

Sonyaja Habathandartha, Yumdna Dali
Punjab, India

Yuri drifted close to the edge of consciousness, a breath away from the pain. He felt himself floating, as if on a sea of emerald green grass and brilliant wildflowers. He could smell the scent of his homeland's steppes in the spring bloom that cradled his cold body. Death was close. Soon...

He watched the hot sun like a golden orb in the azure sky. It loomed above him, calling. *Moi-ya Yuri.*

Yes. I am here. I am ready. The Watcher had finally come for him and soon it would be done. A thread of consciousness touched his mind. It tickled, leaving a strange kind of tingling in its wake. It drew him across the grass, floating toward a woman who sat naked on a soft downy quilt, her arms outstretched, welcoming him to heaven.

I am ready.

He smiled for the first time in what seemed like a century.

The woman took him into her embrace. Their lips met, tongues tangling in a fevered passion that set his loins to burn. Yuri's hands traced their way around the woman's waist and pulled her to him in a tighter embrace. Her skin was so soft and smelled of honey and sun. So long denied any sensation, other than that associated with pain, she felt so good. He thought he would surely die from this simple touching of skin on skin.

It would be an acceptable end.

However, it was not an end. The feelings continued. The fire in his groin burned. The need to sink himself into this goddess and bury his cock fully to the hilt enveloped him. He pulled her atop him, laving her honeyed breasts as she moaned and arched in ecstasy. Her long chestnut curls lightly caressed his nipples as she moved seductively above him. Clenching his cock with her nether muscles, she drew him deeper within her glorious sex.

So, he must truly be dead and this was heaven.

Not bad.

A groan of pure pleasure escaped his lips as he grasped the woman's hips, building a rhythm that threatened his sanity. The beautiful angel moved with him, drawing Yuri closer to a wildly building climax. Stars flickered behind his eyes, punctuating the sight before him. He marveled at the woman's delicate hands as they massaged and played with her own puckering pink nipples. The visual display drove him mad with sizzling desire. His swollen and engorged cock throbbed on the verge of explosion for a single second before he willingly relinquished all control.

Like a backflash, his body flamed, erupting in boiling waves of intensity that rocked the nebulous world in which he lay. Consuming his mind and will, driving him almost beyond the limits of existence, Yuri roared his release, gasping for his last breath. It was more than an acceptable end. It was a glorious end.

Natalia strained to focus and find a way into Yuri's retreating world. She gathered him to her, holding his dying body in a tender embrace. Slowly, excruciatingly, she interjected herself into his mind so tightly closed, it felt as if she were prying open an ancient sealed tomb, dry and fragile. Concentrating, she moved within his mind, assuaging his drifting soul with the only comfort she knew would draw a man back from death; the promise of sexual pleasure. Stroking his mental picture of sensuality and focusing on the essence of the crumpled and broken man held to her breast, Natalia injected what strength she could, hunting for the ability to communicate, probing each tiny crevice for a sign of mental life. Intimately connected to the man she held through her contrived fantasy, she would endure all of the pain he felt. Risky business, if it was more than she could handle. It was a risk she was willing to take. Yuri would not survive for more than a dozen heartbeats now.

She could not allow the last Romanov to leave the world without a choice.

A choice she could provide.

Agony ignited every nerve of her body as Yuri's consciousness slowly emerged. A strangled cough produced a dribble of blood that oozed from the man's nose, the only orifice through which he could still draw a thin trail of air.

An intense, almost strangling wave of pain told Natalia that Yuri was finally cognizant of her presence. Natalia touched his mind with an explosion of thought, explaining in a flash, what she offered the dying man. She could end his miserable existence, or give him life eternal… as a vampire.

Privy to Natalia's communications with Yuri, Elizabetta struggled to hold her silence, and failed. "No Natalia, you cannot do this. He must be able to make a real choice. He is too far-gone to understand. This is not our way." Natalia was aware of Elizabetta speaking with hushed caution. "He will not understand the implications of what you offer."

Totally in sync with Yuri now, and feeling all he felt, Natalia gasped the pain-filled words. "He understands. Trust…me. It is clear to him… He… cannot hold on any longer…" Natalia was panting, straining to hold the connection, awaiting the answer that would guide her actions. She needed Yuri to decide quickly, before his heart gave up of its own accord.

Elizabetta placed a hand over Yuri's heart and allowed the joining to flow through her. As strong as the coven leader was, the shock of the man's condition staggered the woman. Natalia automatically dampened the flow of pain, but allowed Yuri's communication to reach Elizabetta.

Revenge. I want revenge. Give me the ability. I will live as you live. I understand. I want this. A horrible, overwhelming pain stabbed viciously at the three intimately linked minds, as Yuri's heart faltered.

I want this. Do not deny me.

"Alright, do it." Elizabetta kissed Yuri's cracked, dry cheek. She stood, breaking the connection they shared and left quietly, allowing Natalia a moment or two of intimacy which Yuri would appreciate later. As Elizabetta broke the joining, Natalia immediately reeled from the blast of pure agony coursing through her brain. Fighting with every ounce of strength she possessed, Natalia suppressed Yuri's pain for a moment.

I will be with you until you wake. Do not fear the change you seek. I am here, as I always have been. Natalia reassured Yuri as she sank her fangs into his bruised and swollen neck. His heart fluttered, stopping for a brief instant, as life seemed to desert his body. In its place a foreign invader settled in - Vampticious Meticulosus Deliriotum, VMD. In less than an instant, the virus injected itself into Yuri's cell structure and began multiplying exponentially.

It had not been too late. The metamorphosis began and in death's place sprang a new form of life.

She drank carefully, taking just enough to mix their fluids, even though his blood was sickening, tainted and distasteful this close to death. With each sip, she relived his days as a plaything for the maniacal General who directed his ultimate torture and mutilation. She knew his every hurt. She grew more enraged with each memory. They washed across her psyche, bathing her mind in the cruelty Yuri had endured. She had received glimpses of Monique's treatment at the hands of the monks of the Monastery of San Salvador of Leyre. That was nothing compared to what was done to Yuri. It fired her anger. It gave birth to thoughts of revenge so horrible she was ashamed at the extent of her own mind.

"Moi-ya Yuri," she murmured lovingly against his neck as she allowed her virus in their mixed blood to slowly seep back into his artery. It would speed the process. Gently she caressed the seemingly dead man whose blood now coursed through her body. His body was now infected with her mutating virus. She held him with vampiric strength as the changes began to rack his body.

"Never again will you be hurt," she chanted as she rocked the convulsing man. "No more pain. No more illness. You will live free, and revenge will be yours. I promise." Natalia kissed Yuri's cold lips as she lowered him to the floor of the cell and curled around his seizing body.

Soon Yuri's muscles would cease their painful contractions in favor of the death-like state of on-going mutation.

She cuddled him, patiently waiting.

He would need her blood when he woke. She would be there for him. Yes, he would need her blood, and so much more.

He would need. And she would give.

Satisfaction settled in her core as she ignored the guilt that settled in her heart. Fighting her own conscience as she held Yuri close to her breast, Natalia was consumed with the question of what she had done. In less than a heartbeat, she was more than willing to make Yuri a vampire.

Did she turn him to assuage her own selfish desire, or because she truly believed he wanted it?

Was she so quick to act out of her own need, or for some higher purpose?

Would she ever really know?

Natalia sighed. What was done was done, and was beyond undoing now. They would both have to live with the results.

While Natalia lie with Yuri, questioning her own intentions, Elizabetta stood in the dark tunnel outside Yuri's cell fighting the revulsion she felt at the sight of the poor man within. If she had a human heart, it would have broken with what she saw. No wonder the Russian Captain's desire for revenge was so clear and strong in their psychic connection. What was done to that man was so far beyond inhumane, it caused her gorge to rise.

Leaning her head against the cold stone walls of the tunnel, she tried to internalize this particular twist in their mission. Natalia was integral to the job of bringing down the stronghold, but Yuri was not. Her power was strong. She enhanced the other Squad member's abilities to communicate and compel human minds, so much that Colonel Maddox promised they would attempt a rescue, if possible, in order to get her to sign on with the Squad. Nothing was said about turning a dying man to 'save' him. Not to mention, complicating their first mission… the test mission that needed to be a success. Failure was not an option if the Vamp Squad was to prove itself and survive as a functioning and protected entity. Life was good at Olney Farm. They were a coven, a family now. After years of living in fear of discovery, hiding her nature and her life, she wanted this family, this sense of usefulness and freedom.

The ease of living securely in the modern world was carefully planned for by their Babysitters, and that was a perk no vampire had ever enjoyed. Sure, vampire history documented covens that fought and survived by brutal force, but life was hard in that realm. Government condoned existence, a satisfying job, unlimited food supply without attacking humans, and people to protect them while they slept. How much better could it get? As their leader, was she really going to put their new life style in jeopardy? For one man? After all, Yuri was a Russian and now would be a fledgling with all of the needs and challenging desires of a new vampire. How would he fit into their little group? Would he want to?

Too many questions for a mind weary of thinking. Elizabetta sighed.

A commotion further down the tunnel drew her attention. She could make out MorningStar rounding the bend, a huge bundle slung over her shoulder. Now what?

"Ca'cat." The Romanian swear word escaped Elizabetta's delicate lips before she realized what she said. "What is this? Now what have you done?" Exasperation was clear in her tone and in the uncharacteristic wrinkles that pursed her brows.

MorningStar dumped the bundle at her feet and shrugged. Monique stood just behind her snickering, as Susannah shifted from one foot to the other, a few feet away.

"Not my fault this time." The fledgling vamp mumbled as she tried to hold back the giggles. Something was extremely funny but Elizabetta was not laughing.

"Ma soeur, my wild sister is not so nice and calm as she appears. She did not appreciate the behavior of the 'homme bel'. His death was quick. You would have been proud." Monique smiled indulgently at her sister vampire, and kicked the handsome dead man at Elizabetta's feet.

Susannah licked her lips, obviously battling her desire to attempt feeding again.

"MorningStar? You bit him?" Now Elizabetta was as curious as she was worried. MorningStar was probably the most reserved and levelheaded member of the squad. Whatever transgression this

141

soldier had perpetrated must have been very bad.

"The man was disrespectful. I do not tolerate disrespect. I am a Native woman, not a whore. And, I would not dirty my fangs on one such as this. He touched the wrong wire... accidentally. Besides, we need his clothes." Her comment, quick and efficient as always, MorningStar sniffed, then headed toward the parallel tunnel that joined the main intersection beyond where the group stood. "I must set ten more charges." Never one to expound upon a subject, her words were always short and to the point; that was their proud and solemn MorningStar.

"I will return."

"Not to worry, Betta. The well is very deep and the mud is very thick. No one will miss le ordures, this garbage." Monique gracefully bent and proceeded to disrobe the dead guard. Grabbing one leg of the dead man, she dragged the naked corpse toward the well where they stashed the last little 'oops'.

As the corpse slid by, Susannah sighed. "Such a waste of warm blood. Betta, can't we..."

"NO." Elizabetta's command echoed through the deep tunnel. She cringed and lowered her voice. "Absolutely not. At some point these men will be missed. We must not make any more mistakes." Her finger wagged in exasperation at the young girl. "This is not some sorority outing. It is a serious mission, and our lives, as well as our future security, are at stake. Clearly not on anyone's mind but mine. Ca'cat!" The coven leader was back to swearing in her native language again.

"Elizabetta, why are you mad at me? This one is NOT my fault. I didn't do anything wrong." Susannah dissolved into a childish pout, tears running like the proverbial Nile.

The little girl tantrum was back.

On several occasions, Susannah had complained bitterly about her father's discipline. Elizabetta suspected there was another side to the truth. At times, the young woman acted more like a hormonal pre-teen on the verge of PMS, than a highly trained undercover operative.

Susannah plopped down in the middle of the tunnel, her long pathetic sob was interrupted by a deep feral growl. It issued forth from within the cell where Natalia lie with Yuri.

He had awakened sooner than expected.

142

Immediately overcome by curiosity, Susannah's temper tantrum disappeared as quickly as it had begun.

Elizabetta knew Susannah had awakened as a vampire, alone, sealed in a coffin with no source of food or sire. The memories of burning hunger, searing sexual desire and overwhelming fear probably surfaced in sickening flashbacks, as Susannah tried to lean around Elizabetta, peering at the door to Yuri's cell, trying to sense what was happening behind the barrier.

"You and Monique have more charges to set. Now would be a good time to accomplish that." Elizabetta nudged Susannah away from the cell with her foot, pulling the door more tightly closed as they moved away. "They will need to be alone for a time."

Monique materialized from the dark tunnel entrance sans the body she had been dragging. "Oui. I work while Natalia gets to fuck her new fledgling until he can no longer think. Ah, such a world in which I exist. Phew." The French vampire snorted uncharacteristically and swished off down the tunnel, explosives carried daintily in one hand, fifty pounds of det cord coiled in the other. "I will definitely need a hot bath and a serious manicure after this." Her voice disappeared as she rounded a bend.

"Sex? They're having sex in there? Is that..." Less bad memories than curiosity, Susannah was twisting toward the door.

"Susannah! You have a mission to accomplish. Please, just go. Leave them in peace. I can guarantee it will not last long. You saw the man, Yuri has much to recoup." It had been more than two hundred years since Elizabetta had dealt with such a spoiled child. Things seemed to be going south quickly and she did not have the patience at the moment.

"The sex or the peace?" Susannah cocked an ear towards the cell. "Elizabetta, how come..."

"Susannah, please just go!" Now Elizabetta was becoming visibly angry. They were, after all, in the middle of a critical mission. She had one operative wandering through the Taliban stronghold in a tiff about who knew what. Another sashayed through the corridors swinging enough C-4 to blow them all to hell hoping to accidentally stumble upon an orgy she could join in on. Natalia was in the process of helping Yuri awaken to his new life with some truly unwholesome and bloody sex, while the baby of the group wanted to start a discussion about vampire birds and bees. If vampires were susceptible to migraines, Elizabetta would have had a doozy.

She massaged the back of her neck and sent a psyche message to Natalia behind the closed door. *Keep the noise down, Nat. This place echoes like the Chunnel in a traffic jam.*

Chapter 16

Awakening

Awake to the dark, my love,
And find everything you have been dreaming of.
Your fondest desire,
Your heart's on fire.
My need is strong
For eternity long.
I have waited for you to enter my realm.
Now that you're here…

Natalia Vyrubova, Diary of a Vampiress
1984, Siberia, Russia

Natalia felt the man in her arms stir as Elizabetta's mental warning echoed in her mind. He had begun the awakening and soon he would need to drink from her blood. It was the vampire way. The virus was slowly changing his body and mind, growing stronger, mutating the flesh on a cellular level and adapting Yuri's DNA to the triple helix design that provided the enhanced powers of a vampire. It would need copious amounts of blood, her infected blood, to speed the process. And in this case, time was of the essence. His VMD would always be rooted in Natalia's, but would be slightly altered and changed to suit the man, enhancing his particular characteristics and natural strengths, both mentally and physically. She would always be his dama, or female equivalent of a sire, but it was Yuri's human nature and genetic make-up that would determine what gifts VMD would impart after his turning.

Natalia's brain froze at the memory of her awakening. The betrayal. Her brutal rape, then such cold as she had never known. The burning hunger and physical pain of waking from the VMD transformation that had torn at her body and mind, like a vicious claw rending flesh and muscle from bone, tearing the fabric of life

145

from her body. Offering in its place the incredible abilities of being vampire. It had been the last truly physical pain she had to endure. Though vampires could be hurt, wounded, indeed killed, pain was a fleeting thing dampened by VMD, and most healing came in a flash of warm, welcoming renewal. However, not all pain was physical. Unfortunately, there were many kinds of pain other than the physical in Natalia's world. Hiding her vampirism from society was just one of many forms of agony she endured. In her early days, becoming a member of the "undead" world meant losing one's soul and entering the evil realm of the Devil himself. This began a dangerous and often painful time in her life. The worst pain of all was becoming her sire's playtoy. Her greatest joy was the day she removed his head from his body, ending the rogue priest's reign of terror and lust. Unexpectedly Natalia gained a great deal of his power as he died beneath her blade. She would not allow Yuri to suffer, as she had. No one should endure pain like that ever again.

She lie holding the new vampire she made and smiled, remembering those last few moments of her sire's life on a snowy, frozen bank of the Neva River. Though his body was riddled with bullets and he lie exposed to the elements, trying to gather the strength to heal and regenerate, Natalia could find no sympathy for the evil vampire who turned her. She did not even shield her approach, dragging the heavy steel sword noisily across the ice. Having procured the sword from the Royal Armory earlier, she stalked the halls of the palace, waiting to make sure his planned assassination was successful. Natalia knew it would take more than mere bullets and mortal effort to kill the maniacal priest. Natalia would never forget swinging with all her might and the crunching noise the sword made, as it severed the vampire's head from his bleeding body. It was the most beautiful sound she had ever heard. It was the sound of freedom.

Yuri growled in pain, twisting and shivering, as his cells struggled against separation from the human species. His wounds were closed now. The terrible destruction his body experienced was being repaired as part of his turning. His health was rapidly being restored, in a manner of speaking. Natalia scraped at her wrist with a sharp fang. Laying the seeping wound to Yuri's lips, she let several drops of the precious red liquid seep into his mouth.

With the third drop a masculine hand grasped her arm in a vice-like grip, pressing the wound to his eager mouth. Natalia soothed and encouraged with soft mental nudges.

Yuri clamped his lips around Natalia's arm, and drank. In long restorative gulps, he fed. He could feel a new surge of strength with each swallow. As vitality returned, Yuri's vision cleared and he could actually see the woman next to him. She was his angel, the one he had waited for. And, he was drinking her blood! Yuri jerked away and scrambled to the wall, stunned his body moved at his command… and without pain. He sat for a moment on the cold stone, his mind spinning in turmoil.

He could see.

His legs splayed out before him, whole and strong. He glanced at his hands, fingers attached and functional. In typical male fashion, Yuri immediately reached for his groin, feeling the usual tightness and length where nothing had been left intact. After all, a guy is a guy, even if he is a vampire.

"Oh, thank God!" Yuri spoke in Russian as he eyed Natalia, trying to comprehend what was happening to him. One moment he was racked by hideous pain, giving up the ghost in the arms of a gorgeous angel. The next, he was awakening, as if the entire last five months had been some terrible, agonizing nightmare. Then it came to him in a flash of awareness; he had not wanted to die. He had begged for his life as he lie dying in that same angel's arms. Only she wasn't an angel, she was his dark savior. She was an instrument of evil, an enticement for him to sacrifice his humanity in favor of immediate revenge and personal satisfaction.

In favor of becoming a blood-drinking monster?

Yuri growled again, knowing he made his own decision, but wondering if he could live with the results. It was one thing to choose any kind of life when lying helpless at death's doorstep. It was another to face the eventual outcome and lifestyle he would be forced to endure.

He spread his fingers over newly healed kneecaps. Just hours before, the patellas he now massaged had been nothing more than a mass of ruined tissue and smashed bone. His fingers had been missing or smashed beyond recognition. Blind and helpless, he had faced his meaningless death in the dirty, dank belly of the Taliban stronghold.

It came to him like a warm blanket, heating his mind and fueling his rage. He had made the right decision.

What a difference a day makes. Yuri thought of the refrain from an old American song his mother sang to him in his cradle as the old Victrola played its scratchy music on black vinyl disks. What a difference a few hours can make when you have nothing to lose, but your life and your soul!

He felt a presence within his mind as Natalia made mental contact, his first awareness as a vampire. It was weird and unsettling, but somehow comforting. Okay, hearing voices must be part of his new existence. Good, good. He could deal with this. It would take him some time to adjust to this new form of life, but he was a soldier, a captain and he could deal with anything. Obviously anything except his own death. Attempting to mentally respond but not exactly sure how or what to do, he tried to think 'at' the woman.

What? He sent the message.

Natalia found herself jerked from the floor and slammed against the wall. A sickening crack resounded as her head hit stone with an impact that would have killed a human. "Yuri, no. Use your voice, not your mind. I am Natalia. I gave you the life that you now live." Natalia picked herself off the floor and rubbed the rapidly healing split in the back of her head. As she drew her bloody hand from the wound, Natalia found herself tackled, pinned to the floor beneath a snarling, fanged male intent on one thing. Feeding.

Natalia felt Yuri's fangs sink deep into her shoulder as he smothered her body with his. She knew that with the first feeding frenzy came an irresistible sexual need. He would want much more from her than blood. Allowing Yuri to feed as she stroked his back, like nursing a child, she held him close, caressing his body, comforting him.

But unlike a child, this man was exquisite. Excitement infused her body as she ran her hands along the rippling muscles of his back to tight firm buttocks. Yuri groaned as he ground his hips against Natalia, his erection clearly apparent. She smiled, cooing to the man above her, delivering a slight pelvic thrust that drew the response she wanted. Yuri withdrew his fangs from her shoulder and buried his tongue in her mouth. They shared the taste of her blood mixed with a passion that burned as bright as the red blood itself.

Amazingly, Natalia did not feel the revulsion she usually felt with sex. A virgin when Rasputin took her, Natalia's mind associated only pain and disgust with performing for her sire. It was the only sex she had ever known. Completely confounded at her body and the feelings that washed across her mind, Natalia allowed Yuri's tongue to probe even deeper. She could not hold herself back from this man in his time of need.

This was finally right.

This was a shared need and awakening, something she never had.

She sucked and teased Yuri's tongue, filling her senses with the taste and smell of this incredibly handsome and virile male. Her hands roamed freely, touching, learning each intimate ripple of muscle, each secret place that evoked moans of pleasure. At her every touch, Yuri's erect sex responded with a jumping movement that made Natalia smile with satisfaction. This was so incomprehensible. It was power so humbling, it brought Natalia to the verge of tears. Yuri's soft cries were manna to a woman who had never known the pleasure of consensual coupling. She never understood the feeling of strength that giving pleasure could evoke in her, and she loved it.

Continuing to explore Yuri's body, Natalia was taken by surprise when her ministrations were returned by a more than willing mate. Moisture formed at the juncture of her thighs, flowing freely, paving the way for a more intimate touch.

Yuri was overcome with the insane need to bury himself deep in this supple woman beneath him. He explored her mouth with his needful tongue, tasting her essence through the scent of her, mixed with the heady taste of her blood. Like mainlining an aphrodisiac, it was immediate and divine. A fire ignited within his core that he could not, would not resist. He felt her hands softly massage his back and then slide lower. She was teasing a man who needed no teasing. It was a dangerous game. He was so hard, he thought his cock would explode. The intense pressure drove him to find the barrier between them and tear it away. The sound of ripping cloth only added to his crazed desire to be inside this woman, to feel her ensconce him completely, to find the release that would end the sexual delirium that burned his soul. He laved at her creamy breasts, sucking and nipping, bringing each nipple to a hard peak. Hearing her mewing responses, he continued to kiss and lick his way to the soft curls of her sex. God, she smelled good. He could not remember any woman that smelled as enticing and beckoning as this woman, his Dark Angel.

Enhanced sense of smell. The thought settled in his mind, as his tongue began a hectic search for more taste, his nose nuzzling the top of her sensitive folds.

Natalia had never experienced anything like what Yuri was doing to her. She felt his fire through their mental connection, but this was so much more. Knowing her own taste and scent through the mind of a lustful man was so enticing and heady. She wanted more. The last person who had used her body was Father Grigori and it was brutal rape, as always. The pain never left her mind and he never allowed another to use her. By choice, she had never allowed another.

But this was not pain; it was ecstasy. It was heaven, the only heaven she'd known. Natalia cried out and opened herself to her manic lover. She knew this would be crazy, hard and fast sex. Yuri would need lots of this in the next few hours, until he sated himself with her blood and her body. He would need, and she would provide, loving the sharing of his awakening. She owned it, like it was her awakening as well.

In a way it was.

Natalia arched as Yuri's tongue delved into the most private part of her. She felt a coiling energy begin to form in her core. It wound and wound, tightening as it developed into a surge of need so strong she could stand no more. Yet still, Yuri administered his teasing rhythm and filling pressure. She felt his tongue dip deep and she arched again, lifting off the cold stone floor, forcing Yuri deeper. Feeling his fangs against her opening, she knew he would feed as part of the need that burned within his body and mind. Fear tinged the edge of her thoughts but passed immediately, replaced with a precious agony so incredibly wonderful, Natalia thought she would cease to exist. Lightning bolts exploded, emanating from deep within her core, striking every nerve in her body all at once. She screamed, as the mother of all climaxes tore through her body forcing consciousness into a recessed place in her mind. She rode on wave after wave of pure physical ecstasy, aware only of the intensity of the feelings that ravaged her being.

Like an addict in an opium den, Yuri drank the sweet nectar of his Dark Angel, becoming higher with each swallow. Blood consumed during a woman's climax was the most intoxicating substance a vampire could ever experience. It was what encouraged male vampires to become experts in the sexual arena. He had consciously tried to be gentle, as he nibbled her thigh then softly bit, inserting his fangs carefully. Slowly savoring the liquid he withdrew, Yuri's mind spun with fantastic erotic thoughts and scenes. Somewhere, in his cognitive process, he knew to drink just a small amount, more controlled than before. Yuri held Natalia to him, inhaling her scent as his fangs withdrew, leaving a small smear of blood behind. He groaned with lust as he allowed her to slide onto his body, plunging his engorged cock home. My God! She was hot and wet, her womanly fluids combining with the telltale traces of his feeding. His vision blurred and his mind burned, its fever adding to the heat he felt within Natalia.

"Moi-ya Ahn-gel Tiem-no." Yuri spoke the words that fired his heart, "My Dark Angel." It was a mantra he repeated again, and again as he drove himself deeper with every thrust. Buried to the hilt, he grasped Natalia's waist and held her tight to him. His climax enveloped them both with a shared mental and physical connection. So intimate. It raged like a wildfire through them as it grew more intense. Like a vision in two facing mirrors, it multiplied endlessly. On and on, until there was no more infinity. Until there was nothing left to burn, no room left to expand without complete explosion.

Yuri gasped for air and bellowed, spilling his seed with each surge of his cock while Natalia sobbed, limp and satiated. Collapsing together on the floor, she offered Yuri her wrist to slack his thirst. Gently he fed, again just a little, before sliding into exhausted slumber. Spooning together in the cell, they both slept. With the worst, or best, of the awakening behind them, Natalia's dreams were finally filled with passionate encounters and sweet kisses, instead of a mad priest and brutal orgies.

*****

151

General Abdul Haseem Albani looked up from his desk. A strange noise interrupted his thought process and he could not afford the disturbance. Within twenty-four hours the other Taliban Generals would arrive with hungry stomachs, throbbing libidos, and the expectation that they be entertained, catered to and waited on. A representative from Al Qaeda was already stowed in guarded quarters probably strategizing and planning. The sentry had been well briefed by the General himself. The man would go nowhere without a shadow. It would not do to have a member of Al Qaeda roaming the tunnels, possibly getting lost in the dangerous caverns and confusing passageways. More to the point, it would not do to have the man see anything he should not.

The noise came again. A wild animal in the stronghold? It had happened before. The better to keep Mustaffa Al Muffadi in his hole until the generals arrived and settled in for the secret four-day summit. Albani was confident his second-in-command had arranged for appropriate entertainment befitting the celebrated guests. He was not aware of the specifics, but he was sure the entertainment would meet the over zealous desires of the group of generals. Especially, when the men were closeted away from the circumspect eyes of their local ranks. Plausible deniability was a good thing when dealing with traveling generals, and a fanatical Jihadist. Albani always ensured he had some amount of it handy.

Why did he ever considered hosting this summit? Tight security and iron control was the rule of the day, or things could go to the camels in a heartbeat. It had all the potential of a real goat fuck. He had confidence in his small, but well trained security team, and knew Colonel Fashiam would screen his entertainers carefully, but Albani was still nervous. One small slip, and Fashiam would pay with his life.

A pitiful growl echoed through the tunnel outside his office again. The General smiled and returned to his paperwork.

Paperwork... reams of it. How had this war turned into a paperfest? What happened to the original band of young, strong fighters dedicated to wrenching their homeland back from the invading Russians? How long ago was that?

A decade?

A millennium.

The young, strong soldiers were old, greedy men now,

interested in using the war to feed their coffers and their perverted appetites. The religious fervor had long ago dissolved. Control through violent religious indoctrination and financial speculation was now the norm.

So where was the glory?

Where was the freedom?

Fuck freedom and glory. Years ago, they simply exchanged one occupying country for another and still wore the yoke of oppression. At least, Albani's oppression was comfortable and surrounded with enough loot to be enjoyable. Many of his countrymen slept in the dirt and starved for their efforts.

He chuckled at his own convenient patriotism. Once it was different, when he was much younger and more the religious zealot than the practiced businessman. War was business after all. For General Albani, it was big business.

Allah be damned.

His head pounded as he surveyed the stack of invoices before him. In frustration, Albani grabbed his Natchez Bowie knife and viciously stabbed the offending stack, pinning it to his heavy wooden desk. The desktop was littered with small nicks and groves attesting to the level of the General's frustration over the last few years. The knife stuck. One more nick in the dark mahogany. It sprung back and forth. It reminded Albani of a night past, when the very same knife sprung in the headboard of his bed, next to his sleeping whore.

Assassination attempts were a matter of course for Albani. He'd survived more than a dozen in the last year alone. Inside his personal stronghold, he was safe. The only knives he would face here were the ones he himself wielded.

"So much for liberation from paperwork." Albani stretched his legs and rose. At some point, he would have someone hunt down the lost animal and put it out of its pain. It was not his priority at the moment.

Chapter 17

Liberation

In life we toiled to provide.
In death we attempted to hide.
From stares that hurt; hearts that turned
Away from loved ones; a pain that burned.

But now a hope, a chance so dear,
To change the minds so they can hear.
What science holds undisclosed.
The answers for all, a new way proposed.

The Book of Mending, Human vs Vampire
Professor Demetri Valasnikoff, PhD
Moscow University, 1976

Elizabetta leaned against the heavy door and tried to shield Natalia and Yuri's noise. Their combined appetites roared within her head, setting her mind and body afire. The rest of the squad was slinking about the tunnels setting C-4 with blasting caps in preparation for the ultimate takedown. They would have to hurry if they were to return to their quarters undiscovered. With two guards out of commission at the bottom of the muddy well, they would have some leeway. It was risky the longer they remained away from their designated quarters. It seemed like they had been gone for hours.

It was very dangerous to set charges and leave them unguarded. Anyone with half a mind for sabotage would recognize their handiwork in short order. Their saving grace was all of the existing loosely strung wires along the many tunnels and caverns within the stronghold. With generations of additions and remodels, no one would notice one additional wire at a glance. The C-4 they carried was colored a dark reddish-brown to resemble the rock walls of the stronghold. It was easily molded to the surface of the tunnel. Originally, a natural cave system in the mountains, over the years men dug more connecting passageways and added doors. In recent times, the Taliban strung wires for lighting, telephone and Internet. A regular home away from home, Elizabetta snorted. Maybe a home away from home for Fred Flintstone, but not for a vampire. Just being in the bowels of the earth for an extended period of time was way too close to being buried. That was something to be avoided, at all costs.

During their training, Colonel Maddox was adamant they follow protocol and take no risks beyond what the mission required. After all, his daughter was a member of the squad. Elizabetta rubbed her neck. It was becoming a habit. She wondered what Colonel Maddox would think about the recent addition to their little family. She suspected the Colonel was not the kind of guy who appreciated his operatives bringing home strays.

Feeling Yuri's climax, Elizabetta took a deep cleansing breath and knew she could drop her shield for a while. He might be a vampire, but he was also a man. And no man, no matter how virile, could continue that kind of performance forever. Even Viagra could do nothing for a man when Mother Nature shook her pretty little head 'no', and slapped him down for the count.

She snickered just a touch at the mental picture. Mother Nature in flowing robes with an old fashioned fly swatter.

Cute.

Having mentally shared in most of what went on behind Door Number One, Betta was sure Yuri was down for a big count. In fact she could feel him drifting between complete physical satisfaction, and mental satiation. The worst of his turning was passed. She also sensed Natalia was in no better shape. Rubbing the back of her neck again she sent a mental nudge to Natalia. *No sleeping on the job, Alley Kitty. We have work to do. How long before Yuri can move?*

A muddled message came back to Elizabetta couched in a heavy sigh. *Yuri is turned. He is whole and healthy. He will need more, ah, attention later, but for now he is capable of whatever we need to do. I could use a good long nap, though. His turning was somewhat taxing. And, Betta, he has no clothes.*

Right.

155

Taxing?

The entire stronghold heard just how taxing it was. They are probably on their way down here in search of the origin of the sound, it was so taxing. I have clothes, a guard's uniform. The guard will not need it any more.

Elizabetta opened the door a crack, and tossed the uniform inside. She heard movement behind the door and knew the two were madly scrambling to cover themselves with various pieces of clothing. Smiling, she mentally searched for the rest of the squad.

Just as she cast her senses to find her team, MorningStar appeared from a tunnel entrance on the left. Elizabetta felt Monique mentally whispering to Susannah about the pretty red and blue wires. God help us, if the French floozy confuses the colors, Elizabetta thought.

I am not a floozy, Betta. I simply adore the male, and the female, and... Elizabetta frowned at the group's enhanced ability to communicate. Sometimes thoughts need not be shared.

Stop, Monique. I know you adore anything that walks, or crawls, or swims. Just be careful. Get the explosives set and get back here, Elizabetta mentally reprimanded. *And don't forget Susannah. And be quiet, for heaven sakes!*

Quiet? Really? Everyone within ten miles just got a full-blown sound bite of the vampire mambo, Elizabetta. And you're worried about footsteps and whispers? Gee-eeze. Susannah was at her petulant best as she appeared behind Elizabetta tangled in several feet of red, blue and black wire. "Get this spaghetti off me, someone. I need help here. Puh-leeze?"

Elizabetta thought the entire situation looked like a comedy of errors as MorningStar casually went to work on Susannah with a pair of wire cutters in a half-hearted rescue effort. Elizabetta paced the tunnel, watching the three connecting entrances expecting the arrival of the Taliban's finest at any moment.

Monique, on the other hand, leaned against a wall playing with a glob of plastic. Fashioning a very large penis from the clay-like explosive, she lovingly worked an ignition device directly into its oversized head. It was a scene straight out of the Marquee De Sade's Playhouse for Perverts. Pee Wee Herman would have been proud, and probably turned on, to boot.

That phantom pain in the back of Elizabetta's neck returned

with a vengeance.

Nat? How long?

Natalia and Yuri finally cracked the door of the cell and emerged, rumpled and smelling of sex mixed with blood and moldy dirt. Elizabetta cringed as she watched Monique's nose twitch at the scent. The little French vixen rarely reigned in her overactive libido, and was prone to passing fits of flashing jealously.

Ramming the wired ignition device deeper into the explosive phallic symbol, Monique dumped it on the floor and sniffed, "I shall be in my room," then stomped off towards their quarters.

"Ah, Frenchy? Explosive dick. Goes boom. Ya know? Have a snit fit with something a little less volatile, puh-leeze." Susannah stepped out of the wire mess on the floor and trotted after her sister vamp.

MorningStar shrugged, quietly gathered up the carefully crafted penis, the rest of the small pieces of wire, and ditched them in Yuri's cell. She trotted after her departing team members, leaving Elizabetta to welcome Yuri into the coven, as a true Mistress should.

"Welcome, little brother. You have much to learn about your new life, but unfortunately, most of it will have to wait. I can feel your confusion. You must trust us, we are your new family. We will take care of you as you learn to live, as one of us. But now we must go." Betta spoke haltingly as she sent bursts of mental images to Yuri: their mission, the need for stealth and their relationships to each other. With a quick hug she tugged the handsome captain after her down the passageway.

Languages were never a problem as vampires communicated both mentally and verbally. Elizabetta learned to speak fluent Russian during the sixteen hundreds. At that time, her country began aggressively trading with the turbulent countries that, in later history, would compose the Soviet Union. It was probably overwhelming, she knew, but there was no other choice. Yuri would have to go with the flow, as fast as he could. The rest would have to wait.

Yuri shook his head trying to absorb the images across languages and cultures. Still in a state of flux and new to so much of what he would become, he found himself flabbergasted, lost and

157

simply stumbling after a gorgeous Romanian woman with perfect green eyes. From death's doorstep, to incredibly invigorated in no time at all. It was truly mind-boggling!

"Yuri, relax and accept what Elizabetta sends you. It is hard at first, but you can do it." *Relax. Open your mind and feel your power. Hear me. Hear Betta.*

Natalia felt Yuri open to her with a jolt of sexual sensation so strong, she and Elizabetta staggered. "Okay, maybe just listen to me with your ears, for a while, until you get that libido under control. Use your voice for now, but quietly, so we all don't end up with the same accommodations you've enjoyed for the past few weeks." Natalia spoke Russian to Yuri, as she imprinted an understanding of several languages into his mind in small bursts. Although psyche-speak was clear and easily understood without language or syntax, it would be necessary for him to be able to verbally converse with the other members of the Squad. Especially, given the fact that his mental communication turned on every woman within miles, with a jolt. "Let's get back before we are missed. Betta, how do you plan to hide Yuri's presence in our quarters?"

Elizabetta rubbed the back of her neck. It was more than a habit now; it was becoming her signature move. "We can always dress him up in a dancing costume, but that would require a case of razors and some real heavy make-up. I don't know about you, but I am flat out of ideas, at the moment. So, I guess it is up to you to shield his presence, until we can come up with more of a plan. You can do that, right? After all, he's your responsibility, and, you are the super-compeller in the group." Elizabetta was short on patience and long on frustration. "Of all the scenarios Maddox ran us through and planned for, nothing even came close to this one. So we wing it." A mental scowl was apparent to both Natalia and the fledgling Yuri as they hurried up the tunnels toward their quarters.

Showing a great deal more sensibility than was normal for a male, Yuri remained silent.

Natalia stepped in front of the captain. "For now, Yuri, stay behind me and if we run into any guards, freeze and don't make a sound. I can compel several minds at one time, but I am not sure if I can cover your movement and their receptors at the same time. I've never stretched that far in a closed environment. Betta, lead the way." Natalia stretched her mind ahead to check for company. "Our path is clear, as far as I can feel."

The three wound their way through the tunnels following the softly glowing vampire sign. A vampire's movements left a psychic trail that was apparent to most other vampires of their coven. Like a glowing footprint in the dirt, the sign was distinct to each individual. Any vampire could recognize and follow it without training. Even some fledglings just hours old, like Yuri. The footprint also corresponded to the vampire's 'feel' during communication. If a sensitive vampire psychically looked carefully, he or she could see the faint reflection of another's mood. Natalia always thought identifying other vampires through their psychic footprint was a bit like dogs sniffing each other's butts. It was virtually foolproof, but left you with a nasty taste of something very private, as well as a dirty nose. Some vampires never learned the process of identification and could not, or would not see the sign, but it was always there.

Elizabetta turned the last corner before their quarters and felt Natalia still her movements. Natalia had suddenly picked up on Monique's mental turmoil. Someone was inside the room with the rest of the squad.

Monique? Natalia queried with the equivalent of a mental whisper only to Monique.

Oui. There is a guard here asking about you and Elizabetta. I know what he is asking but I can't speak Pashto the way you do. Right now, we are cowering like good Muslim females. Hurry. Tell Elizabetta we need her now.

We're just outside. Natalia broadcast to everyone at once. *I will enter after Elizabetta and work my magic. Stay where you are and act afraid so you will keep his attention.*

Behind the door, Nat heard Monique let out a squeal that would pierce the eardrums of a deaf man. She knew Monique was putting on a great act, pressing her veiled face to the stonewall. Sobbing as if it were the end of the world, Monique mumbled incoherently, as first Elizabetta, then Natalia came through the doorway.

"What is this? Why is my daughter crying? Have you hurt her?" Appropriately huffing and puffing, Elizabetta marched into the middle of the loud scene like the defending mother she pretended to be. "We are here to dance, not provide you with an outlet for your sadistic treatment of children." She stood between the cowering females along the wall and the young soldier who looked, at the moment, frightened out of his wits.

Though the squad members all looked to be about the same age, veils did the trick in covering the physical evidence. Afghani culture provided the rest. Many women acted as mothers or sisters under the Muslim religious umbrella, and it was not uncommon for a slightly older woman to call a younger woman her daughter, if she had assumed responsibility for the care and guidance of the girl.

The soldier must have been all of nineteen years old. Natalia was thankful a burqa covered the smile that played across her lips. An errant child with a toy gun being confronted by an angry mother; it would have been comical, had the child not been a soldier with a real AK-47. And, Elizabetta had not been a member of a vampire squad of military operatives, bent on killing everyone within the stronghold.

This boy's life was measured, and the clock was ticking.

"I swear I did nothing. I could not see your dancers so I searched and found them in the corridor. You cannot leave this room or the Colonel will shoot you. I... " The young man's face went blank as Natalia cleared his memory of the last ten minutes, then motioned for Yuri to come in from the tunnel.

"He will be unaware of the last few minutes and not see Yuri even though he stands here with us. I will plant a memory within his conscious thought processes. He will go and get something to eat because he missed dinner." Natalia closed her eyes, focusing on implanting the necessary thoughts. The man wavered, then turned and left, closing the heavy door behind him.

"Wow, Nat. How did you know he missed dinner?" Susannah was amazed at the length and breadth of Natalia's powers.

"Ah, little one, it does not matter if he just finished a nine course meal. He will go find dinner and eat again. Anything to block his previous memory, somewhat like rewriting one of those new computer disks. One thought replaces the other and the person has no access to the previous memory. I can teach you, but later, when you have grown a bit more." Natalia hugged Susannah, then swatted her on the bottom like a child.

160

"Wow! That's something I just have to learn. Then when I go shopping I can make my dad forget about the bills and I can go again! How totally cool is that?" Susannah was beginning to think about ways to apply her potential powers. Her mind was working way too fast for a fledgling. Natalia frowned. Susannah's father was in for a run for his money, literally.

"Yuri, this is your family. You will know them through the transfer of knowledge you experienced, right after your turning." Though it was unnecessary, Natalia pointed to each as she introduced them, one by one. Having lived with humans most of her life, Natalia liked the social graces afforded by humans who did not have the power of psyche-speak. They had time now, she was sure they would not be summoned to dance until the evening.

"Monique is French and totally committed to experiencing every sexual perversion possible. She is unashamed of both facts."

Monique winked and moistened her pretty pink lips in a coy, but completely obvious flirtation. She blew him a kiss and did a little curtsey.

"MorningStar is a Native American, of the American old west Kanza tribe. On a totally different note, she is dignified, competent, and very good at sneaking around. She has an amazing connection to nature."

MorningStar gave a slight bow and stood her ground, confident and proud.

"You've met Elizabetta. She is our coven Mistress, like a combination of super-mom, commander and big-time CEO. Her word is law, sort of." Natalia watched Elizabetta smile at the description and resist rubbing the back of her neck, hand checked part way to its intended target.

"Susannah is the baby of the group, except for you, that is. She was turned at nineteen, just a few years ago. Her father is the military commander and liaison for our Vamp Squad. He heads up a team of handlers we call our Babysitters."

As if on queue, both Natalia and Elizabetta jumped, their communication implants sounded, alerting them that the aforementioned Babysitters had arrived in Torkham and were in place.

"The Babysitters are in place and ready to provide support, if necessary," Elizabetta announced to the group. All but Yuri had heard exactly the same message as their leader, but when one was born in the fourteen hundreds, verbal confirmations of technologically produced signals was like comfort-food; unnecessary, but nice to have. "Now we wait. We should all rest as much as we can."

"Hey, Daddy!" Susannah depressed the area in her neck where the communication device was implanted for spoken communication. "How do you like lovely, downtown Torkham?" Speech produced by the vocal cords was digitally coded and transmitted by the implant, allowing the user to simply depress the device, and then speak in hushed tones. The receiver picked up the transmission through a microscopic electrode in the ear canal, sounding as if the person were standing next to them speaking naturally. The Vamp Squad's technical equipment development specialist had named the technology 'Vampire Speaking Naturally'. He named it after the well-known computer program that allowed people to speak into a computer that recorded the words as text. Susannah's giggle broadcast across the airwaves loud and clear.

Colonel Maddox responded crisply. "Emergency communications only."

The young woman stubbed her toe in the dirt kicking dust across the room. "Puh-leeze. I didn't know that 'Hey, Daddy' was against the rules. My dad, the high and mighty Colonel, can be such a bore at times." Dumping her burqa on her bag, Susannah flounced over to the mat next to Natalia and plunked herself down with a huff. "Geeze."

Rubbing the back of her neck aggressively, Elizabetta sat down quietly next to Susannah and patted her drawn up knee. "Patience is so difficult for the young. I remember, but Susannah, you must be serious about this mission. You have not endured the lives we have been forced to live, just to exist as what we are. That is why you cannot fathom the importance of succeeding as operatives for the government." Elizabetta took Susannah's hand. "Our safety, lodging, food, support, everything that makes life worth living, is dependent on showing the American government vampires have worth, for specialized military operations. That way they will provide us with a certain amount of protection, and keep our lifestyle comfortable and secret. You have tasted Monique's

162

torturous existence through her dreams. She is deeply scarred by years of abuse as a prisoner. You have seen how MorningStar was forced to feed on the dead and dying of her people, just to live. Natalia survived her sire's despicable life and death with much courage, but much more suffering. I have lived in lonely seclusion, avoiding discovery for many hundreds of years. Do you understand the opportunity that is before us?" Elizabetta put her arm around the young vampire next to her and continued, "We must succeed, for ourselves and for each other. We are a family, a coven now. We must find ways to exist within society and without attacking humans for our food, as some covens do. Those that still feed on people without their consent cause humans to fear and hunt us. We must show the world there is another way, and vampires can exist in harmony with humans." Elizabetta spoke like a nurturing mother to a wild teenage daughter.

Susannah placed her head on the older vampire's shoulder. "I know. I'm sorry. It's just so exciting and then totally boring at the same time. I know I am a vampire now and I can do just about anything I want, but geeze… my dad is such a total geekoid. You have no idea what it was like growing up with a Colonel for a father." She sighed and curled up, head in Elizabetta's lap. "No mom, and Colonel Rambo for a father. Ya know, I actually wrote "Sir" for my dad's first name when I was in the second grade. How totally sucky is that?" The tantrum over, Susannah's lids closed and she relaxed, falling into a much needed sleep.

Stroking the young vampire's golden curls, Elizabetta thought about what the girl had said. She could do anything she wanted? That was an issue which would need to be addressed soon. Vampire or no, Susannah's life would be bound by many rules. She would need a firm hand to grow into a responsible vampire that could control and use her powers, and manage her appetites appropriately. Her immaturity was a threat to their mission but, on the other hand, her exuberance and youthful energy was refreshing. Elizabetta smiled and shrugged at Natalia who watched the interchange with raised eyebrows.

What was a mother to do?

Natalia smiled back at Elizabetta as she watched the touching scene. She would have moved heaven and hell to have a dama like Elizabetta in the beginning of her existence as a vampire. She respected their leader's strength and enduring warmth, but it was the commitment to her coven members that made Betta an exceptional leader, and mentor. She would guide Susannah with a soft, but firm hand.

Natalia motioned Yuri to a corner of the cell and settled him on a mat next to her. She would make sure his turning was as easy as possible. She would teach him and smooth his path. He would not know the perverse fear that shadowed her first days. Already his body lie next to her, slack with exhaustion, and on the verge of day-sleep as she pulled her burqa over them both.

Lying quietly together, Natalia took the opportunity to study the man's features. He had been handsome as a human, but as a vampire, he was stunningly beautiful. Not a single scar marked his perfectly tan skin. Thick, softly curled blonde hair capped aquiline features that tugged at her heartstrings. The Romanov nose and lips she had so loved on Alexei and Nicholas, were even more striking and refined in Yuri. High cheekbones lent a royal air to the man who gazed back at her with eyes the color of the Mediterranean Sea on a sunlit day. His lids half-closed, a sleepy smile played across his lips as he watched her, watching him.

Immediately the fire began to build within her again. She caressed the masculine hand that reached to touch her shoulder with its searing power. His fingers trailed across her collarbone tantalizing and teasing, just inches from breasts that cried for the feel of him. It was sweet agony. Her tongue flicked across moist lips hot with desire as Yuri moved to close what little space remained between them. Natalia sighed in frustration, understanding the desire that drove them both, but knowing rest was also important.

Sleep my love. Soon we will need our strength. Sleep during this daytime, but later... There was promise in the images Natalia sent to him. The grin they brought slowly faded. His lids closed and he fell into a deep slumber.

Chapter 18

Things

I am many things.
I am all, yet nothing.
Bring to me your best,
and I will do the rest.
It does not matter your length or breadth
I shall take your soul without regret.

Duchess Slimova, St. Petersburg
Russia, 1902

The Vamp Squad and Yuri had spent the rest of the day in much needed sleep, and it was close to midnight before Colonel Fashiam sent for entertainment. The twenty or so soldiers he kept as his special unit, lounged around tables filled with empty glasses and cold hookahs. Many of the men snored noisily, propped up in corners or lying slouched against a fellow comrade, too drunk to move. The Colonel had exhausted both whores in an attempt to find sexual release, something more and more difficult to achieve, like the high his hookah used to provide. One disheveled woman lie sleeping on his lap, his cock still flaccid in her slack hand. The other had slid beneath the table, passed out from opium and alcohol. He kicked at the human lump restricting his feet and was not even rewarded with a groan from the unconscious woman.

"Raziq, take this garbage from me. They are useless. Send them to the slavers in Peshwara. Bring me something young and unused. Go." Tipping the table over, the Colonel stood on wavering legs as he attempted to rid himself of the two women.

Sgt. Raziq grabbed the two whores by the easiest handles he could find and dragged the two women towards the door by their hair, one kicking and screeching, and the other simply unconscious.

165

Having been summoned to dance, the Vamp Squad entered on the heels of the loud scene, and froze. Elizabetta was appalled at the way these men treated women. She had seen wars, and witch-hunts, plagues and disasters, but those had not been this kind of senseless cruelty for the sake of pure personal enjoyment. Again she thought, these men deserved the end that was in store for them.

We shall all deserve Academy Awards for our acting this night. Ladies, keep your distance, but light a fire with your dances. Natalia, you are our protection. Put to sleep any man who gets close enough to touch. I will not have anyone in my charge mauled by these animals. The fat one is Colonel Fashiam. He must be happy with our performance if we are to remain and dance for the Generals tomorrow evening. Susannah, stay away. Play the drum from across the room. Fashiam likes them young and you are not ready to handle his unpredictable violence. Your powers are not yet developed enough. Elizabetta's steely resolve was more than apparent in her mental communication.

Susannah moved around the room keeping to the shadows, skirting the soldiers who remained awake and aware. Placing her back to the wall she began a sultry beat, tapping the highly decorated drum in rapid succession with feminine fingertips. Though small with brilliant sequins outlining the ethnic designs, the sound it produced was expansive and mellow. The drum had once belonged to a Tajikistani exotic dancer. Sgt. Miller acquired it during a long weekend in a seedier section of Baltimore. Though his explanation of its appearance was somewhat sketchy, his smile was broad with traces of exhaustion lining his youthful face. No one questioned his story or the instrument, but giggles and snickers followed him through Olney Farm's hallways for at least a week.

From the other side of the room, MorningStar picked up the rhythm and joined in with a long tribal pipe similar to an oboe. The mot'akum was an ancient pipe Sgt. Miller found in an antique store in Georgetown. To ensure the squad's cover, no expense had been spared and no den of iniquity missed in outfitting the women. Still, the pipe was a little hard to justify. Thanks to Sgt. Miller's unique and slightly larcenous mind, it was procured and paid for before Captain Devlin could question the purchase. MorningStar fell in love with it, the moment she laid eyes on the musical instrument. Somehow, she mastered the odd finger placement and strange reed

166

assembly with no problem. After a few short days of practice, she could produce such haunting melodies listeners were moved to tears. Often she would sit in the hayloft at the farm, protected from the damaging rays of the sunset and serenade the oncoming darkness as her sisters of the night rose to go about their evening business.

Now the effect was amazing as the pipe's melody mixed with drumbeats, echoing back and forth through the cavern, multiplying the sound tenfold. Like the organ in the Shasta Caverns in California, the rock absorbed and reflected sound waves in a play of frequencies and vibrations that seemed surreal and enticing.

Monique was the first to sway to the unique, almost eerie sound of the music. Soon she was whirling and undulating, hip movements shaking and pulsing in the traditional Eastern style belly dance. The squad had spent endless hours practicing the tribal dances of the northern areas that bordered Afghanistan. It was not surprising that Monique, familiar with every hip movement known to womankind, excelled at the sensual steps. Natalia and Elizabetta joined in, as the three danced with each other, targeting the mostly drunk soldiers who could not move and lacked the balance to even stand. Surrounding a helpless soldier, they teased and cavorted with him until he fell back in his chair, landing with a thud on the floor. His comrades laughed and teased the poor fellow, as he tried to stand and failed, instead choosing to remain on the floor in a heap, but wearing a huge smile. As the music drew to a close, they moved back to the center of the room, ending the wild carnal dance with only each other, together and safe. The second dance was the same, each dancer preening and swirling with veils flying before a drunk or stoned soldier then gathering in the middle of the floor to end in a swirling dervish of bejeweled arms, ankle bells and zils adding to the frenzy of the music's end.

At the conclusion of their third dance, Colonel Fashiam motioned for the women to dance closer, to dance just for him. He was obviously in a state of complete arousal and planned to do more than just watch the women dance.

Nat? It's time to put these men out of our misery. Can you put them to sleep then give them a cushy memory, one of us dancing and carousing all night?

Sure thing. I'm tired of being looked at like I am a side of beef in a steakhouse full of starving carnivores. Are you sure I just can't give them one of Monique's nightmares? It would be more fun, and much more fitting.

Nat!

Okay, okay! One pornographic fantasy coming up. Would you like that with, or without fries? Super sized?

Nat? Just get on with it, please. Elizabetta dropped her first veil in the lap of a softly snoring soldier who slumped against the table beside him.

Natalia moved to the back of the room and quietly began to work her mental manipulations as Monique and Elizabetta kept the attention focused on them with an ultra sensual dance of veils. The two dancers teased and stole each other's veils, as their hands slid over each other in wildly sexual moves. They ground hips together spinning as one after the other bent backwards displaying their ample bosoms, each on the verge of spilling out of the skimpy costume tops. Finger zils chimed with their movements adding a tinny sound to the rich music. The effect was exhilarating and lust provoking.

Slowly but surely the few remaining conscious men slumped in their chairs, their minds enveloped in the same wet dream. The Colonel was one of the last to succumb to Natalia's mental magic as he watched Elizabetta and Monique sway and spin before him. Like a lion watching its prey, drool dripped from his mouth, his lips drawn up in a frightening leer. As in a hypnotic graphic of white on black, Elizabetta spun, before drawing his sight and mind into Natalia's mental trap.

His eyelids drooped and the Colonel slipped into a vampire-induced fantasy. Finally, greasy chin resting on his hairy, damp chest, Natalia was confident Fashiam slept, dreaming of two gorgeous belly dancers slithering over his moist, manly body. Caressing his engorged member. Bringing him to such heights as no man had ever endured. Natalia caught the Colonel's last waking thought and was appalled by the way he congratulated himself on how well he would be rewarded for finding such entertainment after this night. Thanks to his own over-inflated self-esteem, she was sure he would believe himself a hero, in his own mind.

She grinned, every man should think of himself as a legend,

just hours before he died.

Natalia snorted and pushed her way between two large slumbering soldiers. "Let's get out of here and get the rest of the charges set before these apes wake up with their dicks stuck to their legs." Natalia knew the necessity of keeping the guards contained for a period of time, but was totally disgusted by the way she had done it. To compel or implant a thought, she had to enter the mind. Even the slightest mental touch of these perverts was enough to turn her stomach.

"It's a mission Nat, chill." Susannah grabbed her drum and trotted after the squad members. "I mean really, there is nothing more paramount than the success of a mission in the eyes of Colonel Rambo." She giggled and added a little skip to her exit. "Personally I think we should wire their dicks with a little of that stuff Frenchy likes to play with. Slimy pigs like these guys should have to watch their most favorite appendage blown off their bodies in a flurry of blood, guts and glory, seconds before their puny existences are extinguished. Like a Middle Eastern version of Kill Bill - Kill Mahmoud only blood would spray from their dismembered you-know-whats. No virgins without the gear, guys! So there." Susannah acted the perfect role of Monique as she flounced down the corridor, hips swinging wide, hands flourishing the thin air. "Oui, oui. Let's go."

"Just a little mercenary, do you not think? Our little sister learns quickly." MorningStar followed Susannah's example moving out into the corridor with exaggerated hips and arms. Somehow it looked so incredibly wrong on the proud Native woman, but funny, none-the-less.

"Let's move ladies. We have very little time, and not all of the slimy pigs are sleeping." Elizabetta cautioned her crew as they headed toward their quarters. "Nat, how long do we have before the sleepers awaken?" She pushed her Squad to move quickly and quietly through the sparsely lit corridors.

"As much time as we need, but I wouldn't keep them down more than a couple hours. It seems like Colonel Fashiam's guards are the elite here and they will be missed if they are not at their posts when the Generals arrive. Maybe we should contact the Babysitters for an ETA on the approaching contingents. We need to let them know that Teffas Hamza is going to miss the big bang."

Elizabetta was already depressing the implant as they walked. "Dancer One to Sitter One, ETA on G-Strings?"

Susannah couldn't stop the giggle that escaped at the word G-String. It was code for the string of folks that would show up with every General, hence the G and the string. What it lacked in true covert symbolism, it made up for in imagination and basic junior high humor.

Entering their sparse quarters, each member of the squad heard the same reply simultaneously, "G-One, oh-six-hundred. G-Two, same. G-Three, plus two point five. T-One on site. Out."

Yuri sensed the squad's arrival and rolled over on the dirty mat where he had slept. Slept? That wasn't exactly what he had been doing, but it had been somewhat restful. His body was completely restored and more. He felt a youth and vigor he had not known since his teen years in Russia, streaking across the tundra on his wild stallion, Cossack. He'd been experimenting with his mind and body during the squad's absence. He'd stretched and felt the bulky muscles he worked so hard as a human to build. Now they moved with supple grace. The bones, that had earlier been so much mush were stronger than they were before his tenure of torture. In fact, if he tried, he could sense the elemental structure of his body, enhancing it, if need be.

Playing with his vision, he found it acute, to the point of insanity. He could see as well in the light, as he could in the dark. And, he could see in several spectrums at one time, using the power of his new sight to understand his new life. He'd held a rock the size of his fist and crushed it with ease, as if it had been nothing more than a sweet Christmas teacake. The powder sifted through his fingers like his former life, so many little grains separated from the whole, but essentially the same material, just in a different form. He'd thrilled at each new discovery, testing and retesting, stretching each power, experimenting with limits. He would need to know his abilities and limits when the time came to avenge the weeks of his incarceration. A feral smile crept across his features at the thought. Some base primal feeling invaded his mind and he could taste the scent of each man who had delivered his daily dose of agony. He remembered each man, of each and every day of his torturous imprisonment.

As the women entered, Yuri searched for Natalia. When their

170

eyes met, his groin tightened. What was it about the Russian vampire that made his blood boil, and his heart pound? More than just the virginal deflowering experience as a vampire; more than just a fabulously gorgeous woman, the essence of his reaction to her eluded intellectual analysis. But the puzzle remained on the verge of his consciousness. His cheeks flamed, as he pictured his initial awakening, knowing that the entire squad shared his most intimate experience.

Natalia found Yuri where she had left him, on the pallet in their quarters. He was visibly improved, a glowing vitality apparent to all. She smiled as their eyes met, a stab of excitement coursing through her sex. He was her fledgling, but something was different about this man. Something was happening that she did not understand and had never experienced before. She sent a tight mental message to Yuri that only he could sense. *You are well and rested?*

I am much more than well. This new life is incredible. I have such power, such...feeling and abilities beyond my wildest dreams. How will I ever thank you for this wonderful gift? Yuri rose in a flash and caught Natalia in his arms, as she stumbled against his mental blast, still uncontrolled. His lips traced a trail from her ear to the hollow at the base of her neck. He felt his cock dance with the touch of his lips against Natalia's skin. Her scent was magnificent. Her taste divine. He was loosing control. Lust was taking his mind for a wild ride and dragging his body along.

You are improving with your mental communication. And your tongue! Natalia squeaked as she felt the tingle of excitement begin.

"Oh puh-leeze. Get a room, for crying out loud. Betta, make them stop. Like, make a rule about tonguing in front of us, or something." The petulant adolescent was back in spades. "Don't we have a mission to complete?" Susannah dragged her bag from beneath the corner pile of mats. "Are you coming, or not?" She was ready to put some distance between herself and the single man in their group who seemed to be interested in only one of them, and it wasn't her. Had she been physically capable, her eyes would have glowed green with envy.

"Alright, one more day in this hell hole. The G-Strings should be in place by daylight and the T-Rep is already here. Somewhere." Elizabetta verbalized what everyone except Yuri

171

could hear. "Have a care, security will be very tight this night, even with the lot of sleeping beauties back there." Elizabetta stared at a checklist she withdrew from a false bottom in her bag.

"We'd better do our stuff and get the guards back on their nasty little feet, ASAP. MorningStar, you and Monique set the numbers twenty-two through thirty-six. That leaves thirty-seven through forty-five for Nat and Susannah. I'll do COM here with Yuri, just in case someone stops by for a cup of terrorist tea. All right, to work ladies. And... be careful out there." Elizabetta's favorite TV program of the last millennium was a cop show called Hill Street Blues. It always started with a briefing and that particular statement just before the officers departed for their street patrols. That saying came back to her often during the lonely survival years when being careful left her alive.

The squad members found their bags stashed beneath a stack of dirty pallets and collected what gear they would need. Donning their burqas, the vamps headed out to finish wiring explosives into place for the next day's celebration.

A bar-b-cue was in order and Taliban was on the menu.

I must go. Stay here and rest. You may feel whole again, but it will be some time before you have completed your turning. I will return soon, moi-ya mee-loch-ka. Natalia regretfully disengaged herself from Yuri's arms, took up the second bag of equipment and followed her impatient little sister through the door.

As Natalia left, a feeling of emptiness flooded Yuri's mind, clearly broadcasting his insecurity to Elizabetta. "They will be fine, Yuri. Not to worry. Natalia is the strongest compeller I have ever met. She will protect Susannah, and the rest of the squad as well. Now we must talk of you, and your life with us. Your turning was not part of our mission, but, as it seems, plans change to meet the circumstances. Colonel Maddox will just have to be flexible." Elizabetta tried to look hopeful with the last sentence. Colonel Maddox was probably the least flexible man she had ever met. In fact 'anal' didn't come close to describing 'By-The-Book-Maddox.' "We shall use this time to answer your questions, while I monitor the progress out there."

As Yuri and Elizabetta spoke of all things vampire, the rest of the squad crept about the tunnels, stringing explosives and connecting remote ignition systems. Though disgruntled and snippy, Susannah performed like a pro, setting charges and stringing det cord. Carefully, Natalia tucked the cord into the existing bundles of cable, making sure that the additional 'wire' did not look out of place. Her squad's support team spent hours with mud, grease and oil 'distressing' several hundred feet of cord in order for it to look as though it had been in the stronghold for years. As Natalia tucked the last of the cord into a bundle connecting lighting above their heads, Susannah plastered the C-4 charge against the tunnel wall rubbing dirt across the surface to disguise the slightly greasy looking explosive material.

"This seems a little like over-kill, don't you think?" Susannah whispered to Natalia as they dumped their tools into a carpetbag and turned to leave.

"Of course it does, but I don't want to have to come back here. Do you?" Natalia posed the question she already knew the answer to.

"Point made. Let's make like a bread truck and move our buns." Susannah hefted the bag and trudged toward their quarters. Within an hour the Squad had completed their tasks and were back at their cell.

Natalia and Susannah were the last to return, having spent a good hour lurking about the stronghold. Pausing just inside the door, Natalia took a deep breath, steeling herself to release the sleeping men from their compelled dreams in the club a few hundred feet away. It was close to four o'clock in the morning and sunrise was just around the corner. Methodically she touched each soldier's mind, bringing closure to their wild mental orgies and dropping them into a light sleep state. Leaving Colonel Fashiam for last, Natalia slid from his filthy mind and vomited, falling to all fours. In a flash Yuri was at her side with a bota bag of water, and a soothing touch. He carried her to their pallet on the other side of the room and settled her gently, covering the exhausted woman with a blanket. Looking to Elizabetta for help, he caught the reassuring nod of their leader and knew Natalia would be all right in time.

Chapter 19

Pay In Full

For that which thou hath given me,
I shall pay eternally.

Natalia Vyrubova, St. Petersburg
Russia, 1908

General Albani threw the last stack of loose papers in the file basket and took a deep breath. Almost morning. It would be here soon enough and his men had worked hard to put everything in order for the summit. One last check would not offend anyone's sense of responsibility, and it would calm the growing indigestion that settled in his stomach with the late hours. It pressed painfully against his backbone. He rose and stretched, his cramped legs moving slowly. He would head for the club. Have a drink. Maybe get a bite to eat. When was the last time he'd eaten?

The General strolled through the corridors, like a king walking the battlements of his castle. He was proud of the stronghold and what he had built. From the Russian occupation times to the modern days, he and a select group of freedom fighters earned high marks from their countrymen for their patriotism, and, for the freedom fighter's bank account. However, no one outside Albani's select group of cronies knew exactly how much his own personal accounts grew with the constant turmoil of the country he supposedly loved. And, no one alive knew the extent of his true holdings within the stronghold's storage grotto beneath the plains on which Hafsa Tokar quietly sat.

No one except the snake, Teffas Hamza.

That man, he kept at arms length for good reason. Now, Albani was poised on the brink of negotiating a pact that would bring his forces into collaboration with the Taliban and Al Qaeda, birthing a New Order. In this New Order, General Albani's place would be most near the top, instead of at the bottom with the poor wretched dog fighters. Though he amassed billions in armaments and supplies, he still lusted after the ultimate aphrodisiac; power. This new agreement would provide a way for him to command many contingents, and hold the reins of power that had always been just beyond his reach. He strode proudly through the halls of his domain, surveying all that was his. Today would be a grand day indeed. And the next day he would be a leader lauded by all others. Nothing would be denied him. Ever again.

His chest puffed with the thought.

Albani sauntered through the passageways and paused outside the lounging chamber aptly nicknamed 'The Club'. There should be noise, but there was none. It was just after four-thirty in the morning. The hackles rose on the back of his neck.

Something was wrong.

He reached for the door and his side arm at the same time, cracking the door just an inch to peer inside. He froze, stunned at what he saw.

Colonel Fashiam and his men laid about in various states of dress, slowly waking, several still snoring with the noise of a tramping herd of oxen. Astonished, Albani found Colonel Fashiam slouched against several gaudy pillows in the alcove he considered his office, half clothed, his flaccid penis dangling from a pair of unzipped pants. Evidence of the apparent orgy still dribbled from his limp appendage. The Colonel's eyes were open but not yet focused.

General Albani's mind sizzled with rage.

His blood boiled.

He was beyond reason.

Unlatching the leather strap from the hammer of his American made Colt .45, he slid the pearl-handled gun from its holster. Albani aimed at the largest hookah in the middle of the room. Proceeding to empty the magazine into the huge pipe, it skipped noisily across the floor for several feet, spewing acrid water and hookah scum, as Albani screamed at his men. Pausing to load a new magazine, he glared at the soldiers who immediately startled awake.

Confused and scared they ducked for cover, groggily searching for the infiltrating enemy. The General stomped through

175

the room, firing indiscriminately between pistol whipping the nearest man to him and swearing at the top of his lungs.

Seething in fury, Albani kicked viciously at his second-in-command. Colonel Fashiam rolled to the floor and crawled away from the attacking General, squealing like the pig he was.

"Stand and face me, dead man." Albani commanded. At a critical time, it was insanity to find his commander in such a state.

Colonel Fashiam stood slowly, fastening his pants to cover himself before turning to face the General. The General should have been in his quarters, in bed, long ago. What was this? "Yes Sir."

If it was possible, the man's piddling response irritated the General even more. "You have one second to explain this before I put a bullet between your pathetic eyes." Spittle formed at the corners of his mouth as the General spat the words, wild eyes focused on the Colonel's frightened face. Albani looked like a rabid dog on its way to a pit fight.

"General, we celebrate our imminent success. Allah be praised. You will succeed and be rewarded with the glory you deserve," Colonel Fashiam wheedled. "I have arranged such entertainment to dazzle the eyes and tickle the senses, as you commanded. Tonight we simply wanted to ensure the quality of our dancers was adequate for your esteemed guests. My men have worked so hard, General. It is unfortunate I pushed them beyond their limits. I take complete responsibility for this simple transgression. I throw myself on your mercy." Fashiam fell to his knees and placed his forehead on the dusty boots of his General, praying silently for his life, but without a great deal of hope.

"Son of goat dung, do you expect me to believe such dribble? Stand up!" the General screamed, shaking his gun in disgust. He was on the verge of apoplexy, currently housing a dangerous member of Al Qaeda, facing the biggest negotiation of his life and now dealing with a group of screw-ups who were more interested in sucking the hookah juice than securing the stronghold. "You will return to your duty. Now. Clean this mess up. And wash your filthy body! You smell of opium and sex. I warn you only once, do your job and stay out of my sight!" General Albani stormed out of the club in a fit of frustration.

Shocked, but relieved to be among the living, Colonel

Fashiam vomited... for several minutes. His men scrambled to remove any evidence of their supposed celebration, each silently wondering about the party he had and how it ended. Each embarrassed to admit he smoked too much opium, and did not really recall the orgy that followed.

*****

Elizabetta lie on her pallet, exhausted and in need of serious rest. As a vampire, she always loved to lounge and doze away the daylight hours, reveling in the dawn of night. While others celebrated the sunrise's golden approach, Betta celebrated the softening of the day, as the reddish glow of its end settled into the velvet arms of night. Under the ground, day and night were irrelevant, but rest was not. She sighed and rolled over, tired, but restless and unable to find the call of day-sleep's help. According to her watch, it was close to eight am. The Babysitters indicated that the visiting Generals and their retinues would be arriving between six o'clock and eight-thirty in the morning. The men would be in negotiations all day and want to party late into the evening. Hopefully, the Vamp Squad would begin their entertainment early on to make sure the attendees were in one place. Then they would beat feet out of there, blowing the facility as they departed. They would be clear of any threat from the explosion, according to the plan.

Eighteen hours, at the most. They would lie low, do their job and be home in time for dinner. Elizabetta closed her dry eyes and tried to meditate herself to sleep. Hamza's quick departure bothered her. Was he aware of The Babysitters' approach and setting a trap? Maybe he was on his way to question his brother one more time. She thought hopefully, he just wanted to go home to his wife and children.

Not likely.

Teffas Hamza was the one loose string in the operation so far. Besides Yuri. Yuri wasn't a loose string, he was more like a loose cannon and certainly an unknown.

Across the room, Natalia lie in Yuri's arms, secure and comfortable despite the chill of their quarters. Awake after a short nap, she tightened her thought stream again so only Yuri could 'hear' her broadcast.

You look so like my beloved Tsar Nicholas. When Father Grigori turned me, I was praying for Tsarevich Alexei. He was sick. We were told he would die, so I went to the cathedral to pray for his life. I was but a child. Alexei lived. I did not. No one knew the truth and I could not betray my sire. He held me in complete control. I became a plaything for the Romanov family priest. Just before I took his head, he smiled and blew me a kiss. He was a monster, and he made me one as well. At least, that is what I thought at the time. The myths about vampires were rampant in old Russia and with good reason. He maintained his own coven of disgusting and vile followers. He never understood the simple truth about what he became. What I have since learned of my life.

Yuri whispered, not completely trusting his psyche-speak in such close proximity yet. "What do you mean, he didn't understand the simple truth?" His breath against her ear was titillating and played with her focus.

The truth about vampirism. We are mutated by an infectious virus called vampticious meticulosus deliriotum, or, VMD. It's a complex virus that needs more blood than our bodies can produce, so we have fangs to suck blood right into our system. The virus keeps us healthy, makes us extra strong, allowing us to use one hundred percent of our physical and mental capacity. We seem to die, while it takes over our bodies, mutating our DNA, but it's just a kind of viral induced coma. Then, when part of the job is done, we are reborn with partial viral adapted bodies. We age at such a slow rate, it seems we are immortal. The only serious drawback is a reaction to sunlight. Full, natural ultraviolet light causes rapid cell deterioration. Unlike the legends of Dracula, and modern vampires that look like Tom Cruise or Brad Pitt, we can exist in sunlight, it just takes a huge amount of blood to remain intact and a recovery period to heal any deterioration that may appear. Many years ago, a German doctor developed V-screen, ultraviolet block-out. It's good for a few hours only, and then our skin begins to blister.

Natalia snuggled closer and turned to face Yuri, breathing in the scent of him. *All the crazy stuff about churches, crosses and holy water is just that, crazy stuff. Although I did have to give up garlic, it seems to conflict with the virus and gave me gas. But that's okay; I never really liked it anyway. Silver makes our skin react as well, but only if we live on human blood. Synth-blood has mitigated the reaction to silver metal somehow.*

"So, I can go to church if I want to? Yuri smiled as his lips traced a little line across Natalia's forehead.

Sure. Contrary to popular belief, VMD doesn't take our souls or damn us, or anything. It's a virus. Not good, not bad, just a little organism that changes us. It makes us more than we were, able to accomplish unusual feats. In return you have to give up sunbathing, limit your daily exposure to UV, and learn to control your appetite for blood and sex. But you can still go to church. What church did you attend before? Natalia could feel the fire begin to burn within her mind and body. Each of Yuri's kisses fanned her fire like gasoline on an open flame. It was becoming increasingly difficult to focus and project her conversation.

"Didn't. I was just checking, in case I wanted to, at some later date. And, why would I control my appetite for sex?" He tickled her ear with his tongue and blew on the moist lobe. Yuri paused in mid lust. "So how do we actually…I mean, I have these fangs. How… do we really bite?" Yuri was finally considering the primary issue that set vampires apart from humans. Taking blood from a human would be the main thing that changed his lifestyle forever.

In the old days, it was our way of feeding. We killed our victims. Or at least, that is what I thought. It was what I was taught. Some vampires still do. Each coven is different. The smart leaders teach their coven members not to kill, just take what each human can give, without taxing the body to the point of death. Now-a-days, most vampires use modern methodology, you know, blood bank and synthetically prepared blood supplements or synth-blood. Some covens still believe in feeding the ancient way, to stay in touch with what they call their 'inner vampire'. They see humans as a food source, as inferior. Like the way humans see cattle and chickens. They make it impossible for the rest of us to live openly, and they keep the myths about blood sucking monsters alive, scaring people for fun. Natalia scrunched her nose and made a face in disgust. *My sire was like that. He killed for food and sport. He was a true monster. In a modern world, there is no need for such foolishness and violence. We have a kind of self-policing body that*

179

tries to mitigate problems that arise from the back-to-basics crowd when they cause difficulties with their nasty lifestyle. But, as far as I know, the Vamp Squad is the first-ever, government supported and protected group of vampires. Our coven actually serves the country, and does something good for humans. Well, the Nazi's did some research and actually used vampires in their SS. That obviously wasn't for good.

"I guess, that depended on which side of the fence you sat, in those days. But, I have to admit, even the Russians disliked the cruelty of the SS and the horror of the extermination camps." Yuri hugged Natalia close, loving the intimacy of talking and playing at the same time. His hands wandered, smiling every time Natalia gasped or wiggled. "But I do remember the old wives tales my babushka used to tell me, as a small boy. She said, there was one who lived forever and watched over our family. Watched over all of the Romanovs. My family kept our identity secret because of the communist government. The KGB, one way or another, would have exterminated us, if they ever found out the Romanov line continued to exist. The Communists always feared returning to the old ways with a Tsarist government and now, the government just fears. The Watcher had special powers to keep us safe and secure. When I was growing up, sometimes I actually felt...I know it sounds strange, but I felt like someone watched me." Yuri was quiet and still for a moment.

"It was you, wasn't it?" He growled against her throat, nipping and licking his way towards the cleft at the base of her neck. He literally purred at the taste of her skin. Like an addictive perfume, the more he had, the more he wanted. His hand slipped beneath the burqa that covered them as a blanket, searching for the taut, silk encased nipple that puckered at his caress.

Yes. Yes. Natalia arched into his touch, her rock-hard nipple straining against the wisp of material that was the top of her costume.

"I knew it!" Yuri sat up and looked hard at Natalia. "I knew you were always there, my Dark Angel. I have always felt you, here and here." He tapped his head and then his heart. "And here, too." Yuri maneuvered Natalia's hand to his bulging pants that hid the throbbing cock beneath.

Natalia started, as cold air touched her skin. She frowned at the beautiful, dumb man above her. *I didn't mean yes to that, Yuri. I meant yes to... ach!* She scowled, disgusted with the apparent tunnel vision of the man beside her. She abruptly turned on her side to face the wall. *Really Yuri, you sure know how to douse cold water on a hot beginning.* Facing away from him, she curled her arms around her middle and closed her eyes.

"So, will this virus that made me a vampire, make me understand women?" Yuri whispered, frustrated and unsure of what he had just done, but knowing somehow he'd made a big mistake.

No such luck, Captain. Go to sleep. You will need your strength tonight. Natalia slipped from Yuri's mind and lie there, stewing about a book she had read while at Olney Farm. It detailed the difference in thoughts and behaviors between men and women, attributing those differences to the fact that men were from Mars, and women were from Venus. Squeezing her eyes tight in exasperation she thought the author was definitely correct. Men must truly be from Mars because they certainly were not from the same planet as women.

"But, I don't want to sleep. I want to..." His arm snuck across her shoulder, and pulled her close to him, spooning again. Her silky skin and feminine warmth felt wonderful against his chest. Beyond his control, 'Little Yuri' leapt to life, prodding Natalia's back with small pulses. And just as quickly, it died on the vine as Natalia giggled at his clumsy attempt to return to their previous lustful state.

Sighing, she relaxed against Yuri's body. A hundred years and nothing changed, she thought, as Yuri's breathing slowed and his arm lie heavy across her chest. Sex, sleep or food, men were basically the same through time, across borders, and despite genetics. Unused to being held, it took a while before Natalia finally drifted into a dreamy sleep fraught with sensuality.

*****

Languorously, she lie in a soft green field of moss surrounded by a riot of color: bright blue Siberian squill, neon yellow zharki and darker blue iris. Far below, her castle's golden domes glittered, sparkling brightly against the deep blue waters of Avacha Bay. The

181

tiny flowers covered the landscape, as far as the eye could see. Clumps of daffodils dotted the land punctuating the shallow hills and gullies of the Russian arctic tundra. The weak midnight sun warmed her skin and enhanced the drowsy feeling that invaded her body along with the heady aroma of the Siberian blooms. In the distance, a man gathered wildflowers as he strolled toward the thick bearskin on which she reclined. Siberia was beautiful in the hot summer months when the sun burned for twenty-three hours a day. Life was abundant, in a hurry to live before the snows of winter covered the world with their killing touch, and darkness enveloped the landscape.

Natalia watched the man approach, delighting in the picture he presented. It was a true woman's fantasy. Like an animal on the scent of something deliciously promising, a shirtless Yuri ambled closer, arms full of gay flowers. Pollen clung to the soft blonde hair covering his muscular chest. Like a kiss from the sun, it lent a bright yellow gleam to his body, as if he were a golden God. His six foot four inch frame was topped with dusty golden curls that accentuated his brilliant smile, a smile that glowed just for her.

She breathed in the air knowing the smell of him, exalting in the feeling it produced in her soul. She could feel the excitement build as moisture formed within her sex. Her breasts pressed against the satin and lace of her bodice, as she stretched to take the bouquet from his offering hands. He planted a soft kiss on her wrist, his lips caressing her skin so slow and seductive.

On his knees before her, Natalia let Yuri draw her toward him, flowers drifting around them in a cascade of lively colors. She was encircled within his arms, the tip of his tongue touching her velvety lips softly, but with defined purpose.

Like an explosion of energy, Natalia was struck by the sensual heat that ignited her body. She was amazed that his touch could produce such a reaction. A shower of sparks settled behind her eyes, as she felt his heartbeat quicken. Surely a woman could die from such exquisite pleasure.

The sun warmed her flesh as Yuri warmed her heart, both a power beyond reckoning, beyond human ability to comprehend. In matters of the heart, there was no comprehension, no need to intellectualize. Only to feel. To consume what each offered the other.

Gently she lie back, pulling Yuri with her, feeling the enticing weight of her golden lover's body above her. His lips found her neck as he teased and licked his way to the border of her bodice. Ever so slowly, pulling the satin laces with his teeth, his move released the bonds that held her breasts within the gossamer covering. She gazed at her lover, as he nosed the satin confection away from her creamy mounds, teasing her pert nipples with his curls. Gently caressing her, flakes of pollen drifted about them. The air shimmered with a shower of golden flecks as Yuri continued to play with her breasts. His tongue worked its way downward. Flames of pure heat flicked across her abdomen and tangled in the deep chestnut curls between her trembling legs. His tongue continued its journey as Natalia gasped for breath, arching against his mouth's ministrations.

She pleaded for more, unable to resist.

Adding more pressure, she felt Yuri growl his need. She was vaguely aware of the tearing sound, as the covering material that kept him from his prize, gave way. It lie in tatters amongst the flowers strewn around them.

His fingers explored the depths of Natalia's velvety folds.

Holding her breath, she opened to him freely, offering up her most private and intimate places to his touch.

Yuri sought her nether lips, licking and kissing her opening. Driving her to new heights of delirium. She bucked and cried out as he cupped her buttocks with strong hands, pulling her to him, thrusting his tongue deeper, swirling and sucking. Her juices flowed around his mouth, coating his face and chin with her scent. Again he growled nipping gently with his teeth, teasing. The vibration sending her over the edge.

Her body exploded in a million pieces, as Natalia rode the waves of orgasmic pleasure. At each crest she screamed her ecstasy, until she could no longer breathe from the pure joy of the dream.

✵✵✵✵✵

Startled, Natalia jerked awake. Covered in sweat, she shook from the intensity of her sensual fantasy.

Sweat? Vampires didn't sweat. Ever since this connection

with Yuri deepened she had begun to 'feel' human things again. What was happening to her?

Carefully she stole a glance at the man who slept, wrapped around her. His breathing was even and constant. His beautiful face revealed no indication of having shared in her sleep-induced reverie. She automatically sensed the sun was near setting outside of the rock fortress in which she lay. She had slept much of the day and it was close to night again.

Wiping the moisture from her forehead, she slithered from beneath the scratchy burqa. The cool air within their cave quarters sent chills across her damp skin as she quietly stood, leaving Yuri to sleep on, undisturbed.

Betta, are you awake? Natalia softly touched Elizabetta's mind.

No. A lazy reply preceded a sharpening of the message. Their leader woke quickly. *What is wrong?* Elizabetta's eyes flew open, immediately alert for trouble. *What? I just got to sleep!*

Shhh, nothing is wrong. If I am to feed Yuri when he wakes, I must also feed. I have lost a great deal of strength in turning Yuri and compelling the soldiers. I need blood Betta, I am having trouble focusing and I think there is no more in our supplies. Natalia stumbled towards the door. *I sense no guard outside.*

I listened during the day as I rested. No guard returned throughout the day. But I heard soldiers go by. They spoke of the Generals' arrival and some kind of trouble with Colonel Fashiam. Seems he got caught sleeping on the job. Betta mentally snickered. *From the gossip I heard, General Albani almost shot him on the spot. Dissension among the ranks is good. They will lose trust with one another and spend time checking up on each other, not us. It will make our job easier. Go, but be careful and please do not kill your victim. The well is filling up rapidly!* Elizabetta closed her eyes and rolled over withdrawing from Natalia's mind and quickly sliding back into sleep.

Silently, Natalia slipped from their quarters and cast her senses down several tunnels, as she hid in the shadows. She could hear men shouting, laughing and talking from different directions. She could feel groups of soldiers together throughout the stronghold, but she could not sense one alone, separate from the rest. She would need that, a loner, or someone wandering alone,

184

away from the rest in order to feed in secret. Her vampire sense was slow and unfocused.

After exploring one particular corridor for several hundred feet, she heard a single heartbeat, close and strong. It beat rapidly with the rhythm of fear. Curious, Natalia followed the sound, moving silently and in sync with the person's footsteps and breathing pattern, closing the distance between herself and the oncoming frightened heart.

Up ahead a weak light appeared illuminating the robed figure of a tall thin man. His long beard and mustache hid most of his features, but his rapid heart beat and shallow breathing told Natalia this man was not where he should be, and he was afraid of being discovered. A miniature flashlight, the kind that spies carry, splashed a tiny pool of light across the floor as the man hurriedly picked his way down several flights of crumbling stairs. He was coming directly towards Natalia who stood in the shadows of a connecting passageway, hidden in the recessed darkness.

Though hungry enough to take this man's blood immediately, Natalia was curious about who this secretive man was, and to where he thought he was sneaking. Slowly she backed farther into the passageway and remained silently hidden as the man stumbled by. Just as silently, she followed. Reaching out with a refined touch, Nat probed the man's mind, looking for clues to his surreptitious trek. Twice she pulled back and froze, as the man stopped, mumbling to himself and surveying the tunnel behind him. On some level, he was aware he was being followed, but chose to continue on his intended mission anyway. He was not, however, aware of the mental connection to the woman who tracked him.

Again Natalia reached out, this time she found what she was searching for. She scanned his thoughts with the finesse of a master illusionist. Through the jumble of mental pictures and verbal diatribe she gained an understanding of this man's true mission. He was the official representative of Al Qaeda supposedly here to negotiate an agreement with the visiting Generals. In actuality, his real job was to discover the extent of General Albani's secret supplies. If the Al Qaeda intelligence had been half correct, Albani's accumulated wealth and strategic resources were treasures Al Qaeda could not pass up. Taking the General and his men out of the equation through assassination, left the jewels ripe for plucking. The man's name was Mustaffa Al Muffadi and his mission was much different than General Albani thought.

Al Muffadi scurried on with his little spy light flashing back and forth, oblivious to the woman who followed, delicately pilfering his thoughts. Sounding alot like a small rodent scurrying for its life, his sandal clad feet made tiny, almost inaudible scraping noises in the dust as he moved through the passageway that led deep into the mountainside.

Weeding through the mind's occupying fear of being discovered and the determination to move quickly, Natalia sorted the quips and details she gained from the Al Qaeda operative's thoughts. He was supposed to be resting after a long day of negotiating, but had dispatched his guard, placing the body in the bed in his quarters, in case anyone checked.

Following a hand drawn map of indeterminable age, he smuggled into the stronghold with his other papers, he searched for a disguised entrance that would take him to a vault thought to contain billions in riches and supplies.

Natalia picked up on snatches of skepticism floating amid fears of being caught, as the man wound his way through tunnel after tunnel, stopping to check his map at each turn. Al Muffadi thought himself to be a very careful man. He was pleased with his progress and confident that the map would lead him to whatever there was to find, whether it be riches or a dirt cavern of rodents and filth.

Now more interested than hungry, Natalia followed. Catching a whiff of the negotiations discussed earlier in the day, she drank in the man's thoughts. Like breathing as lightly as possible in a hiding place, she forced her mental lungs to take as much information as she could without betraying her actions, slowly and gently.

During the meetings, Al Muffadi acted the religious zealot, pressing the malleable Generals to join the cause of Al Qaeda. Mustaffa Al Muffadi was a master at surreptitiously manipulating and influencing men. The kind of men whose primary desire revolved around personal greed, beautiful women, the illegal gun or drug trade, and oil. His mission was to use them to find their resources. He had no concern for the men who deserted Allah's purpose to feather their own nests with worldly goods, and illicit women. So, he wound their desires with fanatical dreams of power and wealth, while entwining their loyalty in the supposed root philosophy of his cause. It tickled his perverted sense of humor to play the game, one schemer manipulating another for the ultimate prize.

Natalia listened to the ebb and flow of Mustafa's philosophical diatribe, as she followed him deeper into the stronghold. She felt Mustaffa admonishing himself for allowing the philosophical wanderings of his mind at such a critical moment. It would not do to lose focus and be caught before he discovered what lie within this stronghold. Still hesitant and doubting the source of Al Qaeda's intel, Al Muffadi personally considered the miserable informant's endless description of riches, a little beyond belief. If a third of the pitiful spy's reports to Al Qaeda were true, General Albani had done well for himself. And, if the story was indeed completely correct, he had done very well for Al Qaeda.

Natalia tripped on an unnoticed stone and hissed, mentally kicking herself for making such a stupid mistake. She must be in a more weakened state than she thought. Mistakes were expensive, and often lead to death, or worse. Al Muffadi immediately extinguished his light and froze. Natalia watched with her vamp vision, as the man cocked an ear and stared hard into the inky blackness. For almost a minute, Al Muffadi stood motionless, listening, waiting for the feared deathblow that would come out of nowhere to end his life. Natalia could hear the pounding of his heart, the surge of his blood racing through his veins. She could smell the cold sweat that dripped from his body, betraying the terror that enveloped his thoughts.

Natalia slid into that terrified mind and eased his fear. Softly, she mentally whispered to him. *It is nothing. Only a small animal follows. Do not fear what the shadows conceal. There is nothing to worry about. No one comes this way. It is forbidden and you are safe.*

She continued to compel his mind, as she crept closer, her mouth watering as the scent of the man's blood filled her nostrils. She had passed the safe zone of self-control and now fought her pressing need. Fangs extended of their own volition and Natalia felt the blood lust begin to rise, threatening to consume her conscious thought in the wake of the approaching feeding frenzy.

Hang onto your control Nat, she chided herself. She was too old to act like a fledgling, lusting after a container of blood with no thought for the source or their ultimate mission. But the smell of fear-impregnated blood was a heady enticement and she was losing mind control of her target in favor of hunger and feeding. Natalia stole closer, swallowing hard to control the saliva flooding her mouth. She licked her lips and tasted the man's scent just inches away. Breathing deeply, Natalia pressed her fangs to Al Muffadi's neck and drank.

God and the Devil, it was good! Caressing the man as she drank, Natalia wrapped his mind in a fantasy of sensual feelings, mixing the pain of her bite with the pleasure of his fantasy. Al Muffadi groaned and leaned back, rubbing against Natalia's breasts, sliding his body closer, feeling her luscious body behind him.

Thank the powers that be, even religious zealots never seemed to lose the lust for a woman's flesh. Their minds connected, Natalia reveled in the strength she drew from his blood, brimming with adrenaline. She had rarely experienced live blood from anyone but her sire, and that was so tainted, her body often revolted at the very thing that sustained her. Later, after she dispatched the fiendish priest to his ultimate end, she existed on non-human blood, content with her lot, but unable to face taking that which she found so repulsive.

Now, out of necessity she broke her own rule. Like sipping a rich after dinner cognac, the warm liquid burned her veins with excitement and fueled her slacking strength. No wonder many modern vampires would not give up drinking warm human blood!

Control Nat, control. This is not your way, only a band-aid for an emergency situation.

Finally, she drank slowly, savoring each tiny drop, stretching out the wonderful feeling of feeding. She hadn't really considered the effect of human blood after living without it for so long. Now she knew. She tasted Yuri, but his blood had been so used and void of anything living by the time she found him, it did not nourish her. Though guilt nagged at a part of her mind, Natalia needed to feed, and live blood was the only way at the moment. So she carried Al Muffadi with her, mentally exchanging her exhilaration in feeding for a sexual exhilaration that fired his libido and pummeled his senses. An even exchange… possibly.

Finally, reeling from the heights of passion and blood loss, the robed man crumpled, pulling himself from Natalia's mouth. She allowed him to drop to the floor, licking her lips daintily, like a cat that just finished a saucer of milk. At odds with herself, disgusted at what she'd done but preening just a little, she kicked the unconscious man away from her. He would sleep for some time then wake with fuzzy memories of a clandestine encounter deep within the stronghold. Though Natalia could not afford the time to follow Al Muffadi to the end of his quest, she implanted a memory that he'd found nothing after searching long hours. When he awoke he would be well convinced that the Al Qaeda spy was wrong and his trip had been for naught. The cave system's rugged floor simply caused him a bad fall, and his head hit harder than expected.

Like a child who had stolen cookies from the cookie jar without permission, Natalia exhilarated in the taste and strength of Al Muffadi's blood. She seemed perfectly able to momentarily disregard the nagging guilt taking his blood had created. Like teenage sex in the back of a sports car, it felt way too good, whatever the consequences would be later. She spun on a dainty toe and retraced her steps, easily navigating the winding passageways back to the Vamp Squad quarters and a waking Yuri. Reminding herself he would need to share her bounty when he awoke assuaged some of the niggling guilt in the back of her mind. She promised him she would make his awakening as painless and easy as possible. Taking Al Muffadi's blood was required to fulfill that promise, or at least she worked on convincing herself as she stole through the stronghold.

He would also need more of the kind of attention he received shortly after awakening. That could prove problematic in their small cell with four pairs of curious watching eyes. Natalia sighed; so little time, so many problems to solve. She would find a way to take care of Yuri. Her veins throbbed, sated and happy, the vampire equivalent of a full tummy. Despite what she had done, Natalia's steps were light and quick.

Chapter 20

<u>Sunrise, Sunset</u>

Sunrise, sunset. Sunrise, sunset.
Swiftly flow the years.
Once season following another,
Laden with darkness and fear.

from Fiddler on the Coffin
Racine Medalliar, Paris
France, 1966

Elizabetta stretched, feeling deep in her bones the rhythm of the planets and the sun. The sun was setting outside on the surface. VMD provided a kind of circadian rhythm that kept its host aware of the sun's position at all times. As a self-protection mechanism, it was fairly effective. As an alarm clock, it was infallible.

She sensed her squad members were beginning to wake as well and Natalia had not yet returned. Yuri still slept soundly, but it would not be long before he woke. When he did they would face a new problem. His overpowering need for blood could be provided for, but the rest? Well, she did not need to ride herd over an orgy. And an orgy it would be, with Monique primed for just about anything, any time. Susannah was raring to see what she missed out on in her own awakening. And strangely enough, Natalia did not seem to be capable of resisting Yuri's sexual needs any more than she could deny him her blood.

Elizabetta thought hard on that particular issue. There was something she could almost catch hold of in the back of her mind. The more she chased it, the more it eluded her grasp. Had she not seen a relationship, something like this before? A darkness descended to envelope her train of thought. It had not ended well, she could recall.

But how had it begun and why? How? She would ask the

190

Librarian when their mission was over. It would cost her, but they were old friends. Few secrets existed between the two old vampires and often Emilliano allowed tidbits of valuable information to enter into their casual conversation that gave Elizabetta exactly what she needed to know.

Just as Elizabetta reached for the back of her neck, Natalia bounced into the room, a brilliant smile plastered across her face, "Good evening Betta. Sleep well?"

"As a matter of fact, no." Elizabetta rose and stretched again. Her body ached and she was beginning to feel her age. And she was old. "I assume by the smile and the skip in your step, you actually found what you were looking for? And there were no problems?" Her auburn eyebrow arched speculatively.

"Everything worked out just fine. No new additions to the well, and I am back to my old self." Natalia smiled sweetly at Elizabetta as she knelt to kiss Yuri awake. It was like a scene out of some Norman Rockwell painting; beautiful Russian belly dancer kneeling seductively to offer her soft lips for the hero's plunder. The whole scene was so right.

Well, except for the fangs, bloodstains and that animal growling thing.

Betta chuckled to herself. She was sure the well-known artist wasn't into painting Norman Rockwell's Paranormal America, but the thought was entertaining for a swift second. "All right then, we should get everyone up, and make sure the equipment is ready to go as soon as our evening engagement is over. Hopefully it will be a fast exit."

Elizabetta heard Monique giggle, then draw a sensually deep and rapturous breath. Following the French vampire's line of sight, she turned to catch Yuri plastering kisses up and down Natalia's arm. His eyes were glowing blood red and the pearly fangs protruding from his full lips caressed the bulging veins in Natalia's wrist. "Okay, then. Let's ah…"

Yuri sank his fangs into Natalia's wrist where the throbbing vein pulsed, sucking at her skin as he drank. Their eyes met and souls melded in a flash of sensual pleasure. Natalia gasped, accepting Yuri's sexual broadcast with no regret. Drinking in his powerful need, she combed her fingers through thick blonde curls that so recently appeared with his healing. She loved the hair that now hung to his shoulders, framing his handsome features. He so resembled a vision of angelic masculinity her mouth watered with anticipation. Except for the little trickle of blood on his chin, Yuri could have passed for a Greek god. Natalia was afraid she was losing her mind like she lost her heart years ago. It was a dangerous mixture.

Elizabetta immediately threw the equivalent of a mental bucket of cold water on the two. Natalia squealed and Yuri growled as the chilling psychic shot cooled more than their ardor.

"Betta, ease up. Yuri is still turning. He needs this." Natalia faced their leader, hands on her hips, the wound at her wrist already closing.

"Of course. But I do not need to have an orgy on my hands. We have a serious situation here. Feed him but restrain yourselves. We can't afford to have soldiers show up at our door and figure out that we have a new boytoy on our hands. Someone is bound to miss the two men in the well, sooner or later, and we still need to make sure the Generals are in place before we blow this popsicle stand."

"Wow Betta, I didn't know you could talk jive. I'm impressed. How did you learn that stuff in some dank crumbling castle in the mountains of Romania?" Susannah, a product of public education and little travel was unaware of Elizabetta's comfortable and modern home. The girl hopped up and danced around checking her costume and warming her cold limbs.

"Before Olney Farm and you, my little daughter, I lived in a chateau in my beautiful Transvaal Mountains. My home has nine bedrooms and eight bathrooms, tennis courts, a pool, theater, and satellite dish. Over five hundred channels and high speed Internet. I may be old, but I am *not* out of date. I sometimes talk that way out of habit but never underestimate this vampire." Elizabetta sniffed.

Natalia had to laugh at their erstwhile Mistress. She had to give the elder vampire credit for keeping up with the times. Like herself, and many older vampires, Betta was flexible, knew world politics, kept a hand in several financial interests and maintained a more than comfortable life style. However, after over five hundred years, even that was a little tedious. So, what did an ancient vampire do when she had everything she needed? She adopted a new daughter and became the leader and coven Mistress of a misfit group of independent and strong willed vamps, whose mission was to defend the free world by engaging in covert operations. Natalia just had to smile. The only thing that seemed to be a given in the vampire world was change. If you lived long enough, what change you could see!

"Let's be ready when the guards come for us. It's after sundown and their negotiations should have broken for the evening. I imagine it is close to seven or eight o'clock." They sat in a close group, gathered around Elizabetta who spoke softly for added effect. "Check your gear and costumes. Susannah, remember your place is at the rear with your back to the wall. Do not get within an arm's length of any soldier, straight or drunk. Monique, you target the Colonel and keep his attention, but stay safe. Natalia, your job is to keep the communications flowing and zap anyone who gets carried away."

Though the Vamp Squad was well aware of the plan and their individual parts to be played, Natalia was glad Elizabetta showed her concern in the warnings she handed out with efficiency. Not for the first time, Natalia thought of the loneliness and cruelty she experienced at the hands of her own sire. He was the Master of the only other coven she had been a part of, but he cared only for his own pleasures and the power of being a strong vampire. He learned to draw on the coven to increase his power and control of politics, as well as the royal family. In the end, it lead to the downfall of everything he sought to hold, and eventually his own death.

His end was one of Natalia's better moves. She never regretted killing her sire, but always wondered how his incredible abilities transferred to her as he expired. The relationship between their mutated VMD was as close as it could be. She was his direct progeny, but had never seen or heard of a transfer like that, in all her years, alive or dead. Maybe, her VMD was close enough that his virus sought its offspring, depositing its own unique characteristics, instead of dying with its primary host.

She could postulate all day and still find no concrete answers. Some day she would pose the question to the Librarian.

"Someone's coming, Elizabetta. Yuri, in the corner. Get under the bags and mattress. Hurry." Natalia was in a panic. She sensed three guards outside the door and hoped they would wait just a second. She knew she could compel their minds to ignore the presence of a man in their midst, but why take a chance? "As soon as we leave, get the equipment together, consolidate the bags and be ready to go. We'll be coming through on the run. It's a ways to the entrance, and we may have to fight our way out. Bullets can't kill us but they still hurt." Natalia whispered to Yuri as she tried to cover him with a filthy mat.

"I know another way to get out, if we need it." Yuri whispered back and planted a soft kiss on the lips of the woman he had come to trust and desire in such a short time. He winked seductively, bringing a smile to the same lips he just kissed.

Ducking beneath the last mat, Yuri effectively disappeared from sight.

Natalia stood as the guards entered. Turning slowly she shot a bolt of control at the three. Each man affected a dopey smile and remained in place, standing dumbstruck and immediately lost in their own secret sensual fantasies. "From my mind to your libido. Enjoy. Betta, are we ready?"

Each member of the Squad collected their veils and musical instruments and stood ready. Elizabetta depressed the communication device in her neck and transmitted the commencement code to the Babysitters.

"Babysitters,V-1. Party's ready. We're gonna dance all night." Elizabetta imitated a southern drawl as she spoke.

They all heard the response, "V-1, Babysitters. Kick it, babe. Out."

"That had to be Miller or Devlin. My dad would never use the word babe." Susannah snickered.

Natalia released her mental hold on the three soldiers and waited while they recovered their senses. Slightly startled, the lead guard glared at his two subordinates then issued orders to the women.

"You go to dance. Now." The man ushered Elizabetta and the others through the doorway at gunpoint, shouting, "Go now. Colonel Fashiam does not like to wait."

So the Colonel is in a hurry to die. I'm good with that. Natalia mentally nudged the rest of the Squad as Susannah stifled a giggle. They all trudged through the passageways between the guards contemplating the mission and how to stay at arm's length while entertaining a room full of perverted terrorists.

They heard the carousing long before reaching the Club. The loud sound of the men echoed through the passageways. Cheers and leers rang out, as the women entered the room. The place was packed, but an area in the middle had been cleared for the dancers. Colonel Fashiam's men had set up small couches around the dance floor for each of the Generals and their aides. The rest sat crammed around small bar tables, complete with hookahs and plates of seasoned goat meat and rice. Laughing and hooting, the men grabbed and slapped at the women as they made their way to the center of the room.

Betta, what do I do? I can't get to the wall. Susannah was frantic and beginning to shake. The soft red glow emanating from her eyes was rapidly turning to blaze red.

Hang on, little one. I will take care of this. Move to the pillar over where the women are sitting on the laps of those soldiers. Their hands are full. They cannot hurt you, unless they drop their doxies. Put the pillar at your back and stay there. Betta swirled and pointed to where Susannah should position herself in a graceful, flourishing movement. It was a seductive move that introduced her musician but also directed Susannah to where she needed to be. Next to the pillar, a man sat, neatly dressed all in black with a black turban secured by a huge gold emblem. He leered and squeezed the breast of the scantily clad woman on his lap. She buried her hand in his crotch and rubbed possessively. Her green eyes and light skin betrayed her Romanian descent and she wore the coined and sequined short veil of her tribe. By the look of her age and adornments, Elizabetta knew the woman was an expensive addition to the General's stable. Obviously there were other women stashed in the stronghold beside themselves.

Too bad for them.

MorningStar moved to the opposite pillar and began to pipe a haunting tune. Susannah twirled and drummed her way to the pillar Betta had designated. Placing her back to the stone, she began to beat a rhythm that complimented the piping. The three remaining dancers circled the floor with tambourines encouraging each group of men to root competitively with the others. A contest of cheering broke out as the Generals threw money with jewelry, and attempted to grope the dancers as they undulated by. The entire scene resembled a competitive mud-wrestling event at the Mustang Ranch. When the crowd was near frenzy, the music paused creating an eerie silence, as the dancers moved to the center of the room and posed, ready to begin their entertainment. All eyes turned to the three women, veiled and ready to dance. The silence stretched for several moments adding to the anticipation of the crowd.

Elizabetta counted as she rounded the room. *Nat, They are not all here. All four visiting Generals and their men are, but not Albani. I don't see the Al Qaeda rep either.* The music started once again and the dancers began to move, winding their veils, circling each other with sensual steps and swinging hips.

Monique laughed and teased as she danced, completely in her element.

The Al Qaeda rep will not be a problem. He is deep in slumber, renewing his blood supply somewhere in the bowels of the stronghold. I cannot tell where Albani is. He should be here. Natalia stretched her senses searching for Albani as she caught the edge of a veil and pulled it from a spinning Monique. Elizabetta caught the next veil and removed another layer from the twirling beauty. Now completely revealed, Monique bent backwards, thrusting her hips into the lap of a very drunk officer, smiling, beguiling, her hips aggressively working his crotch as her hands worked the zils in time to the music.

Monique, cut the physical contact unless you want a wrestling match in front of everyone. And they won't be rooting for you to win, that's for sure. Two more dances and we go for a wardrobe change to cover our retreat, then beat feet out of here. Elizabetta was becoming uncomfortable as the crowd pressed and the dance floor shrunk. Men crushed closer and closer, as the soldiers in the back inched forward for a better view.

I'm just having a little fun Betta. Come on, cheri. Monique executed a perfect back walkover using the General's knee as support, and then twisted around to land in his lap once again. Obviously inebriated and off balance, the man slid from his chair to land unceremoniously on the floor on his rump. The crowd jeered and laughed, throwing beer cans and pieces of fruit. Things were rapidly getting out of control. Again performing a back walkover, Monique slid her foot from the man's crotch to his chest;

touched his chin with her decorated toes and kicked backward over his body. It was a perfectly executed escape that worked well with the music and dance. Monique was amazing.

The drunken officer lurched for Monique's foot, as she deftly extricated herself from the entanglement and returned to the ever-decreasing center of the dance floor. *Oui Betta, you were right, mauvaise idée, very bad idea!*

All three dancers remained in the center of the floor in a tight circle, teasing the men from afar and dancing with each other for the final two songs. As the music died and the dancers bowed, Elizabetta announced they would return after changing their costumes into something 'very special' for the next set of dances. Hoots and cheers followed them to the door but no one blocked their exit, depraved expectations clear amid greasy faces and bleary eyes.

Leaving as rapidly as they could before reaching hands and drunken debauchery detained them, the squad ran toward their quarters. Elizabetta explained to the guards as they ran by, that a quick costume change would take a very short period of time. They knew the way to and from their quarters and would return in a few moments. The guards had watched the dancing and leered as the women ran by, but did not follow or stop them. Natalia compelled the guards to agree and stay at the Club enjoying a quick drink until the dancers returned. The women were finally free and unaccompanied, but not for long. They would have to hurry.

Chapter 21

<u>Why?</u>

Why do we live in fear
Of the human so near?
Hiding in shadows, afraid to say?
We should be proud of our race, the role we play.

It is not we who are the monsters
Yet accused we do live.
Confined to darkness,
And still, we forgive.

Bouduin Melinar, The Awakening of Mankind
Paris, France, 2000

General Albani stood outside Mustaffa Al Muffadi's quarters as two guards removed the body of a young soldier. Al Muffadi had supposedly retired after a long day of negotiations to rest and pray. Now his guard was dead and the Al Qaeda puke was on the loose.

Where the hell was that piece of Al Qaeda shit? How long had he been free to wander the fortress? What had he discovered in his wanderings? This did not bode well for the summit. It did not bode well for Al Muffadi, either. If he found anything of use to Al Qaeda, he would never be allowed to return to his superiors. Accidents and ambushes happened all the time. That would take care of the sneaky Al Qaeda pig, and keep Albani in the clear. It was rapidly becoming apparent that Al Muffadi had ulterior motives in his mission to negotiate an agreement with the Taliban Generals.

"Find him!" Albani growled out the words, a burning cigarette clenched between two gold teeth. Six heavily armed soldiers saluted and took off at a run. "And check the Club. Bring me

198

Colonel Fashiam immediately." Albani's face was red with anger and his fist shook at the guards that remained.

The last three soldiers headed for the Club as fast as they could. It was not safe to be around their General when he was furious.

Albani stomped toward the armory. He wasn't sure what was going on, but something was up, and he wanted to be ready. He hadn't lived as long as this without being prepared for surprises.

The armory held a huge cache of weapons and resembled Q's workshop right out of a James Bond movie. Stainless steel tables and drawers held all manner of handguns and assault rifles. Ammunition was displayed in organized racks for easy access. The light blared cold and white reflecting off of the highly polished work benches, contrasting with the deadly black weapons hanging from their specially designed brackets. Highly organized and efficient, Albani's armory was as antiseptic and useable as the death its tools provided.

Quickly, the General selected a Belgian made FN Five-Seven and grabbed five extra mags. Each magazine held 20 rounds. It was a handy and deadly little tool. Albani fastened the holster and weapon to his side, then shoved the mags into his pants pockets. Grabbing an FN P90 from the wall along with two spare magazines, Albani scrambled into a bulletproof vest, packed the mags in the vest's appropriate holders and strapped an Afghani tribal long knife resembling a machete to his right leg.

He was ready.

Cocking an ear, he heard a commotion in the passageway outside the armory.

Colonel Fashiam and the soldiers appeared out of the gloom as Albani exited the armory looking like a walking arsenal. "Dead son of goat's dung, where is Al Muffadi? You were supposed to keep track of the Al Qaeda spy. Is there nothing you can do right?" Albani kicked the Colonel in the groin, smashing the man's head with the butt of his P90. Fashiam crumpled to the ground with a grunt. "Take this incompetent piece of shit from my sight, before I decide to end his pitiful life. Find me Mustaffa Al Muffadi." Albani spun and headed for his office. "Bring my personal Guard to my quarters, immediately."

Two soldiers picked up the injured Colonel and dragged him

towards the armory. Fashiam was popular with his men, for obvious reasons, so it was in their best interest to treat him with respect, even if their General did not. Life was tenuous in the terrorist business and protecting your supplier's back was important. Gingerly laying him out on a bench, they left Fashiam to his pain and ran back to the Club in search of the General's Guard. Fashiam may have been a soldier's man but Albani was God. What Albani wanted, Albani got, and as quickly as was humanly possible.

*****

Natalia hit the door first, quickly followed by the rest of the squad members. "We have about ten minutes before we will be missed and someone will come looking. Don't bother to change. Just get your stuff and let's mov…" A pair of hot wet lips interrupted her directions. Yuri enveloped her in a bear hug, plastering wet kisses across her face and mouth.

"God, I missed you. I need your taste. I need your scent. I…"

Natalia cut him off. "Yuri, we have to move. Control. You must wait." She pushed at his chest, trying to escape his capturing arms, but found herself restrained in his hot embrace.

"I can't wait. My body is on fire. I need you now. It's like I have to have you or I will explode." The other vamps with their enhanced hearing easily caught his whispered words.

Monique whistled softly.

MorningStar simply ignored the couple and quickly set to arranging her equipment in a bag. Pulling and twisting the hidden pockets, she transformed the tribal carpetbag into a versatile backpack. Elizabetta was already hefting her transformed pack onto her back.

Susannah stood in the middle of the room observing in disgust. "I'd tell you two lovebirds to get a room, but we are in a bit of a hurry here, Nat. Yuri, get it?"

With a dark look from their leader, the sarcastic teenager flew into high gear stuffing her backpack and changing into a pair of tennis shoes. "Gotta love my Asics Gels for days when you just seem to be on the run. Did I ever mention, I used to do track in high school? Never thought all that practice would come in handy

200

when I became an undercover vampire operative for a secret government agency. Okay, I'm ready."

Susannah straightened, did a little sexy pose and headed for the door. "Last one out's a rotten vampire operative for a secret government agency."

"Susannah, wait. Albani's men are searching the tunnels for some missing Al Qaeda guy." Yuri's ardor cooled quickly, as he released Natalia and was suddenly all business. "They think he has tried to leave the stronghold. I think they will be heading to the entrance. We should go out another way."

"There is no other way, Yuri." Elizabetta's intel knew of no alternative exit.

"Da, da, there is. I was brought in that way. It's in an ancient dry well at the end of the guard's quarters. It has steps to the surface above. It's a long climb, but clear and safe. Albani's common troops use it to see their families in the village." Yuri pointed the way out on the map as the others crowded around.

The judgment call up to Elizabetta, she immediately changed the plan in favor of Yuri's recommendation. Depressing the communication device in her neck, she spoke, "Babysitters, V-1. It's time to come home. Party's over." They waited for a response, but heard only silence. She repeated the code sequence again with no response. "Let's go. We can't wait. Single file. Nat, you're point. Let's hope we are going in the opposite direction of Albani and his guards. If not, feel free to use that wonderful talent of yours."

The Vamp Squad, plus one, slipped through the tunnels heading toward the alternate exit. Unfortunately, it took them through the quarters of the most ruthless guards in the stronghold. Silently they moved on feather light steps, quickly transiting the clear passageways. To their advantage, most of the guards were searching for the lost Al Qaeda rep near the entrance, or celebrating at the Club. For a while luck seemed to be with them, but it was too good to be true.

Natalia pulled up short and cautioned the rest behind her to silence. Ahead, four guards sat around a circular table hooting and hollering as they played a card game called Teka. The guards, totally engrossed in the plain-trick game, yelled their bids between partners. Seated in the middle of what looked to be a sort of lounge, the men laughed and threw fake punches at each other, oblivious to the oncoming threat.

Nat, can you focus their attention totally on the game so we can pass undetected? I don't want to start anything that will draw attention to us. So far we have been lucky, and any disturbance has been associated with the Al Qaeda rep. I'd like to keep it that way. If we can set the stage to pit the Taliban and Al Qaeda against each other with this operation, it'll be icing on the cake for Maddox. It won't look bad on our resume either. Elizabetta hoped the group would be able to sneak by and continue on without sending up an alarm. These men would all be dead soon in any event.

No problema, mahn. Natalia was in rare form with Yuri holding one hand, and Susannah following close on the handsome officer's heels. Natalia closed her eyes for a second, concentrating on compelling the minds of the card players. Small beads of sweat appeared on her forehead, the strain of compelling clear in her pinched features. As quickly as the symptoms appeared, they vanished. Nat straightened and motioned the group forward. *Walk in single file close to the wall. Try not to touch anything or make noise.*

Her efforts were successful. Tiptoeing across the lounge unnoticed, the group entered a passageway that would take them to the base of the dry well that was their new escape route. Each holding their breath as they moved behind the players, Yuri clamped a hand over Susannah's mouth to squelch a scream at one point as a burly guard threw his cards across the table and flew at his partner. The brawl that ensued effectively covered any noise the teen may have made.

Mon dieu. We could have strolled right through without Nat's talent spécial. Those hommes stupides could not hear a bomb exploding in the next room. Monique's nose twitched as she waved away any concern with a flip of her dainty hand. *Let us be on our way. I definitely need a hot shower and a full mani-peddi. Merde!*

We are not out of danger yet. Yuri, you are sure this is the right way to go? Elizabetta was moving the group as fast as she could, fearing at any moment they would be discovered and forced to fight. A creeping feeling slid up and down her back at every little noise. Her nerves were doing a Tango across her neck and shoulders and her senses screamed under the stress of constant alert.

"Da, da, da. It is the way I came to this house of hell. Soon we will find stairs, then two more tunnels and you will see light from the well." Yuri was confident in his details. "You have no idea how many times I have, in my mind, escaped this way. Steps spiral leading up the well wall and to the village above. Hurry. General Albani is not a stupid man. When he does not find Al Muffadi he will come to the well. It is his way, to never give up. Always he pursues, tenacious like a dog. A mad dog."

Move ladies! Elizabetta's orders were unnecessary. No one wanted to be caught underground as billions of tons of rock came down around their heads.

Just as Elizabetta's urging settled into the minds of each Squad member, all but Yuri received an incoming massage. "Babysitters to VS. Daddy's waiting up. ETA?"

Elizabetta quickly whispered in response as they moved up the last set of stone steps. "Babysitters, V-1. Moving the party upstairs. Unexpected party favor. We'll call mom when we need a ride."

A silvery light appeared ahead marking the location of their exit. A lone guard dozed, sitting against the bottom step. Soft snores disturbed the dusty stones encasing the dry pit, as the young guard snoozed at his post. Silently stepping ahead of Natalia, Yuri dashed the few feet ahead, grasped the young man's head firmly in his strong arms and twisted sharply. A sickening crunch signaled the end of life for one man who chose the wrong path, or, more correctly, the wrong well. Yuri deftly checked the soldier's gun, slung the AK-47 over his shoulder like it belonged there and eyed the ancient stairs. All business now, the Russian Captain signaled the waiting group.

Was that necessary? Elizabetta was surprised at how easily Yuri killed the young man. No thought, just a silent attack, and a quick snap. Alive, then dead. The sleeping man did not even know he died.

Ah, fearless leader, they're all dead men as soon as we hit the top of these stairs. Susannah sarcastically pointed out the obvious, then impulsively attacked the stairs as if they were some new form of stair master in a posh athletic club. *Don't ya just love the moon when it shines down an ancient well to light the way home?*

No guards at the top as far as I can sense. Let's go. Natalia was right behind Susannah, followed closely by the rest of the group. *The less time I spend underground the better.*

I lived for several hundred years in caves. Stone and earth are comforting, natural. MorningStar rarely offered her opinion. In fact, the native woman rarely spoke at all so it was no surprise that her comment drew a gasp from Monique and stares from the others. *The ancient stones we climb have seen many things in their time. They sing of history, of pain and happiness. Though they taste of water, their true strength is hidden in the dust of ages.* She caressed the stones as she climbed, occasionally pressing her cheek to the wall and closing her eyes. MorningStar smiled. *Ah, a song of the ages, beautiful and primitive.*

Well, Kanza girl, we're gonna blow your rock band all to hell, and bury the cockroaches that live inside. Like the Orkin Man on steroids. Pow. Gone. I'm big time down with that. Natalia smiled to herself watching as Susannah kept her mental monolog moving as she crept up the last few stairs. Their vampire senses could tell them if a guard waited above, but nothing was infallible, and caution was the better part of survival. Yuri squeezed Natalia's hand and silently passed Susannah, motioning the girl to wait while he checked the surface. *Men! They always think they are so tough. Hey Ruskie, I am immortal too, ya know.*

Pipe down Susannah. When was the last time you qualified as an expert in hand-to-hand combat? Or crawled out of a well? Patience, malinki devoch-ka. Natalia patted Susannah on the head, like a parent would pat a little girl.

Susannah stuck her tongue out at Natalia, however, common sense prevailed this time. Susannah kept silent and let Yuri go first.

*****

It was several minutes before Colonel Fashiam could sit up without being overcome by nausea. His testicles ached with a fierce pain and he could not feel the fingers of his left hand. Blood dribbled down the back of his neck from the scalp wound Albani had so deftly delivered, with the butt of his gun.

Life was so unfair. He tried to satisfy the General's expectations, but nothing would please the mad man. It was not his fault the Al Qaeda spy escaped. Albani's own Guard was in charge of watching over the man. It was not his fault his men guarded the visiting Generals in their reverie. They were over burdened in the last few weeks, so why not combine work and pleasure? And the women, ah the women. Fashiam's groin tightened with excruciating pain, as he recalled the dancers and their 'special services'. The Colonel rubbed his crotch delicately, decrying the entertainment he was missing at the Club. Damn, he would miss the last and most special dances.

His life could be so unfair.

He tested his legs and stood up carefully, thinking about the Al Qaeda rep. What was he be looking for?

Fashiam considered himself intelligent and devious, or he was sure he wouldn't have been selected as Albani's right hand man. This was his opportunity to make up for the last two days, and prove himself to Albani once and for all. The General and his men had gone chasing after the spy to the entrance of the stronghold. In the same situation, Fashiam would not have done so and was sure the Al Qaeda slime would not go where he could be so easily found. There were two other ways to enter and exit the stronghold that were not commonly known, but if the Al Qaeda pig was sneaking around he could easily stumble on one of the alternate exits.

The easiest to accidentally find would be the old well stairs. It was guarded by only one man. It was supposed to be secret, known only to the families above and the men within, but then again, money could buy anything or anyone. Collecting a few necessities, the Colonel limped deeper into the tunnel system heading for the well exit that he figured was not as secret as it was believed to be.

Within moments of ascending the last set of stairs before the well exit, a vile smile lit the colonel's features. The spy *had* come this way. The evidence lie still and dead at the bottom of the steps that led to the surface. Fashiam leaned against the cold damp wall to catch his breath and massage his aching testicles.

Climbing these stairs will be very painful, he thought to himself, as he kicked the young soldier's body out of his way. A completely self-centered man, his thought for the dead youth at the bottom of the steps was somewhat harsh and coldly calculating. There would be one less soldier to pay at the end of the month. If the young soldier was stupid enough to let himself be killed, he did not deserve pay, or to live. Too bad, Fashiam sighed as he began the long climb to the surface. These days, he thought to himself as he climbed the ancient and worn steps, the younger the soldier, the quicker the end.

He was old and cagey.

He would survive.

Chapter 22

Of Life and Living

What is there of life and true living left?
An image, a touch, of love bereft?
Across the decades time flows anew,
From my blood to yours, genetics askew.
Evolution bides its time
Its message, one most sublime.

The Book of Mending, Human vs Vampire
Professor Demetri Valasnikoff, PhD
Moscow University, 1976

Elizabetta stood several meters from the old well through which they had just escaped. Beneath the eves of an abandoned block building she watched quietly, as the night gave way to day. The early morning rays of the sun had not yet crested the mountains to the east. The air was chilled and dry, smelling of acrid dust and animal dung. The rest of the squad, along with their new addition to the family, huddled inside the building feeling the effects of the oncoming dawn. Elizabetta said a quick prayer for any innocents that might die this day, then depressed the red button on the controller.

Fire in the hole, she mentally announced.

The destruction began as a soft rumbling and grew rapidly. Soon the ground was shaking violently as if it were shrugging off a terrible case of indigestion. Rumbling and shifting, several seconds passed before a cloud of dust and rocks belched from the well to rain down upon the buildings of the tiny village. Rocks and cinders pelted the tile roofs, sounding like a midwest hailstorm. Elizabetta ducked inside avoiding the onslaught.

"Wow. Ya think we may have overdone it a little?" Susannah sat on her rump, both palms flat on the ceramic tiles of the floor as she bounced up and down with the heaving ground. "Dad will definitely be proud," she shouted above the din.

Quiet little one. The villagers will be running around like crazy people outside. They probably think it is an earthquake. We do not want to be discovered, if possible. Elizabetta peered out of the window, watching. "Ca'cat! I do not believe this. Fashiam has escaped. He must have followed us."

"No way! Damn." Susannah scrambled across the floor and hunched behind her leader looking for the incredibly lucky Colonel.

Elizabetta shoved the girl's head below the window frame as the first rays of sun struck the wood. Temporarily blinded, Betta gasped, and sunk to the floor.

"No friggin' way." Grabbing a water pouch from her pack, Susannah pored the tepid liquid over Elizabetta's eyes and dabbed gently at the woman's reddened face. As quickly as the skin pinked, it healed.

"Way." growled Natalia. "He is mine. I have the right to take this piece of filth to meet his maker. He has offended me beyond reason." In rare form, Natalia's eyes glowed as brilliantly as the bright red rays of dawn.

Yuri pulled Natalia into his lap and kissed her soundly. "My little Siberian tigress, you fire my blood and tease my senses when you are like this. Let me take care of this scum. He has offended me more than any. Would that I had the time to make his death as slow and painful as the one he planned for me. You gave me this life so I could revenge my death. Let me have it, my love."

Again Yuri's lips claimed hers. His strong hands caressed her back, as he pulled her atop his body, matching length for length. His need was apparent, and Natalia moved seductively against his swollen and protruding manhood. Their kiss deepened and Yuri groaned into her mouth as his tongue delved, exploring the hidden secrets of her soul. She was helpless, once again, to resist Yuri's lips and sensual broadcasts.

Natalia returned like for like, her mind ablaze with need for this man. Licks of heat trailed up and down her spine as he plundered her mouth. Immediately, all thoughts of Fashiam were gone from her mind. The scent of Yuri was intoxicating, his taste, the sweet nectar of life itself. Her body spun out of control, undulating and rubbing, needing to fill herself with his potent essence. She slithered to straddle him, feeling his hardness press against her womanhood. Only his pants and a thin length of cloth separated them.

Now his mind too, held only delirious thoughts of this woman, her scent, the pressure welling in body and brain.

"Yo, hot stuff, let him go. Our business is not finished. Fat Fashiam ran behind the rickety shack down the path by the well. When I saw him running, he wasn't thinking about stealth. He was covering his head and racing like the devil was on his tail." Susannah crawled across the floor, avoiding the sunlit patches. "We have to find a better place to hole up. It's getting a little warm and bright in here." She fanned her face with both hands.

"Merde. The little one is correct. For once, I also believe we should find cover for our delicate skins until night. The burqa will work for direct light, but why take a chance?" Monique drew her legs up away from the encroaching sunlight streaming through the windows and various cracks in the walls. "Soon, this place will be too hot and light for me. There are too many holes in the roof. Going out now would be akin to suicide for Susannah and Yuri." Monique tucked her burqa tighter despite the heat.

From a quiet corner came the soft voice. "There is a way. Come." MorningStar bent to whisk dirt away from a rope handle in the floor near the corner in which she sat. Pulling the rope, a rough planked trap door opened revealing a small dark hole and ladder. "We must go below until it is dark once again. It is safe below this floor. The stones there are alone and in the dark."

Dragging her mind from Yuri, Natalia disengaged herself and crawled to the hole as MorningStar disappeared down the ladder. Her vampire vision showed the hole to be about ten feet deep with a small rickety ladder descending into the darkness.

"Kanza Girl, you amaze me. How did you find this? What's down there?" Nat's voice echoed slightly as she spoke.

I feel the earth. Come see for yourself. You will be pleased. MorningStar sent a mental smile along with her message.

Natalia looked at Yuri and wiggled her finger seductively. "It's dark and cool. Wanna?"

Yuri's response was a deep growl that sent shivers through the entire squad.

"Puh-leeze, Ruskie. Natalia, would you and Studley cool it for a while. I need food. I need sleep. I *don't* need horndog here, broadcasting his porno prone thoughts for public consumption."

Natalia shimmied down the ladder followed by her 'horndog' in hot steamy pursuit. As Natalia reached the last rung, she whistled softly. The ladder ended in a small hole. It connected to a tight passage through which she could see a large room complete with a couch and a small serviceable kitchen. Feeling the wall, she found a switch and pushed the button. Dim lights appeared with a buzzing sound, slowly brightening, as the sound faded. Light wasn't really a necessity with vamp vision, but it was comforting just the same. Natalia could hear MorningStar shuffling around in one of the rooms, obviously exploring their newfound accommodations. Natalia squeaked and jumped forward as Yuri found the floor with his feet, and her backside with his hands.

"Stop that… for right now." She giggled as his hands snaked around her waist, pulling her against his chest. She leaned into his embrace, bent backwards and planted a quick kiss on his chin. "Come on, let's see what's down this little yellow brick road."

"Yellow brick road? There are no yellow bricks here." Yuri's lips trailed a string of kisses down Natalia's neck and out her shoulder.

"It's an old American movie with witches and, ah, wizards and, a lion that talks." Natalia gasped as her body ignited.

She had to break this wild attraction. Distance. She needed distance. She pulled away, as his lips sought a lower target. "Let's look around before I melt right here." Natalia took Yuri by the hand pulling him toward the main room of the basement.

The others in the squad descended the ladder one at a time, each hoping the rope and stick structure would hold as they climbed. Several times the ladder groaned and swayed under the weight of its climber.

"Holy shit." Susannah dropped the last three feet, squeezing past Yuri and Natalia, skipping out into the main room as MorningStar appeared from a side door. "This is like the Hyatt after where we've been." Like a typical teenager, she ran across the floor straight to the kitchen area and popped open the ancient refrigerator.

"Phew! Bad idea." Slamming the door, Susannah flapped a

hand in front of her nose. "Who ever left this place, didn't bother to clean out the frig. It's growing green hairy aliens in there. A real junior high science project."

The rest of the squad walked around the room while Yuri pulled a blackout curtain across the opening, effectively closing off any light that could be seen from above.

"This will do, for now. " Elizabetta pronounced the verdict with relief.

"Wait, I shall return." He swept Natalia into his arms for a deep, wondrous kiss that set her mind spinning, then he was gone.

Scrambling up the ladder, Yuri stood on the top rung and brushed the dust and dirt on the above floor to cover their tracks if anyone should look. Always a tactician, and versed in the ways of covert operations, he carefully lowered the trap door and blew through the cracks letting the dust above settle naturally. They would be safe through the day and could relax in peace.

He was looking forward to a little peace.

Yuri appeared in the passageway and pulled the blackout curtain back into place before affecting a royal bow to the ladies. "We are set for the day. You are most welcome."

Monique and Susannah clapped as Natalia curtsied in the fashion of a court attendee. Yuri appeared next to her in a vamp-flash, taking her hand to plant a solicitous kiss on her upturned palm. "Moi-ya me-loch-ka, my love."

The mood light now, Yuri pulled Natalia into his arms to swing her around the room in a loose interpretation of the Troika, an old Russian folk dance.

"Alright, enough play for now. We must rest and plan our egress. Fashiam escaped. We will have to deal with him at some point, and who knows how many others may have gotten out as well. The last thoughts I picked up told me General Albani was headed for the exit to catch the Al Qaeda spy. He may have escaped the blast as well. Our great plan seems to have gone to hell in a hand basket through no fault of our own."

Elizabetta depressed the com device in her neck. "Babysitters, V-1. Party's over, but some stragglers left behind. Time for sleep. You cooking dinner?" The pre-arranged code let Colonel Maddox and the support team know the Squad had accomplished their mission, were clear and safe. It also told them the squad suspected some had escaped.

The com implants buzzed. "Babysitters, V-1. Dinner for five on ice. Call mom when you need a ride."

Natalia glanced at the rest of the Squad who were looking directly at her after having heard the transmission. Dinner for five? Should she tell Maddox about Yuri now, or let it be a surprise? She knew the man did not like surprises, especially surprises that involved potential problems.

"V-1 out." Betta shrugged at the group as she responded, a frown marring her pretty features for a moment. Their fearless leader wasn't about to spill the goods before it was necessary.

"E-liz-a-betta! Ooh man, you're not going to tell him, are you?" Susannah was smirking. "Not that I blame you at all. I have to tell you, he is really gonna be pissed." She flounced onto the couch producing a small cloud of dust. The young vamp choked and coughed between laughing and shaking her head. MorningStar sat cross-legged on the edge of a worn Persian rug, tracing the patterns with her index finger.

Natalia was amused that everyone was avoiding the subject of Yuri. While she was not looking forward to breaking the news to the Colonel, she had done what she needed to in order to save her Russian Captain's life. She wasn't sorry; nor would she apologize.

Though it had never been a consideration in any of their scenarios, turning Yuri had been the only answer at the time. Natalia still did not know if she acted out of personal desire or because Yuri himself wanted it. Had she planted the thoughts in the dying Captain's head, without recognizing it? Yuri was adapting well to this new life, but what would happen when the mission was over? She had the option to stay with the Vamp Squad, but would the Americans accept Yuri as well? Would he want to go home with her to Vilyuchinsk, a place where his family and friends, human family and friends, still lived? Even though he was a vampire now, would he work for the Americans or consider it defecting?

She would not leave him in the world alone. So many questions and no answers, only avoiding the issue. Natalia sighed.

Yuri watched his woman.

She was his woman?

Of course she was his woman.

212

At the realization his groin tightened and a smile played across his lips. Something was going on in the pretty brunette head of hers. The wheels were turning, but he was not privy to the thoughts. "Natalia? Shto bu-eet? What is it?"

"Nee-chevo." Natalia smiled waving him off. "It is daylight and I grow tired. We should find a place to sleep. Soon you will not be able to stay awake." Natalia pulled away and busied herself searching the adjoining rooms.

The main room contained a couple of couches, one of which Susannah claimed and was on the verge of sleep herself. Down a short hall, one door lead to a small sleeping room. An alcove toward the end looked to have been an office or workroom of some kind. Now only a small table and stool sat against the far wooden wall. It was covered with old papers pinned haphazardly along the woodwork.

As Natalia returned to the main room, she heard Monique scoff. Leave it to Frenchy to have discovered the only reflective surface in the place.

In a cloudy mirror Monique studied her reflection, fussing with her hair. Vain to the end!

Elizabetta rubbed the back of her neck. "You all get some rest. I'll take the first watch at the entrance. " She moved to sit next to the blackout curtain and groaned heavily. It had been a long night.

Peering down a semi-dark passageway on the other side of the main room, Natalia spoke excitedly. "Elizabetta look." She quickly disappeared then reappeared with a wide smile on her dusty face. "There's a toilet in the bana-ya! And running water! Water's cold but clear. There's also a bedroom with a mattress, and a thick metal door at the end of the passageway back here. It's sealed and frankly I'm too tired to explore anyway. If nobody minds, Yuri and I will take the bedroom. Pretty nice digs actually." Natalia glanced seductively at the man who held her hand.

Searching for anything on which to focus besides Yuri, she remembered, "Our historical perspective from intel said often a teacher would live at the local schoolhouse. Accommodations were almost always in the basement to keep the rooms cool in the summer and warm in the winter. I'll bet the building above was a school." The country suffered such devastation by its own government, as well as the endless string of occupiers over many

213

years, not much was left in small villages like this one.

The longer the vamps remained awake, the more their strength faded. Monique perked up enough to castigate Natalia. "Va chéri! Why do you get the only bed here? I have slept on the floor with cockroaches, cleaned up after our little sister, danced for a hundred perverted soldiers, traversed tunnels stringing tons of explosives and have broken three fingernails. And you will not share the only available man around worth looking at. C'est injuste!" She hit the mirror on the wall, mumbling as it shattered in a million pieces. "Bah, seven years of bad luck. What is that next to what I have been through in the last forty-eight hours."

"Monique! Quiet! We are below the floor but sound travels. Share the couch with Susannah, but quietly. Natalia, you and Yuri can have the bed, but no noise. And I mean none. We are all tired. Everyone, get some rest. We'll be out of here tonight. Keep it together for another twelve hours. Please." Elizabetta was disappointed with Monique. It was difficult for a vampire, whose life revolved around sexual escapades to be in close proximity to a newly turned male. New males required large quantities of extreme TLC. Monique's nerves and hormones were wearing thin.

"Com'mere Frenchy. Don't worry about your nails. They will grow back before you know it. You can sleep with me and the dust bunnies." Susannah cooed, patting the couch next to her, sending up another mini cloud of dust.

Immediately Monique calmed. Natalia smiled to herself as Monique licked her lips and sauntered across the floor. Cuddling up with Susannah, the two women settled under a burqa to giggle and whisper before drifting off to sleep.

Natalia tugged Yuri toward their private but sparse room. A green army blanket lie folded on the foot of the mattress. Natalia shook the dust from the wool blanket and lay it down as a barrier between the filthy mat and the couple. She and Yuri lie down together, quietly spooning, simply enjoying the reassuring touch of their bodies, finally safe and together. Both were exhausted and in need of sleep, their desires muted for a time.

Natalia relaxed listening to the rhythmic breathing of the man who encircled her body, a protective arm across her waist cupping her breast. She felt secure and warm. For the first time in many years, Natalia considered what a truly loving relationship might be.

It was not something within her comprehension. Her sexual experience, before Yuri, had been brutal and emotionless. She had no idea how to develop a relationship with someone who was gentle and protective. She had eagerly given her body and been amazed at the lack of pain. In fact, sex with Yuri felt wonderfully good. But giving her heart? Even though there was this incredible and irresistible attraction to Yuri, she wondered about real love. Natalia loved Yuri from the day he was born, but with complete surety that a true relationship could never be. It was a safe kind of love. It was love from a distance with no threat. She could go anywhere with her own fantasies, as long as they were fantasies, but the real McCoy? That was a troubling thought. She said the word often enough and thought the word easily enough, but feel the word? Would she even know real love if it came in search of her?

How much of Yuri's reaction was the physical need of turning? How much was the beginning of love? Would he hate her for turning him after the mission was over and he had to live with his new life?

Yuri kissed her ear, sending little electrical sparks throughout her body, pushing exhaustion aside. She arched against him, feeling his length and hardness pressing her backside. Hot moist lips touched her neck just below the two tiny scars left by her sire's fangs so long ago. Natalia froze, terrifying memories flooding her mind. Fear invaded her soul and she could not breath.

"It is okay, my Dark Angel. Relax. I will never hurt you, moi-ya me-loch-ka." Yuri's tongue trailed a path from her ear to her collarbone.

Forcing her mind to let go of the old fear, slowly she relaxed in Yuri's arms. Incredibly titillating, Natalia moaned softly and threw up a psyche shield around the room, affording as much privacy as she could for them. Feeling she owed Yuri an explanation for her strange reaction to his ministrations, Natalia attempted to verbalize something that had been held deep inside for a century.

"Yuri, it is hard for me to trust. There was such pain and evil in my life. The evil is gone, buried with the devil that made me what I am, but the pain remains. It is difficult…" Natalia was at a loss for words. Her body heated, but her heart remained cold now that the real Yuri lie next to her. This was no longer a carefully designed fantasy kept within the confines of her own mind. It was a very frightening reality.

"Give me the pain and I will lock it deep within my heart. I will surround it with love. Then, when you reach for it, you will only touch love. No more hurt. Da? Open to me, Natalia. Share with me so I can understand." Yuri punctuated his words with whispered kisses, as he gently caressed her breasts.

"You can not know the depth of my pain, the loneliness, the isolation. I could never share such intimate agony." Tiny tears of blood pooled in the corner of her eyes. Natalia fought for control, pulling away from Yuri.

Yuri pulled her back, not allowing the separation she sought. "Moi-ya maleen-key dedush-ka, you learned so much yet so little in a century of life. Between two lovers is much sharing, the good and the bad. My babush-ka used to tell me that true love means never having to say you're sorry." Yuri slid his hand lower, tickling her naked abdomen with little sensual circles.

Natalia giggled at his touch as well as his silly comment. "Yuri, during that century I did get a television. Ali MacGraw was not your grandmother. I knew your grandmother, and she never would have quoted an American movie. I saw Love Story, Yuri Milassoviech." She swatted at his roving fingers.

Caught, his hand paused and he stiffened in an attempt to keep from laughing. "You can't blame me for trying, da? Besides, it's true. My parents survived much in their thirty-six years together because they truly love each other. My father is not an easy man to live with, and neither is my mother a simple partner. But their love is strong and they share all. All of my life, I have looked for a woman with whom I can have what my parents have. I believe I found her." Yuri tightened his hold, pulling Natalia closer, breathing his words softly against her ear. "And she is a vampire. But then, so am I. Nechevo, neh doo-my-you?"

Natalia twisted to face the man who had just spoken the words she never thought she would hear. Her arms escaped his hold and she reached to caress his beautiful face. Her lips sought his and she was rewarded with a soul-wrenching kiss that shook her to the core. Tongues entwining, Natalia couldn't release his mouth, wanting to kiss him until the end of time. She could not get enough of his taste, his feel, and his love.

Love.

Love?

He loved her. He did.

But could she trust him with her past? Would he still love her when he knew how she lived, and what she did to survive? He was a Romanov, and she was sworn to protect all Romanovs. Never in a million years did she imagine she would find herself in the live arms of one who talked of love and sharing their lives. She witnessed his birth and watched as he grew to manhood, and now she held him as a lover. The 'ick' factor was there again and boggled her mind a little less as her confused senses sought satisfaction. After all the contrived fantasies and wistful contemplations of a life she could never have, Natalia actually found herself lying in Yuri's arms! Fear bubbled up surrounding her heart and mind, building a wall between her and the man whose hands played her body so well.

Yuri stretched to see Natalia's face, looking deeply into her eyes. "Trust me Natalia, my love. Eternity is a long time to be alone and without love. If we are truly immortal, or close to it, I don't want to live forever without someone, without you. In fact, I don't want to live another minute without you."

Fear clenched its boney fingers around her troubled heart. She needed time to figure out what was happening to her. She played for time, stalling. "You have just begun a life that you do not even understand. Go slowly Yuri. You may find there are things that you cannot accept. We have time. Do not be in such a hurry to offer something you may regret later." Natalia could not look at the man who held her. "I am your creator, so it is no surprise you feel this way right now. You awakened and tasted my gifts, but there are other vampires you may find attractive. We, as a species, are not necessarily monogamous. The rules of human society do not apply to vampires, but we do have requirements to belong to a coven. These are all things you must learn and consider seriously in your new life. I do not want to confuse you in the beginning."

Yuri rolled to his back and stared into the darkness, contemplating the words his lover had spoken. He closed his eyes sighing long and deep. "Slowly? I do not need slowly." He rolled on his side taking Natalia back into his arms, cradling her once again. "But if it is what you need, I shall attempt to be... patient." Yuri kissed her cheek tenderly, and closed his eyes. "But can we still enjoy nash-a tee-ella? The feelings you awaken by just breathing test my limits and tease what little control I have. Odd, but I do not feel this with others now. In my past life I would have taken liberties with any woman worth looking at. Now I can only see your beauty shining with such light it blinds me to all others. This I do not understand."

Natalia smiled and snugged her bottom against his crotch, wiggling seductively. She could no more resist his body, than he could hers. Even more, she did not want to, as long as it was only her body. "I see nothing wrong with enjoying each others' bodies. But remember, you can make no noise!" Her hand snaked between them, unzipping his pants and massaging his hardening cock. He groaned and again Natalia giggled. "No noise, Captain. Where is that famous army discipline? Shhhh!" Twisting and stretching she hissed into his ear, nipping the lobe as she ran her tongue down his neck. Rewarded with another groan, Natalia continued to work her fanny against Yuri's hot body, slowly, grinding her ass cheeks in small circles.

Yuri buried his face in her hair and breathed deeply. She was maddeningly sensual, and he could not resist her teasing movements. Placing a hand flat against her stomach, he held her tight to him, feeling the electricity that flowed between them. He slid a hand between her dancing girdle and silky skin. Slipping lower, his fingers touched the soft curls above her sex. God she was an angel, his Dark Angel. An inch lower and he would feel her moist heat.

His hands had a mind of their own as one sought to fondle her full breasts, the other slipping between her nether lips to caress her swollen clit. He smiled against her cheek as she let out an unexpected gasp. "Shhhh! No noise me-lotch-ka."

He was torturing her. Yuri's fingers worked little circles around her most sensitive place causing jolts of pure ecstasy to envelope her entire body. She held his fingers tighter, wanting more pressure, more movement. She needed him to fill her in every way. Her breasts ached for more of his gentle touch. Her body screamed for release.

Yuri deepened the pressure once more. His fingers pulled

aside her costume to allow his cock access to the precious space where his fingers played. Together they began a slow, rhythmic assault on her senses. She was wet with anticipation, her fluids coating his fingers and manhood. Leisurely, he slid into her tight opening, holding her pressed to him, entering her with deliberate, measured movements. Natalia hissed and pressed back against him. Yuri denied her the hurried coupling she sought, opting instead to draw out his seduction. He strained to hold on to a shred of sanity, to go slowly, to tantalize and tease. Blood pulsed through his cock, causing little, almost painful jerks. Obviously his body did not want slow either.

Natalia pulled at Yuri's hand drawing it to her lips. She licked a finger, tasting herself on his skin. "Mmmm. I love to share." She twisted to run her tongue softly across his lips leaving her scent for him to taste.

Yuri licked his lips and growled deep in his chest. Pulling Natalia tighter, sinking himself into her as far as he could, he held his breath. On the brink of madness, he strove to control his movements, easing out and back in again. The ancient timbers that made up the bed frame on which they lay, creaked and strained with each movement. Yuri froze for half a second before he could contain himself no longer. Pounding into Natalia, Yuri hissed and groaned into the wadded shirt that served as his pillow.

Natalia moaned, her hand clamped over her mouth to stifle her cries of pleasure. Faster the bed creaked as Natalia felt her climax build. Like a whirling tornado, powerful and mind-blowing, the energy built, until she could no longer contain the strength of it. Attempting to muffle her cries of passion, Natalia clamped both hands over her lips and closed her eyes as tight as she could while her entire body exploded in a million pieces. She held Yuri deep within as her muscles clenched his shaft, contractions moving through her body with waves of incredible feeling.

Yuri tensed, his muscles flexing with the fight to maintain self-control. He realized, as he felt Natalia clench his cock, the fight would be lost within seconds. Wrapping her in his arms he drove into her one last time. Groaning deeply, he emptied his seed into the woman he had come to love above all others.

Unfortunately, his world shattered at the same exact moment as the bed frame.

Clutching each other and crashing to the floor, the couple, the mattress and their bedding hit the dirty tiles with a resounding noise that could not be mistaken. From the adjoining room came several hisses and one fit of giggles.

"Shhhhh! So that's your idea of no noise, Captain Milassoviech?" Natalia chuckled softly against his neck. "Breaking a creaky old bed?"

"Nyet, me-lotch-ka, I did not accomplish this feat alone." Yuri pulled her into the crook of his arm protectively. "So we sleep on the floor. At least now we don't have to worry about breaking the bed. Da?" Yuri could see the smile play across his love's face.

Rearranging a few broken pieces of wood and several lumps beneath them, Natalia settled in the crook of Yuri's arm, feeling his coolness and strength even in rest. Within minutes Natalia felt Yuri relax. His rhythmic breathing slowed and she knew he slept.

Tears trickled down her cheeks and soaked the blanket beneath her head with deep red stains. He was so wonderful, and handsome, and in love. Would she ever be able to return his feelings without thinking of her sire? Without feeling the brutality of her early years? Could she bury her past and begin again? This time with a clean heart? Would he understand? Would he want her? After he knew everything? Natalia thought of Vlad and Rivka, happily expecting a child, their love combined and sealed in a new human being. Would she ever share such closeness, such a love? She lie awake for several long minutes searching for answers that would not come.

Finally, exhaustion won and she dropped into a tense sleep.

*****

Natalia remained on her knees through the entire Divine Liturgy. It was freezing inside the Cathedral of Peter and Paul, but she was determined. Alexei lie in his royal bedchamber in the palace, and Father Grigori had been clear. Only through dedicated prayers would the Tsarevich survive his latest bout with the bleeding disease. So Natalia knelt on frozen knees, shivering on the ancient, icy stones of the old cathedral, praying for the boy who was like a brother to her. She remained in place and prayed throughout the day and, now long into the evening, all for the young Tsarevich's life… and for warmth.

At the tolling of the last bells, Natalia struggled to stand and found her legs would not oblige. Pulling herself up onto the oiled wooden pew to sit, she attempted to rub feeling back into her deadened limbs. Her cold, stiff fingers almost glowed white against the dark thick wool of her stockings. Her breath created small billows of steam that circled her elegantly styled chestnut curls. She tried to massage life back into her limbs that had been still on the frigid stones way too long. Hot flashes, like pins and needles, stabbed at the soles of her feet. Her joints screamed in cold agony. Whimpering, she tried once again to stand, wrapping the fur lined cape closer about her shoulders. Her thin court attire was beautifully designed in diaphanous drapes exposing her voluptuous décolleté. It did little to provide warmth in this coldest of Russian seasons.

Concentrating on the simple but painful task, Natalia, at first, did not notice the small group of noble women file into the cathedral. They were lead by the Dowager Duchess Slimova. However, their unseemly laughter immediately caught Natalia's attention, as she covered her mouth to hide an astonished gasp. Quietly, she slid to the floor and remained in secret, silently watching the most unseemly display. It would not bode well to draw the Dowager Duchess' eye. In fact, in the uncertain political climate of the day, it could well mean banishment to the steppes, or even death. While Natalia was no threat to the Dowager Duchess, her tranquil beauty and graceful composure won her the notice of the Tsar and endeared her to the Tsarevich. She and Alexei were now fast friends, allied against a tumultuous world the two sheltered children could not comprehend.

Palace rumors often flew about the Duchess and her practice of the sacrilegious rites of the Khlysty sect. Though Natalia always ignored palace small talk in favor of a young girl's play, it was commonly believed the Duchess could exert complete control over the members who practiced with her. Natalia had been warned about the iniquitous royal by her Aunt Anna Vyrubova, the Tsarina's best friend and confidant. When Aunt Anna first invited Natalia to court as a companion for the youngest Romanov children, she talked at length to her naive niece about avoiding the Duchess. Veiled in gentle terms, Aunt Anna explained the mystery behind Slimova's grooming methods. Anna also pointed out the unfortunate fate of girls who'd been caught in the black widow's web of power and control. Natalia lived in fear of the woman's disconcerting stare and brutish manner, and made sure she was never alone and unprotected around the Duchess. It had taken no more than a few days at court for Natalia to understand the seriousness behind her aunt's concerns.

In the darkened sanctuary Natalia held her breath, pulled her dark winter cape tightly about her and slid its voluminous hood over her chestnut curls, hiding the long glorious hair that had become her trademark. Crouching upon the floor between pews, she watched the group of women slowly move toward the gilded altar room doors. Attempting to become lost within the shadowy recesses of the cathedral, Natalia pressed herself lower, ignoring the bitter cold floor, as she hid frozen in place.

Clad in sinuous white robes, the women moved as if in a trance. Dowager Duchess Slimova danced and twirled as the silky robe twisted about her rotund figure, tangling around her bare legs and feet. The others followed, robes and limbs moving to some mysterious canon playing within their minds. The Dowager Duchess' daughter, Katarina Limnovich reveled in the imaginary beat, spinning like a Whirling Dervish in ecstasy. As the girl spun, Natalia caught fleeting glimpses of pale skin and alabaster breasts, nipples erect in the chilly air. It was the dead of Russian winter and these women danced without slippers and wore only thin pieces of cloth over their naked bodies! Natalia's naked fingers held her cape in a painful grip, aching in the cold.

From deep in the dark shadows of the rotunda, behind the iconostasis of the cathedral, Father Grigori appeared. Standing before the huge golden doors, naked to the waist, arms stretched in a parody of Jesus' crucifixion, he watched the procession approach. The women hissed and screamed, running to kneel and supplicate themselves in obeisance before the priest. Natalia heard his deep baritone resonate within the cathedral as Slimova tore at her robe, revealing her obese torso, breasts hanging huge and pendulous. Slimova knelt directly in front of the priest as he unwound a coarse, knotted rope that held his peasant pants about his hips. Stunned, Natalia peered above the pew behind which she hid and watched her beloved priest as the decadent scene played out before her. Framed by the huge, ornate doors depicting The Last Supper, Father Grigori's pants slid down naked legs as Duchess Slimova took his free, engorged cock into her mouth, slurping and sucking with the abandon of a wanton whore. Face contorting in illicit pleasure, Father Grigori shouted out scriptures, as he lashed the back of the Duchess, again and again. The women circled closer stroking the priest, licking and kissing the man, fondling every part of his body within reach. As the scene continued, the momentum grew amazingly unfettered by the conventions of God's house.

Shocked to her very core, Natalia watched in abject horror as Katarina drew her robe above her waist and wrapped her thighs about the priest's leg, humping him like a street dog in heat. Her hands cupped his dangling balls, working the skin with less than tender attention. The more intimate and violently exhilarating the ministrations, the more mystical and thunderous the priest's ranting became. Soon the sanctuary and altar room echoed with the screams of the women and Father Grigori's mad recitation of Orthodox scriptures.

Unaware how deeply she had become enthralled in the act she was witnessing, Natalia's head swam and her vision blurred. Excitement built within her core, as if she was an intimate part of the orgy in the sanctuary. Trying to focus on the huge, golden relief of Jesus and his disciples that covered the altar room doors, her eyes remained locked on the scene before her. She could not seem to look away.

The rope struck *her* back.

Her mouth watered, tasting the priest along with the other women.

His hand slid beneath *her* bodice, as she touched her own pebble hard nipples.

Licks of fire flicked throughout *her* body igniting her mind with exciting and forbidden fantasies her naive mind did not understand.

The hood covering her head fell, exposing her hair as she rose and moved forward, inexplicably compelled toward the insanity before her. As she approached the altar room doors she could see the women tearing at their clothing, gouging hunks of skin from their bodies. The Dowager Duchess lie in a heap at Father Grigori's feet, her massive shoulders and corpulent torso bled freely where

223

the rope whip kissed her fleshy body too many times. Her daughter, taking the place of the unconscious Duchess, moaned and rocked, burying the priest's engorged shaft deep in her throat, a masculine, bejeweled hand grasping his red, swollen testicles, as the girl worked to take the Priest to some higher level.

Natalia stood, paralyzed by the scene's astounding display of violence and sexuality in the cathedral of The Lord. This was wrong. It flew in the face of everything she knew to be righteous and virtuous. Her mind screamed. The desires coursing through her body would not cease their assault on her senses. She was compelled by their complete control. She could do naught but watch the horror before her unfold in its decadent glory. The frenzy of the group continued to build, and Natalia thought she would die for release of... release of something unknown and totally sensual.

At once, the women screamed in unison and Natalia felt an electrifying energy pulse through her, like an explosion of incredible, all-consuming heat. Then, there was nothing. Floating as if in a void, all was black emptiness until she felt the icy stones of the floor touch her cheek.

For some time she was aware of the cold, so cold. Natalia could just make out a voice seemingly far away, but so close. "So Father, what do we do with this new little convert?" Natalia recognized the Duchess' voice.

"Father Grigori?" Natalia rasped through stiff, frozen lips. "Father?"

He was her priest.

He would help her.

Shivers wracked her body and her limbs would not obey. It must be the cold. She was becoming hypothermic and could do nothing to move, to help herself.

"Yes, my child?" The priest's familiar baritone whispered seductively near her ear and she felt his hot breath on her cheek.

"Father, help me. I can't open my eyes." Her voice was the embodiment of fear. Now the shivers came from more than just the cold. A hand passed over her face and slowly she lifted her stiff lids. Soft candlelight illuminated the faces surrounding her.

The Duchess stood fully dressed next to the priest, now completely clad in the robes of his office. Katarina appeared at the end of the altar upon which Natalia lay. The sneer on her face was startling. Small fangs protruded from her pouting red lips.

"Maybe she should be my companion, mother." Katarina whined. "I never get to have any fun. Alexei's going to die anyway." The girl's smile widened and a look of pure hunger passed swiftly across her twisted features, as she leaned closer.

"No daughter, not this one. I think the good Father can take care of our little Natalia." The Duchess bowed slightly, jerked her daughter by the hand and quietly departed leaving Natalia alone with the priest.

"Ah, devoted, innocent, little Natalia. What shall we do with you, my dear?" The priest circled the altar as he ran his hands across Natalia's body.

She fought the feelings his action evoked but could not deny the sensations seeping into the juncture between her legs. A soft moan escaped her lips as she squeezed her eyes shut once more, willing herself to lie still. "Please, don't. I can't… please Father."

"I love to hear a virgin's pleading voice. Do it again, Natalia. Beg me." Father Grigori's lips touched her throat delicately. She heard the long intake of breath, as if he delighted in her scent. His lips traced a line down her throat to the apex of her cleavage. "Beg for it, Natalia. Beg." He nipped at her breasts through the thin cloth that covered her bodice. "I want to hear it."

"No, Father. It's wrong. Let me go. Please." Quivering lips rasped the breathy words. "I cannot." Excitement impregnated fear as Natalia fought the feelings that arose, provoking tiny muscle movements she had never been aware of before. Her mind flashed to the erotic scene she witnessed just before fainting. "I only wanted to pray for Alexei, Father. I didn't mean to watch. I swear to God, I didn't mean to be here."

The priest's smile drove fear deep into Natalia's soul. "Ah Natalia, there is nothing wrong with watching, child. In this way you learn. And what is it you learned, little one?"

Natalia closed her eyes, squeezing her lids as tight as she could.

"Open your eyes. Look at me." The priest's voice was once again strangely compelling and Natalia could only obey his command.

Candlelight flickered, its tiny flames dancing in the black of the priest's eyes. Held by some dark power, Natalia lie immobile, watching in abject fear as the priest licked his lips and slid a ruby encrusted, sacrificial dagger between her breasts, slicing the front of her gown. The ripping sound grated in her ears but her body felt tingly and tight, as if on the verge of something wondrous and secret. She was confused and frightened; how could the mind know one thing and the body feel another? Her thoughts roared with innocent bewilderment and she could not breathe as the priest slide the knife lower. Her clothing came away at the touch of the blade, leaving her exposed and self-conscious. Twisting and straining, Natalia finally understood the reason she could not move.

Ropes restrained her arms and legs. She felt the rough fibers cut into her wrists and ankles, multiplying the sensations that coursed through her body. She felt moisture form where there should be none, and clenched her legs as much as the ropes would allow. No dark power worked here, just the conventions of an evil man and the riotous feelings of an untried girl. Natalia knew her religion warned about these feelings in the sacred scriptures.

Natalia knew a little of the happenings between a man and a woman, but she was no woman and he was certainly no ordinary man. Her fourteenth birthday had just passed, and he was her priest. She was an innocent and knew nothing except that she would be damned to hell for the things she was feeling and thinking. What was happening to her? Hands felt for her pert nipples, squeezing with delicious, forbidden pleasure.

Natalia watched through hooded lids as the priest devoured her body with his gaze. At once she knew he would have her. She could not resist his touch as she twisted and moaned, inciting the priest's manhood to pound and throb, rhythmically moving the cloth of his robe. Against her own will she begged for his touch, his taste, begged to assuage his need. God would damn her for this act, but it no longer mattered. An irresistible desire burned within her mind and body, spurring her on. From deep within amber eyes, a fire began to burn as red full lips whimpered and moaned.

With practiced ease, the priest slipped from his vestments, grazing the edge of the altar with his erection. At the sharp intake of his breath, Natalia's eyes flew open and locked on the man she thought served only God.

The priest stood before her, naked. Natalia had never seen a naked man before this night. Half curious, but frightened beyond words, she struggled with her bonds. This was not right. This had to end. The rope holding her wrists was soaked with blood, *her* lifeblood, but still she struggled wildly, thrashing, secured to the altar. Her scream split the silence of the cathedral and was quickly stifled by a cold set of wet lips. Natalia choked against the tongue that invaded her mouth. The priest climbed upon the altar, crawling to straddle her and pressed his body to hers, grinding his engorged erection against her as he ravaged her mouth.

Natalia could not breathe.

She was dying.

Pain shot from her hips through her back and straight to her brain, paralyzing her limbs once again. The priest forced himself between her legs. Her second scream was muffled by his assaulting mouth. She tasted blood and felt the priest's excitement grow, wrapping around her mind like a rushing tide, drowning independent thought. She was carried along on a wave of pure ecstasy that lapped at her will and ate away what fears were left to her. Slowly fear receded into a misty haze mired in overpowering sensuality. She felt probing pressure between her legs and lie, helpless to stop the assault, opening to the shaft that pressed against her most private place. Panic rose in her throat, momentarily blocking the priest's compelling control of her mind. She had lost command of her own body. Instead, it responded to the priest's manipulations as if she were a puppet in some macabre play. With one swift thrust, he entered her. Pain exploded in her body and still she could not move. Lying, tied to the altar, the priest rutted within her.

Helpless, tears flowed freely from her eyes. Her lungs cried for air crushed from her chest. She could do naught but survive this horrid encounter then hide her shame from the world. If anyone found out, she would surely be blamed for allowing this, not the crazed priest who rammed his shaft into her, taking her innocence, her virginity and her future.

Little did Natalia know this was only the beginning of her nightmare.

For an eternity, she lie supine, a raw, bleeding receptacle for the mad priest's rock hard cock. When she thought she could endure such brutality no longer, the torture ended as the priest rasped and collapsed on her bruised and battered body. He lie there, crushing the life from her, inch-by-inch, still hard within her bloody, aching sex. The silent tears continued to flow as Natalia prayed, not for Alexei now, but for herself, for death.

Connected both physically and mentally Natalia felt him forcing his way into her mind, ensuring she shared the height of sexual satisfaction he had just experienced, despite her pain. He raped her body and now would rape her mind and soul. Natalia tried to scream but what issued forth from swollen lips was but a tiny mew.

The priest she'd once trusted, shifted atop her. Just when she dared hope he would slip from her body and leave her to die, a pressure throbbed deep in her brain. Terrified yet sickly fascinated, Natalia felt the first wave of thought wash across her mind: *my luscious little toy. How blessed I am to have found you.'* She recoiled, but just as his physical body had forced hers, so did a flood of hot thoughts and feelings Natalia knew were his alone. The transmitted waves of wild sexual satisfaction overwhelmed her and she tried to scream, but the invasion continued cutting off her pleas for help. The rape of her body had been horrible to endure, but the rape of her mind was so much worse.

Sharing this sick mental connection, she felt his perverted joy. Her mind wrapped around a truth too frightening to evoke complete comprehension. Having found his new plaything, Natalia knew he would never let her go. In the breadth of a heartbeat, she understood somewhere in her innocent mind, his all-consuming need to have her again, and again would never end. He would continue for the rest of his despicable life.

She was without hope. After all, how many times could one man be damned to hell for what he did to her?

Still hard and ensconced within her, she felt Father Grigori shift his weight. Her eyes flew open as his lips nipped the skin of her neck in a burning caress. Licking the tiny trickle of blood his kiss produced, he pulled back to see her expression. Fear replaced revulsion as she looked into blood red eyes and saw the man above her for what he truly was: a hideous monster of Gypsy folk tales. Still held captive, she lie frozen in time like a stone statue, as Father Grigori Yefimovich Rasputin sank his fangs into her soft young neck, and drew what remained of her human life to him.

*****

Natalia woke fighting for her life. She punched and kicked the monster that clenched her neck with his fangs. A strong hand covered her mouth, smothering the cries that struggled to escape.

"Natalia, wake up. Shhhh! It's okay, me-lotch-ka. You are safe in my arms, calm yourself." Yuri's lips breathed the soft words on deaf ears. A solid knee caught him in the groin and he was forced to let go of the wildcat in his arms.

In a flash Natalia was on her feet, backed against the far wall, panting like a cornered animal. Her eyes blood red, her fangs extended, Natalia crouched growling and hissing.

"Ah, pa-zhal-sta, Natalia, can you not aim for something besides my testicles? I just got them back, woman. Do you not understand what it is like for a man?" Yuri groaned again, curling on his side, one hand massaging his aching balls, the other fending off the attack that was sure to follow.

Natalia shook her head vehemently trying to extricate herself from the clinging nightmare, and make sense of the voice she heard through the fog of fear. As her heart slowed to a racing pace and fangs withdrew, her eyes cleared and she saw Yuri a few feet away, huddled on the floor waving off some mysterious attacker. Quickly she scanned the room. They were alone. Confusion wrapped around her mind. What just happened?

"Yuri? What?" Natalia crept closer to the quietly groaning man. She tentatively touched his outstretched hand, entwining her fingers with his.

Yuri rolled to his back and winced. "You either woke up extremely mad at me and decided to perpetrate the most intimate punishment you could think of. Or, you had a bad dream and I was in the wrong place at the wrongest of times. I am hoping it was the latter." Yuri propped himself on one elbow, still rubbing his groin. "Is that a word? Wrongest?"

Natalia collapsed on the blanket burying her head in her hands. "It happens. I dream of the night I was turned. It was horrible, and I have never been able to purge the nightmare from my mind. I am so sorry, Yuri." Blood tears seeped through tight white knuckles and dropped softly onto Yuri's arm. Emotions out of control, it seemed, after years of no tears at all, they now flowed with irritating regularity.

Yuri pulled Natalia into his arms, cradling her like a small child despite her tears. "Cry, my love. Let the agony go with your tears. You are here in my arms and I will never let you go. I may take to wearing a cup to bed, after we make passionate love, that is, but we will get through this together. Me-lotch-ka, listen to my words. Rasputin is gone, and I am here." He tightened his arms and rocked Natalia, planting small tender kisses across her brow.

"But I hurt you. I can't be trusted, even in sleep. Oh God, Yuri. You must think me horrible." Her tears flooded his shirt turning the dark fabric a deeper color and still he held her.

"I think you are the most beautiful woman who has ever destroyed the front of my shirt. Do not be ridiculous, Natalia. It was a bad dream, nothing more. Let me take this dream from your mind and replace it with enough love to fill those dark places that seem to haunt you so. Give me your heart and let me guard it forever, and I promise I will never let anyone hurt you again." He softly kissed the tip of her aquiline nose.

"Yuri, you say such wonderful things." Natalia kissed his warm lips.

"I don't just say them, I mean each word with all the honor and strength of a true Romanov. Let me protect you, Natalia. Let me love you, me-lotch-ka." His lips covered her mouth. Yuri's kiss deepened and Natalia felt heat begin to build in her sex. Would it ever melt the ice that encased her heart? Rasputin's legacy seemed ever impenetrable.

Natalia could not resist Yuri's touch and soon her mind, if not her heart, was engulfed in a passionate fire that slowly melted away her chilling fear.

Chapter 23

This Thing

This vampire thing I find irresistible.
I feel the power of centuries mystical.
In my cells the strength abounds.
But what of my humanity? Lost or found?

Diary of a Mad Vampire
Kelly Petrokoff
Oxford University, 2005

Colonel Fashiam ran for his life. Rocks, dirt and pieces of splintered wood rained down on his head as he ran. Deaf from the explosion he barely escaped, Fashiam watched the villagers chasing each other, their mouths open, obviously screaming. No sound reached his neural pathways to be decoded by his rattled brain. Hardly aware of the continual ringing in his ears, the Colonel desperately sought cover, ducking into an open shop. His sidearm firmly clenched in his fist, he shoved the shopkeeper into a corner, screaming insults and threats. Quickly searching the small tin shop, he settled on a stool behind the worktable that served as a counter and a production area. He was safe and out of sight for the time being.

"Allah be praised. I am alive." Fashiam shouted, shaking his head and pounding his ears. Pointing his weapon at the frightened little shopkeeper, he continued to shout. "He is here. Have you seen him? A stranger? Tell me now."

The little man cowered and covered his face as if he could ward off a bullet with his bare hands. He mouthed an answer and crawled behind a large basket full of hammered tin cups.

"Fool. Answer me." Fashiam jumped up, lifting the little man by his robe and jamming the 9 mm into his mouth. "Speak."

The shopkeeper's lips moved. His mouth opened and closed.

231

Colonel Fashiam could see the man was talking but clearly no sound could be heard. Fashiam dropped the villager, kicking the man viciously across the dirt floor. Shaking his head, it finally dawned on the Colonel that the loud ringing was no longer noise from the explosion, but a result of damage to his ears. "Ahhhh!" He could not even hear the stream of foul oaths that issued from his own lips.

Fashiam fell to his knees batting at his head as if he could knock away whatever blocked the sound from his ears. No noise alerted him to the rapid departure of the shopkeeper as the man fled in a silent shower of flying tin silverware and dishes. Fashiam's head ached and his vision blurred. Dawn's brilliant sunlight stabbed at the pain in his head, multiplying it tenfold. He was alive, but this was not a good way to begin his day.

On the south side of the canyon below the cliffs that rose to the plain above, General Albani and his men had just reached the entrance to the stronghold when the massive explosion shook the cliffs. Stumbling, clutching at the sides of the cliff walls, the men fell to the ground and held on as the entire valley shook and rumbled. An enormous dust cloud spewed from the mouth of the cave entrance. Forced out by the power of the explosion, it covered the men with a film of desert grit, spitting small shards and gravel for hundreds of yards.

Hugging the rock walls and dodging falling stones, Albani screamed in frustration. "What the fuck is happening? This is obviously an Al Qaeda plot. That sneaky mother of camel dung will die!" Albani was beside himself, pounding at the rock and kicking up gravel clouds, spittle flying from his sneering lips.

The six guards who sat on the ground watching, held their tongues. Experience taught his men how unhealthy it could be to remain in close proximity to Albani when he was aggravated. It would mean death to laugh at the General's obvious temper tantrum.

"I will find this evil insect and tear his testicles from his body. He will never stand before Allah as a man. I will find his family, and they will die horribly before his eyes." The General was winding up for a complete blowout, and he was well armed.

"Get up you idiots. We must catch this pile of pig shit before he escapes." Albani waved at his guards with his pistol, ushering them down the narrow tract.

"General Albani, Sir?" The Sergeant asked timidly. "Sir, would we not be able to see this pile of pig shit from here? He could not be so far dawn the valley yet. Our surveillance teams would have radioed. He must still be in the stronghold. He is surely dead with the rest." The man paused, looking backward at the rock and dirt clogged entrance to the General's subterranean headquarters.

Albani studied the cave-in then scoured the valley with high-powered binoculars. "That is possible. If he did not come this direction then he may have gone to Hafsa Tokar. We must go to the village and search it. Quickly, before it is too late." Albani shifted his armaments to his back and set out at a jog.

No one spoke, but all followed closely on their General's heels.

Halfway down the valley, Albani and his contingent ducked into a well-camouflaged crevasse and began climbing the cliff with the assistance of rope ladders and several man-made platforms. None of the sentries Albani questioned, saw a man fitting Muffadi's description move through the canyon. The creaking wooden walkways and rope extensions made the way difficult and dangerous but saved the soldiers more than five miles of trudging through the hot valley. Terrorists, like snakes, could not have too many exits.

Orange licks of light played across the red stone as dawn illuminated the way, casting shadows that crawled among the outcroppings, hiding handholds and footsteps. The hemp rope rungs tangled around black boots, as the guards climbed. Gaining the summit, General Albani set out for Hafsa Tokar at a trot. He seemed to be able to run without tiring. Several of the guards paused to say a quick prayer for their safe delivery from the rock and rope climb, then followed their leader, running all-out to catch up. It would not do to fall behind.

Cresting a rise near the village, Albani's first sight drove sanity from his thoughts. Rage descended to smother all rationality as he aimed his pistol directly at his Colonel standing in the open in front of a small shop. Just as he pulled the trigger, Fashiam stepped into the shop.

"Damn that idiot! I shall kill him three times over, then feed his bones to the rats. He shall beg forgiveness from his mother for his miserable birth." The General was literally hopping up and down as he ranted. Clouds of dust billowed around his boots.

"Possibly the Colonel has followed the Al Qaeda spy and awaits our help to capture the man." One of the General's guards commented quietly, from behind another soldier. "Colonel Fashiam has always been loyal to the cause, and to you, Sir."

Albani spun and shot the man between the eyes, the soldier in front ducking at the last second. The young man dropped where he stood as his gaping compatriots looked on in horror. "Let us proceed. NOW!"

The General ran toward the village. This time, his men, maintained more than a safe distance behind him. As they gained the last rocky hill, it was clear the villagers were terrified and running scared about the streets. They were shouting something about an earthquake. The appearance of soldiers led by a madman, did little to allay their fears.

Albani ran straight toward the small shop where he had seen his second-in-command enter, just minutes before. His men remained outside, confused as to where to begin searching, but knowing better than to enter the shop.

Several of the small buildings were damaged or destroyed as a result of the explosion. The well entrance to the stronghold was clearly collapsed, completely filled with stone and debris.

The villagers noticed the soldiers' arrival and shied away from the elite guard denoted by the all black uniforms they wore. None of the elite guards had family in Hafsa Tokar. The General liked it that way. There was no one near to cloud their loyalty or give reason to disobey. As members of the General's personal guard, the men were highly trained killers, skilled terrorists, and expendable.

Albani appeared at the door of the shop dragging Colonel Fashiam who held his head while screaming platitudes. Thrown to the ground, Fashiam squinted into the sun, trying to make sense of what people were saying around him. He was at a loss to understand anything without his hearing. What he did know, was that he was in serious trouble, the kind that he might not survive. His General was hopping up and down obviously shouting something at him. The man's face was red as a beet and he spit as he shouted. His sidearm flapped around in the air as he pointed to the well, the cliffs and the village. Albani was definitely in a fit. Clearly the Al Qaeda spy had escaped, and the guards were in pursuit.

Fashiam's mind began to work, firing slowly on damaged cylinders. "General Albani, I came through the well entrance. The guard was dead so I continued up the stairs. I am sure Mustaffa Al Muffadi used this way to escape. As I gained the last step, something exploded." Fashiam shouted, still banging at his ears. "I can't hear. The explosion..." The Colonel shaded his eyes and looked up, directly into the barrel of the General's highly polished FN.

General Albani mouthed the words, over enunciating so the Colonel could read his lips. "You will die for this, idiot. But now we search. We must find the spy and kill him before he can escape." Albani motioned to the closest guard to help the Colonel up.

"He is your responsibility now. If you let him escape, I will personally make you wish your parents had abandoned you to the desert at birth. Now search the village. Find the spy." Albani stomped off to look at the rubble clogging the well.

The soldiers quickly organized themselves, a young pale guard held Fashiam's sleeve, guiding him as they moved. Ducking into the small shop, the guard produced a pad of paper and a pencil with a whittled tip. Handing it to the Colonel, the guard wrote, "What happened?"

"I do not know. I found the soldier at the well with a broken neck and knew the Al Qaeda spy had escaped. I thought I could catch him so I climbed the steps. As I got to the top, the whole place exploded and blew me out, or I too, would be dead. What happened down there? Who set the explosion? Where did you come from? How did you and the General get out? What about the rest? Are they safe? My head feels like my wife took an iron pot to it. I can only hear ringing. Ach." The Colonel was rambling as he continued to pound at his ears.

The guard quickly scribbled answers to Fashiam's string of questions. No one yet knows who set the explosion. Mustaffa Al Muffadi is the prime suspect. The guard was unsure if anyone else escaped the explosion. The visiting generals were obviously dead, as they were left to enjoy the scheduled entertainment of food and dancers at the Club. Those who escaped came up the cliff halfway down the valley. They did not find hide nor hair of Mustaffa Al Muffadi, and did not know where he went. They were only six strong.

The Colonel read the scribbled answers and, after processing the information more slowly than was usual for him, swore loud and long. "We will find this son-of-a-bitch and teach him the name of pain," Fashiam, still unaware he was yelling, shouted at the guards who all nodded in agreement. Pointing as he continued to shout orders, the Colonel split the guards into two groups and sent them in different directions to search. "Turn every rug. Look in every corner. Find that spy. Report back to me, as soon as you have found him. He must be here. Somewhere. There has not been enough time for him to escape. Do not fail or we shall find our lives in serious jeopardy."

Fashiam returned to the tin shop and sat down against a rolled rug. His head ached beyond reason and the continuous ringing in his ears would not stop. It was making him crazy, and he threw a basket of tin plates across the small shack. He and his men would have to find the Al Qaeda spy, or the Colonel knew their lives would be worthless. Over very quickly, but not painlessly. That he knew. General Albani was insane in pursuing the spy and would hound his men until he got what he sought. If his men did not provide what he wanted, they would die.

The Colonel sat contemplating his situation. Why did the Al Qaeda spy destroy the stronghold? He came to sign a pact to collaborate. Did the man discover Albani's stash? Had his true purpose been to destroy the strength of the freedom fighters all along? Fashiam's General had spent many years accumulating what Albani lovingly referred to as, his 'insurance policy.' It would be a pretty little feather in the cap of Al Qaeda's war, if Albani's wealth was found and usurped.

Few knew about the fortune upon which Hafsa Tokar sat. Many of the people of the village starved in the best of times while the terrorist stronghold beneath them prospered. The men lived in luxury and ate well. Albani made sure he footed the bill to keep his men happy and loyal. In the current political climate, a man's loyalty was usually for sale, so it benefited the highest bidder to keep the perks rolling in. And, rolling perks cost precious Euros on the open market.

So Colonel Fashiam was back to the question; why did the spy set the explosion? If he did find the stash, his actions buried it. Why didn't he just play out his role and leave, and then return with a force to take the stronghold? Could someone else have set the explosion? The only other possibility was a traitor, or the visiting troupe of dancers. Women who wore slips of silk and teased the men around them with undulating hips and sensuous lips, could not have accomplished such a thing.

The Colonel was sure of his men. It was inconceivable that a traitor existed within their ranks. "Puhhh! And stupid women know nothing about war," Fashiam scoffed to himself. He did not believe a group of dancers could have had anything to do with destroying a terrorist stronghold. Anyway, Teffas Hamza checked them out thoroughly before bringing them to the stronghold. They even carried their own small bags and nothing more. Fashiam banged at the sides of his head trying desperately to stem the distracting noise. The women were no factor in the explosion. Those sluts were good for dancing and fucking, nothing more.

General Albani's face appeared in the doorway of the shop, still bloated and red with anger. Fashiam struggled to his feet and stared at the General's lips, attempting to understand what the man was saying. The Colonel stumbled toward the doorway offering the pad of paper and pencil. Hopefully, his superior would take pity and leave him alive for a few more minutes.

General Albani snatched the paper and scratched out two words. SEARCH. NOW. Raising his gun directly at the Colonel's face, Albani's finger moved to squeeze the trigger. Colonel Fashiam ducked beneath the barrel and ran from the shop. He sprinted down the street catching up with two guards who wandered through the village, ducking in and out of buildings as they searched. He yelled at the men, "Anything?"

The Sergeant shook his head negatively and scratched in the dirt. "You are shouting."

"I am? I can not hear a thing except this damn ringing." The Colonel was back to banging on the side of his head.

Pointing around to all of the villagers picking up pieces of their lives, the Sergeant shrugged, indicating there was little to find. Buildings that stood tenuously on their own before the stronghold had been destroyed, now looked like they had existed in an active war zone. Almost all suffered damage in the aftermath of the explosion. Bricks and roofing lie strewn about. The villagers scurried around picking through the ruins, looking for whatever could be salvaged and used to rebuild. No one seemed to consider leaving or packing to moving on. One poor Afghani village was the same as the next, just poor. They would simply pick up and rebuild their hovels.

A lone woman clad from head to toe in a black burqa crept to the edge of the dry well that served as an entry to the stronghold for more than a hundred years. Peering over the edge, she studied the rubble-clogged hole, then shook her covered head and turned away. With slow measured steps she returned the way she came, head hanging in what appeared to be grief. The suffering of the poor decrepit village folks never ended. Loss was a way of life.

The sun was now high in the sky, baking the small village as the General's men moved methodically from one dilapidated building to another. Waves of heat could be seen wafting from the ground, blurring vision and limiting the guard's sight. By late afternoon, most of the village was declared clear.

Abandoned and empty, the schoolhouse was last. Three guards entered the shell of a building and stood in the shade drenching their heads with water. They spoke quietly between themselves, cursing the General's obsession with finding the Al Qaeda spy who undoubtedly lie dead, along with their compatriots, right beneath their hot tired feet. Obviously the spy died below with the rest and their search was in vain.

One young guard squatted against a crumbling wall and wiped a filthy hand across his sweaty brow. "We should go south to Landai Kohl. I have a cousin there with a factory. He produces munitions. I can get you a job, if you want. We would be safe from Albani. There are too many different warlords in the mountains between here and there who hold no allegiance to our General. Frankly, I am tired of this constant fighting. Always worried about when the next bullet will come my way." Despite his dark hair and swarthy skin, a sunburn showed around his uncovered cheeks. The guard complained in a low voice watching for any ears that might overhear his comment.

"Do not say those words when there is a chance General

Albani will overhear. You will no longer worry about the next bullet. It will be between your eyes. I, too, yearn for a less complicated life. The General has lost everything and that means we will have nothing as well. I will consider your offer, but very quietly." His fellow soldier spoke softly as he surveyed the village through the empty window casement. There hadn't been glass in the building for a decade. He picked at the deteriorating wood slats that once held shutters. "There is nothing here for us but death, either way."

The third guard shook his head and frowned. "We cannot leave. There is no choice with this madman. You will not live to see the next hill you climb. The bullet will not be between your eyes but between your shoulders as you run away." It was a depressing thought, but true, nonetheless. He slid down in the corner with his back to the walls, joining his friend, contemplating the dirt before him. Picking up a handful of the powdery mix, it filtered through his fingers like flour, right into a crack in the floor. The guard watched the dirt disappear for several seconds before he spied the rope handle attached to the door, but covered in dirt.

"What is this?"

Both of the other guards turned to see the object of interest as their fellow soldier stood to lift the trap door. Creaking as wood scraped against wood, the men cautiously peered into the hole.

"It has a ladder."

"We should go down and see what is there."

"This has not been opened in a long time. Clearly the dust was not disturbed."

"What do you think we would find?"

"Why don't you go down and see?"

"Why me? Why don't you go?"

"Surely a spy would not crawl into a hole and hide so close to his enemy. There is probably nothing there. I see no reason to crawl down that rickety ladder."

"The Americans found Saddam Hussein in a hole like this, remember?"

"Ah, yes but he was a politician. A spy would not be so cowardly, I think. We should look at least."

"The ladder is not safe. It probably won't hold my weight. I could break a leg."

239

"It looks very old. Unsafe, I agree."

The larger guard pointed to his friend, "You are the smallest. You go down."

The slender man stared back, "I do not like rats. I think, more and more, that I like the idea of a factory job."

Chapter 24

Dark Escape

What would the world say of my darkness?
My heart? My spirit? My likeness?
Is there a place for me?
Should I come on bended knee?

Or just play along,
with what is wrong,
Hoping for more,
But knowing the score?

Poems of Darkness, A Collection
Michelle Le Bouff, Poet Laureate
Dartmouth College, 1945

Natalia sat by the blackout curtain that covered the entrance to the surface and dozed. She liked to stand the last watch, just before nightfall, feeling the onset of darkness in her bones. She rubbed her arms together warming the skin that prickled with the chill of the basement. As a vampire, her body temperature was naturally lower than a human's, but she still felt the chill. Sighing, her head rested against the back of the chair in which she slumped, letting her mind wander.

The soft sound of dirt and small pieces of gravel hitting the floor drifted through the heavy blackout curtains reaching her enhanced ears. The sound of scraping wood came next, alerting Natalia that they might have company. Freezing, she strained, listening with both the psychic and enhanced hearing of a veteran vampire. Easily following the dialog from above, she reached out to touch the minds of the reticent men above. Sifting through their thoughts, Natalia gained the information she needed to compel the men's minds.

241

The pit is unstable. It is simply an old storage hole full of garbage and insects. It is not necessary to crawl down the rickety ladder. It probably wouldn't hold your weight anyway. There is no light to see. Leave it. It would be smart to find another career before you too die, like your compatriot. Leave the crazy General and go south before it is too late.

She mentally teased the men, playing to their individual insecurities. One was afraid of insects. Another feared injury and death. The third hated garbage and darkness. All three men worried about surviving the General's rampage. Natalia concentrated, her mind control extremely successful. The men closed the trap door and sauntered out of the building. They talked about their wasted day, the heat of the evening and their growing need to leave the General's service. They each thought about seeking safety in the south at Landai Kohl. Smiling to herself, she was sure they would go south at the first opportunity.

Hey, gang, time to rise and shine. But do it silently. We've had company above. It is almost sundown and we need to leave this resort. Natalia gently conveyed the message into the sleepy minds of the squad several hours after sunset. They had time to catch a few extra winks so Natalia let the squad sleep longer than usual. Watching as the waking women stretched and rose, she caught each with a quick glance, placing a finger to her lips, signaling quiet.

What's up? Natalia caught Susannah's smirk as she pointed a dainty index finger toward the floor above. Psyche communication definitely had its benefits when hiding out from Middle Eastern terrorists and fanatical jihadists.

There is a small group searching for Al Muffadi. Three guards came into the building and found the trap door. I compelled them to leave, but I am not sure if others may come. I don't know how many are in the village, but I know General Albani is above, somewhere. Looks like our extermination plan only got some of the vermin. At least a handful of rats seem to have escaped.

Clothing rustled lightly as the women changed from sexy dancing garments to more conventional gear for the transport out. Their traditional tribal garb was more serviceable for travel than their highly decorative and skimpy costumes. Yuri cleaned up the broken slats and straightened the bed and blankets, leaving them as if nothing happened in the private bedroom.

Well, sort of.

A soft smile played across his face as he folded the old wool blanket. It smelled of Natalia and sex. There was not much that could be done for the broken bed. Again he smiled and his groin tightened. His woman was incorrigible and he loved her beyond all human limits.

Actually, well beyond human limitations.

Stashing their things in their packsacks to leave no evidence behind, Elizabetta contacted the Babysitters as quietly as possible. "Babysitters, V-1, on our way home. ETA one plus zero zero."

Natalia listened by the curtain, waiting for any noise that would signal they had been discovered. Her drawn long knife gleamed even in the darkened room, a testament to the battle ready vampire of a past century. She was competent with firearms, but the long knife or sword remained her weapon of choice. Together they made an efficient killing mechanism.

The response from the support team was immediate and broadcasted in all the squad's implanted receivers at the same time. "V-1, Babysitters. Fly safe."

The Babysitters were waiting and the only thing left to do was escape. It rankled Natalia that Colonel Fashiam, at least, survived the explosion. He had much to atone for, and she felt dirty leaving unfinished business behind. Maybe… *Elizabetta, what about cleaning up after ourselves? I want Fashiam.*

Right now it seems they believe an Al Qaeda spy set the explosion. We should leave it that way. As far as they know, we died in the stronghold as well. No need to set the record straight. Let's just get out of here undiscovered. Elizabetta wanted her Vamp Squad out and safe, as easily and quickly as possible. *You have Yuri. That should be enough.*

Elizabetta had a point. Natalia felt Yuri's warm arms encircle her from behind, his hot breath tickled her ear. "I thought once that I wanted nothing more than to kill the bastard, as well. Now I have a new life and I have you. I do not need revenge. His stronghold is gone and he is without men. That is enough for me."

His lips trailed a moist path from her ear to her throat where he nibbled at the sensitive juncture. Pulling her tight against him, she felt his ardor grow. This was ridiculous. Every time she felt his touch, heard his voice, mentally connected with him, her body flamed beyond control. She relived each and every touch. Her mind refused to focus on anything except the man who stole her heart, and how much she craved his body. Natalia mentally shook herself and stepped away from physical contact with Yuri. *Yuri, please. I can't think when you are so near.*

"You, mon ami, are out of control. Oh, it is so mignon, so cute. Our powerful Natalia, always such tight control. Ach, no longer. Le coeur est détruit! The heart is lost to our handsome little brother." Monique danced around, sliding her hands seductively over both as she circled the couple, trying without success to suppress her hushed giggles.

Monique, stop. Leave them alone. Elizabetta wanted this whole thing over as soon as possible. She could feel the tension building, and knew things were set to boil out of control at any minute.

Oh, oui. Every time we leave them alone, the furniture mysteriously breaks. Monique planted a sly kiss on Yuri's cheek, and quickly danced away.

Yuri's face reddened as he moved to swat at the teasing blonde's round fanny. Monique evaded his half-hearted attempt, dancing across the floor to hide behind Susannah with a provocative giggle.

Elizabetta rubbed the back of her neck and shook her head. *Why do I feel like a middle school teacher with an unruly class of hormonal thirteen year olds?* She stood next to the blackout curtain and cast her senses above to the dilapidated building. *The schoolhouse is empty. I sense no one above but we must be careful. Natalia, you must keep Yuri with you if we are to fly. I will take Susannah with me. Nat, you have point, then Yuri, MorningStar, Monique, and Susannah. I'll go up last. Let's get out of here.*

The basement lights were shut down and Natalia drew the curtain aside. Slowly she climbed the creaking ladder and raised the trapdoor an inch. Casting her senses and peering out in both directions, she motioned the rest that the coast was clear. Propping the door against the sidewall, Natalia snuck out of the hole and crept to the window looking out on the street. The moon, almost full, sat low on the horizon. It shone with a silvery light, casting bluish shadows across the village. Natalia sensed people but saw no movement. Anyone with a lick of sense was probably behind closed doors and bedded down for the night. She moved to the back of the building.

Yuri followed, taking up the lookout position on the other side of the building. *I don't see anything.* Without thinking he once again attempted to communicate mentally. The power of the attempt hit the entire squad like a physical blow.

Natalia flew against the wall with a resounding crack. MorningStar, half way out the trap door, fell against the vamp below her, starting a cascade that ended with Susannah shrieking as she landed atop Elizabetta at the bottom of the hole.

Yuri, for God's sake whisper, don't psyche! You haven't exactly mastered the mental finesse it takes. You're blasting us all. Natalia rubbed the side of her head that had contacted the cinder blocks of the wall.

"Sorry." A sheepish smile played across his handsome features and Natalia's heart lurched in her chest. "I don't see any movement on this side." Yuri whispered toward Natalia, his hand cupping his mouth to channel the noise.

Ah, yeah, we got that much, Studley. Susannah pulled herself off Elizabetta and untangled Monique's feet from her hair. MorningStar tried the ladder once more, with the others following, as quickly as they could manage the ancient ladder. *At least don't psyche until we get up this ladder. I don't like wearing a waffle imprint on my forehead from Frenchy's boots. It's just so not cool.*

With everyone out and laying low on the ground level of the schoolhouse, Natalia watched the back street for movement. A stray dog wandered near the village pump, licking water from shallow puddles that reflected the cold moonlight. A lone man walked with purpose toward a ramshackle hut at the end of the block.

Natalia cast her senses. She found jumbled thoughts and stray emotions, but no sign of Colonel Fashiam or the guards she'd heard before.

I can't feel any of the guards or Fashiam. The villagers are scared ...sad ...depressed ...they, ah, some are hopeful that the cave-in was not as terrible as it looked. Some know they will not see their family members again. Natalia focused a tight beam of thought scouring the village for any little clue to the whereabouts of the soldiers. *Ah ha! I found them. The guards are searching the south road, probably on their way to their next jobs, courtesy of my little mental nudge.* Natalia provided a commentary as she continued to mentally search the village. Small beads of perspiration appeared on her forehead and cheeks, seeping together in little rivulets to trickle down and drip to the floor. She panted, drawing in deep draughts of air, reaching to stretch further than she had ever extended her psyche powers before. Her forehead wrinkled as she squeezed her eyes closed, focusing. *I cannot feel Fashiam. I do not know where he is.*

Then let us go, quickly and quietly. Behind the building, we will morph and fly from here to the caravan at Torkham. The Babysitters will meet us, as arranged. Somehow Olney Farm seems like a comfortable old shoe, like home, even though I have only these last few years come to live there. Natalia thought she detected a wistful, but determined note in Elizabetta's comment. She snuck to the back of the building to peer out the empty window frame into the dark alley.

Natalia felt Yuri's heat behind her and knew the Russian Captain was scanning the area directly outside, looking over her shoulder for danger. He was such a man, such a soldier, such a…hot, luscious. *Ach, Yuri, what did I tell you? PLEASE keep your distance. I can't think.* As she turned, she found her body engulfed in a pair of incredibly strong arms, her lips enveloped in a blazing kiss that devastated her thought processes. Fast and hot, she moaned into his conquering mouth.

She was completely lost.

Again.

Yuri chuckled, and held her from him. Like a rag doll, Natalia hung for a heartbeat before recovering her wits. This was getting to be a bad joke. She glared at the Captain, slapping his hands away from her arms. "Be serious, Captain. This is business." She spoke the words for emphasis.

"Ah huh, monkey business." Yuri continued to scan the area as he teased Natalia. "Damn, I love the little extras that come with being a vampire. I can see as if it is day, only in different colors." The whispered words tickled her thoughts and made her chuckle. She couldn't remember ever being without the benefit of VMD and had no idea what challenges the modern human condition actually presented. She just never considered the things she came to take for granted. There was little she could not do. As she grew older, her powers increased, unlike humans, who seemed to grow weaker and more frail with age.

Across the room Susannah scoffed, psyching at the same time. *Cool, we have sight just like dogs. I guess the next time someone calls me a bitch I should happily agree. Not.*

Let's go. Be careful and stay together. Elizabetta moved to crawl out the window accepting the helping hand from the man behind her. Landing on her feet, she ducked into the shadows, watching as the rest of the squad came through the window and melted into the darkness.

They assembled in the shadows of the back alley. *Yuri, hold my hand and let me take control. You will need help to morph and fly. Trust me and let me be the guide in this.* Natalia and Yuri linked hands as he closed his eyes and let Natalia enter his being, taking control of his body and mind, with an easy familiarity.

The first shots grazed Yuri's ear as his eyes flew open, breaking the connection before Natalia could morph them. A hail of gunfire peppered the wall behind Natalia, as the squad hit the ground and crawled for cover. More shots sprayed the schoolhouse as guards shouted to each other, moving in the darkness. Natalia listened to the names and mentally searched for information as she ran, ducking for cover each time another round split the silence. *Betta, General Albani is close and Colonel Fashiam is with him. How many more could have escaped the explosion? Why didn't I sense them?*

Yuri leveled the AK-47 he took from the well guard, returning fire, as he covered the retreat of the squad. They ran down the alley, ducking and weaving. Susannah dove into a small shed, rolled to her feet and provided a distraction with a couple grenades from her pack. *Just like pitching on the varsity baseball team. I could do this all day.* She tossed three more grenades at the oncoming guards with amazing accuracy. Two went down and the third slid under a turnip cart. *I don't have to worry about wearing a flak jacket with this lovely tribal ensemble.*

Don't get cocky little sister. The bullets will not kill you, but they still hurt when you get hit. Stay down. Elizabetta hid behind a stack of tribal rugs watching the lone guard. He was trying to figure out who the enemy was, and from where had come the grenades. Yuri did a perfect dive and rolled through the open window, back into the schoolhouse. Landing on his feet like a cat, Natalia waved him down from the edge of the shack directly across the way.

Immediately, General Albani appeared in the middle of the alley, the P90 riding at his hip. Firing rapid rounds, the General advanced, spraying bullets in every direction, screaming obscenities in Pashto. The one remaining guard crawled further beneath the cart, then collapsed flat on the ground. A gaping hole seeped blood from the back of his head. Albani fired several more rounds into the still body, then kicked viciously at the dead man's head. Obviously, the General was totally insane and shooting blindly at anything that moved.

Everyone, stay in hiding. Do not move and make no sound. Elizabetta sent her message with the mental equivalent of a stern finger shake.

Colonel Fashiam, flanked by his last two guards, ducked into the alley, surprised to see the General kicking one of his own men. Still banging at his head, he shouted, "What the hell is going on?" The guards behind him fanned out and knelt to fire at the source of the assault.

Albani turned, leveling his weapon at the Colonel and guards. Screaming a nonsense string of curses, the General paused to emphasize his anger, then spun, lowered his gun, and stomped toward the end of the alley, right past Elizabetta's hiding place. Susannah squeaked, ducking behind a stick and rope door too late to avoid the General's view.

Albani froze mid-stride. Staring at the young woman through the sparse cover of the door, he drew his FN. Elizabetta, with the speed of a mother bear separated from her cub, dashed across the alley, grabbed the General by the back of his uniform and threw him against the shack wall. Twisting as he fell, Betta was rewarded with a look of pure surprise. Used to acting on survival instinct, the General fired, emptying his magazine into the woman who stood in front of him, a feral grin twisting his features.

Recoiling from the bullets, Elizabetta shrieked at the man and launched herself. Fangs extended, eyes flashing neon red, she flew at Albani. Pinning the General to the building wall, she sunk her fangs deep into his neck and ripped. The tissue, muscles and organs tore, splashing blood across both herself and her victim.

Growling into the terrified eyes of the choking, dying human. Elizabetta cooed in Pashto, "Bad dog. No bone. Didn't your mommy teach you, it's not nice to shoot at defenseless women?" She slid her tongue up the man's cheek, tasting his blood in a final caress as Albani drew his last ragged breath. Elizabetta released the man's torn body as it slumped against the building, and slowly slid into the dirt of the alley

As Elizabetta moved away, the holes in her chest closed beneath the coarse shirt she wore. Out of the side of her eye she caught sight of Fashiam standing dumb-founded, his men paralyzed with fear. Delicately she drew an arm across her mouth, wiping the remnants of the attack from her face. Her bloody fangs glittered in the moonlight as she smiled sweetly at the stunned men.

MorningStar appeared with Monique behind the two frozen guards. In less than a heartbeat, the women dispatched their targets leaving Fashiam standing alone in the alley. Elizabetta slowly stalked toward the unarmed Colonel who stood rooted to the dirt. He was shaking so violently, she thought he would crumple at any minute.

From her hiding place, Natalia joined Elizabetta as they continued down the alley. It was definitely a Charlie's Angel moment, only with more blood and less fashion sense.

Yuri vaulted through the window and stepped toward the Colonel, amazed that the man stood his ground. "So you have no bravery when you do not have an army behind you, Colonel Fashiam." Yuri watched the Colonel as he sauntered toward the man. It was a pleasurable experience to see recognition dawn in the eyes of his torturer. Fashiam promptly peed down his own leg, urine, soaking his pants and pooling around his black boots

"No, it can not be. No, I do not understand..." Fashiam could not believe what his eyes told him was true. He knew the legends of the blood feeders called vampires, but these were dancers. They were all sluts, women of no consequence. They danced for him and his men. He was sure he tasted the flame haired one. She had serviced his need only yesterday, and he remembered it was extraordinarily good. He could still feel the silky hair she drew across his engorged appendage. The heat of her as she bucked and taunted him. Her screams as he thrust himself punishingly deep within her.

"What is it you do not understand, Fashiam? That I stand before you, alive and well? Or that I walk beside these beautiful women, who you thought took such good care of your men?" Yuri smiled, revealing his fangs. Indicating the men laying behind the Colonel, he chuckled. "Not so fierce when you stand alone, eh? Ladies, he is mine. I will have my revenge, and it will be sweet."

"No Yuri, he is dangerous and you are newly turned. You do not know what powers are at your command." Natalia grasped Yuri's hand turning him toward her, she planted a desperate kiss on his handsome chin.

Fashiam could not understand how he came to be in this place with these demons. He did know, if he did not escape immediately he would surely die this night. If the Russian Captain had not expired in his cell and was now a vampire, the man had much to avenge. He backed away tripping over the two men who supposedly protected his back. Terrified to look, but drawn to the bodies, he stared in horror at the gaping wounds on the necks of his men.

"Allah save me from this…"

Monique smiled tauntingly, licking a dribble of blood from her pouty lips. "Oui, Oui doux Colonel. Allah no longer listens and I think you have a petit probleme'. " She drew an index finger from his nose to his chin, and down his neck.

"Do not touch me, demon of Malik, Djin of Evil. I shall put an end to your pitiful existence." Fashiam raged at Monique, brandishing a curved knife from somewhere up his sleeve.

Monique giggled and moved with the speed of light dancing on the wind. One second she was before Fashiam, and the next, she and Susannah stood behind Yuri.

"End the pitiful life of this piece of trash. This man surely deserves to feel the hand of he who has died in his care." Monique was disgusted by Fashiam's clumsy attempt to imbed his little pig sticker in her chest.

Yuri cautiously approached the Colonel, watching, as the man tossed his knife from one hand to the other. A deadly gleam, lent fire to Yuri's eyes. "I will send this pig to his own hell. Come

Fashiam, we have unfinished business."

"Allah, give me strength to defeat this self-possessed Djin. But what power do I have to face Malik's agent? If I am to die this day, then I shall take many with me to the fires of Malik's House of Hell." Fashiam charged Yuri, slashing viciously with the decorated tribal knife. Its jewels glittered in the moonlight as he moved with practiced strokes. Ducking and weaving, Fashiam and Yuri met in the middle of the alley. Dust flew in great billows as the men tangled.

Yuri, you are so much stronger and more agile. Use your enhanced strength. Natalia's mental message did not go unheeded. She watched the men fight, wondering at Yuri's strategy.

I will use only my human skills. I will defeat this garbage as a man, in a man's way. It is a matter of pride. Yuri's mental response knocked Natalia from her feet.

Picking herself off the ground, she dusted her hands on her pants and snorted. Men. Would they never learn?

Fashiam's knife sliced through Yuri's shirt, opening a bright red wound. The Colonel snarled, encouraged by the success of his first strike, only to see the wound begin to close as quickly as the steel left its mark. On the attack once again, Fashiam dipped low carving another wound in Yuri's calf. It seeped bright blood and looked more serious than the scratch it was. Laughing with abandon, Fashiam stroked the air wildly, confident that his skill would win the day and Yuri would finally die by his hand.

Pain coursed through his leg, but Yuri ignored the sting. Years of combat training taught him much. It taught him to deal with pain and insignificant wounds, but already the sting was gone. The wound was healed. All he needed was an opening, and that he was trained to make himself. Looking clumsy and accepting a couple of scratches would allow the Colonel to believe Yuri was at a disadvantage in hand to hand combat. It would stir the Colonel's confidence and bring him on.

Successful at the ruse, Fashiam acted as if he had nothing to lose. The Colonel put one hundred percent of his strength and skill into the battle, holding nothing back. What the wild Colonel did not consider, was that each of Yuri's wounds were closing, something that would occur with each strike.

Fashiam charged, surging forward, the knife poised to deliver

251

a deadly gut wound.

Yuri easily countered, channeling the charging man's power and direction to his benefit in a quick parry and chop.

Fashiam stumbled under the unexpected strike, and rolled away to face his opponent again. Rising to his feet, the Colonel approached more carefully, slashing the air in quick figure eight motions. An experienced dagger fighter, the Colonel expertly fingered his knife feeling the camel bone and lapis lazuli handle inset with the jewels of his family. It settled against his palm with comfort. His Mashook steel had met tissue twice now. The famous knife-maker would be proud to know his work was well used in this fight. Fashiam knew this Russian Captain was no match for a veteran freedom fighter, used to defending himself in filthy ditches and caves.

Again the Colonel slashed the air, a broad sneer gnarling his normally unpleasant features. Panting, sweat dripped from his forehead and nose with the effort of fighting. Too much hookah juice and sweet meats had taken their toll on his once lean and hard body. But it was too late for regrets. Now, he would have to depend on his experience, and the cagey methods learned in the desperate battles of his youth. Stalking Yuri, Fashiam rushed, closing the distance between himself and his unarmed opponent

Studying the Colonel's eyes, Yuri knew when the final attack came. He had purposefully dropped his guard to lure Fashiam in. Slipping out of the way, he put the Colonel on his face in the dirt with a simple sweeping maneuver. Dropping onto Fashiam's spine with both knees, a loud crunch could be heard above the screams of the prostrate Colonel. Grabbing a chin in one hand, and the back of the head in another, Yuri snapped the Colonel's neck in one swift movement. The screaming ceased as Fashiam's body slacked in death.

Yuri rose to stare at the man who had been the instrument of his pain and torture. He had subsequently been party to Yuri's death and rebirth. A feral smile contorted Yuri's features as the euphoria of victory swept through his mind.

Yuri, we must clean this mess up and go. Natalia pressed close.

He felt her fingers softly touching his sweaty face. Pulling away from his lover, Yuri's eyes glowed blood red. A growl began deep in his chest issuing forth as an animalistic scream of victory. Falling to his knees, he sank his fangs into his vanquished opponent, and drew the still warm blood to him. It spread through his body firing every nerve and cell. Like a mainlined narcotic, the high was incredible.

Again he howled, loud and long.

Reaching for Natalia, he plundered her mouth, ravaging her mind through their undeniable mental connection. He held her body tight to him with strength that would have broken the bones of a mere mortal. His hands roamed her figure, passion fired to the point of eruption. The entire Vamp Squad felt their crazed ardor, and shared in the orgasmic delirium Yuri broadcast with the strength of a lightning strike.

"Holy shit, Hot Stuff." Susannah sank to her knees, a hand holding her chest. "Oh man, what a feeling. Why haven't I ever felt like this? Beats the hell of out anything I have in my little toy chest. No nine-volt batteries needed. Jee-sus Natalia, make him turn it off before the entire village has one giant orgasm." The youngest vampire in the group was panting and caressing her breasts as if she were on the verge of climax.

Monique knelt beside Susannah embracing her little sister, cheek to cheek, both ensnared in the throes of Yuri's passion. Elizabetta stood, leaning against the roll of rugs, her eyes closed, allowing the sexual rapture to move freely through her. The only member of the Vamp Squad unaffected, seemed to be MorningStar. She sat on the windowsill of the schoolhouse lazily observing her squad mates in the shared thrall that filled the air following a vampiric feeding frenzy.

Natalia allowed the power of Yuri's feeding to slip through her shield as she reveled in the encompassing passion of shared contact. Her body felt like quicksilver, moving and forming, to reform with every touch of Yuri's exploring hands. Streaks of power slithered through her mind, shifting colors and patterns of thought. Yuri's tongue tangled with hers in a dance that sparked jolts of electricity through her most sensitive areas. She felt moisture form with need, pulling closer to her lover, their kiss deepened even more.

Elizabetta recovered her thoughts enough to throw up a mental shield, blocking the couple's psychic broadcast. Panting, she tore herself from the psychic projection, and concentrated on muting Yuri's incredible explosion of pure sensual emotion. She would have to speak privately with Natalia, at some point, about the strength and depth of her relationship with Yuri. It was unusually powerful and uncontrolled. Possibly, the open nature of their shared emotions was part of the natural ability of Natalia to compel, but it was also a dangerous thing when wild and free, uncontrolled to the point of incapacitating those near. Elizabetta could already feel the effect of his broadcast on the villagers.

Natalia, Yuri! We must go. The mental slap accomplished its objective. Slowly Natalia disengaged herself from Yuri's arms, with a seductive smile and a pat to his inflamed cheeks. *Gather the bodies, we need to cover our tracks.*

We will place the trash in the schoolhouse basement. MorningStar hefted the nearest body, tossing it lightly through the window from which they escaped before the firefight. The Native American vampire's communications were curt, and to the point, but always helpful and efficient.

The squad began moving bodies into the empty building as MorningStar opened the trap door. *Hand them down to me then I shall set a charge to collapse the building. No one will find these vermin for a very long time. The villagers will believe it an aftershock. Then, we go home.*

Elizabetta rubbed the back of her neck and shrugged. Why was MorningStar immune to Yuri's emotions? Unusual. She would figure it out later. Now there was business to attend to, at the moment. *Make it so.*

"Whoa! Now who's acting like a captain? Daddy would be proud, Elizabetta. Come on girls. Warp five. Then home to the Farm. And a hot bath." Somewhat recovered, Susannah patted Monique on the ass as she moved to lift the last body through the window.

"Oui, what I would give for a hot bath and a peu de massage'. How I miss the sweet smell of clean." Monique sighed, flinging dirt over a spot of puddled blood where Colonel Fashiam died. "How I shall truly love to sit for hours in the scented water, simply... simply loving... myself." She giggled, and hopped through the window following the rest of the squad into the abandoned building as the last body dropped into the hole leading

254

to the subterranean quarters.

The sound of scuffling and something being dragged floated up to those above, as MorningStar took care of the bodies, placing them out of sight. It wouldn't really matter after the building was leveled and the underground entrance covered in rubble, but being careful was always a good thing. A dim light appeared in the hole accompanied by a mental message.

I will be but a minute. I will put them behind the locked door and jam the lock. Then we need not level the building. This village has lost enough. A crunch followed by a screeching metal sound was heard, then silence.

Kanza girl? What's going on? What's behind the door? Elizabetta was concerned at the mental and environmental silence. *MorningStar, are you okay?*

Yes, I am fine. You all must come here and see this. The excitement in MorningStar's communication was evident. The Native American vampire was not concerned or afraid, but truly astonished by something. Whatever she found would be seen only by descending the ladder, and joining her.

Susannah scampered down the ladder and hit the main lights. The dull humming sound returned with the cold blue illumination of iridescent lighting. As the room brightened and the humming disappeared, Susannah let out a whistle that could be heard clearly by the squad members above. Curiosity getting the best of them, the others descended, one after another, and closed the trap door once more.

Natalia, last down and jumping from the second rung, landed on both feet and let out a gasp. Through the small opening she could see the huge metal door at the back of the main room. It stood open, the lights beyond burning brightly… as far as the eye could see!

"Oh my God. Can you believe that?" Her jaw dropped open as she stumbled forward and tripped over Fashiam's body. It lay forgotten, across the entrance. Caught in the process of falling by Yuri's strong arms, Natalia could not take her eyes off the scene before them. Finally, stepping across the body, Natalia took Yuri's hand and followed the rest of the squad into the mammoth chamber beyond the quarters where they'd spent the previous night.

Susannah squealed as she danced through the metal doors. Monique sped past her sister vampire, running without direction, looking both ways, taking in the numerous connecting passageways and chambers. *Be careful, these rooms may have booby traps or guards. It might be connected to the stronghold. We could run into more terrorists. This stuff got here somehow, and it did not come down that ladder.* Elizabetta warned as she followed the group, casting her senses for soldiers. She could not feel any other than her squad. *Nat, can you feel anyone near?*

Betta, I don't feel anyone. As far as I can tell there is no one else here. Natalia stood, staring at a chamber that seemed to be as long as a football field. It was brightly lit and she could see hundreds of gleaming cars, parked in nice neat rows, polished and shiny. The hoods of the cars in the first row sported the little tri-star of Mercedes Benz. *We could always grab a ride and drive to the end. Just to see. Where is the end?* Natalia's expression was more smug than questioning.

I feel no movement in the air of this place. There is no opening, other than the one we came through. All believed MorningStar's statement. She spent more than four hundred years living in caves and was definitely the expert on spelunking. Long ago tuned to the earth and natural elements, her vampire senses were infallible. *There may be a sealed door somewhere, but I have not seen or felt evidence of it. This place sings of completeness.*

"There has to be another exit, but it could have been through the stronghold and now collapsed. Let's see what we can find." Elizabetta depressed the com device in her neck, "Babysitters, V-1. Stopping to check on a surprise. More later."

"V-1, Babysitters. Problem? Need a ride?" Sergeant Miller was heard over the receiver with some concern evident in his voice.

"No problema mahn. Just a little shopping." Susannah responded before Elizabetta could speak. Her quick imitation of Arnold Swarzenegger was cute, but only seemed to confuse the sergeant.

"Come again?" Colonel Maddox's voice came across the air waves loud and clear in their ears. In his tone was a curt reprimand for his child's comment.

Susannah, please let me handle this. Elizabetta depressed her

256

com. "V-1, no problem, just a little stop to look-see. Patience. Out."

Oooh. Daddy doesn't like to be put on hold. He's gonna get freaky if we don't let him know what's going on. Susannah was smiling like the cat that swallowed the canary. She was getting a great deal of satisfaction out of keeping information from her father. *He has no patience, believe me.* She danced off into a chamber that held chests and large metal containers with drawers, all sealed with sturdy padlocks and metal chains.

Watch for booby traps. I have no idea who amassed this Aladdin's Cave, but I suspect it is well protected. Always the worrier, Elizabetta was surveying the floor and different corners for explosives, and traps set. *Use your senses before you move. Be careful. Now that we survived our first mission, I don't want to lose anyone in this giant...Mall of Amazing.*

"Oh, oui. I love the sound of those words. Anything with mall in it, just seems to roll off the tongue and lips. Eeehhhhh! Susannah, come here little sister."

Elizabetta turned and ran toward the cavernous room where she had last seen Monique and Susannah. Just barely beating Natalia and Yuri to the site of the scream, she froze in mid stride.

Several yards into the room, Monique danced around Susannah winding her in jewels and long strings of pearls. Millions of dollars in diamonds, rubies and emeralds dripped from the young girl, as she giggled and spun in delight, a heavy tiara sitting cockeyed atop her dirty matted blond curls. Broken locks lie strewn about on the floor. Drawers stood open, half full of unset jewels. A scatter of glittering stones lie strewn across the ground. Monique undulated, laughing and preening, several diamond-studded belts crisscrossing her torso. Huge emerald globs hung from her ears. A gold and onyx Egyptian mask covered her pretty features, held in place by a grimy hand.

God bless vampire speed. Elizabetta could not keep herself from laughing at the two women drenched in glitter. How in the world they managed it in a blink of an eye, was a question Elizabetta did not even want to consider. Of all the massive rooms filled with various treasures, armaments, explosives, vehicles and other supplies, of course, Monique and Susannah would find this one first.

Elizabetta shrugged at Yuri who stood at the doorway, gun poised to defend. "No gun could protect your little sisters from their passion, Yuri. I believe, it will take much more than explosives to separate these women from their little discovery."

"Lends a new meaning to bling." Natalia laughed at her sisters covered with millions of dollars in sparkling jewels dancing about each other.

"Meaning of bling? How about the value of bling! I do not believe the American word for fake jewelry is quite appropriate here. In fact, me-loch-ka, you would not look bad in this. Only this." Yuri pulled a web of gold chain and polished onyx from a case sitting askew on a huge wooden box banded with metal straps.

"Basic black. Oh so classical and sophisticated. But I fear this would be somewhat breezy, my Captain. I would definitely feel the chill of the Russian winter if I wore only this." Natalia held the chained stones to her neck pirouetting for Yuri to see.

"I would have to wrap my arms about you, my love. I would keep you warm with my heat." Yuri took her in his arms and nuzzled her neck.

Natalia did feel a heat begin to build at his simple touch only it wasn't body heat, but heat of a very different nature. Her cheeks flamed as she moaned at Yuri's caress. Dampness formed in her sex as she pressed closer, feeling each rounded stone between them. It was an erotic feeling that only served to add to her fire. She felt Yuri finger the lacy chain loops at her neck and heard his muzzled growl as her body felt the mental excitement of his need ignite and begin to grow. Pulled so close, her body matching his, she could feel his manhood grow as well.

"Moi-ya ahn-gel tiem-no." Yuri was broadcasting waves of sensual pleasure as he breathed in the scent of his woman and tasted her skin. Natalia could almost feel him purr as his mouth covered her neck and ear lobe with hot wet kisses. She was drowning in his mental and physical arousal. His lips found hers and she opened to his plunder with a deep passionate moan.

"Puh-leeze. Nat! Yuri! Stop. Get a room. But not this room. This one is definitely mine. Go find the room with sex toys and batteries." Susannah threw her tiara into a trunk of treasure and stomped over to the couple. Yanking at the chain and onyx Kirdan vest, she swatted at Natalia and Yuri with a pout. "Give it a rest, girl."

Natalia pulled out of Yuri's embrace and shook her head to clear the intoxicating effects of his touch. "Ah...I...ah..." Natalia shook her head again and cleared her throat. "I think we should see the rest of this fascinating facility, da?"

Since Monique's scream was due to pleasure and not fear or pain, and Natalia wanted to put some space between herself and her squad, she took Yuri's hand and wandered off to survey the other storage rooms. Each was filled to overflowing with treasures and supplies.

"Did you ever see the Mummy movies with that American actor, Brandon something-or-another? This reminds me of the place they found in the City of the Dead. Rooms and rooms of treasure. Wow, Colonel Maddox will be happy to see all this stuff. At least he won't have to worry about financing the Vamp Squad anymore. In fact we could just move here and live forever." Natalia sauntered down corridors and passageways, pausing every few feet to kiss Yuri.

"All I need is a soft bed and you." Yuri pulled Natalia toward a stack of blankets all folded neatly in low stacks. "Or just a place to lay my tired head for a few minutes." He grinned at the woman he towed along behind him.

"Your head is not tired, Captain." She glanced toward his crotch with a smirk. "And it's not your head you want to lie down." Natalia giggled as she pushed Yuri down on a pile of wool blankets and flopped on top of him, wiggling outrageously.

Yuri captured Natalia in his arms and stretched beneath her, feeling the contact of their bodies deep in his soul. "Why is it, that each time I touch you, I want you more? I cannot seem to get enough of you. My mind goes to mush and my body takes over. I cannot resist you, my love." He whispered the last words into her mouth as his tongue sought to explore the depth of her need.

Natalia's body tightened in response, as she teased and sucked at Yuri's searching tongue. Since his transformation, he always seemed to taste of hazel nuts and chocolate, her favorites combined in one. She slid a leg between his and caressed his groin with her knee. Her hands tangled in his soft blonde curls that continued to thicken as his turning progressed.

"Mummm. I will never tire of your taste and feel." Pressing

259

her breasts to his chest, she could feel his ardor rise with each spinning tendril of excitement that touched her mind. His tongue traced patterns across her jaw and down her neck. Goose bumps covered her body and Natalia thought she would explode from his sensual foreplay. Tugging at his shirt, she giggled as the fabric tore like tissue paper. Her mouth sought and found a small tan nipple.

Yuri gasped as Natalia took it in her mouth teasing the tip with her teeth. "Aghhhhh, you will torture me, my love. Have I not endured enough in these past months?" His hands roamed her back and clenched her buttocks, pressing her tighter to him as his cock jerked and grew even harder.

"Ah, such torture, my Yuri. You wish me to stop?" Natalia pulled back and peered at the wondrously beautiful man beneath her. Her heart wrenched in her chest.

"I am sure we can find many more important things to occupy our time. We are in the middle of a very serious mission." She bent, starting at the top of his head with feather kisses, then nipped at his ear lob.

"And there is much still left to do." The whispered words did nothing to still Yuri's need.

"We should help the team discover all of the secrets of this fascinating place." Natalia blew cool air across Yuri's chest and watched as the fine hair moved and his nipples perked. She licked lightly at each for a heartbeat, then slid lower.

"They will, no doubt, need our support." Propped on one elbow, Natalia drug a single dangling curl across his neck and down his chest.

"Such amazing treasure we have found." Leaning down once again, she tore each button with her teeth, slowly revealing Yuri's bare skin, one button at a time.

"So much left to do and so little time." Her tongue swirled circles around his well-defined muscles. She smiled lustfully at each groan her teasing movements evoked.

"We have a job to complete, Captain." She released the top button of his pants, dragging her long silky hair across his navel.

"You have not answered my question." She pulled at his zipper with her teeth, sliding it down excruciatingly slowly. "Should I stop?" Her breath tantalized the tip of his cock, extending out of the opening, engorged and hard. Her tongue flicked at the head and it leapt to life, jerking toward her moist lips.

"What is your answer, Captain?" She took the head of his penis in her mouth and sucked gently watching his reaction, enjoying his attempt to form a sentence between gasps.

"I do believe you are speechless, Captain." Natalia's words vibrated around Yuri, as she sucked and mumbled. Then she took him deep, using the back of her throat to work the head of his cock. Natalia was enjoying herself. Mentally wired to Yuri, she could feel everything he felt.

Yuri bucked and growled. "Nah...don...stooo...ooop." He knew it was a loosing battle when it came to Natalia. She was in his blood and his desire for her flowed through his veins with the life giving liquid. His body convulsed with wave upon wave of pleasure, building until passion flared too hot to contain. Giving up, Yuri succumbed to Natalia's sexual ministrations and roared his release. His body exploded in a million particles of charged electricity, as the energy of his orgasm vibrated throughout the caverns, echoing and rebounding, growing in strength until it dissipated in a flash of pure ecstasy that infected the entire squad, sending up a sensual howl that shook the walls of the mammoth facility.

Natalia felt Yuri's orgasm trigger her own, and released her mind and body to revel in the pure pleasure of it. Somewhere in the caverns, the entire squad was doing the same thing.

When breath finally returned to Yuri's body he sighed heavily, pulling Natalia to his chest. Nestling her against his shoulder, he wrapped his arms around her, and promptly fell asleep.

Natalia lie for several minutes listening to Yuri breathing before she too slept.

Chapter 25

Historical Perspective

It's an ancient story
Written in blood and glory,
Older than time and space.
The length of which, buried in haste.
Became the legacy from which we hide
Nursing our wounds, concealing our pride.

A new millennia begs our witness
From darkness to light, a path of swiftness.
Now free to show our heart's desire
From the frying pan to consuming fire.
We run with light minds and powerful egress
From light to dark, a deadly process.

Digressive Research of Nazi Germany
Dr. Amelia Jung
Berlin, Germany 1985

Natalia was there again, in the frozen cathedral. But this time it was different. She seemed to hover above the scene, no longer the victim *in* the nightmare, but an observer *of* the nightmare. Detached from the pain and fear, she watched as Rasputin conducted his perverted ritual. The Devine Liturgy echoed in her ears as she watched the Dowager Duchess Slimova service the vampire priest. The noise the woman made was repulsive and Natalia tried to turn away, to force herself to wake with no success. Fear began to etch itself into her mind slowly, like water carving a canyon over decades, a molecule of stone at a time, each grain of sand scouring a landscape, an unstoppable force.

Natalia cried out, clawing at the air. The scene played on and on; the sex, the beating, the chanting. Finally, she watched, outside her own body, as an innocent girl lie tied to an altar, the priest poised over her battered body, his disgusting appendage engorged and pulsing. The child screamed as Rasputin perpetrated his vile rape of her body and mind. Natalia screamed with the girl, again and again. Natalia screamed and fought until strong arms shook her awake.

"Natalia, wake. Do not fight me. Wake up. You are safe. Shhhhhh, me-lotch-ka, shhh." Yuri rocked the shaking woman in his arms as he spoke.

Slowly, Natalia opened her eyes. Her mind was still mired in the horrible dream of her turning, afraid of what she would find. What she saw, was Yuri's concerned expression tempered with such love, the like of which she'd never seen before.

"Oh Yuri. I did not hurt you, did I?" Tears rolled down her cheeks.

"Nyet, moi-ya me-lotch-ka. I am fine and whole. Was it your dream again?" He knew the answer before he asked the question.

"Da. I shall never be free of that monster. After a hundred years, he still haunts me." She buried her face in his chest, sobbing disparagingly.

"Ah, my sweet, I will find a way. My love is strong. Together we will manage." He crushed her to him and held her for several long minutes.

"Yuri, my heart is not free to love as yours is. What if I cannot tear free from the haunting? What if I must spend eternity fighting the fear and hatred?" Natalia whispered between sobs. "You will not want a woman with a past that seems so alive and real she beats you in your sleep."

"Shhh, Natalia. We will get through this. My heart and my love are great enough for both of us. Let me love you. Let yourself be loved."

Natalia wiped her eyes and sat up. "You are a wonderful man, Captain Yuri Milassoviech. Maybe some day I will be worthy of your love. And maybe someday I will be free to love you in return." Turning away, she rose straightening her clothes. "We should go. How long did we doze?"

"Not long, about half an hour. I apologize for falling asleep on you. I was so…ah, what can I say? I'm just a man." Yuri reddened as he shrugged and smiled at the woman who just gave him the best orgasm of his life.

Natalia giggled. "Well, it was something, wasn't it? I think the entire squad will agree with me." Still giggling, she strode toward the main corridor, hips swaying seductively.

"The what? You mean…" Yuri ran after Natalia. "They heard everything?"

"Heard and felt, Captain Studley." The broad wide smile that shone with glee, lit Natalia's face.

"What am I to do? I cannot face those women after they shared something so…intimate. How do I turn this thing off? Natalia?" He was running after Natalia who was now trotting toward the main passageway in search of her team.

"Natalia, wait!"

"Yuri, come on. Don't worry about it. They all understand. We are a coven, a family. We share everything." Natalia waved off his concerns as she continued on, peering into each warehouse style room as they moved along.

Embarrassed but unable to do a thing about it, Yuri followed.

The next three caverns contained crates of missiles. At the entrance to the second storage area Yuri paused in his tracks. "My God, Natalia. Do you know what these are? Zvezda KH-31." Yuri was amazed at the stash of ordanance but knew Natalia had no idea what he was talking about. "Look at this. There are several hundred crates of anti-radar missiles. They are Russian made, and can carry up to a 100 kilogram warhead of conventional explosives. I do not understand. These must be launched from an aircraft. Why would Albani have this many?" Yuri wondered out loud as he walked to another crate and read the label, now engrossed in his impromptu inventory.

"If this tag is correct, these contain anti-ship cruise missiles, the 3M82 MOSKIT. These are supersonic missiles that can carry nuclear warheads or conventional payloads. The Raduga Moskit anti-ship missile is perhaps the most lethal anti-ship missile in the world. The MOSKIT is designed to fly as low as 9 feet at over 1,500 miles per hour. That is faster than a rifle bullet." Yuri shook his head and counted crates with the same tag. "My math is not that good, but I calculate there are some two hundred of these missiles here. General Albani was either contemplating declaring war or, selling arms." Yuri looked at Natalia who stood with a

264

blank look on her face.

"Yuri, this must have been the stash the Al Qaeda spy was searching for. Surely Albani was dealing. There is way too much here, and such a diverse inventory."

"Ah…French made Roland anti-aircraft missiles. These are fired from a mobile launcher and have been very effective with low flying aircraft. We used them against the Afghan forces on the border last year. Where do you think he got all of this?"

"This entire facility must be worth, heck, I don't know - well off the scale. What comes after a billion anyway?" Natalia kissed Yuri's cheek, and pulled him on. "You do know your missiles, Captain, but there is more to see. Come, Captain Milassoviech, before you get ideas about starting your own army. Look over here!" Natalia dragged Yuri faster, obviously excited.

"Oh my! Have you ever seen this much art in one place?" They stood at the entrance of another large storeroom. All manner of paintings, rugs, wall hangings, ancient pottery, vases and glass statuary littered the room. Wrapping paper and packing material was strewn about between boxes and framing crates.

"Yuri, look. It's an original Salvador Dali." Natalia danced on between crates. "My God, a Monet. Isn't that a Picasso in his blue period? How in the world did Albani get these?" Natalia stood with her mouth open, a delicate finger touching the frame of the Monet.

"You do know your art, my Dark Angel. Come, we have much more to see." Yuri took Natalia's hand in an attempt to pull her from the room, only to be yanked back.

"This painting hung in the Hermitage, when I lived there. Look, it is a da Vinci, the Benois Madonna. I studied all of the artwork at the Hermitage. I used to roam the halls when Alexia was ill. It took my mind from worrying about the Tsarevich. I was always so afraid he would die in childhood." A somber look passed across her features. "As it was, he and Anastasia were the only two Romanovs to survive the bloody Bolsheviks. I hid them for a time." Her mind wandered back to the good old days, when things were so bad.

Yuri pulled Natalia into his arms and held her close. "Do not fret about the cold years. Had we not traveled the paths we have, I would now be dead at the hands of that pig of a terrorist, and you would be long dead and buried. I would not hold you, love you, and want you so much that I burn. We have a chance to begin a very long life together. Do not have regrets for each trail, every footstep, the many turns in life. For all served to bring you to me." His lips brushed hers with such tenderness her eyes began to tear. Nuzzling her ear, "No tears, only smiles and kisses. Have I told you, that your kisses set my mind ablaze with wanting and..." He pulled her tighter to him, pressing his groin close so she could feel the effect she had on him with only a simple peck on the cheek. "Well, I think you get the point." He smiled and nipped at her slender neck. It was becoming his favorite thing to do.

"Yuri, stop." Natalia gasped, pushing at Yuri's chest with both hands. "I don't seem to be able to resist you, either. Please, we should see what else this place contains, then be on our way. We..." Her pleas were cut short, hearing a mental message from MorningStar.

I may have found the exit. I am at the end of the main cave. Come.

Chapter 26

Dear Diary...

How do I love *me*, let me count the ways.
I walked among humans today and did not feel the
overpowering need to kill.
I think I'll shop for a new pair of shoes.
Maybe even a matching handbag.
I deserve it.

A Personal Journal
Susannah Maddox, Vampire
Olney Farm, 2008

The facility was truly incredible. Besides the jewelry room, and the missile room, and the art room, there were huge storage caches of just about everything. Munitions, building materials, medical supplies, and chemical weapon suits stood in huge crates. There was an entire vault of foreign currency stacked in trunks by country. The alcohol collection would rival the most educated collector. There was food and water enough to feed a small army. The furniture, and the luxury vehicles stored in other chambers came from not just one, but many countries.

Elizabetta was aghast at the smallest of the many large chambers. It was stacked, floor to ceiling, and wall to wall with raw cocaine, containers of meth and crack, all packaged, color coded and boxed for shipping. Within a filing cabinet in the drug storage, was a binder listing contacts and deliveries. Who would have thought General Albani kept intricate records of his buyers?

"Albani was not as smart as he thought he was, to keep these records." Yuri fingered through the pages. "These dealers are in every country. This will be handy if the Vamp Squad goes into business hunting drug smugglers. It also contains the means to identify how drugs are smuggled. Look here... he noted the

267

shipping methods. He was either an incredible idiot, or a very confident businessman."

Elizabetta stood near the door watching carefully. Monique was licking her lips, eyeing the drugs as if they were water and she was dying of dehydration. Elizabetta could feel the woman's ticklish need, a haunting desire just touching the surface. She funneled a subtle message directly to Monique. *Consume any drug you wish. The virus that has made you what you are, will not accept its interference. Like alcohol will have no effect on your system, unless it is bloodwine. VMD neutralizes the toxic chemical just as it heals tissue and bone. Whatever mood altering substances you placed in your body before becoming a vampire, will do you no good now.*

Monique snorted, and flounced from the room with a rude comment.

"Frenchy, what? Hey, wait for me." Susannah ran after her sister vampire, confused at the woman's actions. "So you can't stand drugs. I don't like them either, but really."

The group gathered before a huge cascade of boulders and dirt almost a mile from where they initially entered the cavern, behind the basement door of the schoolhouse. MorningStar sat on a large rock feeling the ground like it was a sentient being that could speak to her. She worked her fingers into the dirt, sniffing the air. Obviously their little fireworks display sealed this exit as well.

We are close to the air, beyond these rocks. It smells fresh and sweet. Past the exit, it does not lead to the stronghold. We are too far away, and this facility is in a different direction. Beyond these rocks is the trail we followed in the truck. Colonel Maddox can easily find this place. MorningStar closed her eyes, feeling the ground.

"Ya, right. Come on Kanza, how do you know what direction we walked? We're underground." Susannah was ready to be above ground and headed home. The shine had worn off the jewelry, she was tired and becoming grouchy. They'd spent several hours in the caverns and dawn was approaching. "Anyway, we have to go all the way back to get out. My feet are killing me. We should have hot-wired a car and driven down here." She sat down hard on a rock, and rubbed her instep through the tennis shoes she wore.

Possibly, but we may find a way here. This exit was large

enough for cargo. I believe there may be a smaller door for foot traffic. Another exit. Still sniffing the air, MorningStar rose and traced the wall for several feet in each direction, carefully observing the way. Touching as she moved, like a doctor looking for a broken bone or injured organ, she moved slowly and methodically, feeling for the cracks and breaks in the stone. She paused often, laying a cheek against the stones, whispering in soft, almost seductive tones.

Yuri sat with his back to a large boulder, pulling Natalia to sit between his legs, resting against his chest. They had been exploring the storage facility for several hours and would need to bed down for the day, if they did not leave soon. His mind was full of questions about the contents they'd discovered, as well as what the American Colonel would do with the wealth of resources. Russia and America were still opponents in the grand scheme of things. Yuri kept his thoughts and questions to himself. The members of the Vamp Squad may be his coven, or vampire family but he wasn't part of the Squad, and probably never would be. He was a Russian citizen and a soldier, albeit his status as a human had significantly changed.

"The stone speaks! Elizabetta, I have found a door." MorningStar pulled on a hanging tarp that had been air brushed to look exactly like a stone wall. Without touching the material, it appeared to be part of the stone wall of the cavern. Sliding back, the curtain revealed stone steps that lead to a heavily bolted metal door, recessed in the stone. With a quick flip of the wrist, MorningStar twisted the bolt, breaking the lock.

The door opened with a great woosh of warm air. Brilliant moonlight flooded the steps and created a halo around the sultry woman standing within the exit. Slowly and silently MorningStar disappeared, ascending the well disguised steps, watching for booby traps and guards near the exit opening.

It is clear. You may follow. There is a small cave camouflaging the exit. It opens into a valley. I can see the road we traveled that leads to the stronghold. We must be near the end of the valley. Come and see.

Elizabetta was right behind MorningStar. They stood for several minutes, quietly observing the valley with enhanced sight.

"Do I believe my eyes? Is that not our Babysitters, there on the road to Hafsa Tokar? What in the world do they think they are doing?" The coast was clear and Betta was working up to a decent rage.

"Babysitters, V-1. Respond!" She was more than working up to a rage, she was totally pissed!

"V-1, Babysitters here. Where ya been? Daddy's concerned. Pick-up on its way. Hang tight."

Elizabetta launched skyward with a feral growl. In seconds she appeared next to what looked like a slow moving caravan of traders. Purposeful strides took her to within an inch of the old, crippled donkey driver.

"Just what the hell do you think you are doing?" Elizabetta demanded, fangs barred and eyes glowing red as the oncoming dawn. "Why did we drill for weeks, practice all kinds of scenarios, memorize your stupid protocols, if you throw them out the window the second you begin to worry about us and get a wild hair up your nose? Ahhh! Men." Elizabetta calmed as she spoke pointedly at Colonel Maddox.

"Ah, ma'am. We thought you were in trouble. Your communication was strange and we wanted…" Sergeant Miller looked confused and more than a little frightened. He'd never seen Elizabetta in her vampire best.

"What part of patience, did you not understand? You could have compromised the entire Squad; my women, your daughter, and Yuri. I thought you military types followed the rules ALWAYS!"

"Ma'am, standby. I mean, please keep your voice down and calm yourself. We simply chose to move the support team closer. It was a command decision." Colonel Maddox was not in the habit of explaining himself, but in light of the vampire's anger, he thought it would be fortuitous to attempt to present some kind of excuse. He still did not totally trust the promise that his squad members wouldn't bite, if they were truly provoked.

Elizabetta looked truly provoked.

"We're here to support you, to help in any way we can. We can do that much better, much closer, okay?"

Sergeant Miller stared at the Colonel as if the man had lost his mind. "Ah, Sir? Maybe we should find out what's going on? Ah, before we, before you make any more command decisions. Just a thought." Miller flinched, and stepped back as Elizabetta leveled an angry glance his way. "Do you need medical support for the Russian? I believe you mentioned Yuri. I assume you meant Captain Yuri Milassoviech."

"Your sergeant has more sense, than the entire American Army. Yes, Yuri is with us and he does not need medical assistance at the moment." Elizabetta was careful how she explained Yuri's presence. "Go back the way you came, and take the path that leads around the backside of that cliff." She pointed out the way toward the cavern exit and MorningStar. "I will meet you there. We found something." With her last words, Elizabetta morphed and leaped skyward. "Hurry, it is almost dawn," she called from the sky.

Sergeant Miller shook his head. "I see it. I still don't believe it. With all due respect sir, if I were in your uniform, I don't think I'd push the envelope with these ladies." Miller grabbed the reigns of a string of pack animals laden with trading goods. "Big teeth. Never mess with the one with big teeth." He pulled on the reigns and started the animals back the way they had come. Mumbling to himself more than anyone, Miller said, "I wonder what they found?"

Chapter 27

A Comfortable Compromise

We shall exist together into the future and beyond
For one depends on the other, neither one fond,
Of the style, the life, the ways of the other
Symbiosis? A family? One brother to another?

Not in this world or universe wide
Shall both exist side by side.
One lives life to the fullest extent,
The other sees food, a meal content.

A Vampire's Tale
Kalila Muligan DuMont
New Orleans, Louisiana 1892

Elizabetta landed with a soft footstep, on the ledge she left a few minutes before. "The Babysitters will be here soon. We can wait for them inside. The sun will rise soon."

"Did we not have a plan to go to them? Why do they change their plans, without consulting us?" MorningStar was confused and a little insulted.

"Apparently, rules and plans are for us. They do whatever they want. This will be something we must discuss at a later time. Now we shall take cover and wait. Hurry up and wait. Finally, I understand that human saying." Elizabetta was frustrated, but the sun would be coming up and the Squad needed protection. "Come. Let us go inside, and, hurry up and wait."

As they joined their compatriots within the storage facility, Elizabetta could feel the approach of the Babysitters. Apparently she had spurred them on, and they were pouring on the speed.

"They should arrive within an hour." She looked at each member of the Squad thoughtfully. "I do not suppose you will consider replacing your, ah, loot? A soldier should not be wearing a million dollar tiara and two miles of pearls, I think. Susannah, your father would frown on pilfering the goods, even though the earrings compliment your complexion beautifully." Betta sat wearily on the steps and smiled. "Where are Natalia and Yuri?"

"Êtes-vous étonné ? Surprised? They are behind that pillar by the last corridor. And we? We must hold down the fort, so to speak and face the big bad Colonel, all alone." Monique flounced across the floor, playing the fearful little girl. "But then, it only delays the inevitable. The Colonel will have to learn of Yuri, at some point."

"Oh yeah, and Daddy's gonna be pissed. Do you have any idea, how hard he had to fight just to get the Joint Chief's to recognize the existence of vampires in the first place? If Elizabetta hadn't gone strolling in, fangs a blazing, they would have laughed him out of the Pentagon. Then, they refused to fund the project. Daddy called in all of his markers to put this together, and there was no guarantee that it will continue after this mission. I think this little storehouse may help convince those stuffy bastards." Susannah snickered as she twirled her pearls like a fifties flapper.

"So you have finally come to understand the importance of succeeding on this first mission." Elizabetta was relieved that Susannah had come to grips with the importance of their initial mission's success. However, she had a sneaking suspicion the pearls had something to do with it.

"Oui, little sister is completely serious about her jewels! And the Colonel should be very happy about what we have found. Possibly, he will make his own little army, no? Or maybe just make a very big deposit in some bank on a very little island. In any event, we now can do as we please, and foot the bill ourselves. C'est doux, no?" Monique wrinkled her cute little nose.

"Betta, puh-lease. They're at it again." Susannah was rubbing her ribs and scrunching her shoulders. "If we're gonna work as a team, they have to just…stop it." Susannah squirmed as she picked up on Yuri's energetic broadcast. Abruptly, she sat on a wooden crate, sticking her chin in her hands and balancing her elbows on her knees. Her pouty lip stuck way out for emphasis.

Elizabetta rubbed the back of her neck and sent a quick mental nudge to Natalia. *Shield yourself Nat, unless you want Monique and Susannah joining you. The Babysitters are on their way and we must be prepared to explain your new paramour.*

*****

Natalia giggled and snuggled closer. They found cots, blankets, and tents and other items a regiment would need to set up a base, right near the exit. Obviously soldiers camped here at some point. It was close to dawn and Yuri was in dire need of sleep, blood and sex. It was less than forty-eight hours since his turning, and he was going through the last stages of the process. She felt his lips on her neck, then the warm wetness of his tongue. He traced a path from her ear lobe to the cleft at the base of her neck and back. His favorite move. Her favorite feeling. Her senses jangled, and she could not breathe. Why did Yuri's touch inflame her in so many ways, and to such an incredible extent?

She had heard the tale of a vampire bonding such as this when she and Petra visited the Librarian. It was documented, but only once. The two individuals were extremely strong, old vampires, heroes among those who carried VMD. They shared everything, communicating through psyche-speak and rarely spoke to others. For hundreds of years they lived within each other's minds and bodies, as if they were truly one and the same.

At the time Natalia thought it was a legend, a fantasy love story that every vampire looked for. To live with a mate who fired your senses for thousands of years was a dream come true. To have the kind of love that connected you directly with the human you had been, was even more precious. Natalia often thought that every vampire she knew would give their right fang to return to being human. Anything that made vampires feel mortal was akin to reverent.

She did not feel that way.

She did not deserve humanity when she had failed in protecting the only humans that accepted her, needed her.

There was that guilt again.

This connection began even before Yuri was turned. Was this a universal comment on fate or just a coincidence?

Or something even stranger?

She felt Yuri's electric touch and sighed. What connected them so strongly that a simple glance would initiate all kinds of fantasies and send her concentration off into the ozone layer? Her heart was not free, but Yuri gave his freely to her. Could she learn to love him despite the monstrous dreams that haunted her sleep? Was it just because she was his creator? Was this a normal pattern? It surely had not been like this between Rasputin and herself. Or was this something more, something outside the norm even for vampires? She lie her head on his warm shoulder, and closed her eyes, letting the feelings envelope her.

Yuri felt Natalia relax against him. He was in heaven. Wishing that he could be this way the rest of his life, however long that might be; a year, a thousand years. He loved his dark angel with all of his soul. He chuckled. Yuri was relieved to know he still had a soul to commit. He was just as astounded to understand, a virus made him the way he was, not some demonic curse of the living dead.

He pulled her closer and softly kissed the top of her beautiful brunette head. She would need time to adjust; he understood that much about the woman he held. He was a patient person, a soldier used to waiting for the right moment. He was also a man, used to having his way with women.

However, Natalia was not just any woman. She was something incredibly special and fragile. Strength, powers, intelligence, courage, heart... she was so much more than he could ever wish for. And she was his, at least for a while. It was up to him to make it forever. He would find a way if it was the last thing he did.

"Moi-ya me-lotch-ka, ya-lou-blue-ya vas. I love you and I always will." Yuri whispered the soft words, despite the response he knew he would get.

"You do not yet know what it is to love as a vampire, Yuri. You must go slowly into this new life. I have lived as such for a long time, and I am not sure I still believe there is love for our kind. For us." Natalia raised her head and peered over his chin. "Right now you feel as if you will die without sex. But, I think it is only the turning. When it is done, you may move on. I will understand." She was giving Yuri every out to leave her, if, in fact, their connection was due to the process of turning and not the will of the heart. She was so unsure of her own feelings, she would not trap Yuri by his. This was entirely new territory for Natalia.

"This thing we have is something more than a viral reaction. I

275

am no vampire specialist, but I know how I feel. I think I know how you feel, too." He kissed her lips tenderly. "Your turning was brutal and filled with violence. Had you the experience I have had, you might feel differently. I don't truly know, Natalia. What I do know, is that we have time to find out. If what Elizabetta said is true, then we have about a hundred thousand years to knock around the idea. Is there some book, or record, or scroll or something that will help us understand? Maybe the Internet can provide answers. Heaven knows, you can find just about anything if you search long enough. How about we Google vampire love and see what comes up?"

"We don't have a computer handy, Yuri, and the only thing I want to oogle is you." Her hands went to work, drawing his mind away from the topic at hand, a successful strategy to sidetrack such talk of intimacy and true love.

"That's Goog... ah, yes, yes." Yuri's body took control of his brain, and he was stretching to offer Natalia a better handhold. "Moi-ya me-lotch-ka, you have the oogle of a sainted angel. Don't stop, ever."

His lips captured hers, as his tongue sought an opening against velvety lips. Finding what he needed, he ravaged her mouth.

She returned the pleasure, sucking at his assaulting tongue.

A feral groan escaped with his ragged breath. His body ached to be ensconced within the woman he held, the ache eliciting both pleasure and agony. He felt small hands unlatching the pants that contained his throbbing manhood, then cool air, as he was freed from confinement.

Working loose from his arms, he felt Natalia's tongue draw lazy circles down his chest to his navel. Her teasing tongue burned like hot wax, then chilled with her soft breath. She was a master at using her glossy hair to tease and tantalize. Silky hair trailed across his cock, as it lurched and bobbed at each strand's movement. Again, she drew her hair across his stiff appendage, this time adding little butterfly kisses with her eyelashes. She was a teasey hellion who wanted to torture him, and yet a beautiful savior that would give him release from his body's anguish.

Those same velvety lips that his tongue caressed, now encircled the head of his cock, swirling and tantalizing. He jerked and groaned, close to losing control. Waves of pleasure assaulted his senses beginning at his groin, working their way steadily to his brain, with ever increasing frequency. He rode the crests, straining to keep from drowning in the overwhelming lust that drew him on. When he thought he could contain himself no more, Natalia quickly shed her clothing and slid atop him to straddle his cock. Pausing for a half heartbeat, she smiled then took him deep into her sex, feeling his full balls draw across her bottom with each pump.

Completely locked into Yuri's pleasure, Natalia felt his strain. She glanced toward his face and saw the ripple of his abs as he arched and fought for control, his face a mask of tension. *Let go my love. Enjoy.*

It was all the encouragement he needed. Thrusting deeply, Yuri surrendered to the intense pleasure as the mind numbing orgasm tore at his consciousness. Mindless and surfing on wave after wave of incredible feeling, he bellowed his release. Natalia, body and mind locked around his cock, felt the jolt as if she were on the receiving end of her own ministrations. Sailing with her lover, she cried in pleasure, sharing each wave of feeling with Yuri.

Collapsing onto the cot, Yuri tried to relax but Natalia clung to him, feeling her muscles clenching in rhythm with her heartbeat. "Nat, stop. I cannot take any more. I… ah…" This time an animalistic groan split the silence of the room. Again, he was catapulted into orgasmic delirium to rise to the top of an even higher crest to plummet, as if riding some mammoth pleasure coaster. "Ahhhh….no more. I must breathe. You will surely kill me."

Natalia pulled away licking her lips in a sensual gesture. "You are all but immortal. You don't really need to breathe, Yuri. You will not die of pleasure, no matter how hard I try." She sunk her mouth onto his still softening cock with a loud sucking noise and a giggle.

Yuri winced, gasped and tugged at her hair. "No, really. A man has his limits love, and I think you found mine. I have never experienced the kind of, ah, experience I experienced, just now. It was quite overwhelming." Yuri was becoming tongue-tied as he pulled Natalia up into his arms. He frowned, "Do you think they heard us?"

"Did you not feel them with us? Trust me, we were not alone." Licking a small trickle of cum from her mouth, she passionately kissed her lover. "I felt all that you did. And now you taste all that I did."

Yuri never tasted himself on any woman's lips and found it incredibly intimate. Now he knew what women felt when he shared with them their own taste in his kisses after making love. A heady sensuality filled his being and he curled around Natalia, holding her tightly, unable to get enough of her body touching his. "Is it always this way with our kind?" He never felt multiple climaxes before, and the level of intensity was astounding.

"I don't really know. I cannot say that I have had a lot of experience making love. Rasputin always took me how and when he wanted, with no thought to my feelings. He raped my body and mind." Natalia's voice was small and faint. She buried her face in Yuri's chest to cover the sad look that enveloped her features.

"I gave you my pleasure, now give me your pain. I will take it and send it to hell with it's maker." Yuri covered the top of her head with little kisses. "You must let it go, my love."

Natalia looked into Yuri's eyes with a tentative question. "You cannot know, Yuri. But I will show you." She focused on his eyes and let him share her memories.

In an instant Yuri was catapulted into Natalia's memories, chained to the freezing altar, feeling everything Natalia felt. Hearing every word Rasputin spoke, screaming the words Natalia had screamed. His heart was torn apart, finally understanding the torture she endured as Rasputin raped the little girl who came to the church, only to pray for her sick childhood playmate.

Yuri's eyes stared into the maniacal eyes of the priest, felt the man's putrid breath on his face, knew the intense pain as Natalia's body ripped to accommodate the size of the mad monk. He felt the warm blood flow from him as the priest grunted and rutted within a virginal girl who did not understand what was happening. He felt the betrayal, the bewilderment, the fear, the violent attack with its pain. He knew the hatred. He knew the moment when Natalia ceased to be a living human as the virus entered her body through the fangs of the deranged priest. He felt her slip away, broken and battered, still chained to that cold altar, hating herself for not dying, before the priest could damn her to hell.

278

The feelings poured into Yuri's conscious mind as he held Natalia tight to him and felt her tears flow. He too, cried for the naive little girl who had experienced something no one should have to endure. Something that changed her, literally forever.

"I have hated him for so long." She was despondent, sobbing in long painful cries. "You don't know how I dreamed about killing him, in so many ways. Over and over. He always knew and laughed at me. It excited him to know my hate, my desperation. He fed off of it. Only when I learned how to block him from my mind did he begin to doubt me. By then it was too late. He taught me well, and I was a good student. I laughed at the gurgling sound he made when I cut off his head. His eyes never left my face, even as his head rolled to the snow."

"Shush my love. He is long gone. Now forget. It will not be easy after holding these memories for so long, but let them go. You avenged yourself, and now it is time to begin anew, with a family. With me and with love." Yuri gently rocked his woman like he would a newborn baby, cooing to her softly.

"But you don't understand. There are things I did. Bad things. Rasputin made me do some of them, but later, on my own I did unspeakable things as well. I survived, I am ashamed to admit." The sobs continued as Natalia poured her heart out to Yuri. Once she began, it seemed everything she feared, everything she did, every insecurity came spewing out of her mouth. She could not stop producing the hateful words.

"Ah, moi-ya me-lotch-ka, you also did good things. Don't forget you were my Dark Angel, my protector. You saved Alexei and Anastasia from the Bolsheviks, kept them hidden and safe, for how long? You watched over the remnants of the royal family for over one hundred years. You risked all to rescue me, and, I, for one, am grateful." This time he kissed her forehead with a loud smacking noise.

Despite her tears, Natalia smiled. "Yes, but I killed more than once."

Yuri imitated a German accent, "Yes. But they were all bad men."

"How did you know?" Natalia cocked an eye at Yuri speculatively.

"It's a line from a movie. You know, the one with the woman

who dances real sexy, the one with great legs. And the Austrian body builder, the actor fellow who became the governor of the US." Yuri smiled, showing off his knowledge of western movies and celebrities.

Then Natalia did have to giggle. "He was the governor of California, not the US. The movie was True Lies, and the actress' legs you so fondly refer to belonged to Jamie Lee Curtis. By the way, I hate to burst your bubble, but she had a body double for those legs." How did their serious conversation turn to movies and jokes so quickly?

"No! Don't tell me that and ruin years of fantasies. I saw the movie as a young man when I was in military training. We all fantasized about her legs wrapping around us with those fabulous heels digging into, ah, never mind." Yuri feigned a duck, as Natalia aimed a playful punch at his chin.

"No matter, what we do to survive, good or bad, is just that, survival. Human's have perpetrated some of the worse crimes on their own people, for more self serving reasons since time began. Rasputin did unthinkable things to you. What you did to him was justice. What the Bolsheviks did to the royal family was butchery. What you did to protect what was left of the Romanovs, was necessary. Let it be, Natalia. We all have pasts. We may not be proud of them, but they have brought us to this place and time. I am content to be where I am, here, with you, despite both our pasts. Let's move on together. Let love take us into our future." He stroked her back as he spoke, lulling the guilt and pain away, comforting his love.

"Yuri, you are a good man and I do not deserve your love. But I will take it." She smiled weakly at the man who held her so securely. "You have no idea how I have longed to leave my nightmares behind. How much I wanted to forget the evil that has clung to me for over a century." She kissed his chin and snuffed loudly, shuddering just a little.

"Then concentrate on the light of my love, see only me. Leave the nightmares and evil in the dark where they belong." His tongue, once again sought hers with its warmth and sweet passion. Their hot fires satiated for the time being, their kiss was gentle with the promise of a future together.

Chapter 28

Sensual Hunt

I can feel your heat, your need, your want.
I sense your flame and find your haunt.
Within the walls you find so safe,
I will take my pleasure in that place.

I will take your blood, your life, your seed,
I steal from you to assuage my need.
There is no law unto my kind
I simply take what crosses my mind.

The Book of the Hunt
Madelynn Courdree, Huntress
Mandalay Bay, Dutch Antilles 2001

Monique perched on a flat rock just inside the cavern, fanning herself with a jewel encrusted fan from the Spanish Civil War. The painted silk of the fan depicted ladies in a garden surrounding a handsome prince. Each vied for the man's attention except one, who stood to the side, shy and reserved. The prince eyed the child-like girl with obvious interest.

"Mère sainte de Mary, what ever Natalia has done, Yuri is now silent. But I am se sentir chaud, feeling the heat, you know. Do you think she has killed the poor man?"

"Monique, don't be silly. You of all people, should know what a man, or woman for that matter, needs when turning. I am sure Yuri will survive. What puzzles me, is the intensity of their relationship, and the fact that he is not interested in anyone except Natalia. In my experience, it is most unusual."

Susannah's little ears perked and she looked critically at Elizabetta. "Why is that unusual? I don't understand."

"Vous écoutez, little one, when a man turns, he needs three

things: blood, sex and more sex." Monique smiled and chewed at a broken nail that was quickly returning to normal.

"That's only two things, Frenchy." Susannah snorted.

"Ah cheri, not with our kind. You were locked away when you turned, but do you not remember the burning hunger, the sizzling need that tortured your dreams? My sire was a notorious lover, experienced and adept at, how shall I say, instruction? I still dream of the monster quite fondly at times. But, a male vampire's drive can be intimidating and exhausting." She finally worked the nail to the quick and stopped chewing at it. Within a few seconds, it began to reappear. "But what Betta refers to, is the fact that most males take from any female that is willing. Our Yuri does not even notice other females. Moi, for instance. It is, as you say, puzzling. This is not a thing I have ever heard of, Betta. Strange, indeed."

"I seem to remember, a very long time ago, the story of a vampire couple. They were mated, connected somehow by their mental powers. But it was much more than choice, they remained together for centuries, never stepping outside their relationship. When the Contessa died, her mate walked into the morning sun. I always thought it a Romeo and Juliet version for vampire romantics, but possibly it was true. No one ever explained the how or why, it was just a legend, a story to whisper about with others of our kind when we occasionally gathered, or in the Council chambers behind locked doors. A hope for the kind of love some humans have." Elizabetta rubbed the back of her neck aggressively. "If this has happened to Yuri and Natalia, for whatever reason, it could be a serious problem."

"Yeah! We will all go insane trying to block out the two nymphos on our team who can't keep their hands off each other. Monique will have no fingernails left, from chewing them to the quick and I, the equivalent of a vampire virgin, will walk into the sun myself from sheer frustration. G-a-w-d!" Susannah pouted, obviously already frustrated with the lack of sexual experience in her new life form.

"Patience, little sister. Males can be dangerous and unscrupulous. They take, not give. You should have a man who gives you pleasure many times over. A man who worships at your feet, and lives to please only you. Oui?" Monique's fantasies were often embellished to suit her mood.

"As Monique says, Susannah, patience. You have many years to add experience to your life but you must learn some basics first. Crawl before you walk, and walk before you try to run."

Elizabetta cautioned the young fledgling. "And of course, run before you fly."

"With all due respect Mother Superior, I can crawl, walk and run just fine. When do I get to fly and fuck?" Susannah was startled by the deep voice emanating from behind the curtain.

"That was crude and uncalled for, Miss Maddox. Apologize at once." Colonel Maddox stepped from behind the thick painted tarp. He eyed his daughter, then nodded toward Elizabetta. Morningstar stood silent behind him.

"Yes, Sir. I'm sorry Elizabetta." Susannah sat back down on her rock, drew up her knees, hooked her arms around her legs and looked sullenly at the floor. Monique moved to sit next to her with a sisterly hug, and conspiratorial look.

"So, madam, what is this surprise you want..." In his strict adherence to manners and family discipline, the Colonel was focused on the desire to have his daughter apologize for her comment, at first. Looking up, his jaw dropped open as he took in the length and breadth of the cavern in which he stood. "Holy shit!"

His comment was echoed by the two men who followed Morningstar into the room. Sergeant Milo Miller and Captain Robert Devlin both stood, gaping at the place.

"Ah, Bob? Do you see, what I see?" The Colonel could not believe his eyes. He looked from one to the other, noticing the men could not tear their eyes away from what they saw. He looked at Elizabetta and noticed the *I-told-you-so* smile on her face. Next his view took in Susannah and Monique perched on their rock, clad in casual coveralls, but covered in jewels and pearls.

"So, Daddy, I guess 'holy shit' is on the list of okay things to say now?" Susannah was twirling her pearls and obviously smirking at her father. Her comment did not even register with the Colonel who continued to stare at the long corridor.

"Ah, Sir? Colonel Maddox, Sir?" A few feet away, it did not take vamp-sight for Elizabetta to see the wheels turning in Miller's brain, as he spoke. The man was a wheeler-dealer from the word go, which landed him in the brig, then on the Vamp Squad as a kind of punishment. His skills had been invaluable over the last year or so, but this was definitely letting the kid loose in the candy shop. His stunning smile clearly resembled a shark moving in for the kill.

"Frank, the team's a little short." Devlin quietly commented to his friend and commander.

Sgt. Miller, ever the true Babysitter with the style and technique of Mash's Klinger, began to assess the team and noticed the missing Natalia. "Ma'am, we seem to be missing someone. Is Natalia with you? Or was there a problem we do not know about?"

Susannah gave a little snort, "Ah, she's okay. She's…"

"Susannah, I believe I should update the Colonel on our mission status and the team." Elizabetta had stepped in quite eloquently, and was now at a loss for words.

"Okay, have a go at it. This should be interesting… Ma'am." Susannah added the respectful title, as a last minute thought. No reason to push her father's buttons when Elizabetta was going to do it for her. In a big way.

"So, report Ms. Zoeltel. I'm waiting." The Colonel was all business, but continued to look down the length of the cavern, squinting, unable to see the end. Obviously the Colonel was curious as to what else might be stashed in what seemed to be an endless facility.

"Well, Colonel, the mission was accomplished satisfactorily. The stronghold was destroyed with four Taliban Generals inside. General Albani, Colonel Fashiam and the Al Qaeda man, we efficiently dispatched. A couple bodies lie at the end of this cavern, ready for disposal. In the effort to hide the bodies, we discovered an entrance to this facility. It is connected to the stronghold, or rather *was* connected, by an underground passageway about half way back. A trap door exists under the schoolhouse in Hafsa Tokar and the only other exit, is the one you just came through. This facility contains several storage chambers, one of which is missing a few pieces of jewelry. " Elizabetta nodded at Monique and Susannah. "The rest is intact, as it was, when found." She paused gathering the words to explain about Natalia and Yuri.

"And?" Susannah smiled sweetly, as she deliberately prodded.

"And the only little snag we ran into was in rescuing Captain Yuri Milassoviech. Ah, actually, it wasn't a little snag, just an unexpected occurrence. More like an unplanned happening. The scenarios we practiced did not include the problem we, ah… ran into. But it was solved, and all is well." Elizabetta realized she had no words to explain what actually occurred.

"If all is well, Ms. Zoeltel, then why are you talking in circles and saying nothing? What's going on here? Where is Ms. Vyrubova?" Colonel Maddox stood with his hands on his hips, glaring at Elizabetta.

"She is here, safe and sound, Colonel. No need to be abrasive."

As the words left her mouth, Natalia and Yuri, hearing the commotion, appeared in the doorway of their private little love nest, grinning silly, holding hands. Natalia kissed the man lightly and dragged him forward.

"Colonel Maddox, this is Captain Yuri Milassoviech." Yuri slung his arm around Natalia's waist pulling her close. For effect, they both smiled broadly, matching fangs gleaming in the iridescent light.

The Colonel's jaw just didn't seem to be able to stay shut. "Holy shit."

Once again, the statement said so much!

"Told ya Daddy was gonna be pissed." Susannah high five'd Monique and reached for the string of diamonds designated as the pay off for their private bet. "You gotta love predictable men. And good old Daddy dearest is military predictable." Susannah hopped off her stone and trotted over to stand behind Yuri. She casually slung her arm around him and smiled, her fangs matching those of the grinning couple.

"We have a new brother, Daddy." Susannah planted a sisterly kiss on Yuri's cheek before returning to Monique and her rock seat.

Milo Miller mumbled to himself as he backed up. "Not another one. It's bad enough I have to watch out for five women with fangs, now we have a guy running around looking for a neck to bite. He better stay away from my carotid. I don't swing that way." Vampaphobia was a term Miller invented when he first met his new team members. Still fearful of being alone with a vampire, Miller was careful to keep his distance from the women he worked with. Now he had homo-vampaphobia to worry about as well.

Unconsciously he rubbed the sides of his neck.

"You are correct about one thing, Ms. Zoeltel. This was never a consideration in our scenarios. I suspect, we will have to expand the selective options for our computer simulations generator." Colonel Maddox frowned, considering the implications of this new turn of events.

The only one not completely taken aback, Captain Devlin strode across the dirt floor and extended his hand to the Russian Captain. "Strawz-vuit-ya, Capitan."

Surprised, Yuri took the hand and shook it vigorously. "Nice to meet you." Yuri grinned at Natalia like a little boy. "I can speak English! What is this?" His tongue pronounced the words carefully with a Russian accent.

"Yuri has much to learn about being a vampire, sir. He was turned only a short time ago." Elizabetta recovered her speech and was smiling like a proud mother.

"Apparently. And this happened how?" Colonel Maddox glared at Natalia. "I believe, our agreement was to rescue the man, not add him to the collective vampire community. He is a Russian soldier, correct?"

Yuri stepped forward, unable to remain silent, and let Elizabetta or Natalia protect him. "Was, Sir, was a Russian soldier. I am no longer sure what I am, except incredibly in love and happier than I have ever been." He pulled Natalia to him kissing her soundly.

"Oh puh-leeze. This is becoming ridiculous. Dad, do we have to keep him? I mean really…"

"Susannah, Yuri is not a pet to keep or abandon. At present, he needs our support and we will not fail him. What comes of this remains to be seen." Elizabetta admonished the pouting teen. Turning to the Colonel, she was all business.

"Colonel Maddox, despite this unique situation in which we find ourselves, we have successfully completed our first mission and discovered an amazing cache of goods. Both of which will undoubtedly surprise and please the Joint Chiefs. Sir, consider what this can do for the Vamp Squad." She extended her arms toward the corridor. "It is a considerable and timely find. You should see the extent to which Albani has collected, not only arms but illegal drugs, and many of the world's most prized treasures."

286

Elizabetta took Colonel Maddox by the arm and deftly escorted him toward the passageway that led to the drug room. "Albani kept meticulous records as well. This intel will be invaluable in squelching the opium and cocaine trade, Colonel. But what I find most enlightening, is his warehouse of missiles and bombs." For the warrior no truer words were ever spoken and now, she had his complete attention.

"French, Russian and American weapons, sir." Yuri followed them with Natalia on his arm. In any other situation, the two couples may have appeared to be enjoying a romantic stroll through some exotic marketplace.

"Missiles?" His eyebrows rose as he looked past Elizabetta to the Russian Captain.

"Zvezda KH-31s, several hundred 3M82 MOSKITS, grenade launchers, American made anti-personnel mines, enough to supply a medium sized coup, serious ordanance, Colonel and, possible chemical agents, Sir. Certainly chem-suits and respirators." Yuri pulled Natalia closer, looking deeply into her chocolate brown eyes. Inadvertently, he licked his lips, feeling heat ignite in his groin.

Elizabetta mentally warned the newest member of her coven. *Yuri, focus. Colonel Maddox knows little of our kind and it would be beneficial to keep it that way, for as long as possible. I do not believe he has ever experienced a turning, or observed the resulting, ah... needs.*

"Obviously, Captain, you have a weapons background. It may be useful." Colonel Maddox continued his review of the many storage rooms. Strolling through the passageways, he mentally chalking up the extent of the holdings. Natalia, Yuri and Elizabetta hurried to keep up. Colonel Maddox was a man on a mission, like Rambo in a WalMart for weapons. By the time he reached the third storage warehouse off the main chamber, he doubled his stride and was whistling to himself.

Chapter 29

Soulless

He took my blood, my life, my soul.
And left me dead in a deep, dark hole.

I'm not so easily left behind,
That is the truth, you will find.

My Life, Death and Life
Bella Montague
Sterling, Scotland 1654

Monique licked her lips and giggled. *Susannah, let us have a little fun with Miller. I can smell his fear. It is so sweet. Would that he'd allow me to feed. His blood would be delicious with so much adrenaline!* She breathed deep.

No way, not me, Frenchy. My dad'll be really pissed if we fool with his men. Susannah wagged her finger at her sister vampire. *You don't know the true meaning of pissed, until you've seen the Colonel on a rampage.*

Ah, little one, we will not really bite him, just play a petit jeu, small game. Monique stood and sauntered seductively toward Sergeant Miller. *Watch. He is so afraid. I find it endearing, and just a little cute.*

Miller, deep in conversation with Captain Devlin, did not notice Monique's vamp-rapid approach until he felt the warmth of her tongue on his earlobe.

"Ahhhh! Don't do that. Get away. You're not – normal Ms. Merchant. Beggin' your pardon, Ma'am." Sergeant Miller jumped, bumping into Captain Devlin, who laughed and shoved the Sergeant back toward Monique.

"Ah, mon amour. Do not worry your delectable little head over such things. I simply find you...irresistible." Monique

288

allowed her fangs to extend as she licked her lips and smiled seductively. Her hands snaked around his neck pulling him closer as she whispered, "Come, I will show you what I mean." Purposefully, her eyes glowed blood red, as she looked deep into the Sergeant's eyes, as if to mentally compel the man to her.

"No way. Absolutely not. Back off. Leave me alone. Don't do that, that- that mind thing you can do." Miller was squawking and flapping his hands, like a drowning duck.

"Come on, Frenchy. Leave the little guy alone. He probably wouldn't taste good anyway." Susannah hopped up and crossed the floor, scuffing at the dirt. "Too much cholesterol, and not enough protein, if you know what I mean." Susannah managed to insult Miller's physique as well as his sexual prowess in one sentence. Dragging Monique by the arm, she headed for the nearest pile of blankets. "I feel the need for a nap. The sun is coming up."

Monique sighed heavily as if she lost out on the opportunity to dine on a nine course meal. Together, hand in hand, the two wandered off to find a place to bed down for the day.

"I hate it when she does that. I never know if she is serious, or joking at my expense. Why did I ever agree to this assignment? Vampires? For God's sake." Sergeant Miller whispered to Devlin and slid a shaking hand across his forehead, wiping away beads of sweat.

"Probably because you had no choice. Twenty-five years in Leavenworth, or assignment to the Vamp Squad. That's a no-brainer in my book. Come on, man. It's not so bad. Working with gorgeous women fighting terrorism, covert ops, all the high-tech toys we can find, travel to lovely garden spots of the world like Afghanistan. What else could a soldier want?" Captain Devlin lifted his arms and spun a circle. "And now we are going to be rich beyond our wildest dreams. I am sure Colonel Maddox'll keep a little on the side, in case the powers that be decide to end our little Shangri-La. I've known the Colonel for a long time. He's a great soldier and a really great friend, but come on? Bazillions of dollars in booty? Not likely to keep a man completely on the up and up. Know what I mean?"

"Yeah, well I notice they all leave you alone. You're an officer. You can order them around. Why do they pick on me?" Miller was not being side-tracked. Fangs were still fangs and they could leave two little holes where they settled. Miller was not going to allow those little holes to be on his neck. No sir-ee.

Devlin shot the Sergeant a profound 'well duh' look. The answer to Miller's question was obvious. "Because you are clearly afraid of them. Frenchy gets a kick out of teasing you, and you fall for it every time. You know they promised not to bite any of us as part of their working agreement. Elizabetta keeps a firm hand on the ladies. She will not allow it. Besides, if you did go for it, you could finally tell us what it's like, and dispel some of the mystery around these ladies and their, sexual prowess. You would be serving your fellow soldiers and officers."

"They're not ladies, they're vampires. And they're dangerous." Miller was pacing back and forth, wearing a trough in the dirt. "And you can't order me to get bitten. It's un, un…unconstitutional, and down right uncool, Captain, Sir."

"Miller, they are ladies *and* vampires so I suggest you begin treating them that way, and maybe they'll quit teasing you. I'm going to check on the animals outside. You'd best find the Colonel, and figure out what our next move will be." Devlin ducked behind the painted tarp and was gone.

Sergeant Miller stood, mouth agape, as he watched his only security depart. "But…but… ah, shit." Miller snuck a peek at the two 'ladies' curled up together on a pile of old army blankets. Susannah snored softly, her blond hair floating with each noisy breath. Miller tip-toed by and then sped down the passageway in search of the Colonel and the rest of the squad.

*****

The last thing Captain Devlin remembered, before the entire world went black, was stepping through the doorway into the dawn. A pistol handle descended on the back of his neck and then there was nothing.

Teffas Hamza snickered and kicked the unconscious man at his feet. "Take this trash and tie him up." Hamza pulled a dirty rag from his neck and whispered. "Gag him. We need no noise to alert his friends."

Two burly soldiers dressed in Albani's black uniforms grabbed the unconscious man by his arms and dragged him behind a large outcropping of rocks. The remaining three waited for their orders.

"We must be silent and careful. There are at least two more soldiers inside, and Allah knows how many more await us. The General is dead and so is Fashiam. Allah has chosen me upon whom to shine his light. I shall take up His holy fight with the might Albani provided in death." Hamza was smiling like a cat that just ate the rat. "You and you," he pointed at the two who stood closest to the entrance, "go through the doorway. Clear the way."

The two soldiers took tentative steps toward the entrance and paused.

"Go. Be filled with the courage of Jihad. Praise be to Allah." He rammed his rifle barrel into the back of the last man. His point was taken, as both men moved through the doorway as quickly and quietly as possible, afraid of what they would find on the other side but more afraid of the 'courage of Jihad' held in Hamza's hands behind them.

"Fadique, slowly." The trailing soldier warned his comrade in a hushed whisper. "I do not wish to join the General in meeting Allah this day." His gun was raised and ready to fire at the least provocation. His hands shook as he prepared to squint into the darkness of the cavern they were about to enter.

"Hush. Do not shoot me in the back, you idiot." The first man moved behind the curtain to peer into the cavernous room beyond. "There is no one." Surprised by the brightness, he spoke in a loud voice. "The place is empty. Come." They stepped from behind the curtain and moved out into the huge room, checking the nooks and crannies, behind boxes and around rocks.

"Mamoud," Fadique whispered, then motioned to his friend with a finger to his lips. He pointed to the sleeping women on a pile of blankets near one wall. A perverted smile lit his features as he moved his hips in a humping motion.

Fadique shook his head in warning and moved toward the women, his gun leveled at their heads. "Wake up!" He kicked at Susannah who moaned sluggishly and curled tighter around Monique.

"Get up, bitch." Mamoud grabbed Monique's leg with a vicious jerk. "Get up now."

Monique took a deep breath and forced her eyes open. A burly angry man in black waved a gun in her face. She sighed, and shoved the barrel away, closed her eyes again and mumbled, "Merde."

Mamoud looked at Fadique with a puzzled expression. He prodded the sleeping women with the end of his gun, and got no response. This was strange indeed.

Fadique reached down and shook the snoring blonde, again with no response. He leered at the women, set his rifle down next to the pile of blankets, and began to untie his pants.

Snickering, Mamoud followed suit.

"Do not even consider it." Hamza stood just inside the curtain, his rifle pointed directly at Mamoud's growing erection. Behind Hamza, two soldiers dragged a still unconscious Devlin, now tied and gagged. The third soldier held a pistol to the Devlin's hanging head.

"Holy shit…" Sergeant Miller heard the commotion before he saw it. Rounding a bend, he reached for his gun, then froze.

Two soldiers stood, one on each side of Monique and Susannah, their rifles now pointed at the pretty heads of the sleeping vampires. Two soldiers flanked a slumping Captain Devlin and one big ugly guy stood in front of them a few feet away, aiming an AK-47 straight at his Miller's chest.

"Uh oh. NASA, I think we have a problem." Miller raised his hands. "Colonel?"

Behind Miller, Colonel Maddox, Elizabetta, Natalia and Yuri surveyed the scene. Maddox calmly stepped in front of Miller, as if he was moving to officiate some formal ceremony.

"All right, let's all calm down now. No need for anyone to get hurt." He held his hands in front of him as if he were in complete control and confident that everyone would follow his directions without question. "Do you speak English?"

Hamza screamed and fired a spray of bullets across the room. Colonel Maddox dropped to a crouch, as Miller ducked behind a box of medical supplies. Elizabetta stumbled as several bullets impacted her body with enough force to throw her backwards. Natalia caught her as she tripped and fell. Yuri charged Hamza then froze in his tracks.

Hamza held Captain Devlin in front of him as a shield, his men lined up directly behind their leader shielding themselves from gunfire. "Go ahead, and I will take this man's head off with one shot." He sneered. "And my soldiers will make a very messy end of some very pretty dancers. Dancers, eh? I don't think so." The real facts of the situation were beginning to dawn on Hamza as he finally recognized the sleeping women dressed in something other than their burqas.

Elizabetta lie in Natalia's arms, already recovering from her wounds, but weakened. Natalia's mind screamed with rage. Her blood boiled as she watched the holes in Elizabetta's chest slowly close of their own volition. Her fangs grew with her anger, and her eyes glowed neon red. She lay Elizabetta gently to the floor and rose to face the man who she would soon kill. She was a vampire, immortal. She was a super compeller as well. She could, if she truly wanted, end this pig's life with a thought.

Yuri watched his beloved and knew her anger would keep her from acting rationally. This was no time for irrational behavior. He was a soldier and knew how to handle the situation. He screamed, "No, Natalia, let me…"

Then all hell broke lose.

Natalia closed her eyes in concentration as Hamza hissed in agony, fighting the mental pain that threatened to explode his brain. Without the ability of true conscious control, he fired randomly, emptying his gun into the room. Yuri stepped in front of Natalia to shield her from the rain of fire, taking the hail of bullets into his own body.

Devlin, now awake and somewhat confused, watched in horror as Yuri's body seemed to explode, blood and tissue flying across the room. The men holding Captain Devlin crumpled to the ground screaming in torturous mental agony seconds before starting their journey to meet Allah once and for all. Mamoud and Fadique, standing over the two sleeping vampires, looked surprised as 9mm slugs from Miller's Beretta lodged in their chests, one after the other in rapid succession. Maddox ran toward Devlin, catching the man as he toppled toward Hamza who lie on the ground writhing, dying as blood oozed from his nose and ears. A terrified look was etched into his frozen features.

"Yuri!" Natalia shrieked as she watched the man she had earlier vowed to love forever, collapse in a puddle of his own blood and organs. "Nooooo," she screamed.

Instantly, she knelt cradling what was left of Yuri's mangled body. "Oh, my God, Yuri. Why did you do that? Yuri, you can't die now. I love you, moi-ya me-lotch-ka." Natalia sobbed rocking his body. How could she lose him now?

Elizabetta rose, completely healed but still unsteady on her feet, and ran to Natalia's side. Quickly assessing the damage, she spoke quietly, "His heart and brain are intact, Natalia. He can be healed."

"No Elizabetta, I am too weak now. The sun is up and there is too much damage. Even you can not do this for him."

Yuri's breathing was shallow and he choked as blood dribbled from his mouth and ears. A gapping hole in his mid section slowly filled with body fluid, floating damaged organs that threatened to spill down a torn and ragged side. Shattered ribs stemmed the flow for a time, but not long. A split femur shoved its way out his leg, a leg which lie at odd angles to his body.

"Natalia, you can draw what power you need! Like before. I will give what you can take." Elizabetta wrapped her arms around Natalia hugging the woman tightly, and kissed her cheek.

"It will not be enough, Betta. Even now his life floats away. He only wanted to protect me. No one has ever done that before." Natalia still held Yuri, stunned, simply watching as he drifted toward death.

"Can we help?" Miller always eves-dropping when possible, overheard the private conversation. "Can you maybe, what? Use us, somehow? Captain, Colonel, get over here, ah, please, Sirs. The ladies need help." Miller was issuing orders as nicely as he could, considering he lacked the rank to even comment in the Colonel's presence.

Maddox untied the Captain and pulled Devlin to his feet. They rushed to Elizabetta's side and pulled up short, shocked at the sight of the Russian Captain. Devlin, still woozy from his head wound, immediately turned, hit his knees and vomited in the dirt.

"Sorry." Devlin mumbled through the rag he held to his mouth. "I've never liked the sight of blood. Ah, so much, ah-" He turned and vomited again, wiped his mouth, and mumbled his apologies one more time. Considering the fact that he was a trained fighting machine, he was handling the scene fairly well.

"So what do we need to do, Ms. Vyrubova?" Colonel Maddox

swallowed hard as he studied Yuri's wounds. He had his doubts anything could actually be done for the man, save a quick death, and that was plainly on its way, at warp speed.

Yuri choked, his body shuddered struggling for breath.

Yuri, hold on, I am coming for you, my love. Natalia insinuated the message deep into Yuri's cognitive processes, reaching for a thread of life to follow.

Chapter 30

Possibilities

Can it be?
There is a future I see?
Of love's warm embrace,
My heart encased,
In arms so strong,
My life in song,
Played to the beat of singular desire.

Author Unknown, Bathroom Stall 2
Sanctuary House Hotel
London, England

Yuri drifted, close to the edge of consciousness, a breath away from the pain. He felt himself floating, as if on a sea of green grass and brilliant wildflowers. He could smell the scent of his homeland's steppes in the spring bloom that cradled his cold body. Death was close. Soon… again… here again, in this place?

He watched the hot sun like a golden orb in the azure sky. It loomed above him, calling. *Moi-ya Yuri.* It had called in the same way, once before.

Yes. I am here. I am ready. A thread of consciousness touched his mind. It tickled, leaving a strange kind of tingling in its wake. He knew that tingling. He felt it before in the same way. It drew him across the grass, floating toward a woman who sat naked on a soft downy quilt, her arms outstretched, welcoming him to heaven.

I am ready. He smiled for the first time in what seemed like a century. She was so beautiful, his Natalia, his Dark Angel.

She took him into her embrace. Their lips met, tongues tangling in a fevered passion that set his loins to burn. Yuri's hands traced their way around Natalia's waist and pulled her atop him in a tighter embrace. Her skin was so soft and smelled of honey and

296

sun. She felt so good, he thought he would surely die from this simple sensation of skin touching skin. It would be an acceptable end, here in the arms of his beloved Natalia... just like before, but different.

Something was different.

Again, he thought the end was near, however, it was not an end, the feelings continued; the fire in his groin, the need to sink himself into this goddess and bury his cock to the hilt. He pulled her along his body, laving her honeyed breasts, as she moaned and arched in ecstasy. Her long chestnut curls caressed his nipples as she moved seductively above him, clenching his cock with her nether muscles, drawing him into her glorious sex. Ah yes, he was home.

A groan of pure pleasure escaped his lips as he grasped the woman's hips, building a rhythm that threatened his sanity. This beautiful angel moved with him, drawing Yuri closer to a wildly building climax. Stars flickered behind his eyes, punctuating the sight before him. He marveled at Natalia's delicate hands as they massaged and played with her own puckering pink nipples. The visual display drove him mad with sizzling desire. His manhood throbbed on the verge of explosion for a single second before he willingly relinquished all control.

Like a backflash, his body exploded, erupting in molten waves of intensity that rocked the nebulous world in which they lay. Consuming his mind and will, driving him almost beyond the limits of existence.

Yuri roared. His eyes flew open. He gasped for breath. But there was no sight. Pain sliced through his body, a pain so intense and invasive it challenged his consciousness. He fought it, wrestling the waves of searing agony until they were beaten into submission. Again, and again, the miserable pain reared its ugly head, only to be trampled by swift steps and a strength that came from... from where? Yuri knew not, but was grateful for the tiny moment of respite. After a time, respite outweighed the pain and he could fight the waves away with little effort.

His breath came in more even gulps now and his body seemed to float on a cloud of veiled agony that thinned with the gentle breeze blowing through his mind. His eyelids hung, just a speck too heavy yet to lift. Soon... it would be soon.

"Moi-ya me-lotch-ka, rest Yuri. I am here, and you will be fine." Yuri heard Natalia's voice through the neural channels in his ears. His ears? He felt a gentle hand caress his cheek.

Felt?

Cheek?

Yuri forced his eyes to open.

This time he saw.

His Dark Angel appeared, a brilliant smiling beacon in the fog that surrounded his vision. "Moi-ya ahn-hel tiemno, I love you." His voice rasped and he tried to reach for her.

"No, no, Yuri. Lie quiet and heal, my love, my heart." Her lips braised his. "I almost lost you. I will not allow that to happen again." Natalia settled his head in her lap and smoothed his matted curls.

Yuri tested his movement, hunched his shoulders and rolled his head, looking around. "What happened, I don't quite remember."

Elizabetta hovered above Natalia looking tired and somewhat drawn. She was pale and her eyelids drooped in exhaustion. "You were wounded quite badly, Yuri. We have helped you to heal. It was somewhat...taxing." Elizabetta looked toward the three men who sat panting on the ground at her feet, too spent to even stand.

Devlin was ghost-white.

Maddox slumped, his head in his hands, sweat soaking his clothing, but still sitting somewhat upright.

Miller lie, curled on his side holding his stomach, breathing deeply as if fighting a bout of overpowering nausea.

The humans? What had happened? Yuri was puzzled.

"We must all rest now. Your healing has taken more than I thought from each of us. But the important point is, you shall survive." Elizabetta stumbled on her feet wavering slightly, then shuffled a few feet and proceeded to flop on a pile of blankets, and curl up to sleep.

Morningstar lie curled between two large rocks, her hands snuggled into the dirt.

Devlin pulled himself to stand. "I'll secure the door." Mumbling as he wandered toward the exit behind the curtain, "we have several hours until sunset. Should be safe." He kicked a body out of the way and almost fell with the effort of it.

Maddox crawled to a blanket and collapsed, snoring within seconds.

Miller rolled to his back, pulled his collar tightly to his neck, smiled at Natalia and promptly fell into a deep sleep.

They had placed Yuri on a pallet of blankets before attempting the healing meld and now Natalia snuggled down beside her love, pulling a loose blanket over them both.

"Natalia, what happened? I can't seem to remember…"

"I will tell you all later. Now, I desperately need sleep, Yuri." Natalia closed her eyes and relaxed.

"But I don't want to sleep." Yuri was feeling very fit and healthy, and energetic. His hands made their way across her breast finding a nipple. "I want to…" Natalia murmured something unintelligible, swatting half-heartedly at his hand then burrowed deeper into Yuri's arms.

"Natalia? Me-lotch-ka?" Yuri could hear soft rhythmic breathing issue from beneath the chestnut curls that hid the face of the most beautiful woman in the world…who, obviously exhausted, now slept in his arms.

Yuri shifted, drawing Natalia's hair from her face with his free hand. God, she was gorgeous!

God he was hard.

What happened?

His thoughts were fuzzy and his mind could not find an answer, no matter how hard he concentrated. Somehow his wounds were healed, but wounds from what? Natalia shifted with a sigh and flung an arm across his chest absently caressing his breast in her sleep.

"Helluva note, Captain. You're the only one fit for anything and everyone else is flat out gone." Devlin stumbled toward a stack of tarps next to the Colonel. "Need sleep." Devlin crumpled onto the tarps, pulled an edge over his legs and chest and closed his eyes.

"Wait, Devlin. Tell me what happened. Was there a fight?" Yuri pressed for answers in a quiet voice, though he suspected even a shout would not wake the sleeping humans, or vampires alike.

"Big fight. Got em all. Messed you up. Something fierce. Natalia linked with us to fix you. Incredible thing. We were all connected inside her. Tired…" Devlin was mumbling, as if it took all his remaining strength to speak. "Loves you. Did it for you…" He was gone mid-sentence.

The returning memories struck Yuri like a lightning bolt out of the blue. Energy sizzled across his neurons building a picture of the firefight and subsequent miracle of his healing. His dream… She had come after him. Right to the door of Hades itself. To bring him back to her.

She loved him!

Yuri pulled Natalia closer, hugging her to him.

She was magnificent.

She was incredible.

She was his.

And he was hers.

Yuri inhaled the scent of her, and felt his groin tighten. He'd won her with patience and determination, a little more wouldn't hurt. Well, it wouldn't hurt, but it was damn uncomfortable, he thought, as he closed his eyes and mentally squelched the raging hard-on beneath her carelessly flung leg. They had a lifetime to love. He could wait a few hours.

He calmed his thoughts and settled Natalia beneath his chin. Within moments, he too slept. A silly grin was plastered across his face.

Chapter 31

To Paint a Future

When all is said and done,
The love of a woman hard won,
Is all that truly matters in life.
It makes worthwhile haste and strife.

When all is said and done,
The love of a man, no matter how won,
Releases the heart to accept its mate,
Finally gone is the terror, the panic, the hate.

Bouduin Melinar
The Awakening of Mankind
Paris, France, 2000

The fall colors were spectacular at Olney Farm as the setting sun turned the leaves every imaginable shade of yellow, red and brown. The sleepy meadow, in the middle of which the old farmhouse sat, seemed kissed with sun and covered in deep green grass. Bees buzzed busily around the last of the autumn flowers, manically gathering nectar to sustain the hive over the coming winter. How like those bees they were just a few short weeks ago.

Now, like the bees in winter, the Vamp Squad rested and contemplated the changing of the season. Natalia sat in the shadows of the coming twilight, on a wooden swing suspended from the roof of the porch.

After conning the Joint Chiefs into an agreement that gave half the sum total of the booty to the Vamp Squad, Colonel Maddox called in a hastily formed detachment to catalog and tabulate the contents of the stash they'd found in Afghanistan. At some point he would pay for his audacity. No one held the Joint Chiefs hostage to intel, but for now, the American military

301

leadership was ecstatic over the success of the Vamp Squad's first mission. The subsequent spoils of the Taliban were still not completely tabulated. But, General Albani's business ledger of drug deals was passed on to the DEA, along with a tidy support contingent of extra resources and manpower.

Natalia fingered the huge pink diamond on the fourth finger of her left hand. Maddox never mentioned the few baubles and trinkets the Squad managed to smuggle home as souvenirs of their successful mission. Yuri was such a romantic, and she loved the fact that he selected the ring in secret, saving it until they returned to the safety of Olney Farm to present it on a warm evening under the stars. His proposal had been a passionate event, tinged with a sweetness that their love seemed to thrive on.

Natalia's staff back in Siberia had yet to meet the new Yuri, but everyone at home was ecstatic about the turn of events. Petra and Natalia skyped daily, about everything and anything. Petra took care of business from Natalia's castle, and kept her boss well informed.

Petra forwarded a formal notification from the Council of Elders just the previous week. Surprisingly enough, Frabriaci and "The Brat" finally received the official nod from the Council of Elders. They were formally sealed for all time. In Siberia, it was business as usual for Petra and the rest of Natalia's staff.

Natalia had yet to return home, but there was a new happiness in her tone evident to everyone. Rivka's baby would soon make his appearance, and Natalia sent packages almost daily to the expectant mother.

Natalia thought back to the firefight in the cavern. She was terrified that she would lose the first man she ever truly loved. It still touched her heart that both the humans and vampires of the Squad banned together to help her heal Yuri, when she doubted herself. Knowing full well they may have been injured or died in the process, the humans did not think twice. Yuri sacrificed himself to save her. They were willing to sacrifice themselves to help her save Yuri.

How could she turn her back on the squad now? How could she leave this place and these people to return to a castle halfway around the world, in Siberia? Despite her staff, whom she considered family, how could she return to an isolated life that she now knew was a lonely substitute for real living? A blood red tear slid down her cheek. When she thought about leaving Olney Farm and the Vamp Squad, Natalia actually felt like she was abandoning a new baby, birthed by pain, but a true miracle of renewed life.

"A penny for your thoughts, me-loch-ka." Yuri crossed the porch and sat next to Natalia, taking her hand to his lips for a soft kiss.

"My thoughts? They're worth much more than a penny. Maybe a million." She smiled at her lover.

A tender finger wiped away the tear. "I believe we have it, my love. A million and much more." Smiling, Yuri lifted the damp finger to his lips and licked away the blood. "Have I ever told you, I love the taste of your tears? I intend to spend the rest of my days kissing them away until only happiness glows in these wonderful Russian cheeks."

Natalia had to smile back at her passionate Captain. "I was just thinking about how this all began, and everything we've been through. I never promised to stay after the mission. I just wanted to rescue you so I agreed to help. I didn't care about the American's operation or the Vamp Squad, or any of this. Now, well… things have changed. I feel a responsibility, no, that's not the right word. I feel as if…" Natalia floundered for the right words.

"You feel as if you found a new family, a place where you belong? You feel a kinship to these people who risked their lives to help you save me. Yet there remains your old family in Siberia. I know. I understand. My family is also there, and Kraz." He pulled Natalia onto his lap and kissed her moist lips with such tenderness, she thought she would cry again.

"Yuri, wait. I can't think when you kiss me. Listen. I'm trying to…" Again she was without words.

"Ask me if I want to stay here? To be a part of the Vamp Squad with you, and the rest? If I would give up my country and home to be here? With you?" He was working hard to keep the chuckle from his voice. Natalia thought she saw him actually bite the side of his cheek to keep the emotion from his voice.

"Well, I… I've been thinking. The Russian government thinks you're dead. They never knew I was alive. My home is a remote castle in Siberia. It's not really a bad place to live, in fact fairly comfortable, all things considered. But…no central heating; no synthetic blood supply. No armed guards to look after us. Only my staff to keep me, I mean us, safe. Your family and friends are there still. We risk being discovered or recognized. You are no longer human. It poses certain problems. I have Internet access like here, and we have…" She was listing the pros and cons as if trying to weigh the two against themselves.

Yuri's lips covered hers and he mentally communicated, *you think too much, my love. It is not so complicated that we cannot have the best of both worlds.* His kiss deepened, and Natalia's world spun out of control. His kisses always seemed to do that to her and she was beginning to like their effect. Her hands sought and found his neck, as she pulled him tighter to her.

I do think too much, don't I? Natalia felt herself lifted from the swing as Yuri carried her toward the barn and their favorite hayloft. *I love you, Yuri Milassoviech.*

And I love you, Natalia Vyrubova Milassoviech. Yuri was having a good deal of trouble walking with a woman in his arms and an erection that left not an inch of room in his jeans to accommodate the swagger.

Not yet. Natalia's tongue tangled around his.

He stumbled.

She sucked his lower lip sending frenzied emotions through them both.

I'll have to remedy that soon, but first things first. The last of the soft orange sky turned to velvety blue, as he gave up on the impossibility of walking and teleported them directly to the loft. He had practiced in secret for quite a while and perfected the new skill just that week. He was adapting rather quickly to his new life and stretching his skills every day, just like a dedicated soldier in training…

"You are just full of surprises, my Captain." Natalia knelt before her lover in the soft warm hay, sliding her hands up his muscular thighs in search of a liberating snap. Finding what she sought, Natalia slid her warm hands into the opening of Yuri's pants and massaged his sex.

"Ah, moy Bog! My God, you tease me so." Yuri's fingers laced through her thick chestnut curls. "How can I ever give you up? Not for a million dollars, a slice of the moon or even for world peace." His deep sigh turned feral and sensual as his cock grew with each stroke. "Were you to leave this world, I would follow. You can run, but you can never hide from my love… or my…ah, Natalia!"

Yuri's knees gave way, and he collapsed on the hay with a deep groan of pleasure. Slowly, imitating a stalking cat, Natalia crawled to his chest, pulling at each button of his shirt, as she moved. When his shirt lie open revealing a massive muscular chest covered with fine blond hair, she bent and nipped at his left nipple, then slathered her tongue across his chest to repeat the same maneuver with the right. Smiling lusciously she slid down, playing his abdominal muscles as if each sculpted layer were another challenge, another world to be toyed with and teased.

"God, woman, you kill me. How can I ever expect to be a man around you when all I want is to fall on my knees and beg for your touch? I want to worship at your feet and kiss the very ground upon which you walk. I want to lie you down and bury myself in your heavenly body. That is not seemly for a Captain of the Russian Army." Yuri was gasping for breath, as Natalia slid her tongue lower. He was helpless to stop her hot touch, and, in fact, had no desire to do so.

"Some would say I have already killed you, at least twice over. Others would simply say you now get what you deserve, my love." Natalia eased into the cleft of his shoulder to snuggle closer. "Still others would say that I finally get what *I* deserve."

Natalia let slide the shoulder straps of her silk blouse. Revealing a voluptuous cleavage and pert nipples peeking from beneath the edge of the deep maroon material. "I may not legally be Natalia Milassoviech, but soon I shall bear the name, as well as the brand. Your love has impressed upon me such a presence as I could never deny, or refute. Like a tattoo on my heart, my love, I will have no other in my mind or my life." Natalia raised the huge pink diamond she wore on her left hand as a sign of Yuri's love and promise. It sparkled and shot fire across the loft playing a pattern of stars against the far wall. "Even now, the heavens send their concurrence and bless our union with the dancing lights of paradise."

"I see only my future in the flame of your dark eyes. I see simply the woman I love, beyond life itself." Yuri felt Natalia's hair trail across his chest before soft lips reached to seal his fate.

To be loved both physically and mentally by his Ahn-hel Tiemno, his Dark Angel, for eternity? What else could a man want from death and life anew? As Natalia deepened their kiss, Yuri cried out his answer to the dancing stars that twinkled across the loft. Silken hair caressed his cheeks, heightening sensations, and framing the woman who purred into their kiss. His hands sought and found her soft mass of curls tantalizing his skin and he held on for dear life.

Life? So many questions and so many options. Together, they would figure out life later. Right now... well, right now was right now!

Somewhere in the Vamp Squad's secret complex, deep beneath the old farmhouse, a petulant teenage whine insinuated itself across the minds of those who could pick up the mental-conversation of the coven.

Puh-leeze! Elizabetta, tell them to stop. They're at it again!

Here's a sneak preview…

Coming soon!

Vamp Squad Book 2: The Death of Innocence

Chapter 1

The Awakening of Desire

I feel the desire, in the depth of my cells.
I feel the love, in the beauty of your hell.
I feel your pain and I want it like a drug.
I need it. I take it. Who are you to judge?

Come small thing and bring your blood.
Feed my need. Be my stud.
Your heartbeat slows.
My strength just grows
I need it. I take it. And you still don't know!

Monique Merchant, Vampire
1833

Daytona Beach, Florida, March…

From the shadows of the boathouse, a man stood, watching in the night. He loosened his black satin bow tie, and casually undid the top buttons of his starched and ruffled shirt. Excitement coursed through his body at the sight of such a luscious and provocative morsel. Something else, something foreign, coursed through his body as well, but that would only make the prospective seduction even better.

Susannah slid her toes through the fine soft sand of the beach. It tickled the soles of her feet and spurred her on to dance under the stars.

He watched her giggle at the feeling, twirling and dancing with the twinkling light.

Rich and melodious jazz music drifted on the waves, lulling her toward the bright patterns reflected on the surface of the water. Soft foam slid across her ankles and tickled her calves, calling her deeper. She downed the last of her fruity drink and tossed the little pink parasol into the seductive waves.

A slight frown creased her perfect, nineteen year old features. How many little parasols did she throw away tonight? Delicate porcelain skin glowed with a slight sheen of perspiration. Long blonde hair waved and curled sensuously around her face and bare shoulders caressing her skin like a lover's soft kisses. A petite girl on the verge of stunning womanhood, Susannah hiked her evening dress up and jumped the lines of froth on the incoming waves, playing like a child. With each wild movement, the strapless confection she wore inched lower on her ample bosom showing the cleavage that probably impressed several high school football stars at her alma mater.

The man stood immobile, watching. How many spring breaks had he participated in? How many of these wild scenes had Kellan Burke the III been the sole observer of? Over how many years? It showed in his stance, his every manicured nail, the perfect cut of his evening attire. He was a man who got what he wanted. He was a man who made his own rules, took what he desired, and gave no quarter. Especially in the bedroom, or, actually, wherever the mood struck him. He chuckled deep in his chest and unlatched the top hook of his slacks. His erection was in full bloom, and he slowly rubbed the extended protrusion through the silk of his slacks. A kind of animalistic sound escaped his perfect smiling lips.

Unaware of her observer, Susannah frolicked with abandon, laughing at the top of her lungs. It had been a wonderful eight days and she was definitely taking advantage of her first spring break in Daytona Beach. Even though it caused a hellacious argument with her father, she fought for the right to be a regular college kid, and won.

Here, she was just like all the other girls at her school that came to participate in the wild rites of spring. Here, she could forget the steel cage that held her captive at home during her entire high school years. She was an adult now, and on her own, sort of. Daddy still paid the bills so he had a say in what she did, but a say was so much more freedom than the complete control he exerted over most of her life. This was her adventure, and she was going to do it to the max. No more security details scrutinizing her every move. No more military 'rules of the roost.' No more Colonel Daddy's disapproval at every turn. Just beautiful, free Susannah doing whatever she wanted to do. She was living life on the edge, invincible… and very drunk.

Susannah missed a wave and plopped down on her fanny in the knee-deep water. Laughing uproariously, she tried to stand and failed, initiating another fit of drunken, uncontrollable laughter.

Through the giggles, she felt strong arms lift her to her feet and she turned to face… heaven in a tuxedo. Her savior held her steady as she gazed adoringly into deep brown eyes set in a face that could have easily graced the cover of GQ Magazine.

Susannah smiled coquettishly. Thinking past his seductive smile, she would have preferred to see him gracing the pages of Playgirl, without the tux.

"I think we should get you out of the water, young lady. You seem to have lost your sea legs." His voice thrilled Susannah to the core. She shivered with delight as the deep tones delicately stroked the most base center of her mind.

This could be fun.

Chalk up one more adventure to *Girls Gone Wild at Daytona Beach*.

"You're cold," he whispered seductively, his hot breath caressing her cheek. Kellan knew he had this one nailed. She was a bit of human putty in his hands. Sliding out of his jacket, he draped it around the girl's creamy shoulders. Picking her up easily, he waded for the shore, angling towards the privacy of the nearby boathouse.

He smelled luscious, all spice and expensive wine. His skin was smooth and tan, perfect for her lips. Susannah could feel the iron hard muscles beneath his crisp white shirt, and knew she was in good hands, or better yet, his arms. Snuggling against his chest, she slipped a hand inside the unbuttoned shirt and felt his skin. It was cool, with a light covering of smooth, silky blonde hair.

She accidentally flicked a nipple and giggled at his sharp intake of breath.

Kellan almost stumbled.

Feeling her grasp his breast and squeezed slightly, her hand conformed to his well-toned peck. Again he drew in a deep breath and tightened his hold on her.

Kellan could smell her scent, her blood, and the moisture that began to flow freely with her excitement. She was ripe and ready for the taking. He was ready to take, actually, more than ready.

Using Crysillus Extract made sexual encounters literally, to die for. And, once again, he'd indulged himself in the forbidden drug known in the seedier vampire circles as CE. Indulged just a little too much. Now he wanted release in a big way. And he was holding the way in his arms, and it was holding him back.

He flexed and was not surprised by the sensuous sigh followed by a fit of giggles. Young, full lips caressed his neck as he struggled to stay upright. His strength did not fail him. It was the desire threatening to overwhelm that left him off kilter. They were not yet in a safe place to allow him his kind of seduction.

Susannah felt his erection jump and she wiggled in his arms. The game was to tease and tease, and then, when she knew he would be crazy with need, have her way with him. She wanted this stranger who held her so safely in his big strong arms. She could taste his aftershave on her lips. Slinging an arm around his neck, she let her head fall back offering him a perfect view of her breasts. She moaned with ecstasy as her lover brought them to his lips and covered her sensitive flesh with little nips and kisses. She could feel the neckline of her dress slip below her taut nipples as he took first one, and then the other between his lips and sucked gently.

"Nnnn…a…ame. Your name." Susannah ground out between waves of sensual electricity. "What's… your…. name?" She felt the man pause and chided herself for breaking the mood. But there was no way she was going to seduce this guy without knowing a name to scream when she came.

Kellan could go no further. He was in agony. "Kellan." He mumbled into her ear as he slid his tongue along her jaw line, then towards the back of her neck. He smiled at the goose flesh that rose making her nipples pebble hard.

"Sus…Susann…ah. Susannah." She could hardly talk. Between the alcohol and Kellan's ministrations, she was in heaven. Passion set her mind and body on fire, as Kellan slowly released her, letting Susannah slither down his body. Her arms locked around his neck and she stood on tiptoes drinking in the heat of his chocolate eyes.

Good enough to eat, she thought, licking her lips, leaving a thin coating of moisture to reflect the glittering starlight. An enticing trick.

Good enough to eat, Kellan thought, forcing himself to control the hunger that rose like a tidal wave, threatening to overcome what little grip he maintained on his sanity. For a second, his eyes blurred with blood lust.

Hold on Kellan, he told himself. *It will be better that way, so much better*. He grasped Susannah's hands and lifted her lips to his, devouring them as she hung, suspended in space.

Susannah felt herself lifted off the ground and hung for a second, allowing the ravage of her lips. She closed her legs around Kellan, holding him to her. She took his lips and opened to his probing tongue. It licked and swirled sending delicious little impulses throughout her body. Captured, she captured back, locking her heels around Kellan's hips and rubbing up low across his groin. Her dress rode high over her hips with the motion, eliciting Kellan's deep growling responses. The only thing separating them was the simple draw of a zipper. Susannah tightened her hold, sliding up and down in a purposeful motion.

Kellan held Susannah fast with one hand, devouring her lips, stealing into her mind. The other hand worked the zipper of his slacks. He could contain himself no longer. He was so hard even the gentlest touch was a beautiful pain. Kellan stumbled forward into the shadows of the boathouse, stepping out of his pants at the same time. Freed at last, he plunged himself into the woman who embraced him with her silky legs. He heard her cry of ecstasy from a place in his mind that throbbed, hyper-excited with the forbidden CE. Again and again, he buried himself, each thrust deeper than the last.

Susannah took him stroke for stroke, escalating his lust with her cries. Dragging him back each time he pulled away, she felt the intensity of his passion as if it were her own. Finally, he released her hands and she sunk her nails into his shoulders, riding him for all she was worth.

Without warning, it came, a flood of the most incredibly powerful sensations. Beginning low in her belly, it rose through her body, firing every nerve, exploding her senses. "K-E-L-L-A-N!" Susannah screamed, tossing her head back in the throws of orgasm.

Kellan howled, their minds and bodies locked in a sexual bond held by preternatural strength. He came, ramming into her with one final incredibly deep thrust, and let the climax take him. Any control he thought he could maintain, was gone. The animal lust fired his need for blood. The CE fired his desire for total submission to his need. He could restrain himself no longer and, frankly, had no desire to.

Susannah's cleavage, so deliciously exposed, drew his sight higher. Her slim, young neck, so nubile, so deliciously… delicious. The artery pulsed at the juncture of her jaw and ear, singing to Kellan of delectable promise.

His mouth watered as he sank his fangs into the pounding pulse just below the sparkling crystal set in her dainty earlobe, and tore… and tore… and tore again.

*****

Connect with Miriam Matthews

Each of the first five books in this series are about the Squad's vampires and how they came to be part of Colonel Maddox's group of top-secret anti-terrorist operatives. Each book is also a romance! Book 2, tells how Susannah finally grows up and figures out her future. Book 3 is Monique's story of facing her fears of San Leyre and learning love is more than a great set of pecks wrapped in a thousand dollar suit. Elizabetta finally begins to trust a human man in Book 4 and the sparks fly! In Book 5, Morningstar leaves the Vamp Squad to return to her tribe in Kansas only to find home is not always what she thought it was.

<u>The Vamp Squad Series</u>
Book 1: Strange Beginnings
Book 2: The Death of Innocence
Book 3: The Secrets of San Leyre
Book 4: The Roots of Betrayal
Book 5: A Dark Deception

You can always catch up with me or send your comments to: miriamthewriter@gmail.com.

You can also follow me on Facebook and keep up with my news, new books and trivia questions at:
www.facebook.com/miriam.matthews.773.

www.ingramcontent.com/pod-product-compliance
Lightning Source LLC
Chambersburg PA
CBHW071243170626
46809CB00001B/69